Spinning Real Life

M. L. Fischer

First Printing, March 2003- 100 Copies
ISBN: 0-9672523-3-4
Eclectic Press
P. O. Box 1925
Freedom, CA 95076
Copyright March 2003

Thanks to Denise Fischer for editing and suggesting needed changes.

Other books by M. L. Fischer
Cosmic Coastal Chronicles
Shattering the Crystal Face of God
available from
Eclectic Press
P.O. box 1925
Freedom, CA 95076
www.baymoon.com/~eclecticpress

1.

"Scotty, what the hell is this crap about changing majors?" The old man had gotten right to the point without even a nod to niceties or small talk. It was the moment Scott had dreaded for the last two weeks.

He limply folded his six-foot-two skinny frame into one of his father's plush leather chairs to await the rest of the onslaught.

"Your whole damn junior year, you say. I'm paying this goddamn tuition, dorms, food, women maybe, and you're taking these creative-writing classes. What the hell for?"

His father, a puffy, inflated version of Scott, had worked himself into a red-faced rage, and it looked as if his eyes would pop out of his puffy face. Scott willed his voice calm as he responded to this spiritually impoverished man who obsessed over the narrow world of business.

"I…I w…want to be a writer. I want to experience and write about, you know, real life." Scott stammered. He coiled up and withdrew into the big chair like a snake into a black leather den. And in that position, he had the urge to strike out at his insensitive father.

"What's a matter, the family business not real enough for you? You work hard, make the business grow, take care of your family, and you'll have one soon enough. You become somebody in the community, join organizations, have friends. That's real life, not sitting around some college bar with starving poets and out-of-work actors." The old man was on a roll, and Scott knew he was in for a filibuster.

Scott had set this chain of events in motion during finals week at Long Beach State. There had been a party, and he'd been telling some well built gal about his plans to be a writer. Trips to the keg had made him vociferous and expansive, and when one of his friends interrupted him with, "Did you ever get

3

the guts to tell your old man about your changing majors?" Scott had answered that he'd only waited for finals to be over, and in fact he'd already written the letter.

To Scott, something said was something done, so when he stumbled back to his dorm room, he sat down at his laptop and composed a literary manifesto, a declaration of independence from his father, the boss. Unfortunately, his roommate, an obsessive accounting major, had seen it on the desk and mailed it before Scott woke up. And now he was reaping what he'd sown.

"Pop, I just meant I want to explore how ordinary, regular people live, their pain and their triumphs" He said as justification.

"Regular! Ordinary! What, losers, junkies, drunks? The inept and unmotivated. We agreed you'd study business administration. This business that was supposed to read 'Mukis and Son,' on all six stores. I'm expecting you to help me run this business, and you're writing some damn poetry."

"Prose, actually. I w…want to be a novelist." His voice betrayed his nervousness.

"Oh, yeah. How many of those are making a living. And I guess you want me to support you until you write a best seller?"

"Well, of course not." His face reddened. In the back of his mind was a scenario in which his father demanded he take the money in order to explore his vast talent. The big, black leather chair became quicksand, while his father rose to his feet, displaying the vastness of his 260 pounds.

"You bet your ass, of course not. So, what about 'Mukis and Son'?"

"Becky's the one with the head for business. She's finishing her MBA, and she's already helping you run the business. Maybe 'Mukis and Daughter' would be more appropriate."

The old man slammed his red hand on the desk. "Does this mean you're going to continue with this nonsense?"

Scott nodded weakly.

"Well, you'll do it without my help." He held up a check.

"I've been holding off sending this tuition until we had this talk."
He dramatically ripped it up and dropped it in the trashcan. "You
can pay your own way, or quit school and start working your
way up in the business."

Scott was somehow relieved. Now it was his turn to stand
up and assert himself. With jaw pointed up and out, and his
finger pointing in the general direction of heaven, he insisted,
"I'll manage. I'll find a way to do it on my own." It sounded
somewhat hollow, even as he said it, He'd never worked other
than summers in his father's stores. And before he could stop
himself, he added the cliché , "I'll make you proud of me."

His father's resounding, "Ha!" followed him as he left the
study.

His mother, looking thinner and tanner than she'd been
over spring break, stood in the living room with her customary
martini. "Scotty, dear. I hope your father wasn't too hard on
you, but you really should listen to him. Would you like me to
have the cook fix you some lunch?"

He wasn't hungry, but he needed to think about what
would happen next. It seemed ages ago when he'd met
Original Cyn in old Professor Locklin's poetry class, a class
that was supposed to be a diversion from the dull business
classes. The class and Cyn had changed his life and caused him
to come of age.

They'd gone for coffee after class one day, Scott had told
her he wanted to be a writer. She'd said, "You wanna write
comic books about stupid romances or detectives, or do ya want
to make a difference?" Her dark eyes, under her dyed black hair
had cut into him, making her question more than rhetorical. As
their relationship turned into an affair, he'd begun to see her as
a modern Joan of Arc, and her causes had slowly become his.

After meeting some of the people she was involved with
and attending some demonstrations, he'd started to see his old
life and the world of business as somehow shallow and invalid.
He read Steinbeck's *Grapes of Wrath,* and imagined himself
continuing this bold literary tradition.

Some of Cyn's friends had started a radical magazine, "A Voice in Your Face," and Scott had started writing for it, soon making himself a central figure in the campus progressive, literate, radical circle.

When Cyn had moved on to a painter whose medium was manure and chicken blood, explaining how deep the guy was, Scott had been devastated. He'd missed classes, typed endless, depressing stories over gallons of coffee, and finally come to the conclusion that she'd been nothing more than a dilettante, a paper tiger on the canvas of history. Real changes, he concluded, came from the writers and artists, not the spoiled children with protest signs.

Cyn had seen him through his artistic infancy, but he'd grown up in the last year and was ready to make his mark on the world. He headed for the kitchen, ready to take his mother up on the lunch offer.

I must of cut the cord, he thought. This place doesn't even look familiar any longer. Then he realized that all of the almost new furniture had been replaced with newer and even more ostentatious pieces.

When Becky arrived home the next day, Scott watched the transition with fascination. In the evenings father and daughter would argue about business trends and marketing strategies, things Scott had little knowledge of and less interest in. That first night there was something like an argument. Becky was saying, "Borrow against the stores and start building. Open a new store every two to three months. Cement our niche before any of the big chains take it away from us. We have to be aggressive." She was holding her own against the old man, and he seemed to be conceding her point.

The closer father and daughter became, the more Scott became part of the furniture, treated cordially enough, but not talked with in any depth. Even his mother, who didn't take an active part in the business, had opinions she insisted on sharing.

Scott had always looked up to his big sister. Becky tended to be slender like their mother, but she pumped iron with a vengeance, giving her the lean, hard look of an athlete. She was tall like Scott and his father, but had mother's cool, blue eyes. One day she had her long red hair cut short for a more efficient, business-like look. The final step in the transition to "Mukis and Daughter" was the afternoon on the porch when she lit up one of the old man's cigars. There were the two of them, puffing away, feet up on the porch railing, talking quarterly returns, while Scott helped mother chop onions for the pasta sauce.

After a couple weeks of being humored by his family, he looked out over the homes of the less affluent at the shimmering blue Pacific and knew it was time to start the grand adventure that would be his writer's life. He drew out the $3200 he had in the savings and packed his bags.

"I promise I'll call every week and come home rather than starve." He told his distraught mother. His sister wished him success, and his father predicted he'd come crawling back. He hopped in his fairly dependable compact sedan, drove down the hill, past the traffic mess that State Street had become and arrived at the Highway 101 on ramp. At this point he hesitated, not having a destination in mind. South was the L.A. megalopolis, and his former university. North was new and untainted territory. He absently pushed his long, sand colored hair off his forehead and headed north.

San Francisco held memories of many family holidays. "Can we help you, Mr. Mukis? Theater tickets? Of course, Mr. Mukis." No. He continued on, determined to make a fresh start on new turf. He thought about Oregon the way many idealistic young men think about Oregon, and it became his vague destination. "I'm going to celebrate my 21st birthday in a new home in a new state!" He shouted to the traffic jam in Marin County.

Driving up the Avenue of the Giants, Scott fell in love with the redwoods. They were massive, beautiful, and threatened by greedy timber companies. He leaned out the window. "One day I'll be there to protect you from those business assholes." He promised himself that he'd write a novel about people saving the forest.

7

Hitting rain in Crescent City, Scott decided to turn inland at the 199 toward Cave Junction, Oregon. A few miles past Jedidiah Smith State Park, the rain stopped and the sun came out, casting the Smith River in rich translucent greens. The redwoods towered over both banks of the river, and he wondered at the beauty and what it would do for the creative spirit.

Then he spotted a place that almost shouted at him to stop. Along the highway was a gravel lot with an odd assortment of travel trailers and sagging single-wide mobile homes in a seemingly random configuration. At the front of the lot was a faded wood building, a bit larger than a shed. A sign, painted in whitewash, read, "Texas Jake's Trailer Park and Harley Repair." Below the sign, a smaller sign swung in the wind, "Trailer for rent."

2.

Is this a writer's place, or what? Scott asked himself. He unfolded his long legs from the car and headed over the weed-studded gravel drive to the combination office/shop/manager's apartment, he formed a sudden image of Texas Jake, an image that turned out to be strikingly accurate.

Jake, sitting at his dusty desk, looked like a forty-something Jerry Garcia, with wavy, oily, long black hair. A Harley tee shirt, much too small, stretched over his ample belly, and his arms were decorated with assorted biker tattoos. A stubble of a slightly graying beard surrounded a broad, ingenuous smile. He held out a five fingered ham and said, "Texas Jake. Glad ta meet ya."

As Scott introduced himself and inquired about the trailer, Jake seemed to be sizing him up.

"Oh, it's cheap enough, but then it's only a 24 foot travel trailer, tiny bath and kitchen. Room that doubles as living and sleeping. Say, you look like you don't eat so regular. Sure you got rent money?"

Scott reddened as he explained to the rather paunchy Jake that he eats like a horse but never gains weight. "Fast metabolism, I guess," he stammered.

"Well, you seem OK for a city kid. I'm guessin' southern part of the state, judgin' from your beach boy shirt. Let me show you the place, and if you like it, we'll talk details."

They walked past and over a couple partially disassembled bikes, through a patch of unkempt grass and down the gravel road between trailers of various sizes. Scott noticed that most were small, but there were two double wides, the only ones that looked truly permanent.

The rental place was old but clean. It was cramped inside, and he could see everything but the bathroom from the door, but it had a big awning in front, with a picnic table and two lawn chairs. Scott would spend much of his time outside. The electrical hook up was by the table, making it a perfect place to plug in the laptop. This, he thought, was gritty reality, a novel waiting to be written. He took the big man's hand and said, "It's perfect. I'll take it."

After unpacking the car, Scott realized he had none of the basics for setting up a household, and there were no big stores in the neighborhood, so he drove down the river to Crescent City and soon discovered a thrift shop. After coming out with mismatched dishes, pots and pans, can openers and all the rest, he found a grocery store, picked up a bunch of easy to prepare meals, some cheap towels, and a tacky landscape print. He was now an independent man, a householder.

By late afternoon he had made the place look livable, had some canned pork and beans, chased by a quart of milk, and was sitting outside in front of his laptop, watching the cursor blink and thinking vague but warm thoughts.

A car pulled into the unit next to him, and an attractive redhead got out along with a cute little girl. The girl squealed and said, "Look mom, a new neighbor." She ran over and asked his name. As Scott answered the kid's rapid series of questions, the mother put her bag of groceries in her trailer and walked over.

Scott leaped to his feet as she walked up. She was almost six feet tall and strikingly beautiful for her age. To have a kid that big, she must have been at least thirty. She offered her hand, "I'm Vanessa Vincent, but most people call me V.V.. This is Samantha."

"Call me Sam," the girl giggled.

Scott volunteered a quick account of his life as a student now striking out on his own, and how he planned to be a great writer. Soon the novelty wore off for Sam, and she went back to her double wide to watch TV..

Then V.V. said, "Its been a long, hard day, and I could use a glass of wine. Care to join me?" He quickly agreed, thinking how cool it was to be sipping wine with his beautiful neighbor.

10

She ducked into her place, returning with two plastic wine glasses and a tall bottle of basic white table wine. She settled into one of Scott's chairs and took her turn relating her life.

"I was married. Met my husband in the local community college down in Santa Rosa and dropped out to get married. By the time Sam was a toddler, Ray, a nice but non ambitious guy, got tired of the responsibilities of a family, and one day he went out for an espresso and never returned. I couldn't afford the apartment, so I moved from place to place, job to job. Not having a lot of skills, I ended up waiting tables. The costs and responsibilities of raising a kid pushed me into lower and lower rent areas until I landed, quite by bad luck, at Jake's. I bought this trailer, and rent's dirt cheap, so I figured I'd hang on until Sam graduates from high school in about eight years. After that, who knows." She shrugged her shoulders and poured another glass.

Scott was fascinated by V.V.'s life and her stoic attitude toward its harsh realities. He saw her in a romantic light, as a strong survivor. He said, "You're a noble woman in charge of your own life. You're gonna do great things." While he had yet to attach a label to these new feelings, he was developing a crush on this older woman.

V.V. started to blush from his praise. She looked at her watch and remarked about feeding Sam, and she excused herself, leaving Scott to daydream elaborate plot lines involving her, and a partial bottle of wine to fuel the fantasies.

The next day he hung out with Jake in his crowded shop, watching him work on bikes and drink beer. When he went to the refrigerator and returned empty handed, Scott figured the big guy would be going out for more.

Trying to sound casual, he asked, "Jake, are you making a beer run?"

"Soon," Jake gave him a sideways glance from under a bushy brow. "Why?"

Scott shrugged, opened his wallet and said. "I was wondering if you could pick me up some wine, I seem to have run out."

11

"Why don't ya just trot across the highway? Oh, I get it. You ain't 21 yet"

Scott flushed as he nodded and stuck out a 20 dollar bill.

With the wine cooling, Scott made another quick trip down the hill, returning with two real glass wine glasses from the supermarket. He also picked up a plastic table cloth and a candle. Then he set the table and uncorked the wine. It looked too much like it had been planned, like a date. It wouldn't be dark enough for the candle for three or four hours, so he put it and one of the glasses back in the trailer. He poured himself some wine, and sat back with a book, trying to look nonchalant. By the time V.V. returned from work, he was ready for her.

He looked up as if her return was totally unexpected. "V.V., care to join me for a glass of wine?"

Sam waved and scampered off as V.V. walked over and dropped, wearily into a chair. Scott was in the door and back out with the glass and bottle before her ass settled comfortably into the chair. "I'm learning to find my way around Crescent City," he remarked lamely.

"Not much to see there," she murmured absently. "Did you stop at the State Park?"

"No, but it looks incredible. Perhaps I'll have a look tomorrow." Interesting question, he thought, she could be an environmental activist, like Original Cyn.

She swirled the wine in the glass before taking a healthy swallow, and then looked sort of at him and sort of past him. "Personally, I find it a great place to de-stress after a tough day, customers in a hurry, running back and forth, you know."

Scott leaned forward, face drawn up tight with concentration. "And you like to commune with the ancient trees and touch your primal roots!"

"Well, they're beautiful, and it's peaceful there, but I dunno about communing or any primal roots. I mean, like they're trees."

Scott was disappointed by her answer, but not disillusioned. "Maybe one day you can show me around the forest, a picnic perhaps?"

She shrugged and said something about that being OK, some day when she was off, when she didn't have to take Sam somewhere. Then she gave him a brief account of her day, including the rude and demanding customers.

"It's very noble and courageous to hold down a hard job and still be a super mom. And you seem to take it in stride. I admire that."

She laughed. "It's just life. I got a kid, we gotta live. I do what I have to. We all gotta work, unless we're born rich. What about you? Independently rich? You don't seem to have a job."

Oddly, the thought of a job hadn't slipped into his mind full of book scenarios, the quaintness of his new surroundings, and his fascination with her. He had less than two grand to his name. He needed a job, and he didn't have his father to give him one. A black cloud drifted slowly over his romantic interlude until he remembered the local paper he'd picked up in town. "I'm a writer. I'll go see about a job at the paper." Then, not to seem desperate and poverty stricken, "I'd rather not use up all my savings."

He was hoping that she'd be impressed with his plan to be a reporter, but she said, "Not a bad place to work. Seems they have a big turn over there. Don't know if it's low pay, tough bosses or the crappy winter weather. Anyway, good luck."

Perhaps she wasn't impressed with newspaper work, or maybe just work at a small paper. She would surely be impressed when he had a best seller and was on the book talk circuit. He would be the captain of his fate and would be there to care for her and her child. Then she could fulfill her secret, longed for destiny. He would give her the opportunity to follow her dreams because, well because he loved her. Loved her? Yes, although they hardly knew each other, he sensed the bond, the deep connection. Yes, he was almost sure. It was love.

He asked her if she'd like to read his copy of *The Autobiography of Martin Luther King, Jr.*

"Scott, Dr. King was an impressive person, but I probably

wouldn't enjoy it. I prefer diversion, entertainment, you know, best sellers: romance, crime, courtroom, and historical novels. Sorry."

He tried music, and her taste ran to soft rock. He tried politics, and she was only interested in politicians who were for working people's issues and help for dependent children.

He started talking about his college involvement in social justice, conservation, equality, and the evils of war. She was attentive, asking him questions as he paused in his oration.

"I agree that all that is important, but I don't have the time or energy to get involved. I have to focus on what touches Sam and me directly. Scott, most of us are just trying to get along in this world, get some security and all that. Not everyone has a rich family to fall back on."

That stung. He realized that was exactly how he might appear to others, particularly being unemployed. She likely thought he was slumming and would return home as soon as things got tough. He was determined to prove himself to her and to himself. He would tackle the job issue in the morning, but for this afternoon he'd concentrate on being a sparkling conversationalist and hopefully start winning her over. He started by assuring her that he'd severed his family connection, and that there was no money or support there for him. "I'll sink or swim on my own."

After a couple glasses, he got the idea to do impressions of TV personalities and politicians. She must have enjoyed it, as she laughed and exchanged quips with him until he actually had cause to light the candle. She'd left only long enough to put something in the oven and later feed Sam and bring the rest back to Scott. It was worth the hangover he woke up with in the morning.

The green numbers on the clock radio were flashing, indicating a power glitch, common to the neighborhood. His watch said it was after nine, and he remembered the job thing. Within an hour he was as ready as his muddled head would allow.

Small papers have little formality, so when he asked for the managing editor, he was shown in to the dusty, puke green office without question. The short, middle aged man with thinning blond hair looked busy and slightly distracted. "Name's Rob. What can I do for you?"

"I'm looking for a job. I'd like to be a reporter, perhaps even a columnist" The words seemed to congeal as they left his lips, turning gooey and dripping on the carpet. He felt that everyone in the place would jump up and stare at him. He smiled weakly.

Rob asked about his qualifications, and Scott related his year of writing classes and the underground paper. a crooked grin undulated across the editor's face. "Actually, we don't need any reporters at this time, columnists either." There was a pause where neither spoke. It seemed to last forever. Scott was about to thank him and leave. Finally, the man added, "We could use someone in advertising, on the phones. It's a start, if you're interested."

It was the last thing Scott wanted to do, but the bit about the job being a start cracked open the door of both hope and pride, and he needed to show V.V. that he wasn't a rich dilettante, so he said he be willing to try it.

The classified section manager, a chubby, fiftyish woman named Sylvia, interviewed him, and had him role play a phone call. Finally she nodded her head and offered Scott the job. It didn't pay very well, but rent at the trailer park was low, and Scott had few expenses. It would also give him some time to write, and real people to interact with. He filled out the stack of tax and benefit papers and was told to report in two days.

On the way out he picked up a copy to the paper. He read the whole thing over lunch, finding himself hungry for news almost immediately. He found a liquor store that carried the San Francisco paper, bought one, and called as soon as he got home, to have a Sunday subscription mailed to him.

Making a call, necessitated using the pay phone on the wall of Jake's shop, so he also called the phone company. He had to send them some money, and it would be a couple of weeks before he got service, and he had to buy his own phone. Then, almost as an after thought, he looked up the local internet provider, figuring that he'd need e-mail to send out his work to magazines and publishers.

That evening V.V. had too much to do to stop for wine, but she was pleased to hear about his new job. He phrased it so that his job in classified was just a filler until a reporter's position came up, and that his editor had big plans for him. He had already convinced himself that this was true, that Rob had seen his potential.

The next afternoon V.V. had errands in town, so Scott decided to explore the trailer park and perhaps meet some neighbors. Most of the trailers looked pretty shabby and covered with something like moss. People just lived there. It wasn't like the pride people in his parents' neighborhood had in their homes and gardens. Down at the end of a row Scott saw what looked like graves. When he got close enough to read the inscriptions he was delighted and amused. One read, "R.I.P. original thoughts." Another lamented the demise of the open mind, and there was a sentimental farewell to the last individual. The trailer was painted black, with purple trim, and the steps to the front door were the colors in the rainbow. He marched up and knocked on the door.

3.

The gaunt and shaggy man who answered the door looked not much older than Scott. He was several inches shorter and was very pale. His long dreadlocks were almost black, and he had a full, curly beard. He looked a mix of bleached rastaman and 60s hippie. Rather than a simple hello, he said, "Are you lost, like damn near everyone else?"

Scott was only taken aback for a moment, recovering to say, "I'm Scott, a writer, and I just moved in. I like your graveyard."

"Writer? Sure. OK. I'm Buck Rogers, spaced asshole. What you write, shopping lists?"

"I'm working on a novel based on the real people I'm meeting." Shit, he thought, that sounded lame.

"Like people around here?" Buck gestured around him. "Good, I'll want to read it. You get high?"

Cyn had introduced Scott to pot, but he hadn't had any since they'd broken up. "Sure."

Buck's place was filled with books, magazines, papers, posters, flyers; and everything seemed coated with a layer of dust. There were two old office chairs and a very old desk. They sat down on either side of an old Macintosh computer with every imaginable device daisy-chained to it. "I needed a break from work," Buck said as he lit the joint and passed it to Scott.

Scott took too big a hit from the harsh dirt weed and coughed a bit. He cleared his throat and asked, "Work? What do you do?"

"Shock the establishment and mind fuck the masses. I try to drag the complacent, kicking and screaming, into some level of awareness. Like I'm not just an asshole, I'm a professional asshole."

"And you accomplish this how?" Scott wasn't yet inclined to give Buck much credence.

"I'm associated with a couple other guys. Print set up in

17

town. We do bumper stickers, posters, tee shirts. Check this out." He pulls a bumper sticker out of a stack and hands it to Scott.

"Arm yourself: defend your right to ignorance," Scott read. "I like it."

"Here's another. 'Overpopulation, world hunger: two problems. Cannibalism: one solution'. And this, 'Drive drunk: help bankrupt insurance companies'."

"Weird. And you do these on tee shirts too?"

Buck nodded. "And we do posters and also custom printing work for hire. Pays for the presses and shit."

Scott, stoned and feeling the need to fill any silent moments, started talking about his college activism. Buck nodded in apparently lukewarm approval. Finally Scott's mind came back to his major current interest. "I live next door to V.V.. You know her?"

"Yeah. Nice looking body, but dull as dirt."

"You gotta get beneath the surface. She's a deep woman," An attempt at defending her.

"Hell, everyone's deep. Trouble is, mostly the deeper you go, the duller they are. You must have the hots for her. It's cool to let your cock do the thinking." Buck laughed, obviously pleased with his comment.

Within a few minutes, silence descended. Apparently there was nothing left to talk about, and the inner dialog in Scott's mind kept changing the subject, and he started feeling awkward. "Got stuff to do. Catch up with you later. By the way, is Buck your real name?"

"No names are real. Get your head out of its rut. Stop by any time. Have a nice fuckin' day. Sell your mother into white slavery.,"

Scott staggered off, a bit put off but fascinated by Buck's attitude. Cyn had cared too much about everything. Buck thumbed his nose at everything, but it was a device to break through complacency and raise awareness. It worked; it forced you to pay attention, to think about things. The guy seemed to have a heavy message, and as much as he was put off, Scott wanted to cultivate the friendship.

On the way back to his trailer he passed a very old unit. An ancient woman sat in front in a folding chair. Her face looked like a map of Los Angeles, but her smile was engaging. She glanced in his direction as he passed.

"Hello, neighbor. Do I know you?"

"No. I'm Scott. I just moved in a few days ago. I'm in the next row."

"Scott. Nice name. It sums up an entire ethnic group, a proud and delightfully barbaric group of people who have made great contributions to civilization. I'm Emily Century Conway."

Scott had to pause. There was something about this old woman. "Why 'Century'? The new century just started." He walked over toward her chair.

"Shit! Not this century, the last. I was born December 31, 1900. Sorry about the question. I don't see too damn well at a distance any more. In fact, I don't hear so good either, so step closer Scott."

Scott walked up to her and looked closely. "1900! That makes you over a hundred. Really?"

Emily got up slowly and reached her hand out to Scott. "Age is nothing. You live, and time goes by. I walk two, three miles a day, swim in the Smith during the summer. Hell, I'm living on borrowed time, but so are you."

"Well, I'm not quite 21."

"Statistically, you have about 53 years to live, that is unless you get shot in a war, killed on the highway, or you contract some disease. Scott, you could be dead tomorrow, and I'd be attending another funeral. Do you have any idea how many funerals I've attended in my life? Do you have any idea who took the 'fun' out of funeral? Of course not. Take a seat; have some wine; talk to me."

Scott obediently sat in the other folding chair. He noticed the bottle of wine on the table and picked it up. Everyone in

California drinks California wine, considered the best, but Emily had wine from Ontario, Canada. He picked up one of the glasses on the table and poured some, took a sip, and was pleasantly surprised. "This is great wine."

"87th birthday. Kayak and birding trip. Discovered the wine. Loved it. Case shipped to me twice a year. What do you do to make your life worth living?"

"I'm a writer." God, he was tired of saying that.

"Have you written anything yet?"

The temptation to expand upon his limited writing surged to the fore but was washed away by the honesty of her question. "Nothing to speak of, but I know I will."

"Because you know it, you will. Because you have stopped to talk to me, you are curious. Curious people accumulate beautiful stories. You can't, however, have mine."

Without thinking, Scott responded, "Oh, because you're writing it?"

"Exactly, honey. I even got an editor. You probably don't have an editor." She chuckled.

Scott looked around. "You live alone?"

"Had a boyfriend until eight years ago. Younger than me. He had a heart attack. Ended my romantic life. Really miss it too."

Scott was amazed at this old woman. "You're able to take care of yourself, alone and all that?"

She shook a finger at him. "Don't get fixated on age. Look at animals. They're independent 'til they can't forage or hunt. Then they die. It's the way of the world. Our society takes care of old people, warehouses them. What's the damn point of that? Life happens; then death happens. That's the whole story."

"You still drive?"

"Shouldn't. License revoked years ago. Vision's the shits. Fortunately, store's not too far."

"Emily, I'd be glad to shop for you."

"Maybe." Laughing. "You trying to make time with me?"

Scott grinned. "I would, but I'm kind of interested in V.V., down the way."

"I can see that, given your age. She's damn good looking, but not much the conversationalist. Doesn't have much to say."

Trying to steer the subject away from the object of his affections and avoid having to defend her, he countered. "How long do you think you can stay here?"

"Scott, you have to understand this. I've got no family, I've passed the century mark. I've lived my way all my life. When I leave this place, I leave in a god damn pine box."

For a moment Scott transported himself 80 years into the future. He saw the indignity of age and being dependent. All his life he'd seen old people as simply old people. Talking to Emily made old age real, connected the line from birth to death.

She told him about being a club singer in the roaring twenties, piano player in a jazz band in the thirties, owning a bar for almost twenty years, two deceased kids, half dozen husbands, and an unknown number of lovers. It was clear she could have gone on all night, but Scott was feeling the effects of the wine and was getting hungry.

"I could talk with you all night, but I've got to get home and have dinner."

"Come back any time. Maybe you'd like to walk with me sometime. But you'd have to keep up."

Scott's first day at work was as interesting as his father's accounting sheets. Sylvia taught him about taking ads over the phone. Within a hour he was on his own, taking mostly apartment rental and car ads, helping people cut the wording and abbreviate to fit the basic size ad. It was boring but busy, so the day went by quickly, and soon he was out in the afternoon fog. As always, the sun came out about half way up the hill, and the Smith was liquid emeralds doing a conga line over the rocks. He remembered Emily and her river swims and V.V. and how she might look in a bathing suit. A swimming date! He thought. No, a real date, swimming and dinner.

He caught V.V. before she started fixing dinner, proposing a swim in the river followed by a dinner in town, just, of course,

21

to celebrate his new job.

She reminded him that Sam was part of the package, and he added that the invitation naturally included the girl; although, in the impulse of the moment, he'd totally forgotten about the child.

On the drive, Sam asked, "So you like my mother?" Then when Scott admitted liking her, Sam switched to chanting, "Momma's got a boy friend."

They drove to a deep spot, and walked down the trail. Scott was a bit uncomfortable about stripping down to his trunks. He was kind of skinny and didn't have the buff look he figured women admired. But still, he figured, at least he had "six pack" abs.

When she pulled off her terry cloth shift, Scott was shocked. She wasn't just built, she was chiseled and quite buff. Her slim waist was well defined, her legs firm and strong, and even her arms had solid definition. There was something about her looks that was more than attractive. There was something familiar, as if he'd known her long before meeting her.

There she stood, tall, fiery red hair, trim, hard body, high cheek bones, and pale blue eyes. He had to fight the urge to stare.

They dove in the cool river, swimming and laughing, and watching Sam swing out on a rope tied to a tree and free fall into the deep middle. It was wonderful after a day confined in a dark, green room. Then the sun dropped over the ridge, bring a chill shade to the pool, and they got out.

As he tossed a towel to her, he ventured, "You look really fit. Work out?"

"Yeah, every morning before work. Don't need to be at the restaurant until 10, so I hit the gym, do all the machines plus a half hour on the tread mill. It's too easy to get fat when you work all day and take care of a kid at night."

Scott quickly slipped on a shirt. "Maybe I'll join that gym, now that I'm working." He was tempted to ask her how much she could bench but was afraid it would be more than his best.

Scott wanted to try the old bar and grill near the trailer park, but since it was a bar, they'd likely card, and he didn't want to be embarrassed. Less than two weeks to go, and then they could go out drinking and dancing.

He picked a little Chinese place in town, faded facade, yellowed table cloths, but good food. V.V. seemed to be having a good time. In fact, when he walked her back to her door, and Sam had scampered in to turn on the TV, V.V. kissed him hard and long before saying, "Scott, thanks for a wonderful time." By the time he got back in his place and his erection had subsided, he had become road kill on the hormonal highway.

In Scott's mind, where everything was significant and relationships were important, simple sexual arousal needed a broader context. V.V. was appealing sexually; therefore she was appealing as a person. Being appealing, meant she was interesting, which meant she had potential for great and important things. His lust must be just the surface of a deeper emotion, which, when coupled with her depth and potential, certainly must mean that what he was feeling was love. Yes, indeed. Scott was in love, so it was thoughts of epic romance rather than raw sexual pleasure that kept him awake most of the night.

On Sunday, Scott prepared a picnic lunch and invited V.V. for another day on the river. He had persuaded Jake to pick up some beer for him. The day was cloudless and hot, which meant that Crescent City must be socked in with fog.

They swam, played in the water, drank beer and ate, and with every subtle interaction, Scott's love deepened. Each of her words and gestures took on symbolic meaning. At one point they playfully wrestled over the last piece of pie. Scott, feeling macho, tried to pin her, only to have her flip him off, roll him over and pin him. She sat on him, holding his arms down, grinned and said, "Do you give up?"

Having little choice, he nodded in ascent. "Then," she demanded, "The winner can take her spoils?" She bent over, large breasts almost falling out of her top, and kissed him for what seemed like hours of unleashed ecstasy.

When he could slow his breathing enough to speak, he asked, "Have you taken all the spoils of victory that you want?" He was hoping to offer up as much tribute as she demanded.

"I have something else to get from you, but it will have to wait until we get back." She gave him a wicked smile, and Scott was so thankful she'd found someone to watch Sam for the day.

They got back to her place as the sun was setting. V.V. stopped for a kid's video, popped a bunch of popcorn, picked up Sam, and planted her on the couch, where she'd stay, glued to the screen for a couple of hours. Then she took Scott by the hand and led him to his place.

As she unzipped his pants in the middle of his one room, she sighed, "God, it's been a long time."

For over an hour she unleashed a year of pent up sexual frustration. She seemed to know exactly what she wanted and how she wanted it, and she led Scott through a sexual triathlon. When Scott could no longer get it up, he used his fingers and his tongue. By the time she rolled off him for the last time, settling into a sweaty lump of flesh, Scott was relieved. He was exhausted, done in, tapped out, finished. He was sore and raw and as far removed from horny as he'd ever been. In his vulnerable condition, emotionally and physically naked, he was just about to confess his deepest love, when she looked at his clock and jumped to her feet.

"Jesus, that movie must be over by now. I sure as hell don't want Sam coming over to find me." She slipped into her shorts and top, while Scott lay there, stunned and slacked jawed. He'd expected they would hold each other, whispering endearing things and making plans for the future. Instead, she'd shifted gears so quickly, she didn't seem like the same woman. Then she bent over and kissed him quickly on the lips. "You're a sweetheart, Scott. Let's get together very soon, OK?" And without waiting for an answer, she dashed out the door.

Lying there, Scott was incapable of fathoming the lack of balance in the relationship. While she rushed to her daughter, a very high priority, Scott was building his universe around her.

He had been magically transformed from man to a lovesick puppy who would follow faithfully at her heels. By the time Scott showered and threw on some clean clothes, V.V. had grown to many times life size. He sat at the laptop and started to create a character based on her. This character alternately rescued lost children, made laws for the benefit of humanity, performed difficult, life-saving operations, won international tennis matches, taught courses in several subjects at a major university, and took great care of her husband and children. In the final version of his scenario, she was a professor of literature who had discovered his novels and had brought them to the attention of the world. As the darkness engulfed the forest, Scott's reality flowed quietly down the Smith River and out to sea.

For the next week, she came over almost every night. He tried to have food and wine, to make a romantic date of it. They'd talk for a few minutes. Basically Scott would talk about all the things he would do and the things she could or might do. He also kept handing her books, hoping to interest her in his kind of literature. She indulged his flights of fancy but confined her end of the conversation to practical matters, spiced with a few sexual comments. She also changed the subject, when, after sex, Scott started up with, "Where do you see our relationship going?"

After some conversation and wine, usually within an hour, they'd crawl into his bed for some feverish love making. He continually murmured that she was the best he'd ever had. Actually, there had only been three: his high school girlfriend, when both of them were inexperienced and pretty innocent, a short relationship just after graduation, and Cyn, who had given him his real sexual education.

Scott decided he liked it when she got on top. She instigated all of the experimentation, as he was content to use the missionary position unless something else was suggested. At one point the foggy realization start to form that she might think of him as not much more than a boy, someone to train to her needs

25

and desires. One time she joked, "If you cleaned windows too, you'd be perfect."

To his credit, Scott somehow realized it was too early to confess his feelings. He hinted at it in many ways, with comments like, "You know how much I liked you," or "I think we have a great future together." The one that seemed to make her squirm was, "Do you think there is one perfect match for each of us?" If she saw where he was headed, she gave no indication, responding with affirmations like, "We have a nice thing going, and I really enjoy our time together."

Each night after she went home, Scott would wrestle with the enigmatic comments until he pinned them squarely in the book of love. She was afraid of being hurt again, he figured, but she loved him just the same. That much was obvious.

He woke up one day with a rare thought that didn't involve V.V.. He realized he'd reached the magical age of 21. Quickly, he included her in this thought. He would ask her out to the Tree House, the rustic bar and grill down the street, a place he'd been dying to see since he'd moved there. They would celebrate his birthday, but how would he discuss the subject of age. Neither of them had asked or volunteered that information. Perhaps, he thought, she imagined him to be much older, and that his true age may put her off. Maybe they could just celebrate without the actual number coming up.

Scott found Jake with a bike engine on the bench and mentioned his birthday.

"Well, kid, if I wasn't in the middle of a job, I'd buy you a beer. How about tonight down at the Tree House?

"Actually, I'm taking V.V. there tonight."

"You two must really have a thing goin'. Nice lookin' bod, but a bit old for you, don't you think? Not much fun to talk to, but I don't suppose you're doin' much talkin." Scott's red faced response made Jake laugh. "What the hell, I got my education from my ma's best friend. I was 16; she was around 40. According to the women I've had since, she trained me right well, she did." Then his jovial face contracted and got serious.

26

"Now, I'm not sayin' it's going to happen, but if a some long haired guys that look a cross 'tween hillbilly and early hippie start cussin' each other out, keep an eye on them. If they go for their guns, play it safe and hit the floor. Mind you, they damn near never hit what they're aimin' for, but there's always a chance a stray bullet'll get you in the ass."

Scott was aghast. "They have gun fights there!"

"Not usually, but a weird family runs the place. Hoover clan. Some of the younger generation still livin' the hillbilly life. Can't hold their liquor. Get in fights all the time. Rarely pull guns. Like I sez, most never hit anything. Usually too damn drunk to aim. Law shuts them down for a spell; things cool off. Then it starts again. Probably won't happen. Have a damn good time."

Jake's comments made the place even for desirable. This was more gritty, real life. He was ready for anything.

They carded him but not her. He tried to be as nonchalant as possible about pulling out his wallet and showing the bouncer his license.

When they sat down, she said, "Happy 21st."

"How did you know?"

"Figured it out. Today's your birthday, and for the first time we didn't drive all the way into town. And we haven't gone out to a bar before. Also, you have those cute, boyish good looks." She squeezed his thigh.

They ordered big steaks and a pitcher of Mad River ale, the local brew. As always, alcohol loosened Scott's tongue, and he was over the top about his writing projects, hinting that she featured in current book. He selectively ignored her frown when he mentioned writing about her.

He'd all but forgotten Jake's warning, when he heard someone being called a goddamn, stupid mother fucker. He looked over his shoulder at two of the slimiest looking country boys he'd ever seen. Obviously Hoover boys. He pulled his chair out slowly. "Maybe we should get down."

She looked casually toward the bar. "Naw, they're not nearly drunk enough for that. Probably just go out back and beat each other stupid."

From that observation, it was clear to Scott that she'd been in the place a few times. Drinking in this dive didn't fit his image of the refined, superwoman.

Scott overdid the beer and couldn't perform that night, so he crawled under the sheet and gave her oral sex, even though he only wanted to sleep. He was the kind of man who believed that failure to satisfy a women was worse than being a murderer or traitor.

4.

Dozens of dancing devils doing a perverse version of a chorus line in Scott's head were chased off the stage by an equally annoying sound. "Mukis! You planning on sleeping the whole goddamn day away!"

In his dream state the voice became his father, demanding he get to work. Then again it was his sister yelling at him to do his part of the chores. Whatever it was, it was waking him up. "Wake up Mukis. I gotta talk to you about your car."

It was Buck Rogers. Scott shouted something about him being on his way. He stumbled to his feet, slipped into his sweats, and staggered the dozen feet to the door.

"What the hell's wrong with my car?" He asked, the morning light hurting his eyes.

"The back is naked. You need to do something about that, and I can help." He was smiling and holding some paper in his hand. He was wearing frayed black jeans and a black tee shirt that said, "Nuke a church for Satan."

Scott absently looked at the back of his car. Nothing to see. He did a shrug that indicated a question. "Nothing there."

"Exactly. You must be trying to be mister conservative middle America. I brought you your first bumper sticker. This one's free; others will cost you." He held out the white on black rectangle that stated in block letters, "Lie, Cheat, Steal! It's the American Way."

Scott gave Buck a thumbs up, as he plopped into a patio chair. With the sticker just to the left of the license, Buck sat down in the other chair, pulling out a joint.

"Start the day out right?"

Scott looked at his watch. 9:30. "No, too early for me."

"Suit yourself. Party hardy last night?"

"My birthday. Twenty-one. The Tree House."

"I can see by the lipstick stains vacuous V.V. was with you."

29

That comment pushed Scott's "defend his woman" button, and he launched into a litany of her real and imagined qualities. Buck was wearing the grin of someone who had pushed those buttons deliberately, just to enjoy the effect.

After a few minutes, Buck seemed to tire of baiting Scott. "Since you're legal now, let's grab a beer together one night, that is if your lady will give you a night off. Stop by or call."

Scott was now alone, and it was a quiet Sunday morning. He looked in front of his car to find his first Sunday edition of the San Francisco paper. After looking over the news and reading the comics, he turned to the book review section. They listed a few of the new books that were suddenly in demand. *"The Axe of Compassion*: Gruff, but kind-hearted police inspector tracks and apprehends a serial killer who has killed eleven accountants."

And another book, that while new, sounded familiar. *"Tom's Big Case*: Young lawyer, just passed the bar, helps poor widow sue the Nation's largest and most evil corporation."

And in the non-fiction category, a book by an eighteen year old pop singer, *"My Torrid Life: A True Confession."*

He had to think back an hour. Did he actually refuse that joint, or was he high? He looked at the page again, shook his head, and turned to the Dear Abby advice column.

Scott didn't see V.V. that night or the next. She'd come in late and gone straight inside. He was afraid that she was pissed at him for getting drunk and not performing. He figured that he'd make himself available, and if she didn't show in another day or two, he'd stop by. He would have called, but he still didn't have a phone. The phone company kept making appointments for times when he was at work, even though he explained that he couldn't be home and that there was no reason to come in the house.

Three days without V.V., and Scott was a basket case. He planted himself in a patio chair with a book and bottle of wine and decided to wait. He absently read the same page four or five times before he heard her car pull up. He nonchalantly waved

30

and called "Hi."

She came over and hugged him just as he was getting up, throwing him off balance, his face ending up between her breasts. "Sorry I haven't been around much. Got good news." She waited a few moments for Scott to look wide eyed and to nod in anticipation. "I've been promoted. Assistant manager. The manager's been training me after my shift. I officially start tomorrow. He says I'm a natural. I've always had a head for business. This is definitely my opportunity."

Scott hugged her enthusiastically and told her how happy he was for her, all the while hoping his insincerity didn't show. Business of all things. Not art, education, literature, just business, like his father. His family would welcome her, thank her for settling their boy down and bringing him back to the fold. Why, they'd even build a new wing on the house for them. Shit. What else could happen?

Then her expression changed. "Scott, you know how much I like you and enjoy being with you?" He leaned forward and waited for the inevitable "but."

"But," she slowly added. "Until I get up to speed on this new job, the hours are long. Lots to learn; home late and mentally exhausted. We gotta cut it down to once or twice a week. Not permanently, you understand, just until I get a new routine. I knew you'd understand." She kissed him.

He felt his lower lip extend, and in spite of his best efforts, he was starting to pout. "But, well, maybe you could spend less time at the gym or something."

"Scott, you know how important it is for me to have a balanced life. I have to have my routine to keep it together, to keep from going buggy. You do understand how important this is to me, don't you?"

Cornered like a rat, Scott had no choice but to assure her in the most passionate tones that he was so behind her on this, that he wanted to see her succeed, to become manager in a couple more years, to even end up in the corporate offices some day. He must have convinced her, as she smiled, kissed him again, had a quick glass of wine with him, and went home.

He slouched into his place and came out with a large water glass, filled it with wine, took a healthy drink and put his head down on the dusty, plastic table. He felt that this was the beginning of the end. There was a pen and pad of paper on the table, and Scott started writing a sad love story ending to the book he'd started, continuing until well after midnight, when the wine was gone and his vision was getting blurry.

With V.V. taking up less of his time, Scott was trying to work a modicum of creativity into his job. He started taking a measure of pride in how much he could condense an ad for a customer, allowing more and more information in the basic two lines. He'd been pushing the envelope for days, when Sylvia stomped up to him and signaled him not to pick up the phone.

"Scotty, what the devil is this?" She threw a proof sheet on his desk, put her hands on her ample hips and waited.

"Car ad. What's wrong?"

"Let me read it to you. '92 Fd tk. .75 nw cl, bk, ti, bl pnt. Lo mi. lea in 3G/off.' What does that mean?"

"It's a 1992 Ford truck, 3/4 ton, with a new clutch, brakes, tires, and blue paint job. It has low miles, leather interior. He wants $3,000 or best offer."

"Scotty, Scotty. Nobody can crack your code except you. We are attempting to communicate to prospective buyers." She sighed and started again. "We have standard abbreviations, and they are listed in the paper. Hence, we all speak the same language, advertiser, classified personnel, and buyer. Now, nod it that makes sense. Good. Now you claim to be a writer. Writers communicate. That's what I'd like you to do. Communicate so that people can read it. Please tell me you understand."

"I understand;" Scott replied weakly. So much for creativity. The job, V.V. Things couldn't get much worse.

Things did indeed get worse the next time V.V. came over. She had an arm load of books, which she dropped on the table. "I'm sorry Scott. I tried to read these, but with Sam, the new job and all. Well, you know." She pushed *Remembrance of Things*

Past at him. "Nice writing, but just too much about not much. Next was *Crime and Punishment*. "Just too heavy for the few minutes I have in the evening to read." The last book she pushed his way was *Ulysses*. "Frankly, I don't want to have to work this hard. Reading should be relaxing. Scott, I know you like this stuff. I tried."

She ended up taking him to bed, but his heart wasn't in it. It was like when he'd heard that the host of the kid's show he'd followed faithfully had been busted on some obscenity charge.

He engaged in his usual after sex conversation about their relationship, but she cut him off with, "Scott, do we have to go there now. Can't you see my plate is full these days. Please, let's table this until a less stressful time."

She threw in a few short sound bites of small talk before jumping up and heading home.

The next morning as Scott was leaving for work and V.V. for the gym, she happened to notice the bumper sticker. "Looks like you know that moron, Buck Rogers."

"Yeah, he's a friend. You don't like him?" Another gap seemed to have appeared.

"He's so full of himself. What bugs me is that he considers anyone who doesn't agree with him a fool or some misguided pawn of government or business."

"Well," Scott asserted without much conviction, "He shocks people and makes them think. He's dedicated. I can't see how he's making enough to live on from his stickers and shirts."

"Yeah, right. You didn't look past his front. His real name is Charlie, and he works part time for a guy who does remodels. I met him when he worked on enclosing my porch. I consider him a boorish jerk, but what the hell, he's your friend. Want to come over for dinner Wednesday?"

Discouraged but desperate, Scott eagerly agreed. As he watched the dust rise behind her car, he thought about jumping in his car and driving someplace, any place. But to where? There was always home, but he recoiled at that prospect.

After a day of Sylvia's patronizing attitude and little verbal pats on the head, Scott needed to let off steam. He walked over to Buck's trailer and offered to buy him a beer.

There were few patrons in the Tree House. The peanut shells crunched under their feet as they found a corner table. Scott ordered a pitcher of ale, and Buck launched almost immediately into the absurdities of modern society.

"Companies sell our names and financial histories to people who pester us, and yet we still do business with them and give them more personal information. We play follow the leader, all the while chanting 'baaa, baaa'."

Within a few minutes a loud argument broke out at the bar. They looked over at a couple of guys who looked like members of the Hoover clan cussing each other out. Too many things had pissed Scott off lately, and this was the last straw. "Hey, knock it off over there. We're trying to have a conversation."

"Mind your own fuckin' business," was the reply.

In spite of Buck's gestures to get him to cool it, Scott shot back with, "Can't you guys act like civilized people, rather than backwoods savages?"

It worked, in that it stopped the argument between the guys, but it brought them straight to the table. "My great uncle owns this joint, and we does what we wants here, punk."

The other guy added, "Don't look like he old 'nough to drink. Show me yo ID boy." He emphasized "boy" as to make it a challenge.

Buck had gone paler than usual as he gave Scott pleading looks.

"I'm not going to show you anything. Get lost, Gomer."

The bigger and uglier of the two responded. "You be gettin' lost. In fact you outta here right now."

"We're going to sit here and finish our beer."

"Then we gonna throw yo sorry asses out, which is how we likes it."

Scott suddenly threw the pitcher of beer in the guy's face, jumped up and punched the other one. The big guy caught Scott with a right hook, as the other one went for Buck, who, while an innocent bystander, had no other options. He punched the guy in the gut.

Buck and Scott put up a good fight, but practice makes perfect, and the Hoover boys practiced fighting almost nightly. The battle moved slowly toward the door, and suddenly Scott and Buck found themselves bouncing off the dirt parking lot.

"By the way, Scott," Buck said as he dusted himself off. "I'm a pacifist. Try to keep that thought in your Cro-Magnon brain in the future."

"Yeah, I like the way a pacifist says 'take that, asshole'."

In spite of the cuts and bruises, Scott was feeling much better about himself. He realized that up to the fight, he'd been a passive part of his new life. V.V. ran the relationship, Sylvia treated him like some kid straight out of high school, Jake regarded him with good natured humor, and Buck was constantly preaching to him. Scott was going to take control of his life.

He realized that the fight would make a good story, particularly with the background of violence at the Tree House. He wrote it up and took it into Rob early the next morning. The editor liked it, and ran it. Scott had his first byline.

Sylvia took notice. "Nice piece. You like to write, but can you write on assignment?"

After listening to his heartfelt assurance, she continued, pushing her glasses down for better eye contact. "The guy who does the road tests on new cars is on vacation, and I was thinking of doing it myself. It's part of the advertising section, but that's a long story. Read his last few columns to get the format. We want something for everyone. Comfort, safety, handling, power, economy. Some of that you get from the stats, the rest is subjective. That means you drive the car and tell the readers what you think of it. And no matter what, find something about it to like." Then very slowly, "Do you think you can do that?"

Scott felt like an eight year old getting the job of hall monitor. He wanted to say something sarcastic, but in this business editors, even of the advertising section, are gods. After he promised, she handed him the car brochure. It was the last hold out in the SUV field, the Jaguar. This one had it all. It would do 150, had a stereo with two CDs and speakers mounted in the headrests, so driver and passenger could each have their own music. It had all leather interior, with gold plated instrument knobs. The air conditioning could be customized for each rider. The suspension was adjustable for everything from freeway to off road. The GPS unit also connected to the internet. The list of standard features went on for three pages. He looked at the price. It was more than the two bedroom condo he took an ad for the day before, and he was going to get paid to drive it around all day. Maybe his luck was changing.

"One more thing Scott. Even though we're insured against damage, there's good will with the dealer and the rising price of premiums, so be very, very careful with this car. Tell me you understand."

Again, Scott had to promise. He looked forward to the day he'd get out of this department and would have this tedious woman off his back. It couldn't be soon enough.

He had a ball putting the sleek SUV that handled like a sports car though its paces. Writing about this would be a piece of cake. The only down side was the price, but people who bought Jags didn't concern themselves with cost.

Not wanting to wait until office hours, Scott worked on the story at home and well into the night, even rejecting V.V.s offer for a visit. When he arrived at the paper, he had 2500 words of outstanding prose. He handed the disk to Sylvia, beaming at her the whole time.

Fifteen minutes later. "Scotty, what the hell is this supposed to be? She was storming up to his desk like a stampeding water buffalo.

He shrugged and was wide-eyed with surprise. He didn't understand what her problem was.

I didn't ask for a damn book. And what kind of description is this? "The paint, like a deep mountain pond, draws you in and

36

suspends you in a vibrant sea of color."

"I thought it was a good image."

"'The metallic paint has a mirror finish.' That's an image in a car description. This isn't a bedroom scene from a romantic novel. We are selling cars to people who want to know if this is something they might want. It's as simple as that. Did you read the last few columns." Without pausing for an answer. "Of course you didn't, because you're a great writer and already know better. Now listen very carefully. If you ever want to have another word printed in this paper, you will take this and turn it into 1000 words of straight description, emphasizing the car's good points, and you'll have it on my desktop no later than ten AM."

He picked it up, set his jaw and asserted, "This is quality prose, journalistic literature."

"Fine, go to work for a university literary mag. Or, you could rewrite this and actually get it in print."

Scott could feel his face redden. It was wonderful writing, but he had to concede that it was a bit too long, and the descriptions might be a stretch for the artistically bankrupt business types who would read the column. He sat down and worked feverishly.

Her, "That will suffice," was the highest praise he could ever hope to get from Sylvia. He had written to satisfy an editor, a lesson in practical writing, a discipline that would ultimately help him when book editors suggest minor changes in his novels.

V.V. was getting into the routine of her new job, and she had Saturday afternoon off. It was warm in the trailer park, so they decided on a swim and picnic on the river. It was like the early days of the relationship, weeks before. There was no tension between them, only playful bantering, food and fun. Scott was afraid to bring up anything more serious than his recent successes at the paper, for fear of dumping ice water on their warming relationship. He fought hard to keep things pleasant and to avoid his usual high minded conversations or relationship pressures.

He slipped only once when he asked, "How far did you actually get into *Ulysses*?"

"Twenty pages, perhaps. Ended up falling asleep at 9:30 with the book on my lap. Now here's an interesting book, right off the best seller list." She handed him a copy of *The Axe of Compassion*.

For a moment he thought he'd be ill. "Never mind books right now. Let's go for a swim."

The sex later that afternoon was back to being great again. Scott was learning that arguing with a woman wasn't compatible with getting well laid. He was learning some of the little compromises that make life less of an uphill struggle.

After V.V. went home, Scott wandered over to Jake's shop. "Jake, you ever been married?"

"Once, and that was enough. Woman was always tryin' to change me. I got to know a guy who was like what she wanted me to be. I introduced them, and they ran off together. Heard later that she tried to make him more like me, and he left her."

Scott had a bit of pot he'd gotten from Buck, and he held it out. "Want to smoke some?"

Thanks Scott, but I hadda give it up. Kept getting bronchitis, and the doc says pot was aggravating the lungs. Same thing with cigarettes. Miss the pot more than the cigs."

Scott sat down on a dirty chair. "So, it's true about bikers being big dopers and drinkers."

"Most, not all."

"Guess you did all sorts of drugs and had wild parties. How about coke?"

"Did lots of that. Doctor made me give it up. Blood pressure."

"Isn't the beer bad for that too?"

"Yeah, yeah, I know. And also the weight thing. Doc's after me to lose fifty pounds. Hey. I gave up the whiskey and wine and the good beer, but I gotta draw the line somewheres. I'm down to this piss water lite beer, and if it's gonna kill me, I'll die with one in my hand."

"Jake, moving here is the best thing that's ever happened to me. You helped me make a new home. I wanna say thanks. Let me buy you a beer."

"Over to the Tree House? You ready to go back there so soon?"

Scott wasn't really in the mood for Appalachia West, but he put on his stoic front. He figured that no one would fuck with him with Jake there, and if they did, the two of them could kick ass.

Scott bought a round and was talking about women as a round about way to get to the subject of V.V. The guys he'd fought with a few nights ago were back at the bar, and they were glancing his way.

One of them seemed to focus on their table, and Scott balled his fists in anticipation.

"There's Jake. Howdy Jake. Say, isn't that guy with him the smart mouth kid we trashed the other night?"

Scott felt another fight coming on, but Jake's booming voice cut in. "Yo, boys. Come on over. Want ya to meet a friend of mine."

The big hillbillies lumbered over. "This snot nosed kid a friend of yours?"

"Yeah. His name's Scott. Lives at the park. Works for the paper in town. Says he gave you a few to remember."

Scott flinched at the last comment, feeling a brawl coming up very soon, and finding this conversation very weird.

"Anyway," Jake continued, "This is Dusty and Jo Jo."

The big guy, Dusty, smiled and pointed at Scott. "Shit, he weren't so bad fer a green kid, but he's got somethin to learn fore he can mix it up with the big boys." Then, turning to Scott, "You got you some spunk, kid."

Jake interrupted. "Dusty, haven't seen your old Fat Bob on the road lately. Given up riding?"

"Jake, the fuckin' bike's been cuttin' out, missin'. Don't run worth a shit. Shoved it in the garage."

Jake reached over and rapped on Dusty's head with his

39

knuckles. "Hello in there. You remember who you're talkin' to? Your fuckin' bike's in the garage. Who you gonna call?"

"I know. . . Jake, you don't. . ."

"What? You gonna fix it yourself? Come on, what am I?"

"Aw, Jake. Cut it out."

"Naw, naw. Look, I'm about to buy a round, but you gotta say it first. Come on, let me hear you."

"All right." Both guys said almost in unison. "You're the best fuckin' Harley mechanic in Del Norte County."

Jake waved the waitress for a round. "Good. Now why don't you bring it in? You know that's how I afford to keep beer in my fridge."

"Jake, the road crew's cut back hours fer the summer. Not much work goin on . Ya know last winter didn't fuck up the roads much. Your work, dude, is what they call a luxury."

Jake leaned over, looking more serious than Scott had ever seen him. "Use your brain. That bike's worth a bunch kept up. It ain't worth much for parts. Tell you what. You bring it in, and we set up a payment plan for the repairs. Also, you bring me business, your bill goes way down. Cool?"

"Cool." A fresh round hit the table. Jo Jo asked if Scott rode. Scott, still feeling weird about socializing with guys he recently fought, was about to answer, when Jake cut in. "Been fixin' up a old bike. Be prefect for him. Just waitin until he gets some cash set by. You know, once he climbs on, he'll be hooked, one of us."

They all got a big kick out of that. Jo Jo leaned over and slapped Scott on the back. "Bit of practice, you'd be OK with your fists. Anytime you need more teachin, feel free to mix it up with us. We'd be might glad to kick yo ass till you gets the hang of it. Rule is, loser buys the beer. We drink for free; you gets an education. You can call our ins-tea-toot of higher learnin' 'Black and Blue U'."

Scott was amazed that these guys not only didn't hold a grudge, they considered the whole thing some sort of a game, and they could go from drinking buddies to bloodied opponents in a blink of an eye. Scott felt very much a real man then, and he slipped into the role as if he'd been born to it. "You jokers should know I had a pacifist backing me up. He wasn't much help. Hell, if I'd had Jake with me, we'd have cleaned your clock."

Dusty look surprised. "Jake. Why he hasn't been in no fight for years. What's it been, my man? Six, seven year?"

Jake acknowledged that, but Scott was totally perplexed.

Almost apologetically, Scott mumbled, "Jake, I figured that you a hard core biker and all. . . that you were a brawler."

"Used to be. See, I got this arthritis in my knuckles. Sometimes can hardly hold a wrench. Busted up my hands too much years ago. Punch someone out, and I'm hurtin' for a week. Can hardly work on a bike. Doc says all the fightin' done it." He shrugged, as if to say, "what can you do?"

By eleven that night, Scott and Jo Jo had made friends the way beer makes people friends. Just before Jake dragged him out, Scott had played the bar stool game with Jo Jo. They took turns punching each other on the arm until one of them fell off the stool. On the third round Scott had fallen off his stool without being hit, and Jake had taken the opportunity to drag him to his feet and help him home.

Scott, feeling more the real man, walked into Rob's office two days later and boldly asserted himself. "Boss, you know I can write. You saw the Jag SUV piece, and there was my story about the Tree House." He paused there for a what seemed like hours but was a few seconds. When Rob didn't respond or make an offer, he continued. "I was thinking that maybe you could assign me some stories. I mean, I could still do my classified work. I really want to be a reporter."

Rob folded his arms across his chest and looked absently toward the ceiling. He looked to be in deep thought, and Scott watched the second hand on the wall clock creep imperceptibly, as if counting down to his doom. He found himself fidgeting, unable to find a comfortable stance. He willed himself to stand still, and the pressure had him almost to the point of bolting from the office, when Rob focused on him again.

"You're a nice kid, Scott, a bit odd, but hard working and eager. Tell you what. You could cover the school board meetings." He grinned slyly. "No monumental works of literature. Just straight reporting. You know, what they discussed, how they voted. It's not uncovering Watergate or anything, but it's a start if you're serious."

A start. That must mean that if he did a good job, other assignments would come his way. He saw his future as a full reporter, a columnist, a foreign correspondent, a syndicated national opinion shaper. "I'll do it. Just think, when I win the Pulitzer, you'll be able to say you gave me my start."

Rob put his hand on Scott's shoulder and guided him toward the door. "You know, Scott, that's exactly why I offered it to you."

The next few weeks became a rosy routine. His relationship with V.V. was on a schedule. They had set the two nights that best suited her schedule for their dates, which often included dinner or drinks, but which always included sex. He had the school board meetings every other Wednesday. Once a week he'd have a beer or two with Jake, sometimes including the hillbilly Hoover boys, and about once a week he'd talk with Buck, usually at Buck's place, over a beer and a joint. On his evenings alone, he'd write, usually working on the novels based on V.V. He'd write himself into a corner, delete some pages, and then start over. He had also taken to walking once a week with Emily, surprised at how brisk a pace she could keep. Without realizing it Scott had fallen into one of the deadening routines that take the years away like flower petals down a stream. Summer had become early fall, the warmest time of year on the north coast.

His walks with Emily opened him to the subtle sights and sounds surrounding him. He was forced to rein in his long stride in favor of her shuffle, giving him more time to look around. More importantly, Emily was always insisting that he look at what they were passing. She made him focus on the dance of light on the surface of the flowing water, the convoluted harmonies of the birds' songs, and the rainbow of color imbedded in familiar things.

On one walk she stopped to ask him the color of a redwood tree. Without thinking he answered, "red." Then, after a moment's thought, he amended it to reddish brown. She shook her head and told him to look closely at the tree they'd been passing. He examined the bark and started really seeing the tree for the first time.

"There's some green from what looks like lichen." He said. She nodded and urged him to continue. "I see some orange and a touch of yellow and gold."

He got closer, looking deep into the layered surface. "Black deep inside, and shades of gray." His fascination was growing. "I see some deep blues and more greens. There are many shades of green, a few of red, plenty of browns. Jesus, the whole color spectrum's in this tree."

"That's the idea, Scotty. If you're going to be a writer, you have to be an observer. You have to look like that at trees, at rivers, at birds, at people. There's a world within each thing, and you have to be an explorer."

From then on their walks were magical sensory explorations. He was starting to understand how a woman of her advanced years could still hold a child-like excitement about everything. After each walk, he'd go home and write up his experiences. They were by far his best writings, and he organized them by subject on the computer, planning to insert them in the proper places within the novel he was continually building.

The scenarios he'd been developing around V.V. as a main character were getting harder and harder to work on. When routine moves in, excitement and flights of fancy catch the midnight stage. While he still saw untapped greatness, he was less and less confident that he could coax it out of her. The worst thing is that she now sometimes discussed her new management job during foreplay, making him struggle to keep an erection. He started to convince himself that this was just a natural phase. Once the rush of her new responsibilities subsided, things would be back to normal. He only hoped her boss wouldn't transfer, opening the door for another ghastly promotion.

5.

After the initial weeks of pure rebellion against his family, he had started calling them again, and like the rest of his life, these calls had become routine. Each Sunday morning, he'd call, or his mother would call him. Business was going great. Becky was taking more and more responsibility. She now ran both marketing and accounting, and the red ink had departed the books permanently. Her new title was vice president, and yes, Scott senior was starting the process that would change the name to Mukis and Daughter.

Also, Becky had become a local athletic celebrity. Seems there's a new category in women's body building, called the figure competition. It's less about big muscles than a perfectly sculptured body. Becky was entering and winning.

If all this wasn't more good news about Becky than Scott could stomach, his mother gushed about one more item. Becky was dating, for the first time in almost two years. She was seeing a nice boy she'd met at work, someone in the accounting department, and it looked like it was getting serious. Scott swallowed all this news as if it were box wine and reluctantly agreed to come down for Thanksgiving. It would be the first time home in almost six months.

The phone call put Scott in a funk. He couldn't understand why Becky's life successes troubled him so much. He had chosen not to be involved with the business, but there were parallels in his life. To match her in his field, he would have to be a full reporter at a big daily and have a book out in the bargain. Becky had a serious relationship, and Scott's was in a rut. She was an athlete, and he looked like a grunge rock musician, pasty and dissipated. The main thing Scott couldn't swallow was that she had a firm hand on the tiller of her life, while he was washing in and out with the tide.

Sunday mornings were his time to himself, time to phone, time to write, and time to read the Sunday San Francisco paper. With the phone call out of the way, he tried to lose himself in the book review section.

First he looked at the hot new fiction. There was a glowing review of, "*The Sword of Confusion*: Gruff, but kind-hearted forensic expert tracks and apprehends a serial killer who has killed seven librarians." And another book he could swear was listed before. "*Fred's Inaugural Case*: Young lawyer, just passed the bar, helps poor widow sue corrupt slumlord. He turned to the non-fiction category, a book by an twenty-one year old actor, "*My Nightmare Life: An Honest Memoir*." It was hard to resist the temptation to open a beer.

The morning had sneaked out the door, dragging his self esteem and confidence behind and leaving a snail trail of futility. It was time for a walk with Emily, and the old woman's upbeat attitude would be a blessing after the morning he'd endured.

On this walk they stopped to probe the detritus on the forest floor, observing the many layers, each in a different stage of decomposition. Digging down with the toe of his shoe, he could reach a layer in which all the plant, animal and mineral matter had blended, eliminating any trace of what had once fallen there. This, he thought, was how the days of his life were accumulating and dissolving. They also stopped to watch a newt working its way against the current. Another metaphor for my life, Scott thought.

Back at the trailer park, Jake was in his shop, unusual for a Sunday. "Jake, thought you'd be out riding today."

"Got a bit of carpal tunnel in my right wrist from doin' all this paper work on the computer. Bothers hell out of me when I crank the throttle. Doc says rest it for a week or two, and it'll be fine. Takin the time to clean up a bit in here." He walked over to a bike that looked about three quarters assembled. "Scott, this'd be a great bike for you, lean and mean. Started with a bunch a spare parts, and it's damn near ready to run."

Jake absently reached into the greasy refrigerator and pulled out two light beers. Scott, while not in the mood, just as absently took one and mumbled his thanks.

"Jake, I'm not making a lot of money right now, and well, a bike's not a necessity." He watched the shadow of disappointment move over the big man's face and realized that to Jake a bike is the only necessity. "But you know," he added, "I've been after the boss for more reporter assignments, so maybe I'll be able to buy that chrome monster after all."

Jake's face lit up again, and started explaining all about the bike. To Scott it sounded like, "blah, blah, blah, carburetor; blah, blah, blah, cam shaft." However, he nodded, smiled and tried to look like he understood.

His Sunday ended with uncommitted sex with his part time girlfriend, who, upon his broaching the relationship topic, promptly dressed and rushed home to her child. Scott opened a beer and turned on his small screen TV to a truly boring movie, which he watched for want of anything better to do.

Having become a man of regular habits, Scott caught Rob as he did every Monday morning and asked him if he had any other writing assignments to throw his way. Rob's answer was the usual, "Patience, Scott, patience."

Then Scott added that he was thinking about buying a motorcycle and could use the extra money, even though Scott wasn't a bit serious about spending thousands on a bike.

That perked Rob up. "Scott, I used to ride. Had a Honda 750. Used to run the canyons from here to Cave Junction. What kind of bike you got your eye on?"

Cornered, Scott started explaining the Harley Jake was building, the custom handle bars, all the chrome, the wild exhaust system.

"Jesus, Scott, I've always wanted a Harley, but they're expensive, not practical, and I've got a family and house payment, and all that." He stopped and gazed off into space for a few moments, before speaking again. "There are a couple of other guys here who were really into bikes at one time. I've got an idea. It's like the sales pitch I got last time I was in Hawaii. Time share! That's it! We could get four or five of us together, and buy the bike as a time share. We'd each get it for a weekend, clean it and gas it up, and the next guy would do the same the following week. We got room to store it back in the warehouse. What you think?"

It was weird, but Scott figured it was an OK way to have a bike, and he knew he wouldn't want to ride all the time. A bike would give him a nice macho image, and it was also a way to get on a buddy relationship with the boss and perhaps get more writing assignments. Scott told Rob what he knew about the bike and what Jake wanted for it. Rob called the other guys in, and after a few minutes discussion, they'd put together a deal.

"Time share!" Jake shook his head in amazement. "To me a bike's a pretty damn personal thing. Rather share my woman, but if you boys think it'll work and you can swing it, it's fine by me."

Within a week, the four of them had the deal finalized, and Jake put in the extra hours getting the bike up and running. It took all of Scott's rainy day money, but he figured the bike was, after all, an investment. The damn things hold their value, and he could always sell his share if rough times came around.

When Scott came to pick up the bike, Jake told him that the whole time he was getting the bike ready, he was thinking about the plan, and the more he thought, the more the business man within him was flexing his muscles. He'd never done much dealing in used bikes. They were hard to move at the price he had to charge for his time. He didn't have room to store bikes for months, while he paid to advertise them and all. Repairs were gold. The customers were mostly regulars, and it was in and out, and money in his pocket. He told Scott he didn't need advice, just someone to bounce new ideas off of. "I could put together these here time shares. Then I'd get the bikes, an fix em up. With a smaller investment, I'd get guys who were flirtin' with the life, not just the hard core bikers. I could move me a lot a bikes, and when they break down, I'd have some built in customers. It can't lose."

Scott had to agree with him. It was a great business idea, and naturally, Scott would never have thought of it. Seems he was surrounded with business heads, which made him appreciate Buck more and more. The man often sold bumper stickers for less than they cost him. Scott liked that.

In fact, the back of Scott's car was accumulating a collection of the rude pieces of paper. The latest said, "My Kids are Neutered! How About Yours?" He was actually getting to enjoy the offended looks he got while driving around town.

The time share being Rob's idea, he figured he deserved the first weekend. Cruising around on a chopped Harley all weekend must have put him in a great mood. As soon as Scott started Monday with his usual request for more writing assignments, Rob said that he could cover the city council meetings. Then as an elated Scott was leaving the office, Rob added that perhaps he could do the planning commission meetings also. In fact, since classified hired some part timers, Scott could work less hours on the phone and take more time for his reporting.

This was great. In no time he'd be a full time reporter, covering real news, rushing up to a roped off crime scene with his press pass waving in the air. And Sylvia would have less hours to make him feel insignificant.

He imagined her reaction when she heard the news, but she surprised him. "Good for you, Scott. I'm sure you'll do an adequate job. I knew that once you learned a few basics, you could produce copy."

For Sylvia, this was high praise. But now another problem occurred to him. He would have to negotiate another schedule with V.V. The council meeting fell on one of their regular date nights, and V.V. could be damn inflexible.

"No problem, Scott. We'll just work around it. It's only every other week, and that night's only a problem until this night class ends in December. We have plenty of time together." Scott couldn't believe how cool she was being with it.

They were in his patio, sipping some wine, and listening to

49

that fusion jazz that she liked. Like many educated young men past their twenty-first birthday, he remained a closet lover of heavy metal music. Fans had to deal with a serious image problem, so Scott listened in the car or with headphones on. He always pretended to enjoy this random arrangement of notes, although after a few minutes it faded into something like white noise or elevator music on caffeine. He wished for a few minutes of AC/DC or Metallica.

V.V. wasn't the best company lately. Perhaps she hadn't even thought before responding about the council night. After all, she'd hardly looked up from the accounting text she was buried in. He wanted to grab the book and toss it, but he knew her standard argument. She had so many responsibilities and had to organize her routine, and getting ahead was important to her. He knew he couldn't fight her on this, as it was becoming clear that in her priority system, he was regularly being moved down the ladder. Perhaps the problem was the relationship was becoming dull and routine. He needed to spice it up. "I told you about the bike."

"Yeah." Absently. "Time share. Good business idea."

"Well, my turn this weekend. Wanna go for a ride? We can go through the redwoods, stop for lunch, all that sort of thing."

She looked up quickly and brightened noticeably. "You know, that would be fun. I haven't been on a bike in ages. You do know how to ride?"

"Yes," he said, and it was true. "I've logged many hours behind the handlebars." That part was a lie. Jake had taught him to ride, and allowed him to practice up and down their section of the highway. He'd ridden as far as town, but he felt pretty comfortable and tried to look confident.

He'd been right. It was just the thing to spice up the routine. They rode south, stopping to watch the elk in Redwood Park. Then they continued to Trinidad, where they stopped for lunch and walked, hand in hand, on the beach near the rock, watching the boats and the undulating flocks of sea birds.

A slight hitch occurred when Scott tried to drive up the

steep hills from the beach. With two up it was hard to get moving and stay balanced. He killed the bike four times, the last time almost dumping them on the beach. Finally, V.V. insisted he give her a shot getting them up to the road. He would rather have had oral surgery performed by a blind dipsomaniac with the shakes, but he had no good argument beyond male pride. She fired it up, coordinated clutch and brake smoothly, causing the bike to roar up the hill without a single jerk or buck. Once at the top, she said how much fun it was to ride again, and would he mind if she stayed at the controls for awhile. The question must have been rhetorical, as she pulled into the street and headed for the highway before he could refuse.

She picked up speed, weaving through traffic and leaning into the turns. Scott had his arms around her and was frankly unnerved by the feeling of not having an iota of control. She didn't stop until they got to Klamath, where she thanked him for indulging her and changed places. Scott, unused to two up in traffic, rode sedately the rest of the way home, hating himself for it in the process.

At least they had laughed and had fun, and when they made love, it was like the beginning again.

The passion fired up the one area of thin ice in the relationship, the topic of the relationship itself. He started talking about them making plans and trying to get her to make some sort of commitment beyond the next date.

Had it not been for the afterglow of sex, she might have turned angry. Instead, she just seemed impatient. "We've been over this a dozen times. I'm trying to balance my life, raise a child, build my career, take care of my home, take some time for me, and still carry on a relationship with you. I can't and won't make you the center of my life."

The warmth of passion's nest had turned to the chill of a meat locker by the time she left.

The next morning the paper ran a page one story about a guy who drove his car into a speeding logging truck, just twenty or so miles from where they'd been. The truck driver hadn't been

51

hurt, but the car driver died, and both vehicles had to be towed. There was speculation that it was deliberate. The dead man was an outspoken anti logging activist. Scott feared a pattern, this being too much like the Palestinian suicide bombers. Apparently he wasn't the only one to think that, as a San Francisco editorial writer made that case and predicted, based on an anonymous informant, a rash of these kinds of collisions.

He sought the known quantity of the book review section, fiction first. *The Saw of Humanity* was the story of a gruff, but kind-hearted private detective who tracks and apprehends a serial killer who has killed nine podiatrists. The next new hit was "*Ben Approaches the Bench*: Young lawyer joins struggling partnership and helps a neighborhood resist a big developer's attempt to invoke imminent domain." The non-fiction pick of the week was a book by an twenty-three year old business wonder boy, "*My Rise to the Top: A True Confession.*"

Suddenly Buck dashed Scott's Sunday morning peace. "Did you read about the suicide driver. Great. Shit, it'll be like the massacre in India by the British that finally achieved independence." Buck was waving his arms in excitement.

"Wait." Scott tried to remind him. "That's only speculation. Might well have been an accident."

"Doesn't matter. A few postings on web sites and some phone calls to papers claiming a new organization of activists willing to die to save the trees, and the country will have a fuckin' movement on their hands."

Buck had finally managed to shock Scott. "Don't sound so damn happy. You're talking about people dying here, you know!"

Buck's expression became serious and more subdued. "Only a nut case would die. Well... and besides, it would eventually come out that it was a hoax. Maybe you could make history, rather than write about it."

" Are you nuts. I'm not fucking with this. And you'd better not even think about it. This isn't a game."

"Yeah, you're right Scott. Don't know what I was thinking."

Then with a sly smile. "Hope no one else has come up with the idea." He walked away leaving Scott to struggle with the battle between his insistence on trusting his friends and an uncomfortable suspicion that was crawling around his mind like a drunk in a wine cellar.

Scott had just gotten back to the Sunday paper, when his mother called. It was more good news about the business and Becky's successes, personal, financial, and athletic. His mother had just sent him an e-mail with an attached picture of Becky from her last contest.

As if some demon was guiding his reluctant hand, Scott found himself checking his mail and opening the damned attachment. He gasped as the photo resolved itself on the screen.

Becky was perfect, even more perfect than V.V., which took some doing. Of course Becky was a few years younger than V.V., who still looked magnificent for a woman pushing thirty-one.

After trying for a couple of hours to write, he hopped on the bike and rode up 199 to the rest stop on the border. He stretched out on the lawn, under a tree and tried to clear his mind. There was something about the damn picture of Becky that kept going through him like a rabid rat, running amok in dark mental hallways, ducking through secret doors, and scurrying into the shadows. Why did it disturb him so much, and why did he even bother to save it?

By the end of the week there were four used bikes in front of Jake's shop, and Scott had placed an ad for him. The bikes were on consignment and offered as time share. Jake would put compatible people together, make the deal, and keep the bike maintained. He would make a percentage off the sale and have a guaranteed group of customers. Jake was even thinking that if this worked out, he might even take over the defunct cafe across the highway and someday even open a store in town. Jake was leaning back in his tattered office chair, fingers interlaced behind his head, spinning dreams of future good fortune.

Scott was uncomfortable with this aspect of Jake. The man as biker, mechanic and eccentric park manager was a good image. Jake as astute businessman was like watching the Muppets engaging in unnatural sex acts.

The following weekend the warm season had its last gasp. The rains, now overdue, had not appeared, the days were hot, and the river, while quite low, was a series of warm pools. He saw Emily crawling into her car. When he asked her where she was going, she said, "This is my last chance to swim for the year, and at my age, possibly for the rest of my life."

V.V. was working until mid afternoon, and in spite of Scott's demands, was not going to make time for him. He had no pressing plans, so he offered to take Emily to the river. There was a beach down river with a dirt road down to it, and this late in the year, with the summer visitors long gone, it would likely be deserted. He drove there, taking the dirt road carefully, to avoid bouncing the old woman around. He helped her over the cobbles and into the water before striking out on his own. He did a couple laps of the little pool before swimming over to a boulder near the opposite shore. He climbed up, stretching out in the warm sun, and allowing himself to slip into a current of shifting romantic daydreams and literary fantasies.

Time was doing a slight of hand in his mind. He'd been there for an hour or for ten minutes. He listened to the absolute quiet, which soon dissolved into the softest trickle as the river slipped out of the pool, over the gravel bottom and down to the next pool. Then there arose the almost inaudible sound of dragonfly wings, and the occasional call of a bird far up in a tree. What was missing was the sound of Emily swimming. She probably tired and was on the shore, warming herself, he thought.

After a few moments of lethargy, he forced himself to call out to her. No answer. Asleep, perhaps. Again, but louder. Still no answer. He sat bolt upright and turned around. She wasn't on the shore, so he scanned the water. She wasn't swimming or in the car. Where could she have gone?

Then he looked toward the lower end of the pool, to where it flows over the cobbles and down stream. Emily was lying against the rocks, in inches of water, and she wasn't moving. He cried out again, diving into the water without waiting for an answer. When he got to her and turned her over, listening for breath and a heartbeat was a futile act. She was clearly dead. He pulled her to him and cried, "Oh my god, oh my god. What have I done." In a moment Scott had made himself the responsible party. He was responsible for bring her here, and he was responsible for not watching her. She was dead, and it was his fault. He had let her down. He was a selfish, irresponsible jerk, a disaster in every relationship. Tears were in his eyes as he rocked her limp body in his arms.

The paramedics and police arrived, and Scott tried to be calm, but he realized he was babbling about what happened, causing the authorities to ask the same questions over and over. Although the exact cause of death would be determined later, it was difficult to tell if it were drowning or a heart attack. The paramedics supported the heart attack idea, given the amount of water in lungs and some other professional deductions. That was little help to Scott, who felt that either way he could have saved her, either by keeping her face out of the water and rushing her to the hospital, or by simply pulling her out at the first sign of distress.

He thought about what she'd said as they drove down to the beach. "Each day could be your last, so treat it as both the last and the first of what's to come."

At least she died doing something she likes. Still, she might not have died at all, were it not for Scott's irresponsibility.

The internal arguments were still raging when V.V. got home. As soon as he dashed over to her place, the debate became external. "I was responsible, and I screwed up. I indulged my selfish pleasures while she struggled with her last moments."

After the initial shock, V.V. started getting her impatient look while trying to get a word in with Scott. When he finally paused slightly for a breath, she cut in. "She was very old. You had nothing to do with it. You probably couldn't have prolonged her life more than a few minutes, maybe a couple days. It was her time, and she went out. . ."

"But she was full of life. I should have watched her. Can't you understand what I'm going through?"

V.V. exploded, "It's not about you! Emily's dead! It's about her, not you. Grow up and get out of the center of the goddamn universe!"

Being totally distraught, Scott threw caution to the wind, the waves, and perhaps the fire. "How can you be so fuckin' cold. You're never there for me emotionally, not even at a time like this! God!"

"Scott. I'm not your mother, and I don't want to be. Do I remind you of your mother or something?"

"Don't be absurd. You're nothing like my mother. If anything you're just like my sis. . . Oh my God! Becky!"

"Who the hell is? Oh, your sister." V.V. put her hand to her head and slumped into a chair, while Scott start to pace in double time.

"Yeah, Becky, my sister. I don't know why I didn't see it. You're her. I mean, just like her. You have the same hair, build, features, even this thing about business. Jesus, Subconsciously I must have been in love with my own sister. Oh my God!"

The eight hundred, seventy-three generations, since his distant ancestors developed language and taboos and passed them on with their massive icing of guilt, all came crashing down on Scott. In one day, he'd caused a death and violated something sacred in human society. He lusted after his sister and acted out that lust with an almost double. After ten years of not believing in a general hell, he saw himself creating one of his own, filled with regret and self-loathing.

And V.V. was just sitting there, slack jawed with disbelief. Finally, she shook her head and said in a calm and icy voice, "I don't need this. I don't care about your feelings for your sister, your mother, or anyone. I don't need the drama, the demands, the palpable need. Scotty, my life requires peace and stability. I don't need a volatile relationship. I don't need an immature boy. I can't handle this. I need some space. We need to cool it for awhile, until you get it together."

A huge voice in his head screamed, "Scott, shut the hell up," but he refused to listen, instead shouting the absolutely last words he should have said at that moment. "It sounds like you're trying to end the relationship. If that's what you want, why don't you have the guts to say it?"

She shrugged. "OK, Scott. It's over. I didn't want it to come to a black and white choice, but you're not giving me any choice. It's been great, and you're a nice guy and all, but yes, I guess it's time to end it."

Scott just stood there, staring at her, the voice in his head slowly echoing off into the distance, "stupid, stupid, stupid." He couldn't think of a thing to say. He just stared, until the expression on her face turned into a question mark.

"Scotty. I think that was the cue for you to go. You know, go. Like back to your house, go. Like not becoming a statue in my room and freaking out my daughter when she comes in. Go, just go."

Scott nodded dumbly, turned and started to walk out. He turned at the door and said, "You know I love you and want to build a life with you."

She just slowly shook her head in response as Scott stepped out into a gathering darkness.

6.

It would be a night without sleep. He tried liberal doses of wine, but it wasn't helping. But the wine cleared his mind, and he finally decided that the problem was that he'd challenged her to rise to her potential, and she couldn't handle the pressure. She had opted to live life in a safe routine, and she couldn't do that with Scott around. He paced and carried on elaborate arguments inside his head. Finally, with little room to pace in a small trailer, he walked down to the river and wandered in the moonlight.

Great, mysterious shadows writhed on the ground like anguished ghosts, as he wandered along the leaf strewn bank. The light filtering through the trees cast Jungian archetypal images along the river. He found himself dropping through a psychological rabbit hole to a mythological landscape. A tree alone in a clearing, rising straight to the sky, was the sign he needed. It was a metaphor for his life. His destiny was to rise, alone and misunderstood, from the darkness, and reach for the vast universe of his artistic mission. V.V. had, by a conspiracy of fate, freed him to achieve the fullness of himself.

He stumbled back to his trailer and wrote until just before dawn. Scott wrote the story of Emily's death from his personal point of view. He did it to get a handle on his demons and because he figured it would make a newspaper piece that would touch people. After only two hours of troubled sleep, he was up and starting his Sunday routine. He opened up the paper, and the headlines shouted, "Eco radicals take credit for suicide auto wreck." Apparently, someone had notified the news and authorities that a group, "Mahatmas of the Forest" had organized this suicide to call attention to the destruction of the forest. They had claimed that this was only the first of many sacrifices, and that they would continue until even the most heartless timber baron was forced to turn away from the carnage he was causing.

This smacked of Buck Rogers and his weird way of making a statement. For the first time, he called, rather than walked over. "Buck, you said you wouldn't plant that outrageous story."

The hesitant voice on the other end protested. "Scott, I swear to you that I didn't do it. Really, if I thought of it, others must have. Maybe there really is an organization like that. I used to hang out with Earth First! and ELF, and there were some people around them that were unpopular because they were even too radical for those guys. Scott, trust me. I wouldn't fuck with people's lives to make some lousy statement."

That was it. One thing that was certain was that Scott trusted his friends. If he couldn't trust them, they couldn't be his friends. The argument sort of made circles, but ultimately, the final check point was his own ability to judge people. It was something Buck might have done, but he promised Scott he wouldn't and he swore he didn't therefore someone else had.

That out of the way, he had to tell someone about his broken life. "V.V. broke up with me last night."

"She's thirty something, has a kid, and is obsessed with material success. You obviously are not her type. I'm surprised she hung around this long. You must be a good lay."

Scott did not want to have a discussion with Buck about his sex life, or even think about the kind of crap that ran through Buck's mind. He shut it out and opened the paper.

In the book review section, *"The Cleaver of Perception*: a gruff but kind-hearted insurance investigator tracks and apprehends a serial killer who has killed seven VCR repairmen," was rapidly ascending the charts. *Ted's Fervent Appeal*, concerned a young lawyer who takes on the World Trade Organization for his client, a crippled, illiterate, farm worker. Finally, in non fiction, a new book, *Code and Cocaine* is the true confession of a 16 year old brilliant programmer and hacker and his battle with drugs.

Exhausted, Scott fell into bed early, and he was rested and a little less fragile when he walked into Rob's office and handed him the Emily piece. Rob read the whole thing in that high speed scan newspaper men are so good at. Then he looked up with an almost startled look on his face.

"This is potentially excellent." He handed it back. "You go in there and rewrite it without the whining self pity, and I'll run it."

"Self pity? I was only trying to convey the emotional. . ."

"I know. If you want to write for soap operas, write this way. Is that where you want to take your writing career?"

"Of course not. I hate those shows"

"Fine, you've got to learn the difference between conveying emotion and losing yourself in drama. Learn that, and you could be a good writer. Now, go fix it."

Scott rewrote it and took it to the harshest critic he knew. "Sylvia, would you please read this and give me your honest opinion."

After a maddeningly quick read, she thrust it at him. "Too much drama, and there's this thread of self pity running through it. Maybe it's too recent to write about. Perhaps wait a few weeks."

He shook his head no and went back to his desk. It took two more rewrites to get Sylvia's approval. Then he took it to Rob who gave him a thumbs up and a pat on the back.

Scott buried himself in work, taking on more writing assignments. He got the police beat and even the harbor news. The darkening skies and chill winds worked in his favor. Apparently, those unused to north coast winters were generally good for only one before fleeing to warmer climates. The weather, however, didn't concern him. Whenever he looked up from work, the pain of his loss flared up again, so he kept himself occupied.

With evening meetings to cover, he seldom got home before nine, and then he'd work until after midnight on his novel based on V.V. Actually, it had become two novels, as he couldn't decide if her character should be a crusader for neglected children or a fiery young politician running for state senate. He worked on both with equal fervor.

He looked up several weeks after V.V. had destroyed his life to find that he had a new life. The last tie to classified was severed, and he was a full time writer. Sylvia and Rob had met with him, and during the meeting they started talking to each other as if he wasn't there. They managed to agree that they'd made a writer of him, in spite of his stubborn addiction to melodrama. They congratulated themselves for their fine job and finally Scott for being their good student, for letting these excerpts ferret out his hidden talent. He wanted to be indignant, but his joy at becoming a full time reporter brushed his petulance aside.

He still saw V.V. from time to time, and she often paused to pass a few moments with him, rarely choosing to sit down. She seemed genuinely delighted at his good fortune at work. Her job was stressful as usual. She was working extra hard lately, since the rumor had circulated about her boss being considered for regional management. He had apparently said that he could easily take a long vacation, knowing that the restaurant would be in capable hands.

She asked, "Scott, do your new duties mean a raise?"

He was embarrassed to have to admit that he'd never bothered to ask. Then, for a moment, he interpreted that question as a feeler about his potential as a breadwinner and mate. "I'm sure I'll be making enough to support a family, if that's what you mean."

She shook her head. "No, I mean if you start making more money, you could afford something better." She gestured toward his small, rusty travel trailer. "This place may be available if I get the manager's job. A promotion would my ticket out of this slum."

To Scott the break up was bad enough. To have her leave for good would be devastating.

"V.V., why would you want to leave? You've got the trees around you, and you know the weather in town sucks. It's fog all summer, and rain in the winter. Then there's the big mortgage. You could use that money for a college fund for Sam."

"Scott, I've always lived on a budget. I save now, and I'd save then. I could bike to work, saving gas money and auto maintenance. I'd grow some of my food in the yard. Sam would have a place to play and other kids around. The minute they offer me the job, this dump goes on the market."

"What about all your friends here?"

She laughed. "Casual acquaintances, with an obvious exception." She smiled at him. "This is the fringe of society, a writer's kind of people I suppose. I want a normal neighborhood with normal people."

Scott had kept the conversation going long enough for her to absently sit down. Scott pulled up a chair and nonchalantly poured himself a glass of wine. "Oh, can I offer you one?" He just happened to keep an extra glass on the table.

"Why not. Could use a break before tackling the house cleaning."

It was like old times, the two of them talking about their lives and plans, but this time it wasn't about what they would do, rather what they were doing. Scott mentioned that he was getting some actual stories, rather than just covering beats. Once he settled in and proved himself, he was going to push for a column.

V.V. admitted that the manager's job was just a step. She wanted the corporate office or to run a more upscale restaurant. "My goal by age forty is to own a business." She said it in such a matter of fact way, that Scott new in his bones that she would do it. She really was like Becky, who had always known she'd run the family business someday.

Two glasses of wine did nothing to make her affectionate, to rekindle the passion they so recently had. For Scott's part, the wine had made him want to get on his knees and confess his undying love for her, and then take her straight to bed. Luckily for his ego, he hesitated, for after the second glass, she jumped to her feet and excused herself.

The next morning at work, he checked the wire services and saw a piece that gave him chills. Another car had pulled in front of a logging truck. This time it definitely wasn't an accident. The car had turned and stopped, offering a broadside to the oncoming truck. The side of the car facing the truck had "Save the Forest" painted on it. Within hours of the incident, several people had called the papers and police, claiming to be spokesmen for the group responsible and proclaiming that more blood would be spilled.

Scott sat down and wrote his first column for the paper. His premise was that the first crash had been an accident, and that radical agitators had used it to forge a new organization. The new group, according to Scott, jumped in to grab the publicity and set things up for a real confrontation. He made reference to the film "Network."

Rob liked it and decided to run it, but he asked Scott a question that shook his already fragile sense of reality. "What if you are right about the first crash? But what if the rest is a hoax?"

"A hoax!" He was indignant. "The driver died. Death isn't a hoax."

Rob scratched his head and leaned back in the office chair. "I don't mean the zealous martyrs, they can come independently out of the woodwork. I'm talking about the so called organization behind it. Anyway, being cynical comes with the work. It'll infect you one day. You ever hear of the old Orson Wells radio broadcast of War of The Worlds?"

"Yeah, I heard the tapes. It was part of a class." He stopped and shook his head. "No, no. Radio was fairly new. People were naive back then. Nobody would fall for something like that now."

"Hell, Scott. Maybe you're right. Anyway, good job." He made a hand motion that indicated that the conversation was over, and walked back to his dusty windowed office, leaving his suspicions to haunt Scott for the rest of the day.

The idea was just too twisted. Could someone with a weird

sense of humor, someone perhaps like Buck, take an accident and turn it into something like this as a big joke or to make some statement? And if they did, were there people gullible enough to throw their lives away because they think there is some organized movement? In the world that Scott understood, the world was spared both of these kinds of people. The more he thought about it, the more he figured his take on it was pretty accurate. And he wasn't going to become a jaded cynic, no matter how long he worked in the media.

A column was the new and welcomed addition to Scott's duties, but it didn't have the latitude he'd hoped for. Rob decided that enough people lived up the river to warrant local coverage. Scott's job was to ferret out the people and events of interest. It wasn't the biting social commentary he wanted, but it was a byline.

Obviously, Jake and his business was a major part of the first column, along with the locals' favorite swimming hole. He reluctantly devoted a line to V.V.'s success as assistant manager at the diner. The following week's column would be a bit harder. He realized that he'd only gotten to know a few of the people in the area.

Reading the news off the service was getting depressing. In the last week two more suicide drivers had pulled in front of loaded logging trucks, each with an anti logging slogan painted on the door. In each case there were calls from organizations taking credit. The situation was starting to get national media attention. Scott wondered, since he lived pretty close to the center of the action, if he might be able to dig up some information on the fanatical group or groups involved.

Even though he believed Buck when he said he wasn't involved, it seemed Buck did have some insider knowledge of the people involved. How else would he be able to predict events so accurately. He called Buck, inviting him for a beer and a conversation about the fatal crashes. For the first time, Buck refused the offer of a free beer. He was a bit evasive, but he apparently was very busy with some tee shirt printing, and he promised to get back to Scott in the very near future.

Rob thought the story would be great, but he doubted that Scott could get close enough to the people involved to get the information. After all, the major bay area papers had their best reporters on it, and there were people from the wire services snooping around. "I can't send you out on this, but if you find anything on your own time, I'll be happy to run it."

That was enough of an invitation for Scott. It was his weekend on the bike, and the weather was holding, so he decided to cruise down to Humboldt County to where loggers and protesters acted like Israelis and Palestinians.

He rode to Arcata and talked to the hippie types hanging out in the square. With his tattered jeans, stringy hair, and old Harley, he looked more like some protester than a reporter. The consensus was that a new, more radical group was being loosely formed up and down the coast.

When he got to Rio Del and Scotia, the loggers, who took him for a redneck, were sure it was the work of Earth First and ELF.

He wandered down some side roads off the Eel river, enjoying the massive trees and the way the light and shadows danced over his face. Finally he found some sort of commune with anti logging signs against the front fence. He said he was looking to link up with the protests. Some of the younger guys claimed to have some vague connection to the secret organization. They seemed to regard the martyrs as heroic figures. They knew lots of rumors but nothing substantial. Everything he heard sounded like speculation. However, he did kill a couple of hours with them, smoking their dope and talking about justice for the trees.

It was almost sunset when he got back to Arcata, and he was still over eighty miles from home. He was tired and hungry, and he still carried the warm memories of the Trinidad restaurant he'd taken V.V. to. He pulled in just as the sun dipped below the Pacific in a burst of red and orange that looked like a flock of canaries had crashed into a window. He was so stiff and sore that he could hardly dismount. It took walking from the parking lot to the door to straighten out his aching back.

Being a Saturday night in a good restaurant, there was the typical California wait. He didn't want to hang out for 45 minutes, but he was in no shape to get back on the bike. Scott wandered over to the bar, where there was no wait for a drink. He ordered a beer and couldn't help notice the one other person at the bar, a young blond woman. Being young, male and unattached, he was biologically incapable of ignoring her.

A study of this woman could kill a good part of his wait, so he checked her out carefully, in his gentlemanly way, from head down. He could only see her profile, but she apparently had nice features, which were framed with shoulder length pale blond hair. It took a few minutes for him to decide that the color was natural, before he dropped his gaze.

She was a big woman, not fat, but stocky. She had the look of a Viking woman or a sturdy peasant. Her breasts were huge, her hips full, and her thighs thick. She was actually quite sexy in an earth mother way. He absently tried to guess her height, weight and age. Then with still plenty of time to kill, he tried picturing her naked.

Suddenly, as if his thoughts were audible, she turned toward him, looking more past him than at him. He saw that she looked sad, almost as if she'd been crying. Her forest green eyes seemed to reflect the weight of the world. The naked image evaporated, and he was pulled into her emotion, touched by her sorrow. He wanted to do something noble for her.

He turned back to the bar, feeling uncomfortable. His glass was empty, and he was about to order another, when he turned toward her again. He was suddenly caught, like a deer in the headlights, by her eyes, unable to break the connection. He smiled and mumbled a greeting. Her sad look softened just a bit, and she gave him quizzical look. He was left with something undone. The ball was clearly in his court, but he didn't know what kind of ball or even the type of court. He ended up doing the standard male thing. "May I buy you a drink?"

That seemed to be the right thing, as her look brightened a bit more. She ordered a glass of white wine, he another beer. There were still two bar stools between them, a gap to be bridged that sorely tested his engineering skill.

Knowing he had to take the beer from his lips and desperate for something to say, he went for the obvious. "You seem upset. Are you OK?"

"Actually, no. A two year relationship just went up in smoke."

Good news, bad news. Thought Scott. What he said was, "I'm sorry. I know how it feels. I went through the same thing a few weeks ago." Then as if adding something stupid was a necessary part of his age and gender, he continued, "Were you, like, broken up with?'

"Dumped. The word is dumped, and the answer is yes. You too?"

Was it that obvious? He nodded yes. Then in an attempt to be smooth, he made some comment about the man being foolish to let her go.

He watched her mouth continue to expand into a smile that seemed to rush out in all directions like the big bang. "Thank you. That was just what I needed to hear. Are you into long distance relationships?"

"No." He wondered what she was leading to.

"Well then, why are we shouting half way across the room. If you come over here, I promise not to bite off more than a finger."

Scott felt his face flush as he moved next to her. Only a few inches from her, he felt the full impact of her physical presence. He sensed her raw female energy and could feel her body heat. He was getting excited just sitting there.

She was asking him something, but his focus was on the physical sensation. She waved her hand in front of his face. "Did you go home and leave your body here to keep me company?"

"Sorry. My name, right? Scott, Scott Mukis. And you?"

"Maddie Kobzev. Close friends call me Madd. M-u-c-o-u-s, like in snot?"

"No, M-u-k-i-s. Maddie Kobzev. Russian name? "

"Look at me. Russian peasant stock. Good woman. Work hard in fields. I've never seen you around here. Live near by?"

"No, up the river above Crescent City. I was trying to get info about all those environmentalist guys who've been crashing into trucks. I'm a reporter." With the last comment, his voice swelled with pride.

"Reporter, huh? Interesting job. Those collisions are an interesting social phenomenon. I teach at the university, sociology."

"Wow, a professor. How cool." Scott was impressed. "I dropped out before getting a degree. Wanted to be a writer, learn my craft from real life, you know."

She leaned forward, her breasts threatening to envelop him. "Really? Real life must be fascinating."

Any gesture of interest was all he needed. He started in about the place he lived, his work at the paper, and the novels he was writing about real people, real lives. He tossed in all his theories and notions about literature, his concerns about social justice, the lonely life of a dedicated writer. And, through it all, she sat there staring at him with a Mona Lisa smile on her face. Somewhere in his oration, he signaled for another round, paying and taking a sip without missing a syllable.

As he started to wind down, a smile crept over her face.

She leaned over and kissed him lightly. "What a technique. You just talk until a girl's got no choice. Has to kiss you to get a word in." She winked at him, and he felt his face flush.

"I'm sorry. I. . I."

"I'm just teasing. Don't let it bother you. It was delightful listening to your story."

Scott then insisted that she take her turn. She'd been teaching four years, buying a home walking distance from the restaurant. With some prompting, she gave him an overview of her university years. From a series of casual questions, he learned that she was 29. Another older woman.

Each time she stopped, indicating a response, Scott would fill the space with a series of questions until she started in again. Then the bartender came up, and he saw that their glasses were empty. This time she gestured that she was picking up the round and another pint appeared before him. He was starting to feel it.

"Scott do I make you nervous?"

"Well, um, ah, not exactly." She did. Maddie was self-assured and very forward. There was a sexual question floating in the air, one she'd had the answer to probably from the first. He didn't know what to do, wasn't sure if he were reading her right. It didn't seem likely that a woman like Maddie would come on to a stranger in a bar and have a one night stand. She was an educated, classy woman, and if he made the wrong suggestion, she could be offended, ending whatever dating relationship they might develop. In a way, he hoped he was right. It was happening too fast. He needed to build some kind of emotional relationship. Casual sex really wasn't in his comfort zone.

"Well, don't be nervous. I'm not dangerous. I hope I don't strike you as the violent type."

That comment took him aback, until he watched her smile and ran it through his mind again. "Oh, a pun. I get it."

His table was ready. "Would you like to join me?"

"Why, are you coming apart? Seriously, I'd love to."

Over dinner she explained that she was studying the social dislocations associated with our rapidly changing society. "People need solid social institutions on which to base their interactions with others. When the institutions and the rules of the game change fast enough, people don't know how to react and interact. Society gets fragmented, and people get kind of freaky."

"Sometimes," he added, "they even drive into a speeding logging truck."

She laughed. "Most reactions aren't quite that dramatic, but weird stuff happens, like a writer and a sociologist forging a

69

relationship in a bar." She laughed again.

He told her about his rapidly growing responsibility on the paper, the stories he'd written, and the ones he wanted to write. As he sipped the wine they'd ordered, his candid assessment of himself as a writer grew. Before the bottle was empty, he was talking about best sellers and literary prizes.

The place was almost deserted, and the meal was over. "I guess it's time to go." He blurted out suddenly, getting unsteadily to his feet.

"You plan to go out there and play Hell's Angel?"

"What? Yeah, I'm fine I guess. I should get your number, so I could like call you."

"As opposed to getting my number in order to perform complicated math?"

A light mist had slipped in, giving the night a chilly bite. It started to revive him. Not knowing what else to say, he pointed toward the parking lot. "That's my motorcycle."

"You're not riding that all the way home tonight, are you.?"

"Well, I guess."

"You'd be pickled road kill. Good for the gourmet vultures; bad for you. You shouldn't be behind the wheel, or even the handle bars"

"Maybe coffee or something." He shrugged.

"Or something. Look, Scott, I live a block away. You crash at my place. Ride home sober in the morning."

She was not only right, but she'd relieved him of the big decision. Once back at her place, she'd likely fix him a place on the couch. If she had other plans, it was her turf, her call. He was getting light headed and feeling like going to sleep, so he wasn't going to push for sex in the least.

She had one of those low, wide, plush sofas, the kind you sprawled, rather than sat on. He made some remark about it looking comfortable, and she dragged a pillow and some blankets from the hall closet. As she roughly made up a bed, he looked around. Nice art on the walls, classy but casual furniture. The home of a young, educated woman. He liked it. It was

70

real, not like the continually infernal, interior decorated, anti-septic look of his parent's hall of pretension.

She asked him if he needed anything, and she said it with such sweetness, that he reached out to hug her. They hugged for what seemed a long time, and she was making no effort to disengage, and he was getting aroused, so he chanced a light kiss, which she returned with considerable force. He lost himself in it, kissing her lips, neck, ear lobes. Then he pulled self-consciously away, feeling he'd over stepped.

"Watch it Scott. There are laws." When he looked at her with panicked comprehension, she explained. "Truth in advertising. Your lips made a contract. Is your body going to honor it?"

All he could do is grin foolishly, as she led him toward her bedroom. As he sat on the bed watching her undress her full, voluptuous body, a great fantasy story started building. He found his imagination sailing off with her to new, uncharted worlds.

She gestured at his clothes, which were all still on. Shyly, he started to strip. She watched him intently for a moment before saying, "I feel I should warn you before we go any further. I'll very likely break your heart, and I'm not insured for that kind of damage."

He dropped his pants, looked her straight in her green eyes, and said, "I don't care. I don't believe it, but even so, I just don't care."

Had it not been for the alcohol, he would have come within milliseconds. As it was he lasted until he satisfied her. He felt she had taken him down to his essence. He was laid bare, defenseless. In all the weeks he'd been with V.V., he hadn't surrendered himself so absolutely. He felt he was drowning, suffering a death of pure euphoria. The last thing he felt before slipping into a contorted dream was her moist lips, hard on his.

He woke at first light with his head suspended in a soft cloud, weightlessly bobbing up and down. He opened his eyes and found himself surrounded by breast. She was absently stroking his hair.

"I was going to get up and write you a letter of recommendation, for the next woman you meet."

"After you, I couldn't look at another woman. You're wonderful."

"Great. We have something we both agree on. You do have good taste. I like that in a man."

She kissed him, and he responded with abandon, kissing and groping her, making guttural animal sounds, working his way over her thighs and hips. She grabbed him by his ass and pulled him into place. They made bronco-riding rodeo love until he felt he'd have a heart attack.

After a powerful orgasm, he was too exhausted to roll over. And in that moment of weakness, he swore that he loved her. She rolled him off, and he dozed off again, unintelligible words of love trailing off.

He had a dream that he was a pampered pet poodle on the satin pillow of a rich woman, being fed scraps of prime rib and being bathed slowly and carefully each morning. The sun directly in his eyes brought him around. Madd was coming into the bedroom in a robe, carrying the Sunday paper.

"You ought to see this Scott. Looks like your environmental kamikaze story has taken another turn for the weird."

There was a photo of a nasty crash between a car and a logging truck. Apparently, this time both drivers were killed. The word "ecoterrorism" appeared twice in the story.

She handed him the paper, which she'd finished while he slept, and went in to make breakfast. He started rustling through the sections, looking for more info. Oddly enough, even though the crash happened the day before, there was already an opinion piece denouncing the Mahatmas of the Forest as a dangerous terrorist group, whose real agenda was anarchy, rather than forest protection.

This news depressed him even more than the other crashes. It was almost as if he needed to know that these fanatics were at least totally self sacrificing.

In desperation, he turned to something familiar, the book reviews. On the front page of the section was a review of "*The Shovel of Guilt:* Gruff, but kind-hearted FBI agent tracks and apprehends a serial killer who has killed a dozen Elvis impersonators." The next story was about "*Carl and Dean vs the World.* Two young lawyers, just opening their first office, defend a retarded couple against the World Bank and the International Monetary Fund."

In the non-fiction category, there was a highly recommended book by a twenty-something winner of a reality TV show, "*The Price of Instant Fame: A True Confession.*" Interestingly, the book had come out only three weeks after his victory, while his name was still on everyone's lips.

Suddenly, he had a headache, but it didn't feel like the usual hangover. He wanted to put his head on Madd's breast, and cry for her to make all the confusion go away.

She fed him a nice breakfast, lightly discussing the news. On the subject of the crashes, she rather cryptically commented that something didn't seem right, that there was certainly something else to the story.

Then she said that as much as she enjoyed him, she had papers to grade, and he had a long ride ahead of him. He was becoming aware of her body language. When she stood and talked to him, her hands were on her hips, and her head was high and held back. She was a wall, secure and unassailable, and the statements she made in that position became laws of nature. He grabbed his helmet and jacket.

Before letting him out, she put her arms around his neck and forced eye contact. "Here is your homework for the week. Now listen closely. You are to go home and think about me obsessively until you can't stand it any longer. Then in a few days, you call me and arrange a date. Do you need to write that in your planner, or will you remember?"

"You have my word." Finally learning to pick up on her word games. "I've always prided myself on being an A student, A for amorous." Then feeling quite clever, "I love being

73

teacher's pet."

On the freeway that bypasses Redwood State and National Park in the name of some rabid efficiency, as if anyone is in a hurry to go from Arcata to Crescent City, Scott started to zone out. Attempting to think in terms of her puns, he felt he was going Madd. His helmet was almost too small to contain his contented grin, and the road was hardly more than a sexual vibration. The blast of an air horn brought him around in time to see a logging truck bearing down on him. He whipped over to his side of the road just in time to avoid a head on crash. His heart-pumping fear obscured the obvious irony in the situation.

Back home, he turned on the TV to see what the Sunday evening talking heads had to say. All the conservative commentators were berating what they called the radical environmental community, which to them seemed to include even the Sierra Club and the Nature Conservancy, for the travesty committed against honest laborers who now had to risk their lives in order to make a living and feed their families. Ecoterrorists, they insisted, had placed trees ahead of people.

For some reason Scott felt compelled to call Buck. He asked him if he had any perspective on the situation. Buck seemed convinced that the person who caused the crash was a wild card. He couldn't possibly be part of the organization, as that group had demonstrated sacrifice over violence. Once said, Buck suddenly had someone knocking at the door and had to hang up.

7.

At work, Scott constantly checked the wire services for the latest on what was being called ecokamikazes. By late Monday afternoon there was an update. Someone claiming to represent Mahatmas of the Forest called in an official statement. He said due to the unfortunate death of the trucker, the organization would no longer use vehicles of any kind. They would present only their bodies in defense of the trees, and if anyone used a car that person was not part of Mahatmas of the Forest and was likely from some copycat group. The call had been traced to a phone booth in Klamath.

There wasn't much in Klamath. Likely, someone drove there to use the phone in order to keep from being traced. Scott reasoned that if someone drove, he quickly returned to whatever he was doing. Otherwise he could be noticeable in an investigation. Feeling very much the investigative reporter, that evening he pulled out a map and drew circles at various distances from Klamath. It was reasonable that the call would have come from a strip of the coast from Brookings, Oregon to Eureka. The guy was a local.

The late night guys on CNN debated whether the caller was legit or not. The north coast was full of cranks who had a point to make, and it was unclear what structure, if any, this mystery organization actually had. One highly opinionated commentator had called it "a hoax that had gotten out of hand." With that Scott turned off the TV and went to bed to think about and fantasize about Madd.

He had slipped out with an admission of love, but did he really love her. He'd only met her. It was too soon. Besides, it had only been a few weeks since his break up with V.V. If what they had was real, which he was certain of, how could he love again so quickly? That led to an internal debate about whether there was only one true love in a person's life. That argument kept him from sleep well into the night. By the time he fell asleep, mentally exhausted, he was more confused about his feelings than ever. He would wait and see how he felt on the next date.

By mid day on Tuesday, the first pedestrian report came through. True to the caller's prediction, a young guy had stepped in front of a logging truck on 101, holding a sign that said, "save the trees."

At lunch, he switched on the TV and caught an interview with the driver. The man was visibly shaken. He kept referring to the face of the young man just before impact, and he swore he'd never go through that again. He was quitting, planning to get a short haul job for a grocery chain. Apparently the ecokamikazes had won a round, but at a terrible cost.

It was hard for Scott to concentrate at the school board meeting. Weed abatement at the junior high seemed trivial in light of the bizarre developments of the last few days. He filed his report automatically and headed home. He went straight inside, opening a beer and turning on the TV news. For the first time he didn't look at V.V.'s place or even give her a thought.

By the seven o'clock news two more long haired young men had stepped in front of logging trucks. One carried a sign that said, "Mahatmas of the Forest." "I was right," Scott thought, "the organization is real and well organized."

The next morning Rob casually mentioned that Scott's column could be a weekly feature if Scott took the time to research and write it. With all that had happened, Scott had put his column in a third floor rear unit of the storage locker in his mind. He promised to have something by the end of the week. To get him started, Rob sent him home before lunch and told him to look around.

Back home, Scott realized that he hardly knew anyone in the area. He knew the two weird guys at the bar, Jake, V.V., Buck. He realized that there were thirty of forty other people in the park who he'd only nodded hello to. There must be loads of stories.

He forced himself away from the news shows and started to prowl the park in hopes of meeting someone new and newsworthy.

At the back of the park, near the edge of the gully, there was a place a bit removed from the others, turned at a ninety degree angle to the row, with the front facing out and away. That made him curious. The black paint job on the trailer also made him curious, as the only other black unit was Buck's. He'd heard really loud and cacophonous music coming from that direction from time to time, and he'd assumed young guys with a massive stereo system. He walked around to the back, which was actually the front which had a covered porch the width of the double wide. The porch had a drum set, speakers and amplification equipment. A band. A really bad, punk or grunge band. He figured these guys were good for a story, so he climbed the loose stairs and banged on the door.

A woman around his age came to the door. She was wearing cargo shorts and a tank top and was covered with tattoos. Her blond hair was almost short enough to be a crew cut. A cigarette dangled from her lips. "You here to complain?"

"Complain? No. About what?"

"The fuckin' music. What else."

"No, no. I hardly ever hear it. I live up near the front. Name's Scott." He put out his hand, and she just looked at it as if it were a bug.

Recovering his composure, he added, "I'm a reporter for the paper, and I write a column about the river area. Sounds like you have a band and could use a plug in the paper."

She grabbed his hand, which was now at his side, and pumped it vigorously.

"Jules is the name. The band's called 'Hot Licks Lesbians,' and we do some local gigs. Sorry to come off like a shit head, but Jake gets on our case when people complain. We got the sound pointing out into the woods, and the amps are turned way down, but there's always some asshole making a fuss."

"How many in the band?" He was trying to get past her

rough attitude and act like a professional reporter.

"There's me, Paula Poop, and Lousy Lisa. I'm known as Family Jules." And as if anticipating his next question, "We all live here."

"And, judging from the band name, you're all lesbians?"

"Well, I'm bi. Why you so concerned? You looking for some action?"

At this point a chubby little redhead with the same haircut came to the door. Jules' remark had embarrassed Scott, and he tried to control the color rising in his face. He was also looking for a comeback.

"Actually, I have a girlfriend."

Jules laughed. "Hell, so do I, Paula here." She gestured over her shoulder. Maybe a cozy threesome one day, and Lisa can take the pictures."

The two women burst out laughing, while Scott fought to look composed.

"Look, Scott. Drop by around seven tonight. Hear us practice a few songs. We'll give you the band's yada yada, and you can write us up as a group of rude crazies, which we are and which makes good copy."

Scott agreed, vowing to himself not to go inside or otherwise put himself in a compromising position.

Before going back to the band's trailer, Scott called Madd. He'd made it to mid week, but he didn't want to wait any longer for fear she might make other plans. For some reason he felt nervous dialing her number.

"Hello, Maddie."

"Ah, a male voice. You'll have to give me your name, last name first, so I can look you up in my data base, assuming you are calling for a date."

"B-but, it's me Scott, Mukis, last weekend."

"I know. I'm just teasing. Have you obsessed over me this week?"

"Actually, yeah. I can hardly wait to see you again."

"Good. And you don't know how you can go on living

without me. Right?"

"Well, uh, sure, right. I was hoping we could get together this weekend."

"You're in luck. I do have some free time. Say Saturday night?"

"That's what I was thinking. We could maybe get dinner, see a movie?"

"Don't forget, make love. We could do those in any order. Although making love before dinner and the movie leaves us open to do it again afterwards. You have to excuse me. I'm a teacher. We love to plan."

She was way too forward for Scott's comfort, but she was funny, and definitely not coy. "I'll be there by six. I'm really looking forward to seeing you."

"Naturally. I am, after all, vibrant and interesting, not to mention flawlessly attractive. See you Saturday, cutie."

Things were going far too well to be believed. This was not typical Scott Mukis luck, but he wasn't going to question it.

He was humming some half remembered song as he shuffled through his closet for something to wear. Then it hit him. It's a lesbian grunge band practicing in a sleazy trailer park. If his clothes aren't covered with shit, he's over dressed.

The band wasn't half bad from four or five trailers away. Up close they sounded like a dozen cats fighting in a room full of cymbals. He had brought two bottles of beer, which sort of soothed him during the musical onslaught.

Between songs, Jules brought over a joint, and Scott took several deep hits. She also poured him some wine from a five liter box. Soon the band didn't sound so bad. In fact, he was starting to enjoy the music. A few more hits off a joint and several glasses of the cheap wine, and he was tapping his toe to what he imagined was the beat.

Then the music stopped. Jules and Paula came over. "What you think?"

"Good. I like it. Took awhile to get into it, but your music sort of grows on me."

"Paula here says, give us a good review, and she'll give you some serious head."

Scott started to laugh almost uncontrollably. The outrageousness of the comment plus the wine and dope put him in a semi hysterical state. "He caught his breath long enough to say, "Not necessary. You get some good reviews anyway." Then he felt sort of clever. "Besides, journalistical ethicalities probibit taking bribes or even broads." Having passed over the line to intoxicated, Scott found his remarks incredibly funny, and he launched into another fit of laughter. The women joined in, and another round was poured. Before long Scott realized that he could either walk home right then or crawl home later. He excused himself and left.

The next day he was a bit late for work, as well as a bit hung over. However, he did have a good column. It started with an update on Jake: biker and business man, and the founder of timeshare Harleys. He put in a bit about Dusty and Jo Jo and the latest Tree House brawl. He mentioned some of Buck Rogers' strange bumper stickers, and he finished up with the wild, all girl grunge band that plays to the wildlife in the forest.

Rob read it, laughed, and slapped him on the back, accentuating his headache. Then he said he'd have to show it to Sylvia. The Sylvia thing had been in the back of Scott's mind for weeks. Why did he seek her approval, and why did Rob feel the need to show a column to the advertising manager. He asked Rob what was up with all that.

"Oh, hell, Scotty." Rob pushed the thinning blond hair from his eyes. "You don't know the history. Sylvia was my mentor, years ago when I was a kid reporter like you. She was features editor back east at the Globe. One day, after I'd come out here, she found herself with her kids away to college, a failed marriage, and a five bedroom house to ramble around in. She decided to opt out of the rat race, and she called me for a non writing, eight to five job. She was one of the best editors in the business. That's why her saying you are more than adequate is pretty high praise. Took me a year to get a compliment like that."

Scott shuffled back to his desk, feeling joy in his heart, if not his head. He proceeded to pour his soul into the school board's discussion of landscaping.

By the following afternoon reports of eleven more ecokamikazes came through. Another driver had quit, and several others were saying that someone had to do something about this. The logging company spokespeople were demanding a law be passed making running in front of trucks illegal. The governor responded that there wouldn't be much point prosecuting someone who'd been squashed flat on the highway. The FBI claimed they had evidence that this was part of an international terrorist plot, a vast network of subversives, anarchists and non Christians. The President was appointing a special commission to study the problem.

Scott was still morbidly fascinated with the way this thing was unfolding, but his immediate attention was focused on his Saturday night plans with Madd. He decided to stay home Friday night, to be fully rested for Saturday. He flipped on his laptop and started a new novel. This was about a brilliant and beautiful sociologist who had sacrificed having a personal life to find a solution to human society's morass of violence and ignorance. The more heights she achieved professionally, the more personally isolated and lonely she became. Finally, torn and on the verge of a nervous breakdown, she met a sensitive writer who taught her the meaning of love.

Effortlessly, he knocked out a dozen pages over two or three beers, before his eyes started to droop, and he called it a night.

The morning news detailed two more gristly and very one sided encounters between fast moving logging trucks and sign wielding pedestrians. Every major columnist with a penchant for restating the obvious and every columnist adept at reading their personal agenda into every story was taking a crack at the ecokamikaze issue. These suicidal people were individuals acting in response to heinous acts by industry, or they were part of a fanatical network. They were brainwashed tools of a sinister environmental super group, or they were freedom fighters. They were the hallmarks of the end of the world.

The weirdest column of all related a 1970s study showing that plants can communicate. Plants exposed to a traumatic situation reacted, measured by leads attached to leaves, to a repeat of the situation. Not only that, the plants around it reacted in kind. This columnist, who hinted at some biological credentials, claimed the trees were influencing the activists. The notion seemed totally absurd to Scott. He not only could not imagine anyone believing the idea, but he couldn't imagine a reputable paper printing it. He suddenly felt very superior and well qualified to be syndicated.

As the door opened, Maddie shouted, "Madd at ya." Scott thought he had done something wrong until she dove into his arms and realized, while crashing backward against the wall, that it was another of her puns.

She asked him if he wanted a glass of wine before going out, and when he assented, she said she'd bring it to him in bed.

After a quickie that Scott had not intended to be a quickie, she pulled him to the shower. They drove to Arcata to a funky college hang out for dinner and drinks before catching a late movie. They topped off the evening with a more leisurely session of love making.

During dinner he'd wanted to show off the quick reading up he'd done on sociology, so he asked her about what aspect of the field she'd focused on, and she'd explained that she could generally be called a symbolic interactionist. He'd tried to pretend he'd known what that was, asking her to go into detail, but she'd been too quick for him. "Do you know what that is?"

After he'd reluctantly admitted he didn't, she'd added, "Hell, sometimes I don't think I do either. She'd gone on to explain about how one person can play many roles in a day: parent, child, lover, boss, underling, friend, neighbor, customer. "There are a bunch of us, really boring types, who run incredible amounts of data about this stuff and then do all kinds of statistical studies. We discuss it endlessly, but it can be as dry as a

Southern Baptist picnic. If you really want to get into it, I've got a ton of books you can read, but," she'd reached over and tousled his hair, "you shouldn't bother your pretty head about it."

Even though he'd been getting used to her sense of humor, the remark bothered him. He considered himself an intellectual and expected to be treated as an equal, no matter his level of knowledge of a subject.

Scott, inept in after-sex intimate conversation, opted to bring up the ecokamikaze fiasco. He encapsulated the major theories and asked her which sounded right to her.

Acting serious for a change, Madd told him she didn't feel it was a real organization. A few radical activists, perhaps only one, had seized on a random incident, fed a story to the media, knowing it would be blown out of proportion, and let the idea fester in the minds of impressionable people who desperately needed some meaning in their lives. She stressed that she could be way off base, but that there was something about all this that smacked of an elaborate con or prank.

Scott couldn't accept that. He insisted that it had to be real. People didn't throw themselves in front of moving trucks because of a prank fed to the media. People weren't that gullible, that damn foolish.

"That's where you and I part company, Scott. It's been my experience that people really are that gullible, that damn foolish. Please don't get angry if I call you a bad name, but you seem to be an idealist."

He rose up on one elbow, tapping his chest with his finger. "And damn proud of it, I am."

"When it all comes out, whoever's right gets a free dinner at the place of her, or possibly his, choice."

In the morning he hung around the kitchen, trying to help with breakfast, but mostly getting in her way. Then he suggested that she come up to his place the next weekend.

"Let me see. You live in a 24 foot travel trailer, where the sleeping and living areas are the same. Your ex girl friend lives about 20 feet away, and there's a grunge rock band practicing at the end of the street. You know, Scott, I don't think so. However, if you feel guilty about me cooking breakfast, next time you can do it. You do cook?"

Indignant, Scott assured her that he could cook many things, but while inventorying them in his mind, many became several, became very few. He realized that his food preparations amounted to sandwiches, soups, stew, basic salad and chili. In fact, many of his meals came out of cans or frozen packages. Standing there while she finished the eggs, he was forced to admit to himself that he was a mediocre cook, a typical lazy bachelor in the kitchen. He was not the type to admit failings without immediately seeking a solution. He vowed to purchase a cook book that very day.

He realized that it would soon be time for him to go. There had been so little time. He wanted more. "I wish we could spend more time together."

"We live a long way from each other, and we both work during the week. I have meetings and the like during the week, and you've said you have meetings to report on at night. I don't know how we'd work that." Her voice was very matter of fact, as if she were discussing washing the car or taking out the trash.

"Maybe I could come down Friday nights, and we could spend the weekend together."

She put the plates of food on the table and gave him a benign, insipid look. "Maybe. It would be fun, but we'll have to look at each weekend as it comes along. It's hard to make open commitments."

Her lack of enthusiasm was palpable. She should have added, he thought, that it's hard to make any commitments "But, he tentatively said, You know, I think I've fallen for you."

She was making a strange gesture that he couldn't follow. Then he realized that she was motioning him to sit down. She was already seated, fork in hard, and he was just standing at the table. "I know how you think you feel," she said, "but sex makes people believe all sorts of things. Like, you probably don't think I'm overweight."

He stood there a moment feeling, and probably looking, foolish. He was going to argue the overweight thing as well as his feelings of love, but a trace of wisdom slipped in between his impulses, and he decided not to pursue it, at least at the moment.

Breakfast was followed by a walk on the beach. Gulls and other sea birds were working the air like a stage, and each little off shore island had a miniature habitat clinging to it. Boats bobbed in the regular pulsing of the swell, and the massive rock was doing its impersonation of a work of art. The crisp fall air was a full page ad for nylon windbreakers. They walked hand in hand, taking turns talking about what they enjoyed about living on the north coast. Scott wanted desperately to talk about their life together, but he knew she'd pass it off with a humorous comment. She used humor, he decided, to avoid uncomfortable personal discussions.

He did get up the courage to ask why she always sidestepped the subject of emotional intimacy and commitment.

"Dear Scott. A year and a half committed relationship just ended. I have to process that. I'm not the type to fall immediately in love on the rebound." Then she stopped, turned to him, and gave him a chillingly serious look. "It's too soon to even talk about it. If you push, you're likely to push me away. OK?"

Nearly panicked, Scott backpedaled. "I'm sorry. I care about you, and I don't want to pressure you in any way. I'll call you next week, and if you're free, we'll make plans."

On the way home, Scott decided it was cool with Maddie. They had a relationship, the most she could offer at the time. She would take her time, would heal, and then they would develop a commitment. He was the only one in her life, and the only impediment was time. He was a happy man. Career and Relationship were both progressing at a steady, albeit painfully slow pace.

In this mood of optimism, he took the Redwood Park scenic alternative to the freeway. He saw a trailhead sign off to the left and a place to pull off. The summer people were long gone, and there were no other cars. He followed the trail between immense redwoods, head high ferns and thickets of rhododendrons. The trail wound around and down, the earth below him rich and reddish brown. Finally he saw a clearing ahead, and ended up walking onto a deserted beach. The massive forest was behind him, and the vast, sparkling Pacific was before him. There were no footprints or trash on the beach, and the only sounds were the surf, wind and the birds. A feeling of limitless peace came over him, a feeling he'd never known before, and something in the wind whispered a message to him. The question, "What was it he really needed to be happy?" drifted through his mind. The answer came as if written on the sand just before a breaking wave, and before he could look, it was gone.

Amazingly, the walk back up the hill was free of thoughts of Maddie and his career. He was in the moment for perhaps the first time in his life.

On reaching the highway, the flow of thought came back in a rush. He pulled out his notebook and wrote his impressions.

On impulse, he stopped at a store and picked up a good bottle of wine. As soon as he got home, he took the wine next door and knocked on V.V.s door.

She looked uncomfortable and ready to make excuses, but he thrust the bottle toward her and said, "I don't want anything but to thank you for making my life richer and happier. Here. If there's anything you ever need, just call."

He turned and started back to his place.

"Scott. Thank you. I appreciate having you for a friend."

He turned on a TV news program and crawled into bed. The commentators were discussing the ecokamikazes. "All of the young people who have sacrificed their lives for the trees have been men. This seems to point to some basic differences between men and women, wouldn't you say?"

One of the gray haired suits cleared his throat and offered, "It would seem that only men embody the level of passion, misplaced as it is in this case, to offer up their very lives for a

86

cherished belief. Perhaps women, biologically tied up as they are with issues of motherhood, cannot summon the courage to dash in front of trucks. What do you think, Diane?"

The one woman on the panel responded with, "As I see it, Paul, women simply have more common sense than to step in front of speeding vehicles. Perhaps men are like sheep, playing follow the leader into the arms of death."

"Well, huh, Diane, I guess that is a possibility, smug as it sounds. But Ed, what's the government going to do about this, timber being such an integral part of the economy?"

"As you obviously know, Paul, the President has put together a high level think tank to solve the problem, top cabinet officials, national security people. I expect emergency measures any day. He has to protect the American way from. . . from these people who..."

Scott turned off the set in mid sentence, grabbed a book on sociology and read himself into a deep sleep.

Still feeling renewed and slightly spiritually superior from Sunday's emotional revelation, Scott stopped to smell the flowers on the way to work. There was a clump of bush lupine on the side of the road, and he pulled over and got out to take in the fragrance. Lupine, unlike roses, do not reward the nose, but the gesture was the important thing. He was a new man, enjoying the colors of the forest, being upbeat and optimistic. He'd even risen early and typed up his column, sending it off ahead of him. It was, he felt, a masterpiece.

Rob motioned him into his office. "What is this column?" and without waiting for an answer, "There are pretty descriptions of trees and clouds and all, but there's no content, no people, events, actions."

"I was trying to create the mood of the forest."

"Then write poetry. Sit down. I'm going to teach you a trick of the trade." He called Scotts piece up on the screen. "Now this is a rambling whatever, but it can be turned into something. The forest you describe is the state park?"

Scott nodded, and Rob continued. "OK. Now the piece is

about the park." He started deleting and inserting text, leaving some blank spaces. "Okay, now we have a story about a beautiful park set aside for the people to enjoy, for the protection of plants and animals. You'll look up the history of the park and whatever groups or individuals who were instrumental in its formation. If you're lucky, we are approaching the anniversary of the dedication. If not, we'll romance the angle to make it fit. Plug your research in here and over here, and you'll have a killer piece. Now, go make some magic."

Scott was impressed with Rob's skill, but his bubble of optimistic good will had been busted. Doubts about his ability to produce a great column spilled over to his relationship with Maddie, which began to look shaky again. He felt he was back in the cellar of his writing career. Perhaps no one really understood the sensitive artist in his own time.

On top of everything, two more guys ran in front of a truck. They were holding a banner between them. It read, "When you kill us all, who'll buy your lumber?" The accompanying story was about a trucker walk out. One guy whose photo reminded Scott of a cross between Jake and a professional wrestler was quoted. "People think truckers are big, dumb jerks without feelings, but I'm telling you that we can't do this. We're killing people. You can't live with that kind of shit."

Local lumber companies demanded that the government line all the highways in northwest California with electric fences. A liberal congressman from California responded with, "So, the activists would still die, as would many innocent people, and the government would spend a billion dollars. And a few guys with insulated wire cutters could render the whole thing moot.

The president said he was raising this matter to the highest priority, even above the three hundred thousand people who were camped on hospital steps, protesting high medical costs and lack of coverage.

Scott, for reasons he didn't try to analyze, picked up the phone and dialed Buck. The answer machine droned a cryptic message: "Think chaos theory. A small fluctuation in one place can set monumental changes in motion. Leave a fucking message."

Scott's reply was, "Call me right away. I mean it."

He sat down in the patio, under a bare light bulb and started to work on his novel about the sociologist. He'd only typed a page when Jules walked up, looking very upset.

"Hi. What. . .?

"No goddamn appreciation," she screamed. "Shit doesn't just happen, you know. It was me, my chasing bookings, my pressing rehearsal schedules. Those bitches wouldn't have a band if it wasn't for me." She sort of fell back into the other chair, and her baggy cargo pants billowed as she dropped.

"What happened?" He cautiously asked, not really caring or wanting to be disturbed.

"Pushy, overbearing, bossy! I ask you, does that describe me?"

"Well, it's uh, I mean, possibly."

"I'm a nice person, right? Say, you got anything to drink?"

Scott nodded toward the open door and the fridge beyond. She stormed into his house and came out a big bottle of very cheap red wine and two glasses, assuming Scott was going to join her. She poured him a full glass and one for herself. Then she took a deep swig from the bottle and pushed the cork back in. Her breasts were almost out of her faded tank top, and she wasn't wearing shoes. Her earrings were spiders in webs.

"Now, where was I? Yeah. I do it all, and I mean all, like all the business involved in being a band. I write most of the songs and do the arranging. I mean, like all the fuck they do is get up and play. And they're on the rag about me being boss bitch and all. I had to get the hell out of there. I was close to trashing the whole project. They don't understand me. We live together, love together, and all the time they resent me."

She looked on the verge of tears. Scott couldn't handle crying women, and a woman like that in tears would send him running down the highway, forever plagued with nightmares. Scott felt he should give some advice, although he had nothing of value to give. "Have you tried talking it out with them, explaining your side, your feelings?"

"It's kind of hard talking it out," she shouted, "When you're getting accusations hurled at you. They figure, hey, we're artists and all, but they don't get that I'm also a businesswoman, a damn good one. That's important too, right?"

Scott felt his teeth grind together. "Well, not everyone thinks so. Some people don't think creativity and business go together." He hoped he'd been diplomatic.

"Those kinds of people are idiots. Putting together a deal, planning an album, that's all very creative work. Any damn fool who can read music can play in a band."

She saw her glass was empty, pulled the cork with her teeth and refilled it, giving Scott's glass a fierce look. Seeing his glass almost full, he took a healthy drink. She topped it off. Then she drained her glass and filled it again. "Ya know, Scott, you're a nice guy, sensitive, good listener and all. I judged you wrong when I first met you. You're not really a boorish jerk. Matter of fact, I'm going to give you something, the best lay of your life. I owe it to you for taking me in like this."

"Taking you in. How exactly do you mean that?"

"No, no, I don't mean permanent. I can't face them right now. In a day or two, week maybe, when I calm down, I'll go deal with them."

"And you're planning to stay here?"

"I'm doing you a favor. Wishy washy guy like you probably doesn't get three dates a year. A toast to a new friendship."

The constraints of a middle class upbringing forced him to raise his glass. Her tipsy toasting spilled half her glass, which she refilled after finishing the rest in the toast. He was trying to think of some way to diplomatically get her to leave, but she launched back into her tale of being misunderstood, switching occasionally to the band's few successes. Scott looked for an opportunity to divert both the subject and the drunken woman who had descended on him. He tried to imagine having sex with her, but she was rude, crude, hairy-legged, and bisexual, and it was impossible to think of her sexually.

She got unsteadily to her feet. "Too much wine. Come on. Let's go to bed."

Nearing panic, Scott replied. "Why don't you go in and make yourself comfortable. I have a bit more important work to do. I'll join you real soon."

"Ah ha. You're a bit shy. Ok. I'll be waiting for you." She staggered off.

As Scott suspected, within five minutes, she was snoring. When he was sure she was out for the night, he slipped into bed, still clothed, and hugged the far side.

He woke before his alarm, shut it off, changed quickly into clothes for work, not bothering to shower, and was out the door. He decided to stop at one of the coffee shops on 101 for breakfast. Hopefully, Jules would have gone home before he returned.

He threw his jacket in the back of the car. It was true what everyone said about Fall on the north coast. The fog that had hung over Crescent City all summer was gone. The sun was shining, and it was quite pleasant. He knew he should enjoy as much of this as possible, as the rains would soon come with a vengeance.

He felt lucky when he got home to an empty place. The bed was unmade, and the sink full of dishes. The word, "thanks" was scrawled on a scrap of paper. The phone rang, and he was afraid it was Jules, promising to return that night. He tried to resist the impulse to pick it up, but failed. It was Buck.

"Scott, you scuzzy hound. Getting it on with Jules, huh?"

"No, well, actually . . . It's a long story. Life's getting complicated."

"Sure. You can tell me the details later. So, what was so damn urgent?"

"You've been avoiding me for weeks. Thought you were pissed at me or something. What's going on?"

"Sorry, man. Been really busy. An asshole's work is never

91

done. I figure I owe you a few beers, dude. Maybe Saturday night at the Tree House."

"I've got to get back to you. My girlfriend, not Jules, down in Trinidad. Well, we have tentative plans and I'm not sure what night. You understand."

"Sure, pussy takes priority over beer with buddies. I can dig it. I'm doing a little work around here for Jake rest of the week, so I'll be home. Call when you get a break from the broads."

"Buck, wait. Your phone message. Something about it gave me a weird feeling. Why are you talking about chaos theory?"

"Scotty, my boy. Sometimes you can do a little song and dance over here, and the changes that ripple through the world can be mind boggling. One person, if he's honest about the extent of human shortcomings, can indeed change the world."

"Damn it Buck. You know a lot more about this ecokamikaze shit than you're saying. I want you to level with me."

"Over a few beers, my man. Over a few beers. Call me." He hung up.

Scott's next call was to Madd. "Are we spending the weekend together? I thought we could hike in the woods, see the fall colors."

"Dearly beloved, we'll be gathered here in front God and whomever, but I'm afraid it can't be the whole weekend. I've got a big conference in Boston starting Monday. We all get together and share all those esoteric papers that the general public never bothers to read, because they would bore them silly. Well, I'm flying out pretty early on Sunday, so I'm driving down Saturday afternoon and staying in the city. The bottom line is, if you don't mind driving down after work, we've got Friday night and Saturday morning to play. Will that work for you, wonder stud?"

The need for honesty overcame him. "As disappointed as I am about not spending more time with you, I have to say that I think I'm getting closer to this ecokamikazes thing, and I have a chance to find out Saturday night. I'm sure my neighbor,

92

Buck—remember I told you about him—has some inside knowledge. He's willing to talk to me about it over beer this weekend." Then he mentioned Buck's phone message, realizing as he told it, that it was a critical clue.

"Buck, the bumper sticker guy. You can bet he knows something. He may well be the key to the whole puzzle. I don't think you're going to like the truth of this. It's going to really screw with that loveable innocence of yours."

Scott was getting irritated and needed to assert himself. "I'm not the innocent kid you seem to think I am. I'm a man of the world, and a serious reporter. If there's important news there, I'll get it. By the way, I'll bring down some groceries. I'm cooking for you Friday night."

Scott had forgotten to buy a cook book, but he'd picked the brain of the foods editor and had obtained an exotic recipe for an Indian vegetable dish and a sauce that is served over rice. Lisa Carr, the foods editor had explained how to assemble it, so that the rich flavors belied the simplicity of preparation. He was going to impress Madd, make her realize that he was a mature, sophisticated man of the world.

He called Buck, but oddly, there was no answer. He left a message suggesting they go to the Tree House for burgers and beer on Saturday night.

Hearing footsteps along the gravel path and thinking it could be Jules, he quickly penned a note and pinned it to his door. "Got the flu. Gone to bed. Do not disturb."

He locked his door, turned off all but one light, and set up his laptop in the tiny space that converted from living area to sleeping area. He opened up his novel and started a chapter about his main character going to Boston as a group of terrorists were holding a think tank hostage. It fell upon her to convince them to let the hostages go. She had to summon all her knowledge of human nature to defuse the situation. Assailed by self doubt, she turned to her true love, the cool and objective young reporter, who assured her she had the right words in her heart. She only needed to say them.

8.

There was a rush of meetings to cover for the next two days. Then Friday afternoon the news came over the wire. The President had declared war. His commission had reviewed a decades-old study of plants, the one that demonstrated that plants communicate through some non verbal way and are somehow aware of the events surrounding them. The commission and the President agreed that the trees were exerting psychic influences on the impressionable minds of the young activists. In effect, they were brainwashing the young men into giving up their lives for their nefarious floral plans. The President had declared war on the redwood forests of California and had ordered an evacuation of all wooded areas.

This was, as he pulled into the market on the highway, no way to start the weekend. The world was going crazy. He pulled out his list and shopped in a daze, and he made the hour drive with on some internal automatic pilot. He almost forgot where he was headed and why.

As Madd opened the door, all Scott could say over his bags of groceries was, "Did you hear the news?"

"All the craziness? Yeah. Sounds like the Mad Hatter's taken over DC." She started to giggle, working her way to a serious belly laugh.

An indignant Scott walked past her and put his bags down in the kitchen. "I don't see what's so damn funny. We're in a war zone, and, like these are innocent trees. Something has to be done."

She came up behind him, put her arms around his waist and nuzzled his neck. "Something will be done. I'm guessing that it will quickly get so stupid that even the President will wash his hands of it. These guys opened their mouths before they thought, and they're going to feel damn foolish when their brains catch up."

Scott wasn't comforted a bit, but her lips on his neck switched his priorities, and he pulled out the fixings and impressed her as he put the meal together. She kept commenting about how pleasantly surprised she was.

The meal was great, and Scott listened when she related what these conferences were like. The way she described the stuffy old professors presenting their elaborate, wordy papers, and everyone standing around afterward, using the buzz words of the trade, cracked Scott up. She could tell the funniest stories while keeping a straight face. It wasn't so much that the stories were that funny. She could throw a funny slant on any human interaction.

"Madd, you act as if every social interaction is humorous."

"It is. Even the most serious conversation is absurd if you get past the life and death stuff and concentrate on the way people transact social business. You have to take a step back. You know how it's funny watching chimps dressed up and acting human? Well it's just as funny watching people dressed up and acting human."

"Then you don't take anything seriously?"

"Well, yeah. I take my life, my work, my romantic ups and downs seriously. But I realize that it could look absurd to someone else. What was it someone said. 'When someone else takes a fall, it's comedy. When it happens to you, it's tragedy'."

"God, you are so funny, so bright, so sexy. I love you."

"In that case, you'll probably want sex. I guess I can make the sacrifice." Then she put her tongue in his ear and he felt he was bursting into flames.

He stayed awake long after she'd fallen asleep. His mind was filled not with the human comedy, but with foreboding. This tree thing was scaring him, and Madd going away for a week was bothering him. He knew it didn't make sense, but there was a modicum of emotional safety in the little routine they'd started building, the weekend dates at her place, the mid week phone call. She was going away, and something would get out of balance, and he wasn't sure he could set it right again.

Inside he was in flux, stressed, and worried. She was his anchor in a fucked world, and he needed her to be absolutely dependable.

As they cuddled in the morning, postponing getting up as long as possible, Scott hinted at his anxiety. He told her he was feeling apprehensive, but he wasn't able to bring it into focus.

"In a sentence, Scott, your gut feelings."

"It's just that it's too good. You know, between us. And the job's going well, and life seems to be good."

"Too good to last. Is that it?"

"Yeah. Like I'm this happy, and it can't last."

"So, you don't deserve happiness?"

"No, I think I deserve it. It's like there's always bad luck following good luck."

"You, my friend, are superstitious."

"No. I don't consider myself. . . It's like you and me. I'm afraid something will happen. I tell you I love you, but you never. . ."

She sat up in bed. The cuddling was over for the day. "Scott, you've got to understand. I love you as a sweet guy, a friend, someone I share part of my life with, but I'm not in love. I haven't made that partnership commitment. I warned you about this at the beginning."

"What does that mean for the future? Do we have one at all?"

Now she was up and getting dressed. Scott had stepped into the very jungle he feared. "I have trouble seeing us as permanent. There's too much going on in different directions. I've found my place in this cosmo-comedy called life, but you are still searching for yours and way too seriously. I'm comfortable; you're hungry. Also, I see life as a comedy, and you see it as a tragedy."

Scott started to object to that, but she cut him off. "It's like what you were just saying. The bad has to be coming. This craziness with the trees is almost like Armageddon to you. Your life is a drama. That's all fine, but it isn't where I'm at."

"Nothing frightens or depresses you?"

"Death. See, that's the yardstick. Death is the one thing you can't escape. It'll undo all your plans, end your fun and all that. I compare all the other events in my life to death, and I figure, no matter how bad they seem, I'm alive, so it can't be that big a deal. My paper is rejected by my peers. Oh well, I could be dead. My long time love leaves me, but hell, I'm still alive. I'm alive and hungry. Get your lazy butt up, and I'll fix you breakfast."

Scott was blown away by her viewpoint. He thought of being rejected by his family, his inability to produce a finished novel, his very small part in the world of news, and he told himself, "At least I'm alive." It helped a little, but not nearly enough. He stood in the kitchen playing with this new way of thinking while she cooked. It was a small concept, but the more he tried to grasp it, the more he felt it was the tip of an iceberg. To totally embrace Madd's viewpoint would be to become someone else, to change the Scott he knew himself to be into a stranger.

"I think you've set a new record. This is the longest time you've gone without talking."

He snapped back to the here and now. Glancing at the clock, Scott realized it was still very early. "I know you have to get to the City, but how 'bout a quick walk up in Lady Bird Johnson Grove. I was up there once, and it's incredible."

She looked at her watch. "I can spare a couple hours. Actually, I've never been there. Eat up, and let's go."

They got in his car and turned north on the highway. In a few minutes they were in what's left of Orick, with the closed café and motel on the east side. Then they turned off at the combination federal and state park.

The parking lot was deserted. They quickly crossed the bridge and started walking, hand in hand through the towering giants, mists obscuring the top branches. Head high ferns and rhododendrons surrounded them, and the silence was both eerie and romantic. She actually squeezed his hand, an act of

97

affection he hadn't expected from her.

"You two! Stop!" They turned to see a ranger walking quickly their way. The man was almost out of breath when he caught up. "You're not supposed to be here."

Scott shrugged. "It's a park. What's the problem?"

"Didn't you hear the news? The President has closed all redwood forests to the public. You've gotta leave."

Scott was outraged. "That's crazy. It's a public forest. What, the trees going to jump us or something. Or maybe we're conspiring with the trees to wreck the country or something. You've got to be kidding."

The ranger had a look somewhere between foolish discomfort and anger. "I'm not going to argue with you. You have to leave now."

Scott was about to snap back at him when Madd grabbed his arm and cut in.

"I guess we'll be going. The trees look a bit sinister. I'd keep an eye on those rhododendrons too." She smiled and winked at him.

The ranger's expression changed, and Scott could tell he was working to suppress a smile. "Thanks for understanding. Hey, it's my job, twenty-three years, kids in college and a mortgage. I don't have to agree with policy or even understand it. I'll walk you back to your car." He gestured toward a tree with his thumb. "They won't mess with you while I'm here."

Madd could usually cheer him up, but not this time. All the way back to her place he fumed and muttered a litany of the radical expressions he'd used when he'd hung out with Original Cyn and her friends. He was ready to take to the streets, banners, sit ins, whatever. After a couple of minutes, Madd backed off and let him get it off his chest.

At her door, as she was sending him off, she said, "You should protest. This ban is stupid and probably illegal, and protesting it will make you feel better. I'm sure it will get back to normal in time, but that doesn't mean you can't have a hand in getting it there quicker. I'll call you when I get back. You really are a sweet guy, a bit intense, but sweet." She cupped his face in her hands and kissed him with tenderness and passion.

On the road home the trees had been replaced with question marks. What kind of madness would have forests closed and rangers chasing people from parks? Why did Madd take serious things so lightly? She was an intelligent woman, very astute, passionate, funny and logical. She should be outraged by recent events, by the government's and the timber companies' actions. Yet she seemed to be disconnected.

Crossing the Klamath River bridge, it hit him. The key is sensitivity. For some reason, something had caused her to suppress her sensitivity. She was obviously sensitive, but perhaps competing with men in the academic world, the break up with her ex boy friend, something in her childhood maybe, had made her suppress her natural sensitivity.

Then, he thought, perhaps he was using his own yardstick to measure her and others. He was very sensitive. Things touched him deeply. It was part of being a creative person, an artist. It was his lot in life to be truly moved by events and to be compelled to communicate those feelings to others. He was born to this, to the life of the tortured artist, taking on the pain of society, turning his suffering into catharsis for others. He couldn't blame her, or V.V. for that matter. They were of the majority of people who went through their day, blocking out the painful and soul-wrenching issues. It had fallen on artists like himself to experience these strong emotions and to convert them into literature so that they could be digested by the masses.

These revelations made him feel lonely. Even those closest to him, the woman who would share a lifetime of intimacy with him would never touch that part of him that cried for the world and its broken dreams.

Scott felt superbly noble and absolutely alone. He pulled off the highway, and went back to the road that led to the mouth of the Klamath. At the end of the road he parked above the private camp ground on the beach. The path led past a Native American ceremonial site, a pit with bleacher-like benches around it. He continued down to the edge of the river and out to the beach. The summer people who would have filled the camp area were gone, and the beach was almost deserted. He walked along the broad beach to where the mouth of the mighty river breathed into the Pacific.

There was a solitary surfer off the mouth of the river. Sand bars had formed from the flow of the river and tides and had caused good waves. The guy was catching waves as high as his head, and they broke so fast that it looked like he'd be swallowed by them. Just beyond the breaking waves a huge fin cut the water, gray moving against a gray background. A massive shark patrolled the river mouth, probably a great white, and the surfer seemed aware of it, but unafraid. After each wave he paddled back to within a few yards of the shark. The man was one with his environment, at home with nature and secure in this relationship, and Scott envied his calm and his security.

Driving up 199, Scott saw the park was closed and national guard troops were stationed at the entrance. The usually busy state park was eerily deserted.

As soon as he got home, he went straight to Buck's and got a commitment to go for beer and conversation. In fact, rather than take the chance Buck would wiggle out of the evening, Scott offered to buy food if they left immediately. It wasn't really what Scott wanted to do, being tired and grungy from the road, but Buck lit up at the mention of free food and off they went.

It was early and not crowded. A dog eared poster by the door promised a local bluegrass group later that night. Must be major stars, Scott thought, as they were getting three bucks cover that night.

Scott ordered a pitcher and a couple of burgers with garlic fries. It had been weeks since they'd shared a beer or conversation, so Scott moved slowly, first asking about the latest bumper stickers and tee shirts. He had a new one, "If you can read this, you're not as stupid as your driving."

Scott laughed, perhaps too freely in an attempt to put Buck

at ease. He was about to change the subject when the burgers came. Another beer and an empty plate later, Scott was primed. "So, what's your part in this ecokamikaze group?"

"What group? What part? Where do I fit in?"

"Come on Buck. Don't jerk me around. You know too much about all this. I know you're involved."

Buck put his beer down as if it started tasting bad. "So, what, you playing detective now. Gonna turn me in as a subversive, ecoterrorist, or something?"

Scott had come on too strong. He put his hands up and blurted, "Whoa! I'm not going to turn anyone in. I just want to know. I'm a reporter, you know. Oh, no, I mean, anything I get from you is protected, unnamed source and all that. Oh, what the fuck, Buck, this shit's been bothering me for weeks. I gotta know what's going on."

Suddenly there was a loud noise, and they turned just in time to see JoJo heading for their table backward. He hit the table with his back and slid almost off the other side, scattering what was left of the fries and beer all over the floor.

JoJo looked up and smiled. "Scott! Wanna help me kick this guy's ass?"

"Sorry, JoJo. Got very important newspaper business going on here, but you owe us a couple of beers."

JoJo got off the table and dove into the other guy, taking the fight over near the bar, where barroom fights rightfully belong.

For a moment Scott forgot where he'd left the thread of the conversation, and then the waitress came over with a pitcher. "I'll put this on JoJo's tab. He'll pay, or his uncle will 86 him for two weeks, like the last time."

Buck shook his head and looked at Scott. "Do these guys actually pay tabs?"

Scott shrugged. "Who knows. Weird family. Now, are you going to level with me about all these highway suicides?"

"OK, so you think I'm part of the organization. Are you so sure there is an organization?" He waited a moment for Scott's predictable look of surprise before continuing. Suppose that first time was just what it appeared, an accident. Now, suppose someone who understood the mind set and the frustration of these forest activists made a few calls claiming to represent the group behind it and promising more of the same until logging was brought to its knees. What do you think would happen among these idealistic young people who would try anything to save the trees?"

"Good God! They'd want to be part of the organization, help the cause, and. . ."

"And since they'd not be privy to the so-called organization, they'd act as if they were, taking it upon themselves to help the cause."

"And innocent people would die for nothing!" The idea was sickening.

"No, Scott, not for nothing. Don't you see it?" Buck started making hand gestures as if he were trying to pull something from him. The notion of an organization would bring people together to stand up against the dominant power. Individually impotent, as a part of some omni-group, they'd be buying the salvation of their cause with their lives. It's like the unarmed guys standing up to armed soldiers in order to win the freedom of their people. It's actually noble. Dying is stupid, mind you, but for these altruists, it's noble. Who are we to judge?"

"But it's deceiving people."

"No it's not. It's real, and it's working. Truckers have stopped driving, the companies and the government have been driven to desperate foolishness. After all these years, those poor, fuckin' downtrodden activists are finally winning. It's beautiful, man."

Scott was speechless. He sat there quietly sipping his beer, trying to get his mind around Buck's idea. That this could be a positive thing! A few martyrs perhaps have liberated an entire ecosystem. Would that be worth dying for?

"And you did all this. You made those calls."

"You seem to be jumping to conclusions. I never said I had a damn thing to do with it. I only asked you to suppose that scenario. I may be dead wrong. There may very well be an organization. The important thing is that it will probably work."

A sudden burst of anger rose up in Scott and he lashed out. "Why the hell didn't you step in front of a truck?"

"Hold on there. I'm not a true believer. I'm an asshole and an iconoclast. There's nothing sacred enough for me to die for. There's nothing noble about me. I know that. I accept myself. Accept yourself. Jump in front of a truck, or go out there and try to stop it, tell them you have sources who say there's no organization, that it's all a hoax. Get off the fuckin' fence, Scott. Stick your size 12s in the face of destiny."

Scott swept the pitcher and glasses from the table with a backhand. "Go to hell, you self-righteous, arrogant prick." Filled with an anger that had no form nor object, he stumbled to his feet and stormed out the door.

It took Scott a bottle of wine to calm himself. Then he pulled the laptop on the edge of the bed and started to type. He was nearly drunk, but in a oddly clear-headed way. His coordination was off, and he made lots of mistakes, but his thoughts were intact.

This issue was like a diamond, full of facets, and each time he wrote, he realized that whatever point of view he took was wrong. Anything he might say would be of no help to anyone, and would only muddy things and make them worse. However this had started, it now had a life of its own, and Scott was powerless to undo what had been done. He wadded up the papers, throwing them around his tiny space before crawling off to sleep.

Sunday morning was bathed in the light of reason. The night before had been out of control, but Scott was himself again. He started his Sunday routine with the book review section. The hot new fiction was, *"The Jackhammer of Transgression*: Gruff, but kind-hearted ex-cop teams with coroner to apprehend a serial killer who has killed a dozen funeral directors." Another new hit was, *"Mandy's Portfolio*: Young lawyer, joins struggling firm and sues a company that was poisoning a lake."

The non-fiction de jour, a book by a twenty-eight year old chief financial officer, *"Compelled to Steal: My Road to Corruption."*

Suddenly, Scott felt the urge to throw up, so he abandoned his plan to go out to breakfast and opted for orange juice and cold cereal.

The phone rang. " Scotty, you are still planning on being here for Thanksgiving? You haven't confirmed." His mother impatiently demanded.

"Thanksgiving? Wow, that's a week from Thursday. I've had so much on my mind. Lot of pressure at work. Big stories. Sure I'll be there. The boss'll let me out mid day Wednesday, and I'll hop on the highway. I'll be in very late that night or early Thursday."

"Becky is bringing her fiancée, that nice boy from work. They'll be setting a date soon. I hope you can bring that girl you told me about, the college teacher."

"She's a university professor, a doctor of sociology. She's written books on the subject." He felt his voice rising and took a deep breath.

"Oh yes. Now I recall. Well, anyway, are you bringing her?"

"I think so. I'll have to check when she gets back from a big conference in Boston. She's presenting important papers about her current research. In fact, she's the key speaker. I'll confirm that next Sunday. How's Dad?"

"Doctor found high blood pressure. Told him to take it easy. But with Becky taking over more and more of the daily operation, your father has more time to relax and play golf."

"Well, Mom, tell him I. . . tell him I said hello."

This would be a coup. Becky had some grunt from accounting, and he had a full fledged professor, a leader in her field. It would be great to show her off to the family.

The steady drizzle that had continued since he'd returned from the Tree House was finally letting up, and the sun was starting to nibble away at the dark clouds. Scott thought of going for a walk in the park but remembered the park was closed and armed guys in uniform were guarding it.

He figured he'd stop at the general store to gather community gossip and then wander around the trailer park to talk to anyone who might be around. It occurred to him that after almost six months, he still hadn't met half his neighbors. He could easily get his local news column done today, with the piece about JoJo crashing on his table, and then he could work on his novel, which was actually coming along nicely. His last word count showed he'd written over 52,000 words. He mentally tried to convert that into book pages, and ended up guessing that it was around a hundred and fifty, which made it enough of a book to know he'd finish it.

He tossed on his faded jeans and a sweatshirt and was about to leave when there was a knock on the door. Buck, maybe. Perhaps V.V. He hoped it wasn't Jules. He opened the door and stared in mute disbelief at JoJo. Without the context of the Tree House, JoJo was as out of place as sunbathers on a Crescent City beach. For a moment, Scott thought there'd be a fight, what with the pitcher on JoJo's tab.

"JoJo! Hey man, the beer tab was the waitress' idea."

"That's minor shit, dude. Man, can I come in. I got heavy shit to lay on yuh."

Reluctantly, Scott opened the door, stepped back and let clothes that probably hadn't been washed in weeks settle into his omnipurpose room. "How'd you know where I live?"

"Buck. After you left and I finished gettin' my ass kicked, Buck bought me a few beers. He told me what you guys been talkin' about. I'd been wonderin' what them soldier boys was doin' over to the park. Well, let me tell you, when Buck tol' me that the gov'ment closed the parks and forests and all, I got righteously pissed off. I mean, man I like them trees. Spent many a night drinkin' beer in the woods, sleepin' out under them big ol redwoods. Them trees never been anything but good fer me. Now, I hate the gov'ment on gen'l principles. You know, always fuckin' with you, tryin' to run your life an all." He suddenly stopped.

After a moment's silence, Scott felt compelled to ask, "And then what happened?"

"You wouldn't happen to have a cold one in that there ice box? Need a bit of the hair of the dog to get me right again."

Scott spun around and pulled the refrigerator open in one motion. Knowing how JoJo was, he pulled out two to pretend they were drinking together. After putting the bottle to his lips and only taking a taste, he asked. "So you like the trees and hate the government.?"

"Oh yeah. So all the sudden somethin' just clicked in my head. Like I'd been saying how I'd like to stand up to them pricks in Washington. So, now I'm gonna do it. Got nothing important goin' on round here. So I asks Buck where I might hook up with some of them protester guys, and he tells me 'bout some farm down near Carlotta where they's got a commune of protesters. Well, I figures I'm gonna count fer somethin' in my life. I'm gonna git down there and join up with them guys and fight the gov'ment pricks. I been fightin' all my life, and now's the time to fight for somethin' important."

"Cool, JoJo. So you're on your way to join these guys. How come you stopped by here?"

"Well, Buck says you rilly fired up about all this, and you want to write about how guys are going to stand up to the gov-'ment. He says like you an me'll be a team. I'll be fightin', and you'll be writin', and you'll be wantin my story."

"Well, yeah. I can use your story. You plan to keep in contact?"

"Sure man. I'll keep you posted, and you can tell the world how we'll be kickin' gov'ment ass."

Scott gave JoJo his phone number and wished him well. The guy crawled into a car that Scott wouldn't trust to Crescent City, let alone down to Carlotta, and soon a cloud of blue smoke was all that was left of the little hillbilly.

He had his story. Scott sat down to the computer and started to write without hesitation. "The events that have transpired since the first activist drove in front of a logging truck those many weeks ago, have been bizarre. The reactions to them have spanned the spectrum. Environmental radicals have proclaimed their dead comrades heroes. Logging companies have labeled them outlaws. Many members of the public consider them crazy for giving up their lives for some trees. Some people are convinced that a well-organized suicide organization exists, and that the members would die to save the trees. Others claim that the first incident was a fluke, an accident, and that one or more clever people have manipulated that incident to perpetuate a hoax and to ratchet up the war between timber companies and environmentalists."

"Whatever the truth behind this rash of deaths and the government's radical response, it has had a profound effect on some people who feel connected to the forest.

"A young man, aimless and with no goals other than to get drunk and get into fights, has found a purpose due to this conflict. As I write this, he ventures off to seek the people who stand against the combined forces of government and big business. I do not know if he will live or die, but for the first time he has meaning in his life, and I wish him well."

Wow, I'm writing this without a pause, Scott thought. He looked at the screen and read the words he'd just written as if they were handed to him by the scribe of heaven. "Good," he said out loud. "Damn good!"

He worked the piece over, adding the part about the aborted walk in Lady Bird Johnson Grove, the closed state park, and a bit about how he'd met JoJo.

Rob liked the piece, and called Sylvia over to show her. She actually smiled and said, "You did it." Then she turned to Rob. "Mentor him like I did you back in Boston. I think he's got a future in journalism." And then as if to not get far out of character, "That is if he gives up this nonsense about being a novelist."

As she walked away, Rob smiled absently. "She was the best editor I've ever worked with. Too bad she retired to advertising." He turned his attention to Scott. "I could tell you some stories. I will, one day, over coffee or a beer. You are a journalist, Scott. That, my young friend, is a fact." He added that he'd put it out to the wire, promising papers would pick it up and run it.

The elation stayed with him for almost three days. He'd hoped that Madd would call him during the week, but in the brackish swamp of reality that festered in the corner of his mind he knew that it wasn't her style. She could be painfully independent and unsentimental. At her core, however, she loved him and needed him to make her life healthy and whole.

He had gotten settled back into his daily routine when the bombs started to drop. It came over the service late Wednesday. The President had ordered a preemptive strike against the rogue trees. The first attack came a bit south in Humboldt, in a forest hotly contested over the last decade. It had been the scene of human road-blocks and tree-sits. It was old growth, and that meant a rich, mature habitat to the activists. It meant lots of quality board feet of lumber to the companies.

Without warning, bombs had been dropped on two areas totaling over 3,000 acres. Company crews were poised to move, and as soon as the dust settled, the salvage operation began. The government touted it as a victory; the environmental community called it an obscenity.

Fascinated, Scott went through the motions of his work, all the time watching for breaking news. By Thursday there were protests in every major city on the west coast. Groups insisted they'd ignore the government closures and would return to the forests.

On Friday afternoon, the inevitable finally happened. Bombs were dropped on a place know to activists as the South Fork; 2100 acres were bombed. In the middle of those 2100 acres was something called the Garden of Eden Grove. Over six hundred activists had sneaked in and were staging a rally there when the bombs began to fall. None survived.

Scott was numb. He told Rob he had to go home early. On the drive past the deserted state park, he alternated between tears and the urge to murder Buck.

He had to negotiate a widening array of used Harleys accumulating in front of Jake's. It seems he had half the county riding in shifts, and he'd hired a young biker with a pony tail down his back to help with the work.

He pulled into his carport to find Jules waiting for him. "Scott, do you want to hear what those dumb bitches did at our last gig?"

Pushed beyond the genteel, Scott brushed by her, shouting, "I don't give a fat flying fuck. Six hundred good people just died for nothing. I wanna be alone."

Someone had shoved a tape under his ill-fitting door. It was a song by some band called Jesus Jones, and it was about waking up from history. It apparently was written about the Berlin Wall or the fall of the Soviet Union, but it appeared to have some relation to the forest madness. This was probably a cryptic message from Buck.

He could hear Jules stomping away after shouting that he was an ignorant, Nazi, limp-dick wimp. He listened to the strident music, looked around at the miserable dump he called home, and thought of the senseless slaughter, and he wondered if it could be any worse.

9.

Then the phone rang. It was Madd. She was still in Boston.

"Scott, I have something to tell you, and remember that I warned you."

The next few moments of silence fell on Scott like an anvil on a bare foot. He pictured this bluff in southern Oregon and him jumping into the angry sea.

She continued. "The guy who'd broken up with me? Well, he was at the conference, and on the first night he got all weird about how he missed me and wanted me back in his life. He said he'd bailed because he felt confined, trapped, and all that crap. I said that he was a thirty-three year old educated professional, and the word he was avoiding was 'commitment.' I said that if I wanted a casual relationship, why make it exclusive. It's like staying on a strict diet when you're way underweight. I mentioned you, told him I had a young man in his sexual prime keeping me content. So if he wanted to talk about our relationship, he had to get off the dime. Are you following me, Scott?"

Scott answered with a guttural groan.

Rolling right along over Scott's emotional grave, she continued. "Well, last night he showed up with flowers. Talked about how he saw his life with me and without me, and how he envisioned the two of us raising kids, traveling, growing, and all that. I'll be damned if he didn't end up on his knees, proposing marriage and begging me to give him another chance, and me without a camera or tape recorder. I mean, so what's a girl to do. He knows, one screw up and I'm out of here. Well, anyway, you probably don't want a wedding invitation. Look, Scott, you're a terrific guy. I really hope we're cool with all this."

Inside Scott was screaming, but he said he understood and congratulated her. He added that he'd always love her and would be there when her asshole boyfriend screwed up again.

Then he said that the world was coming undone, and he had to go.

He paced his small room for a few minutes, and then he charged out the door and across the patio to V.V'.s place. When she opened the door, he looked her in the eyes and said, "I need. . . I need to connect with someone." He fell into her arms and let her hold him and rock him. "Why does everything turn to shit?" he muttered, as she stroked his head.

It wasn't planned, but comfort became strokes and kisses and led back to his bed. But afterward Scott felt uncomfortable and tried to reassure her that it wasn't deliberate and that it wouldn't happen again.

"I know it won't," she said, running a finger through his hair. "I just got sucked in by your need. More than that, I've been so obsessed with the job, I haven't had a date since we were together." Then she sat up, the sheets sliding off her ample breasts. "You're right about it not happening again. I'm selling the place. Now that I'm manager, I can afford a real house, in a real neighborhood for Sam to grow up in. Found a cute little two bedroom in town, walking distance from work. We probably won't see each other much in the future, but I wish you luck. You're a nice guy, under all that angst and need." She kissed him, got dressed and walked out his door.

Scott had never felt so alone. He thought of who he might call. He was on the outs with Buck, afraid to bother Rob at home with his family. He could always get ahold of Jules, but he wasn't that desperate for company. He decided on Jake.

He sprinted across the highway to get to the liquor store to pick up a six pack of the light beer Jake drank. He dodged a truck on the return trip, thinking how ironic it would be if he were run over with his article out there. It would be assumed he was part of that organization and had committed suicide. He suddenly understood what Buck had said about how people could be manipulated into believing something.

Jake was watching a syndicated sitcom when Scott knocked on the door.

111

"Wassup, Scotty, my boy?"

"You heard about the bombs and the people killed?"

"Stupidest thing I've ever heard. I thought those guys running in front of trucks were nuts, but the drooling idiots in Washington take the prize. Saw your piece in the paper today. You got some concern about this. Must be bumming you out something fierce."

"Yeah, and I didn't wanna sit home alone tonight, just thinking about it. Care for a beer?"

Jake took one and pointed to a slightly threadbare chair. Scott sank deeply into it, and without thinking said, "My girl-friend broke up with me."

"That college teacher broad down in Trinidad?"

"Went back with her old boyfriend."

"They do that. That's why never take up with one on the rebound. Actually, don't take up with one who hadn't had a guy for a long time, and not if they're too anxious or too standoffish. Shit, when I think about it, it's better you don't take up with one at all. Pick one up in a bar, take her home, throw away her phone number. Advice from a guy what's been there."

Scott pushed out a hollow laugh. "Thanks for the good timing, like shutting the barn door with the horse loose. But, first V.V., then Maddie. Is there something wrong with me?"

Jake waved his hand in the air, attempting to form a gesture, and since the beer was in that hand, it splattered and sprayed. "It's like the old expression. You wear your heart on your sleeve or arm or something.. It's like you got a 'kick me' sign on your back. If you gotta be involved with some broad, find some mousy, needy little thing who will cling to you just as hard as you'll cling to her. You'll have years of mutual desperation together."

The comment made Scott flinch, and Jake laughed out loud. "Won't happen, will it. You'll keep going for the same type and get yourself beat up each time. Glutton for punishment, if you ask me." He reached for another beer.

Then he said he was thinking of getting new furniture,

maybe adding a room. He was making all kinds of money on bikes. Would soon need still another mechanic, maybe a bigger shop, maybe even one downtown.

The conversation had shifted away from Scott and his problems to Jake and his business success. The more Jake talked about business and money, the more distant Scott felt from this man who had become a surrogate father. Opening another beer and listening to Jake's plans, Scott felt even lonelier than before he came. The big biker wasn't interested in Scott's problems. He'd been through all that years ago. He was excited about his life and accomplishments. At a lapse in this one sided conversation, Scott got up and said he had to make some calls before it got too late.

He actually did have to make one call. His mother picked up the phone, surprised to hear from Scott other than Sunday morning. He started talking about the bombing and the dead activists, but his mother interrupted before he could get to his article.

"Those guys are some kind of hippie fruitcakes, jumping out in front of trucks and camping in some restricted forest. Jobs, that's what people like that need. Keep them out of trouble. I hope you're not hanging around with weirdos like that."

Scott had a tapestry of words ready, but his mother's comments unwove it. He only said that he'd be coming to Thanksgiving alone, that his girlfriend was busy with her family.

He put the phone on the cradle and stared at it as if it were a rattlesnake. He grabbed a bottle of wine from the fridge and walked out the door and down the gravel road to the back of the trailer park.

Hot Licks Lesbians was either in the middle of a practice session or an attempt to set music back centuries. They played and argued, calling each other disgusting names. Jules saw him walk up, and said something about him condescending to hang out with them. None the less, they shared his wine and prodded him to take sides on their ongoing battle.

As company, the band was less than satisfying. As salve for a broken heart, they were a waste of time. When his bottle was empty, and the band went back to their assault on music, Scott wandered home. Luckily, he'd had just enough alcohol to let him slip blissfully into a dream that unfortunately was punctuated with bombs and screaming trees, running for their lives.

Along the heavily wooded Smith River, there is little to do with the forests closed. Saturday morning he decided to drive to town to explore. He parked out at Point St. George, and walked along the beach and through the dunes. Most of the others out were joggers or couples. The waves, calm a few week ago, were big and powerful. Four surfers were out catching the scary waves. One stood up on wave much higher than his head and almost immediately fell. It was several seconds before he came to the surface, looking dazed. Getting in that cold water under such rough conditions would take an excess of nerve. Suddenly he felt cautious and somewhat timid. He didn't like seeing himself like that. He vowed to learn to surf, perhaps next summer. He sensed that these were not beginner waves.

He could, he realized, show some instant courage. He would walk into the woods in defiance of the President's orders. He'd stand up and be counted, even if he were arrested. With that thought, the dark cloud over his head started to lift slightly.

That lonely lump in his stomach still throbbed. He was alone, with no one to understand him or even listen. He drove to the first phone booth and called Rob. If anyone would listen and understand, his insightful boss would be the one.

Rob seemed surprised to hear from him and hesitated for some agonizing moments when Scott suggested meeting for lunch or a beer. Rob suggested that Scott come over, and they could retire to his study for beer and conversation.

"I hope I'm not interrupting something," Scott stammered at the door.

"Not a problem. We're all just doing our own weekend thing today. Tomorrow's the family day. Got the little boat berthed in Brookings, and we're taking it out in the morning, weather permitting. But, what about you? You seemed pretty stressed over the phone. Oh, but not out here. Follow me."

It was a newspaperman's study, Scott thought. There was a big desk with a computer. One wall was covered with book cases, with one shelf full of reference books. There was a large world globe on a table, and maps of various parts of the world on the other walls. There were photos of Rob with various senators, congressmen, and broadcast journalists. From the dates, it was clear that Rob hung with the big boys fifteen years earlier. He wanted to ask why the hell he'd ended up in a backwater like Crescent City, but he obeyed his first instinct to turn the conversation back on himself.

"It's been a rough few days. I've really gotten emotionally connected to this forest issue. It's touched me personally, and I think my neighbor is connected to it via some conspiracy. My girlfriend has gone back to her ex, and my ex girlfriend is moving to town. My family are like strangers, and. . . and, oh hell, I feel damn alone."

"It'll pass, Scott. Writing, even for a paper, is a lonely profession. I was on overseas assignment for better than four years, always around strangers, sometimes with people shooting in my direction. It made me a better writer, but I couldn't handle it. The woman I loved was getting tired of waiting, and my friends had drifted off in their own directions. I chucked it, flew home, proposed, sent out resumes, and ended up here."

So, that was the story. His respect for the man was growing. He was more than the quiet, middle aged editor with the suburban family.

"Scott, I'm so glad I had that experience, but I don't miss it. I wasn't much older than you and so ready to take on the world. I was lonely, but I used that to stay sharp, to write with an edge. Now there's no edge, but I'm content and happy, and that's where I want to be at this point in my life."

"I wish I could be."

"You will. You're going through your own trial by fire. It'll temper your mettle, make you stronger and better at your craft.

115

Then you'll find your place, your partner. You're what, barely twenty-one? It's not all going to come at once. You have this life now. Take advantage of it. The other life will come soon enough."

Try as he would, Scott couldn't stop the tears from welling up. He wiped his eyes with his hand and looked at Rob with unconcealed admiration. "Man, that was just what I needed to hear. The others, they haven't been there. You have."

"Ok Scott, now have another beer and tell me about this friend of yours and why you think he's involved."

Scott relayed all he could remember about Buck and his doings since the first activist death. Rob sat still, looking straight at Scott and not saying a word until the story ended.

"He's more than involved, Scott. Sounds like he's the hypothetical guy who took what might have been an accident and turned it into all that's happened. Chaos theory, indeed. Good God, man he admitted it to you."

"But that would make him a monster, a mass murderer. How could he be those things and be my friend?"

"You totally misunderstand. If he did anything at all, it was only to make a suggestion, a small claim of responsibility. There were people out there already primed to do all the subsequent actions. This issue has been boiling for years. There's been violence. Your friend, if I read this right, just brought it to a head, sped up the inevitable train wreck."

"Then should I expose him?"

"You can't. Learn your human nature, Scott. First, no one would believe some hippie, bumper sticker maker in a trailer park could make something so big happen. He flies under the mass mental radar. Second, you can't prove it, so he could sue you and the paper. You can theorize on this in an opinion piece, citing anonymous sources close to the movement."

"Let him get away with it?"

"Away with what? Making a few crank calls? He hasn't really done anything, and that's the fascinating part of it. Look at this another way. History is unfolding, and you've got a ringside seat. I predict this will be the undoing of the President and will usher in some radical changes in forest management, but I have no idea how it will end up."

Suddenly, almost as a non sequitur, Scott blurted out his plan to walk in the woods.

"Good idea. Get a sense of what it feels like to be there, with signs telling you to stay out and with the death of all those people so fresh in your mind. Feel it, write about it."

"If some soldier doesn't shoot me."

"After the bomb fiasco, no one's going to be anxious to shoot anyone."

Since Rob was up and opening the study door, Scott figured it was time to leave. On the way to the door, a perky little blond with a nice body bounced up to them. She was wearing shorts cut high and pulled low, and her navel was pierced.

"Yo, dad, who's this guy?"

"Oh, this is Scott. He's a reporter at the paper. Scott, my daughter Sandy."

Scott awkwardly thrust out his hand, and Sandy looked at it for a long moment before shaking it a bit too vigorously. "Kinda young for a reporter. You don't look much older than me."

"Er, I'm twenty-one. And, you? High School?"

"Graduating in June. Then off to what? Princeton, Yale, Humboldt State? Hey, most of those paper people are senior citizens. You gotta come around more." She winked and pointed at him. "Promise?"

He felt himself flush as he muttered something in the affirmative. The girl was clearly being flirtatious, and it was making it hard for him to look Rob in the eye. The last thing he wanted was to appear to be encouraging her.

"Oh, look at the time. I've got so much to do today. Thanks again. And, oh, nice to meet you Sandy."

On the way to his big errand, to buy a printer cartridge, he thought briefly about Sandy. She was cute, but she was the boss's daughter, and she was a kid. He hungered for a real

117

relationship, a committed one with a mature woman.

That night he lost himself in his novel. Damned if he'd stop, even though his main character had dumped him. The book was three quarters of the way done, and he felt it was strong and real. With the fever of a man who's personal life is empty, he threw himself into writing, knocking out almost eight thousand emotionally charged words before he leaned back and fell asleep, the cursor still blinking and the light on.

The next morning he woke late feeling better with the new day. The sun was shining, but by the time he rescued the paper from the drive and made a pot of coffee, the clouds had rolled in. By the time he finished his ritual with the book review section, the rain started to fall. The top fiction pieces were a court room thing, *The Law of the Forest*, about a young environmental lawyer taking on the Department of the Interior and a major timber company in defense of a tree sitting activist. Another, *The Avalanche of Revelation*, was about a rogue FBI agent investigating the killing of citizens of a small town in the redwood forests. There was also a non-fiction offering. *The Secret Life of an Activist*. A young social justice college organizer tells of the sex and drugs behind the protests.

The rain and wind were rocking his little tin house as he read the lead story. Thousands of protesters were marching in major cities around the country, particularly in the west. They were outraged by the government's murder of innocent forest activists. There were 20,000 in San Francisco, almost 15, 000 in Portland, 17,000 in Seattle, and even in Los Angeles 10,000 people showed up in SUVs to denounce the government. It helped, according to the report, that the organizers were handing out free lattes. Even New York and Chicago had protests numbering in the thousands.

Some of these protests had turned into riots, with tear gas, night sticks, rocks, and baseball bats. Hundreds were injured, thousands arrested, and 170 more people were killed, including three police and an FBI agent. At a huge protest at a forest in Humboldt, the guard tried to keep activists out of the forest.

Almost four thousand protesters charged the guard's line, and the guard, not having been issued ammunition, broke and ran. The protesters took up positions in the forest, vowing that the authorities would have to shoot them to remove them.

The President's party supported him, while the opposition branded him an insensitive hatchet man for corporate timber. People on the streets were comparing him to Stalin and demanding impeachment. Rocks were being thrown through windows in the major cities, and the petty thieves who always follow mass protests were carting home televisions, legal tender in many impoverished neighborhoods.

It was clear to Scott, with an election year around the corner, that the Commander-in-Chief would have to do some serious damage repair damn soon to salvage his job.

All the death and injury of these gentle tree lovers tore Scott up. It was time for him to take his stand.

The rain had become a storm that was washing away his plan to walk in the forbidden state park. He was composing an elaborate excuse for postponing the walk when the image of the surfer blissfully ignoring a huge shark slipped insidiously into his mind and sneered at him. Hell, he thought, it's not a dangerous shark. It's only rain and some weekend soldiers. He pulled rain pants and jacket over his jeans and sweat shirt and, with his jaw set in grim determination, stomped through the puddles to the car.

He parked along the highway, far enough from the main entrance to avoid detection by the two guardsmen stationed at the gate. He soon realized he had to make a stream crossing, and without a bridge, he found a fallen redwood. It was too slippery to attempt walking, so he crossed on all fours. Soon he was deep in the forest, but rather than getting a sense of the forest or communing with nature, Scott was occupied with the discomfort of walking in the mud in a rain storm. Something occurred to him after a few minutes. The rain didn't seem to be coming down so hard. The forest canopy was acting as a buffer, turning the driving rain into a heavy, pervasive mist, with dripping branches. It really wasn't all that bad, but it was getting colder as the cheap rain suit failed to keep him either warm or dry.

It had become a matter of keeping a promise to himself. So, after a half hour he felt he had chalked up an acceptable illegal protest hike, and headed back to the fallen log. This time the crossing was more treacherous, and he almost crawled on his belly. He peered out from behind a tree before stepping out into the open. No guardsmen or even passers by. He crossed the road quickly, hopped in the car and made an abrupt U turn.

Back home, he took a long, hot shower to warm up. He turned on the heat and put on dry sweats, made some hot choco- late and popcorn and flipped on the laptop. He realized that for the first time in a long time, he was comfortable with just his own company. He didn't feel the need to call anyone, mourn his late relationship or anything. He felt almost whole. Then he knew what he needed to write about.

Scott sat down and wrote not about saving the trees or the animals or the watershed, but rather about saving the human psyche. He made a case that woods and other wild lands act as a balm for the stress and anxiety of civilized life. Without those places we become neurotic, needy, obsessed, and unethical. He speculated that perhaps if more people took the time to take to the woods, there would be less corporate corruption, people selling watered down medicines, road rage, domestic violence and a host of other civilized ills. Cutting down the forests, he insisted, would be to doom humanity to a dog eat dog life in a concrete jungle, a post apocalyptic nightmare.

When he finished, he realized that most of what he'd said had already been said in one form or another, but pulling it together at this time and in this place was, in his opinion, an original act and a necessary reminder to the public.

He may not be holed up in the woods, surrounded by soldiers or being dragged off by police in the middle of a protest, but he was getting involved, and that involvement was growing.

He no sooner e-mailed his piece off to Rob's desk, when there was a loud knock on the door. He opened the door to two men in dark suits and overcoats. They had closely cropped hair, black dress shoes, and expressions of icy malice. They held out badges that identified them as FBI.

"Scott Mukis?'

"Why? What do you want?" He tried to hide the nervousness in his voice.

"Don't try to deny it. We know who you are."

"I'm not trying to deny anything. Can I help you?"

"Perhaps we can help you. May we come in?" The question was absurd, as by the time it was asked, they were coming through the door. "It would be in your best interest to cooperate. Have a seat young man."

Scott opened his mouth to protest, but the four piercing eyes acted like force fields, pushing him onto the end of the bed. The two men sat at his two dining chairs.

Without further small talk, one of the men began. "What is your involvement with this radical environmental group?"

"What involvement? Which group?"

"Don't act ignorant. We know all about you and your editorials. Are you working for these people?"

"What people? I'm…I'm a reporter. This is a hot issue in this part of the state."

"Uh huh. You imply that you have sources, people that know who started these suicide missions. If it wasn't you, who was it?"

"Wait. I don't have any information. It's speculation and rumors. I'm looking at all explanations."

"The names of your informants, please."

"I don't have informants, and besides, I'm a reporter, and there's the freedom of the press thing, so even if I did have informants, which I don't, I wouldn't have to tell you." Scott was scared but also getting mad. How dare they come in and accuse him of all this crap. For a moment he considered naming Buck, but he decided that they wouldn't get that out of him, even if they used the rubber hoses on him.

"So, you're protecting your fellow conspirators. I suppose

you were conditioned to take the rap for them."

"Nobody conditioned me to do anything. Besides, what rap? What are you accusing me of?"

"Let's not get ahead of ourselves, Mukis. We have to finish our investigation before we can accuse you. Now what about this guy you wrote about, the one who likes to fight and went off to join the agitators? Suppose you tell me who he is and where we can find him."

"He's just a drunk who hangs around the local saloon, and he told me he was going looking for the protestors. I don't know where the hell he is."

"You're not doing yourself any good, Mukis. We know about your involvement with campus radicals in Long Beach. Is your friend Cynthia Malone involved in this group?"

"Cyn? I haven't see her for almost a year. She's more into human rights, but she does environmental stuff now and then. She could turn up at a protest somewhere."

"So, she's your contact among the protestors?"

Scott found himself almost shouting. "I don't have contacts. I haven't see Cyn since she broke up with me. I just wrote some opinion pieces, and last I heard that's my first amendment right."

"So, invoking the first amendment in your defense." One man was doing the talking, and the other was making notes in a small notebook.

"I don't have a defense. I didn't do anything. What do you want from me?"

"The names of the people in your organization, for openers. How about this Maddie Kobzev? We see she's a social scientist at a liberal university. What's her connection?"

Good God, Scott thought, they know all about me. They probably even know I was in the woods today.

"Was she the one you were meeting in the woods today, or was it Cynthia, or maybe this unidentified local drunk, or perhaps the guy who made all the calls taking credit for the suicides? It sounds like you're in it up to your neck. Make it easy on yourself and come clean right now."

Scott's suspicion and fear of authority was no match for his anger or outrage. "Perhaps you'd better tell me what the hell I'm into up to my neck. As far as I know there's no law against protesting. There's sure as hell no law about reporting and writing opinion. If a guy wants to run in front of a truck or run off to join a picket line, I don't think there's a law against that either. Even if I knew about what those guys are doing, there's no law against that. I'm a reporter and a citizen, and I've got goddamn rights, and my paper has lawyers who'll be down to the jail in a moment to get me out. Now, if you're planning to arrest me, here." He jumped to his feet and thrust his wrists forward. "And, if you do, you damn well better tell me what I'm charged with. Perhaps I'd better call my boss right now, so he can call the lawyers."

"There's no reason to get excited. We're trying to conduct an investigation here, and you're not being cooperative."

"You damn right I'm not. You gonna charge me and arrest me? If not, I've told you every fuckin' thing I know, and I'm not answering any more of your questions."

"Sit down, Mukis." The violence in the voice brought Scott back to the bed. "We're not arresting you at this time. We've noted your reluctance to cooperate with the justice department. For the moment, we have no further questions, but don't try to leave the country. We will be watching you, waiting for you to slip up. Disloyalty to your country is considered pretty cool to you privileged, college types. But, let me tell you, when the security of this nation's at stake, all your father's money won't save your hide.

Now, think about what we said, and if you decide to be reasonable, call us." He thrust a card in Scott's hand as the two of them turned on their heels and walked out into the driving rain.

Scott was shaking with both anger and fear. These guys were cold-blooded. They probably just as soon gun him down as talk to him. The thought of being watched freaked him out.

Perhaps they have pictures of him making love with Madd. They knew he was in the woods, but they don't know everything, or they would have known that he didn't meet anyone. Perhaps they did know that, but they were just trying to fuck with his head and get him to confess. Confess! Shit, now he was using their terms. He reminded himself out loud, "I didn't do one goddamn thing wrong!"

He picked up the phone to call Buck, but stopped. They had likely bugged his phone. He went to the door and looked out. He couldn't see a thing, but he'd remembered the car driving off, so he figured those guys had left. Scott slipped on the rain jacket and walked to the pay phone on the side of Jake's shop.

"Buck, It's Scott. Don't worry, I'm not calling from home."

"Worry? Home? What the fuck you talking about, Scott?"

"The FBI. They were just here, accusing me of being part of a conspiracy, asking me to name people connected with this forest business. But, don't worry, They didn't get anything out of me. Your identity is safe with me."

"Well, gee Scott. Thanks a lot. We're assuming here that the FBI has a reason to come after me."

"Look, man. You don't have to be cagey. I understand now what you're doing and why. I support you. These bastards have got to be stopped. Man, I'm on your side. I even held out my hands for the cuffs and dared them to arrest me. You can trust me."

"Cool, Scott. I trust you; you're on my side, and I like that you stood up to those pigs. The FBI, along with the rest of the government, sucks. It took some balls to do what you did. So, now I can confide in you. I'm Number One, head of SPECTER, and we plan to take over the world."

"Come off it, Buck. I'm standing in the rain at a phone booth. You know what I'm talking about."

"Shit, you and those pigs. Conspiracy theories everywhere. If you want to think I'm the mastermind of some great forest conspiracy, that's fine. It would be great in one of your books. I'm not a leader, Scott. I'm an absurd observer, and you should have enough sense to get in out of the rain. Perhaps we could meet for a beer tomorrow night. If you buy, I'll tell you all about the secret plots I've designed to bring down the world's governments."

"Buck, I walked in the State Park today."

"Excellent. I do that damn near every day. Skipped today, however. Just too fuckin' cold and wet."

"No, I mean, like the park was closed and guarded, and I slipped in and walked there."

"Wow! Next thing you'll be ignoring those 'keep off the grass' signs, and you'll be pulling those tags off mattresses. What a rebel."

"Don't make fun of me. I'm on the FBI's list. They are watching me, and I'm getting in this forest issue up to my neck. I'm not some pampered college boy at a campus protest." Wow, Scott thought, that last comment, screamed through the phone, came from the subconscious. Did he really feel that he was a dilettante, some spoiled kid who went through the motions of being involved and concerned but who never put himself on the line? It didn't matter now. He'd stepped over that line. He was higher profile than the anonymous protesters. He was putting his name to paper and reaching thousands. He was becoming a voice of the movement. He only wished that he knew for sure if there really was a movement.

"I'm sorry as hell, Scott. What you've done is righteous. You got guts and integrity, and I'd be damned honored to drink your beer with you. Tomorrow night at the Tree House?"

Scott agreed, hung up and trudged home for a second hot shower of the day. He was a bit disappointed at Buck's flip reaction. Buck still wouldn't admit anything. Perhaps it wasn't that he didn't trust Scott. If Scott's phone was bugged, perhaps the pay phone was also. Besides, if the feds were that thorough, they might have noted all the numbers he called frequently and bugged all of them, including Buck. He was sure that Buck had been through all this before and had kept ahead of the law by being extra cautious. Scott understood, and their shared knowledge would be hinted at but never named.

Rob liked Scott's latest piece, printed it and sent it out. Turned out that several other west coast papers were picking up his opinion pieces, and he was being read by those who supported forest activism.

At the Tree House, which Scott drove to because of the continuing deluge, Buck was waiting, having walked in full rain gear. The first thing Buck did, after taking a healthy drink, was to hand Scott a book. It was a very thin work. *The Trial* by Kafka. Buck told Scott that he had to read it right away, that it would put his recent experience with the law in perspective. He also gave Scott one of his latest bumper stickers, "I brake for cockroaches"

They discussed the latest events in the forests in a way that interested bystanders might talk, avoiding all references to any direct involvement. Buck seemed to think that this whole mass protest thing, with arrests, deaths and all, might be like the final days of the Viet Nam War. This would, he felt, be the deal breaker for current forest policy and probably for the national leadership. "Scott, it looks like ma and pa middle of the country are finally going to say they want the forests saved. Those activists have put it on the line and pulled it off. Actually, the stupidity of those in power caused it to happen. Whatever, a combination of events has pushed the issue to a head, and I'm dying to see the next chapter."

Scott agreed. People were pissed at the government for letting citizens get killed for the protection of the timber industry, which was the way it was being understood by the press and the people in the street. "We're going to win this one, Buck."

"More of that 'we' shit. Scott, when are you gonna get it? I'm not a true believer of any kind. I don't give a flying fuck about the President and those people who huddle under a tree in the woods. People are just plain fools. The only time they're any fun at all is when I can fuck with their heads. Did I ever tell you that my only hero is Mark Twain, not as a young writer, but as an old dude who had nothing but contempt for his fellow man. Now, Scott, you're a fool too, but you're fun to talk to, and you buy beer."

Then Buck looked around the room for a moment, slugged down some beer, and added, "Remember some saying about, 'I drink to make other people more interesting?' Well, it's true. You're getting more interesting, and I see Dusty over by the bar, and I'm thinking that I've had enough beer to make him interesting. So, what the hell." He waved his arm and shouted, "Dusty, join us!"

The big hillbilly shambled over, long, greasy hair bouncing off his ears and jaw, stubble of a beard catching the bar lights. "Yo, guys. Whatsup?"

Scott really didn't want to talk to the guy, but Buck opened with, "Heard anything from JoJo?"

The big man grinned. "Yeah, but it'll cost y'all a refill to hear bout it." He stuck out his almost empty glass.

This was indeed news, so Scott quickly topped off the glass.

Dusty dropped into a chair, which almost buckled under his weight. "Well, seems like somma them tree huggers got cell phones out in the woods. Hell, they got them a set up out there. There's big tarps, blankets, lanterns, the works. Even with the rain and all, they's pretty dry and warm. Well, JoJo, he be having the time a his life out there. He was with that group what rushed the nash'nul guard, and he punched three a them right good on his way in. Well, he wishing for some action, but they's no fightin' amongst they's self, bein' all brotherhood an all, so he be itching go get into it with the cops, but the cops got more sense then come in them dark woods. An', well, he says the people like family there. They's not much booze back there, but them tree huggers got some killer pot, so JoJo doin' pretty good. An they's this gal, big ass an no bra. Don't shave her legs. Ol' JoJo got some serious hots for her, an he bin busy trying to make some time."

Scott was fascinated. "Did he say anything about the group's plan?"

"Well, from what I hear, they's not much of a plan. They be

127

staying in the woods til the gov'mint promise to leave them trees the fuck alone. That's 'bout it."

Scott managed to extricate himself before getting in the bag. He wanted to be fresh for work in the morning. Buck seemed to be enjoying Dusty's rambling account and stayed around to coax more out of the big man. Back home, Scott parked in a massive puddle, working on becoming a lake. He walked in water a foot deep to get to his door. He reached for the laptop, but changed his mind and turned on the late news. The riots were getting worse. Logging truck drivers were getting attacked by citizens in the streets. Timber company executives were getting death threats over the phone. The White House phones were ringing off the hook night and day. A lumber yard got burned down, and the San Francisco Sierra Club offices had a hail of rocks come through the windows. Some guy with an Earth First! bumper sticker was dragged from his car on the Avenue of the Giants and beaten badly. Everyone in government was pointing fingers, demanding an escalation of the forest wars. The conservatives were calling for mass arrests. The liberals were calling for the President and half of Congress to resign. The environmentalists were saying "take these trees over my dead body," and the timber people were saying that they liked those conditions.

The next day at work was chaotic. All the local meetings had been cancelled. National guard trucks rolled through the town. The police were everywhere, trying their best to keep a lid on the town. Many businesses were closed. The staff could almost look out the second floor window and write the news of the day. At the end of the day, Scott went straight home in the still driving rain and locked himself in for the night.

10.

Wednesday morning Scott packed for his trip to Santa Barbara, and turned on the morning news before heading off for his half-day of work before Thanksgiving. The chaos had reached fever pitch, but there was a lone voice calling for some compromise, some resolution. Some junior senator from one of the empty northern plains states, a Bambi Bottoms, had drafted a bill aimed at restoring order and reaching an agreement.

She had contacted experts in several fields, including hydrology, forest management, and property law and had worked with this group round the clock to come up with her proposal. Without consulting anyone in Congress, she submitted the draft of the bill to the papers.

The first reaction on both sides was a cautious *maybe*. The environmental community didn't think it offered enough protection, but acknowledged that it was far better than anything offered in the past. The timber interests insisted that it gave too much away, but they realized that public sentiment was against them and that the longer they waited the worse their bargaining position would be.

The high points of the bill included a total ban on clear cutting on public and private land, on grounds that clear cutting jeopardized the public interest, just like storing explosives would jeopardize one's neighbors. Issues of sources of water, danger of mud slides, and fishery damage would supercede property rights. Any public lands, including national forests and BLM properties that were already being logged and had roads built, could still be logged, but new, roadless, areas couldn't be opened. Experts were working to complete formulas for the percent of forest cover that could be logged, based on factors such as how steep the hillsides, the amount of annual rain, the types and locations of streams, and the impact on adjacent communities. The figures were supposed to be completed before the Thanksgiving holiday, which meant by the end of the day. The committee that would hear the bill was under great pressure to put it at the top of the list to be heard the following Monday morning.

Then the newscasters gave the public a quick bio on the senator. Bottoms started out as a model in her late teens and early twenties. She graduated to B thrillers and science fiction films. She was often cast as the busty gal in the skimpy outfit. One day she decided she didn't like the local political scene and ran for city council. From there she went on to mayor, supervisor, assemblywoman, state senator and finally senator. She was a study of a popular candidate on the fast track. At 41 she had cemented her place in politics. It was understood that to run against her was more an exercise in the two party system than an actual race, as she managed to win each race with better than 70 percent of the vote. She was considered a populist, a very popular populist apparently.

The station showed a photo of her. Scott was impressed. At 41 she was still a serious babe, big tits, small waist, and long blond hair. Hell, thought Scott, she'd get an easy ten to fifteen percent on the sexual fantasy vote alone.

The monologue in his mind was at odds with the feminism he claimed to endorse. He felt guilty thinking of this woman in terms of her body when she was obviously a skilled and well respected U.S. Senator.

Work was chaotic. Local news had been put on the back burner, unless it was local events in the forest war, as everyone at the paper was calling this mess. Rob rushed out of his office and almost ran into Scott. "All ready for the family dinner in Santa Rosa?"

"It's Santa Barbara," Scott corrected.

"Christ, that's one hell of a drive. You're not needed here today. Get on the road now, before something else happens. See you Monday morning."

Scott started to thank him, but Rob was rushing off to deal with the next crisis.

The car was still warm when Scott jumped in and pulled out of the lot. In five minutes he was on the highway and on the way south out of town. There were a few protesters along the highway at various exits, and Scott imagined that the scenic road through redwood park would be filled with sign-carrying youth. He was curious but aware of the distance and the potential for traffic problems in the Bay Area, so he stayed on the main highway.

Eureka was congested, with protesters on every corner, even with the still-driving rain, but Scott managed to get through fairly quickly. There were no major cities for several hours, so he figured he had it made. Then as he drove up the hill toward Fortuna, it suddenly happened. He heard the radio report about the thousands of demonstrators too late to exit. Just north of the first Fortuna exit the road was blocked with a solid mass of humanity, and the only way out and around would be to go way back down the hill to Loleta, and head out toward Ferndale and the coast, hours out of the way. Naturally with a major highway stopped dead, just turning around was just about impossible for anyone not already in the fast lane. Scott was stuck hundreds of miles from his destination.

He could see a mass of bodies up ahead, and he couldn't move, so he decided to have a look. He walked up to find a sea of tie dyes and long hair, torn jeans and sandals, hand made drums and elaborate signs. This was the group he'd been identifying with, the heroic young people defending our natural wonders, even with their lives. He was moved and wanted to somehow be a part of it. He walked into the mob, picked up a sign that had landed on the ground, and joined the group.

An hour or more had gone by with feeble attempts by the police to push through the morass. Scott had lost himself in the moment, chanting, swaying in rhythm with the crowd, and waving the sign. A megaphone was being passed around. Mostly it was the leaders who picked in up and spoke words of inspiration. As it passed by Scott, he grabbed it and gave a quick speech about how what they were doing today was more than for the trees and the endangered species. It was about the future health of the human species, and that civilization or barbarism would be decided on this spot, on this day. The mass of undulating humanity let out a cheer.

He'd blended, psychologically and physically, with the protesters when the military showed up. Fire hoses, tear gas and tanks pushed slowly into the crowd. People in the middle of the group were panicking, seeing they had no exit, and getting their first blasts of water and gas. Soon the resolve was melting into chaos and fear, and the military kept pushing until they'd cut a swath of empty road through the protesters. Scott, like the rest, found himself backing up.

Suddenly two army officers grabbed him by the arms and told him he was under arrest. Without hesitation, he pulled out his wallet and flashed his press pass. "I'm a reporter, covering this protest."

The men let him go, advising him to get back to his car and clear the area. Scott didn't argue, instead, heading straight back to his car. Soon the traffic cleared enough for him to continue on his way, feeling proud to have been part of it, but guilty for not letting himself get arrested.

He rationalized that his family would be hurt if he didn't show up, that they'd not understand why he let himself get into this trouble, believing instead that he'd chosen to rebuke his family once again. Yes, he decided, he must make this reunion and start to heal the broken relationships.

He put a Grateful Dead tape in the stereo and tried to imagine himself as a sixties hippie and anti war activist. He daydreamed himself all the way to Santa Rosa, where the long traffic nightmare began.

By the time he hit Salinas, it was late and he was exhausted. He found a cheap motel near the airport, and called his folks. He promised an early start and a noon arrival.

Scott had a very late dinner and some beer at an Australian theme steak house, surrounded by large, shouting groups of people in a feeding frenzy. He felt alone and dejected. He was neither activist or regular citizen, not a drop out, but not a successful person, not without family, but not in the bosom of his family either. He was a stranger, a ghost. He didn't belong. He was the tragic artist, looking in at the warm hearth from out in the cold. At least, he consoled himself, the rain had quit somewhere north of Cloverdale.

Forcing himself up at dawn, he managed to pull into Santa Barbara in time for something like a mid day tea on the porch. With a huge turkey dinner, prepared by the family cook, only a few hours away, lunch was out of the question. Rather, it was finger food, tea and a very good white wine.

Scott arrived rumpled from the road. "Dear, you look exhausted. Do go in and freshen up." His mother handed him a glass of wine and guided him toward his room. Her skin had the look of parchment, and her hair was almost the color of buffed gold. It was hard to believe she was not much older than that earthy senator who had promised to save the country's collective ass.

After a quick shower and change, and his wine glass still half full, he was back outside. His father had come out and seemed fatter than before, but more relaxed.

"Scotty. Damn, it great to see you. I hope you're ready to take some of the burden off my aging back." He reached around to his spine for emphasis.

Avoiding a direct answer, Scott replied, "I'm always here for you, to help you out and all. Where's Becky?"

As if on cue, his sister walked in. She looked different. Her long hair had been cut very short, above her ears. She wore a severe suit with a narrow waist and broad shoulders. Her hips were slim, and as he discovered when they hugged, the shoulders were not padded. The two of them looked like bookends, both tall, lean and built to run. The difference was that Becky obviously ran often, but Scott maintained his peak physical conditioning by walking and drinking beer.

Soon company arrived. It was Becky's boyfriend, the man she was talking about marrying. His name was Tom Tremaine, and he was about Scott's age. As they shook hands, Scott sized him up. He was a good two inches shorter than Becky, four inches shorter than Scott. He had the most pronounced V shape Scott could imagine. Tom had broad shoulders and very narrow hips. He wore a polo shirt that showed off a buff body without an ounce of fat. He had chestnut brown hair that rolled in long waves down to his neck. He was flawlessly handsome. He made Scott think of a 1970s rock singer.

With almost perfect civility, Tom said, "Scott, I've heard so much about you from Becky. I'm pleased to finally meet you. By the way, I've been reading your writings about the forest protests, and I'm quite impressed."

After Scott thanked him, Tom excused himself and brought Becky a plate of vegetables and a glass of wine. Then he sort of faded into the background. He was probably a shy young man. Scott noticed that he made polite conversation, but didn't seem to have many opinions. All Scott could pry from him about his relationship with Becky was that he worked in the accounting department, where they'd met, and that they'd fallen in love.

It was logical, both Tom and Becky agreed that should they have children, Tom would quit working and stay home, being that Becky's job was more critical to the company. Tom had added later, at the bar, "After all, I'm just a bookkeeper with a nice title. It's not like a big career or anything. Becky runs the whole company."

"My dad runs the company," Scott corrected.

"Technically, I guess," Tom said. "He's around less and less these days. Becky is everywhere, making all the decisions, hiring all the new management people. I started well before she came in, and it's a different company now. The people running the departments are new, the whole way things are run is different. The company seems more modern, and it's growing so fast you wouldn't believe it. She talks about plans for the future, and it blows me away."

Scott wandered casually up to Becky, who was having a glass of wine with their father. "So, how are the hardware stores really doing?"

His father just said they were doing great, but Becky got into details.

"We've added four stores this year, and we'll have two more before next summer. And, Scotty, we're not hardware stores; we're a home improvement chain, the fastest growing one in the country. We've been written up in the business section of the Times."

It seemed that after saying that she stood a bit more erect and threw her shoulders back a bit more.

"And, " their father added, "we've got the name thing settled. I came up with R.S. Mukis Company. You see, that way it covers the whole family. Your mom, Ruth Sandra, Rebecca Susan, Randall Scott, and soon as you get your head on straight, Randall Scott jr."

"Hold on Dad, I dropped the 'Randall' in junior high."

"None the less, son, it's still your name, and it's now the name on the door, and there's always a place for you in the company. Right Becky?"

"That's right, little brother. In fact, I was thinking that since you're such a wordsmith, perhaps you might be interested in running the marketing and advertising department. We've got some great people in there who can handle the day to day business. You could make the creative decisions, and still have time to work on your novels or poems or whatever."

For a moment Scott was almost tempted, but he realized that his dad and sister would be his bosses, and that however grand the job, he was sure he'd be handled and patronized.

"Thanks for the offer, but I've got a good career in journalism, and I'm working on a gritty, realistic novel. My plate is definitely full."

His father just patted him on the back and said, "Sure Scotty, we understand." He smiled and went off to talk to grandmother, who was holding court in the big easy chair in the den.

The whole weekend was weird. The family treated him like

gold. They all seemed really interested in what he was doing, but none of them asked to look at his writing, which he'd brought on disks, just in case. They wanted to know about the job, his chances for advancement, his pay, his chances of moving to a bigger paper. For a normally self-centered bunch of ego junkies, this whole solicitous business was hard to grasp. During his college days, his father only wanted to know how his grades were doing and if he were getting laid. His mother always asked about his health and diet, and Becky rarely paid him any notice since she'd graduated from high school. The people making a fuss over him this weekend were alien pod people and not his real family.

He was actually glad to be back on the road Sunday. He left even earlier than necessary, citing the possibility of more activist road blocks.

His mother and father were only dimly aware of the situation, and they considered the activists fools who should be working and raising a family.

Becky, however, totally surprised Scott. Just as he was about to get into the car to leave, she took him aside. "You know, I'm on your side in this forest thing. In fact, after Senator Bottoms came out with her plan, I checked her out. Impressive. Looks like she's going to force the normally slow Senate to act on her bill. She's a mover and shaker." Then, as if sharing a confidence, she added, "I called her directly. We had a nice conversation, and at the end, I told her the company had a $40,000 check written, made out to the Bambi Bottoms presidential campaign. As soon as that campaign became a reality, she'd get the check, and probably more. And, as it turns out, we weren't the only ones. She's actually considering it."

Rather than hug her brother, Becky shook his hand with a firm grip, and wished him well. She gave him her card with her cell phone and fax, telling him to contact her at any time for any reason. "You're family, and that's important."

11.

Somewhere near Leggett, in one of the few areas where the highway hasn't been converted to freeway, Scott saw a young woman with a backpack hitchhiking. She was dressed in the north coast hippie style, with patch jeans, an embroidered jacket, and a floppy, felt hat. She was sitting on a huge back pack. Scott felt sorry for her and considered all the weirdoes that might be driving the highway, so he pulled over.

"Where you headed?"

She threw her pack in the back seat and crawled in the front. "Away, north, wherever. How about you?"

"Home, near Crescent City."

"Sounds good to me. Name's Peaches."

Scott introduced himself, adding that he was a reporter. Then he asked where she lived.

"I was staying with my mom for awhile, but her old man can't stand me since I refused to fuck him, and she's kind of a drunk and doesn't want to be bothered with me, so I split. I was in a homeless shelter for awhile. Before that there was a group that had a house, kind of a commune near Boonville. I was in college until the money my dad left me after he killed himself ran out. I got no place to go. Thought I'd try Portland. Old friend from college lives up there somewhere. I'll try to look her up, maybe find a job."

"You're homeless and broke? You can't just wander the road and all. Maybe I can help."

"Dude, you are helping, getting me away from here."

He looked over at her. She was young, maybe eighteen or nineteen tops. She was kind of cute in a plump kid-like way. He liked the way she could be brave in her situation. Scott wanted to help. He couldn't just leave her off on the side of the road in the rain that had started again near Hopland and was getting worse by the mile.

137

"I know folks in my area. Maybe I can help you get a job, a place to stay."

"Oh, like that would be so cool of you. Why would you do that for a stranger?"

"You're down and out. You're hardly more than a kid. Say, have you eaten?"

"Yesterday some time."

There were lots of cafes along the Eel, and Scott pulled off at the first one. They sloshed through the muddy parking lot to find themselves the only customers. Scott ordered coffee for both of them and told her to pick whatever she wanted. She ended up with a double burger and a huge side of fries, which she polished off in minutes.

As he watched her eat, his heart was breaking. This time he wasn't going to be on the sidelines. He'd damn well make sure she was taken care of. Unfortunately, he didn't have a plan, much less a clue. He trusted in good intentions to see him through.

She looked like a little girl. Her round face was baby pink, and she had a small mouth and sad gray eyes. She was round and short, not much over five feet. Her hair the color of dirty straw, hung to her shoulders.

When they got to the 199, Scott considered calling Rob, who had lots of room but thought better of imposing with a stranger at eleven at night. There was nothing left but to take her to his place. What Scott forgot to consider was that his place wasn't big enough for one, let alone two.

He quickly followed his suggestion that she stay at his place with the assurance that he wasn't trying to take advantage of her. He assured her that he just wanted to help her get back on her feet and that he promised to be a gentleman.

She gave him a strange look when they entered his trailer. There was only one sleeping room, and when the bed was pulled out, it nearly filled the room. There was, however, a single bed that could be made from the cushion bench at the table. He was quick to point out that he was giving her his bed and was taking the other, which, he claimed, was quite adequate. She protested for a moment that she was putting him out, but exhaustion took over, and she sat down on the bed, rolled over and fell asleep fully dressed.

Scott threw a cover over her, pulled out his sleeping bag, folded up the table and got into the fetal position on the under-sized bed. This, he assured himself, could only be temporary.

Scott woke with a stiff back. He didn't want to wake Peaches, but in a space that small, there was no way around it. She sat up when he started making coffee.

"Scott, I don't know how to thank you. It's so nice to sleep in a real bed again. But, I feel like I'm a burden, putting you out of your bed and all. Wait, let me help."

She jumped out of bed, still dressed, and took over the coffee making. While she filled the pot and ground the beans, she said she'd make breakfast for him, and that he could take a shower and get ready.

Maybe it wouldn't be all that bad, he thought, as he showered and dressed in the tiny bathroom. When he came out, something seemed to be burning. She was readying two plates of food. She motioned him to sit down and put a plate in front of him. The eggs were overcooked, the toast black, and the bacon half cooked and greasy.

"Looks delicious," he said valiantly. At least he had some good coffee, he figured. He took a sip and felt his eyes widen to saucers. It was as strong as double espresso.

"Umm," he muttered unconvincingly. "How many scoops of coffee did you use?"

"Scoops? No, I just filled this grinder. Don't you like it?" She started to pout.

"It's great, nice and strong the way I like it." He put in extra milk and sugar.

It was almost time to leave for work. "How do you feel about getting a job, at least to get ahead before you decide where you want to settle?"

"A job, yeah. I guess I need one, huh? Any suggestions?"

"I can check at work, and I know the lady who manages the Denny's in town."

"Thank you, Scott. You're so sweet." She gave him a big hug, and he stumbled out the door into a blast of rain.

He had left ten bucks with her in case she needed something from the store.

He stopped by Sylvia's office and told her he had a friend who just got into town and could use a job. She told him she could always use people on the phones, but she wouldn't have time to talk to her for a couple of days.

Then she asked, "So, who is this girl? Where do you know her from?"

He was trying to think of something to say that wouldn't make his sound foolish, and then he nervously glanced at his watch. "Oh hell. Past eight. I'd better get busy." And he darted away to his desk.

The big news that day was the consensus in the environmental community. The big organizations had seized on Senator Bottoms' bill and had come out in favor of it. They claimed that while it lacked many protections they wanted, they were willing to compromise in the name of restoring order, and they challenged the timber industry to do the same. Nice tactic, Scott thought.

Later on a report came in that some industry spokesman said that the environmental compromise meant nothing as long as the militant groups were still barricaded in the woods and running in front of trucks. The public relations war had started.

Scott was beat when he got home. The roads were slippery, and it was dark when he pulled in the carport. He hoped Peaches was alright.

She was lying on the bed, propped up by pillows, watching TV. There were four empty beer bottles on the table along with several bags of cookies and chips.

"Hi Scott. Want some munchies?" She handed him a big bag of cheese flavored chips.

He held them up and looked at them blankly. He didn't

remember buying stuff like this.

She solved the mystery. "I did some shopping. Boy, you can get soaked just crossing the highway."

Apparently, she had spent the entire ten spot on chips and other junk food. Scott opened the fridge and reached for a beer, which he wouldn't have done if he'd only counted the empties first. She'd finished the last one.

"Oh, Scott, I'm sorry. I would have picked up more, but I'm like not old enough."

He assured her that he wasn't mad, threw on his heavy jacket and dashed across the highway for another six pack. Then he figured that with her in the house drinking beer, he'd better get himself a bottle of wine.

She seemed excited about the job, as they sat on the bed, a sit com rerun going unwatched on the screen. She'd ride in with him on Wednesday and talk to Sylvia. If it went well, They'd drive in together until she could afford her own car, and of course, her own place.

He would have loved to turn off the TV and do some writing, but he was too much of a gentleman. He wanted her to feel at home and not like she was a burden. He watched the shows she turned on, only half paying attention, thinking about what would happen next in the forest wars, how long he'd have to put her up, and what would happen if Madd came back to him while Peaches was here.

Peaches said she couldn't have him sleeping on that little bed, and that it was plenty big for her. Scott insisted that she keep the big bed. Then she got what she considered a better idea

"Look, you've got like a big bed, and I trust you and all. There's room for both of us here."

That was a very freaky idea, but he didn't have a logical argument against it unless he was to claim that he couldn't trust himself with her. He had an extra large tee shirt in the drawer, and it worked like a nightgown on her. He went into the bathroom and changed into the pajamas his mother had sent him, but he'd never worn, and they crawled into opposite sides of the bed.

He hugged his side, not wanting to seem like he was trying anything. He felt very weird having this young woman just a foot away. Even though she wasn't at all his type, he got an erection and wasn't able to get to sleep until it subsided almost an hour later.

In the morning, the sky was dark and nasty, but the rain had stopped temporarily. He encouraged her to get up and go outside, take a walk, explore, get some exercise. He didn't want to picture her in front of the damn TV all day.

The big news that afternoon was that a spokesman for the suicide activist group, Mahatmas of the Forest, had agreed to stop the bloodshed and to come out of the forests if Congress passed the Bottoms bill. Naturally, the timber people demanded to know if the offer was from a credible source, the group having no formally identified spokesperson.

The FBI said that the person who had called was the same one who had called many times in the past, the one who had claimed that the group was responsible for the that first highway death. At the time, the man had given the authorities a code name, telling them not to release it to the press, as it was how they could tell the real organization from any copy cats. This was indeed, according to the feds and the police, the real deal.

A few senators were ready to consider the bill without going through all the committee work. They were anxious to calm their agitated constituency.

Scott picked up some food and more beer after the school board meeting that evening, getting home late. He hoped he'd walk into something different than the night before.

At least the bed was made and the junk food bags were stuffed in the trash. He'd seen the glow of the TV as he pulled up, but she'd turned it off before he walked inside.

She took the beer he offered and excitedly asked him about his day. He liked having someone there who took an interest, and he went over it all in detail. Then he asked her how she'd spent the day.

"I took your advice and got out for awhile. Cool trailer park.

Lot's of strange people. I heard some rockin' music and found this chick band. They had some beer and pot, and I listened for awhile. One of them hit on me. That was cool."

"But you're not a lesbian, are you?"

"No, but I'm curious. She was kinda cute and all. Well, anyway, along comes this guy. He looked like an albino Rastaman. Called himself Buck. Said he was a friend of yours. When I told him how we met and all, he seemed to think it was the funniest thing in the world.

That night in bed was no better than the night before. Thinking about her with one of the gals in the band was disgusting, but it gave him a hard on that seemed to never go down.

It was hard to get her up and ready in time to go into town with him. She obviously wasn't used to being a morning person. Scott offered to make the coffee while she got ready.

Sylvia decided to take a chance on Peaches, telling her she could start the next day.

Life immediately spiraled down into a terminal routine. After work or whatever meeting he had to cover, they'd come back, fix dinner, and sprawl in front of the TV. She would take his car to the store while he covered the schools or city hall, so there was always nuts, chips and other snack food in the house.

Within a week Scott was calculating her pay and how soon he could get her into a place of her own. His house was too damn small, and her eating and TV habits were working on him like a family of termites on a wooden leg.

Each day in the news the war of words escalated. The timber industry and the environmental community were calling each other rather nasty names. More activists were slipping by the National Guard and setting up compounds in the woods, and the highway suicides were starting up again, although very few logging trucks were on the road.

The President refused to cave into the people who supported Bottoms, and he pressured the senators in his party to reject her bill. Still, public outcry increased. More and more people, and not just on the west coast, were demanding that something be done, and done soon.

And then Peaches got fired.

"I'm sorry, Scott." He'd been called into Sylvia's office. "She's a sweet kid, but she's a flake. After she takes an add, she chats up the customer, sometimes spending ten extra minutes on the phone. She's tying up the lines and only taking a quarter of the ads she should. I explained it too her, but it didn't seem to sink in. She's got to go."

Scott was dejected. It was beginning to look as if he had a permanent roommate.

He dashed to his desk and called V.V. at work to ask if she could use anyone at the restaurant. She was short a waitress on the morning shift, starting at 6:30. Scott said he'd send Peaches over right away for an interview.

Peaches was picking up her personal stuff, when Scott came up with his keys in his hands. "Go north two blocks, then right to the highway. The manager at Denny's is a friend, and she needs a waitress. She's expecting you."

Peaches gave him a hug and headed for the parking lot. Scott crossed his fingers.

An hour later Peaches was back with a big grin on her baby face. "I got the job. Start in the morning."

That night, she rewarded him by leaving the TV off. She read a romance novel while he tried to write. Then in bed, early because they had to get up at five in the morning to get Peaches to work, she put her head on his chest and thanked him for being so wonderful to her. He knew it would be easy to have sex with her, but he still felt he would be taking advantage of her. He was doing all the giving, and she had only one way to pay him back. It would be, to his way of thinking, an obligation, rather than mutual passion. Besides, he was more than a little sick of having her around. He thought back a few weeks when he was feeling sad at being alone. Now he wished desperately to be alone, to go off somewhere where he didn't have to deal with anyone.

There was a lovely campground on the beach not much more than an hour south. During the summer it would be packed, but during the rainy season, no one would be there at all. He vowed that should the weekend be dry, he'd head down there. If not, he'd stay in that inexpensive, funky Palm Motel down in Orick. One way or the other, he wouldn't spend the weekend with Peaches and her TV shows and snack food.

It was a pain to get up in the dark, with a cold drizzle streaking the windows. They got dressed in a semi dazed silence. It was dark when they stumbled out to the car, and it was still dark when they got to town. He'd brought a book, so he settled into a back booth for breakfast and gallons of coffee for the next hour and a half before he had to be at work.

He watched V.V. show Peaches the ropes before pairing her with a seasoned waitress for training. V.V. looked more magnificent than ever, more fit and self assured. She had cut her hair short, business like. Jesus! He thought V.V. and Becky could pass for sisters. Even though his book was open his mind was on a fantasy of nights of passion. Unfortunately, just as each fantasy scenario was getting good, V.V. morphed into Becky, and the fantasy shattered like a wine glass.

The numbing routine was now slightly altered. Peaches had found bus service that could get her home after work, rather than waiting for Scott. Scott's day now started at five and ended when he got home, usually between nine and ten at night. He didn't even bother eating dinner at home any longer, grabbing a bite between work and whatever meeting he was covering. He'd walk in the door, have a quick glass of wine, shower, and crawl into bed, only to repeat the process the next day. Writing had been put on hold.

This seemed to go on forever, although it wasn't a couple of weeks before the routine dissolved again like a sugar cube house in a Crescent City rain.

V.V. called him at work. "Scott, I'm sorry." Oh shit! He thought. Not again.

"She's a nice kid and all, but a total flake. She gets the

145

orders confused, and she stops to chat with everyone, even when it's busy and people are waiting. She hasn't a clue about a busy place meaning you hurry. She has one pace, casual. This is her last day."

Then she again asked what Peaches was to Scott, and he just reiterated that she was an old friend, this time adding that he owed her father a favor.

Scott was dejected as he drove home that night, letting the windshield wipers lull him into a stupor. She had taken the bus home, and had tried to make him feel better by cooking a meal. Unfortunately, the meat was overcooked and the potatoes undercooked. She tried to talk about it, explain why she hadn't made it at the restaurant, tell him about the pressure of the job, but he told her he was just too tired. "Peaches. I've got a story to chase down this weekend. I won't be back until Sunday afternoon. You've got the place to yourself."

He crawled into bed early, feeling that he was in too deep to get out.

She was still in the mood to talk. "Hey, Scott, what's with the guy who runs this place? Does he fix bikes or sell them?"

"Both."

"You should get a Harley."

"I've got one. Actually, I have a quarter share in one." He saw that she looked puzzled, so he explained. "Four of us bought a used bike in a time share, each getting a weekend. This would be my weekend, but it's been raining, so no one wants to ride lately. That's why it's in the shop. Jake's gonna tune it up first chance he gets. He's pretty busy."

"Wow, a bike. How cool. Let's go riding."

"Maybe, when we get some nice weather. But now, I'm just plain beat. Sorry."

"Hey, I'm sorry too. I'll make it up to you. You'll see."

On Saturday morning the cold and wet gave way to patches of sun, so he drove down to the camp ground, figuring that if the weather changed, he could pack up and hit a motel. Scott fixed some food, took a walk on the beach, and settled into his camp chair with a book. After sitting by a warm evening fire, he crawled into the tent, and with a feeling of peace and quiet he hadn't known for some time, fell right asleep.

Some time before dawn he woke from dreaming of swimming, feeling chilled. He heard the patter of rain on the tent, and the dampness was seeping up and into his sleeping bag. He got up, packed his damp tent and bag, and got in the car as quickly as possible. Cold and wet, he drove into Orick, and waited the ten minutes for the 6 AM opening of the coffee shop. His life and this damn weather were becoming synonymous .

He drove around aimlessly for a few hours before heading home, driving up to Lady Bird Johnson Grove, only to find a closed sign and that ranger standing guard.

Being alone for a time had unwound him, but he still was depressed about Peaches. It wasn't her fault that she was there, dependent on him, and he couldn't just toss her out. Maybe he needed a bigger place. If she had a room of her own, they could survive together until she got her shit together. He'd call that real estate place to see if V.V.'s place was still on the market.

He got home, and the place was empty. Looking out the window at the sign in front of V.V.'s, he got the number of the agent, and called the guy's cell phone. As his luck was going, they had an offer pending.

He poured a glass of wine and felt tears of frustration fall down his cheeks. Then the door opened, and Peaches came in wearing coveralls, which she pulled off and threw in the hamper.

"How was your trip, Scott?"

"It was fine. I did what I needed to do. What's this with you?"

"The coolest thing happened. Don't say anything. Just let me talk. Oh, first I'll refill your glass and get me a beer."

"Yeah, sure, whatever." Scott mumbled without enthusiasm. Whatever it was, it sure as hell wasn't going to be good news for him.

She came back with drinks and sat cross-legged on the bed.

"I went over to meet Jake and see your bike. Nice bike. My dad had the same model. Well, I asked him when he was going to tune it, and he said his guy had quit, couldn't stand the weather and went back to Oakland or someplace. Well, Jake figured you guys ain't riding much in the rain, so he's doing a valve job on that old chopper. So, then I tell him how I owe you mucho favors, and I'll tune the bike. Well he's all with the stuff about it being technical work, with the carbs and valves and all that, and I nod and listen and finally get a word in. I tell him how my dad's buddies used to hang out on weekends with their Harleys, work on them and all. Well, I sez that dear old dad put a wrench in my hand early on, and I was tuning bikes at twelve. Well, he sez he'd believe it when he sees it, so I go, just as pretty as you please, to his tool box and get out what I need and start to work. He's like with his eyes bugged out and his jaw hanging on his chest. See, I got those valves adjusted before he knew what happened, and I'm going for the drain plug. He says stop and put on some coveralls, which I had to roll up cause the guy who'd worked there was tall. So he just stares at me, like waiting for me to screw up or something. And I'm draining the oil, adjusting the carb, setting the timing, even getting the drive belts all cinched up. And all this time he's not saying a word, just looking at me. I got the bike purring like a kitten, and he breaks out in some big ass smile and flat out asks me if I want a job. And I sez, 'if you mean working on bikes, shit yes.' So we shake hands and he's going to pay me more than the waitressing and working those classified phones pay together, and I start tomorrow."

It was Scott's turn to sit there slack jawed. Her account had come in rapid fire, and his tired brain was still sorting the information. It slowly dawned on him, that she found something she was good at, paid well, and didn't require him to drive her anywhere. He also thought that there weren't a lot of customers hanging around to distract her. He roughly calculated what the restaurant and the paper paid, added them together and came up with her being able to get her own place in a few short weeks.

He felt his jaw tighten into a smile, and he reached over, grabbed her and hugged her as if his life depended on it.

"Let's celebrate." He looked at his watch. Still time to run to the store before it closed. "I'm going to get some good wine, and some of that barbecue chicken they have, and we're going to have a little party for your new job. I'm so damn happy for you."

He threw on his coat and ran to the store so fast he hardly got wet. On the way back he saw the light on at Jake's and banged on the door.

"Is it true you hired Peaches?"

"Hell yes, Scott. Come in. She's the best thing happened to me in a long time. Got any idea how hard it is to find a good Harley mechanic up here. I was backed up so. . . Well, anyway she tuned your bike way fuckin' faster than that asshole who bailed out cause he couldn't handle a touch of rain. Where's your brains Scott. If I'd a known you were going to have a permanent roommate, I'd a told you to grab up V.V.'s place. The place is cheap, and it's got over twice the room of yours. Figure loan payment versus what you pay me rent, and it wouldn't have been much more. Now she's working, you could split it and save money."

"Too late Jake. I just called. There's an offer. But man, you're right. We can't both live in a little place like that. Don't suppose you have any other rentals that'd work for her?"

"No. Wanna sit? Oh, yeah, groceries. Look, Emily's place is going through probate. She had family, grandson I think. He paid the rent and hopes to sell the place when he can. Got his number somewhere. I'll lay it on him this way. She pays the rent and keeps the place up. He can't lose, and if she likes it, he's got a built in buyer. I got the guy's number here some-where. With luck, we'll have her out of your hair by end of next week. Learn to think man. Figure the angles, plan. Don't let all that pussy you're getting cloud your mind."

"Jake, I'm not touching her."

"Fuck! The younger generation's goin' to the dogs, sure as

149

hell. Get out of here 'fore I put a boot to your ass."

As he walked back to his place, he realized that it was December 18, a week before Christmas. He'd been so wrapped up in this quagmire, that he wasn't paying attention. This news was the greatest Christmas present of all, and he would buy her a nice gift. She was a good kid. He'd helped her find her place, just as he'd hoped to do. He'd been a moody shit around her lately, but he'd make it up. None of it had been her fault.

They drank wine, ate and talked. He put on some music for awhile, and finally decided to turn on the TV for a sappy film about being sleepless in Seattle. They propped themselves up with pillows and, as the movie got more mushy, they started holding hands and exchanging smiles.

When the movie was over, they embraced and fell into each other's arms. All the pent up sexual frustration of the past weeks burst through, and they had two hours of Chinese acrobat style hot sex.

"It would have been perfect, had she not ended the evening with, "Scott, you are my hero. I love you. I really do."

He worried about that admission all the next day, wondering if she meant it as a friend or as being in love with him. The thought constricted him like a starched shirt and tie on a hippie musician, but it didn't stop him from doing a repeat performance the next night and the night after. She was a bit chubby, but she had a cute body, and she was an uninhibited lover. It was, Scott kept telling himself, just two close and intimate friends sharing something special. She didn't really love him, as in being in love with him.

Jake made an exception to his two week pay period and paid her at the end of her first week, assuring her that should she keep up her performance, she'd get a fifteen percent raise after a month. He also told her that she could have Emily's old place on a month to month, and that there was a chance she could buy it.

Scott offered to clean it up, make it livable for a young girl, even help her buy all the little things that make a house a home.

As they talked, he grabbed a quick look at her pay check. Add fifteen percent, and she'd be making more than Scott. Give her a year with Jake, and she'd be making a hundred more a week. Apparently, unlike reporters, good Harley mechanics were worth their weight in gold.

That weekend the strangest thing appeared in the sky. It was, as best as Scott could recall, the sun. Drops of water hanging from the tips of leaves and needles sparkled like jewels. The grass along the road was the color of an Irish calendar. White clouds danced over the trees. The guy who was scheduled for the bike was out of town, so Scott took Peaches for a ride up to the Oregon border. At the rest stop, she begged him to let her take the controls. She could barely reach the foot pegs, and he didn't like the idea, but she talked him into it. She handled the bike as if it were an extension of her body. He was totally confident in her as he relaxed and watched the scenery fly by.

The rest of the weekend was spent cleaning the new place and getting towels and dishes to replace the old stuff Emily had. Buck wandered by and helped move furniture around and did some odd repairs.

By Sunday night, the place was ready for Peaches to move into. Everyone was exhausted, and Peaches started doing her nesting thing after kissing Scott goodbye.

Scott had taken the opportunity to make his noble speech. "I've thought it over, and I know that your feelings for me are probably based on gratitude for my helping you and all. I don't want you feeling obligated to me in any way at all. You don't owe me any misplaced loyalty or sex. In fact, you can see other people. It won't be a problem for me."

"Sounds like you want to cut it off with me."

"Peaches, I know we're just good friends. We're not really cutting anything off. I like you, but you have a right to go out and find happiness. I don't want you to feel I have some claim on you. I want you to feel free."

"Free? I see. As in unconnected, not a couple, a single, young female. Got it, Scott. Well, I'm tired and ready to crash.

Thanks again."

After all the time Scott had wanted her out, now that she was gone, he was lonely again. He missed her bubbling monologues, her constant junk food, her sappy TV shows, her body up against him at night. Scott definitely didn't love her, but he didn't not love her. The ambiguity was back in his life. He turned on the news and was blown away.

12.

The military, in an effort to drive the activists out of the forest, had flown low with a helicopter to drop tear gas. The chopper had flown too low and hit a tree. It burst into flame and crashed, killing the helicopter crew and the thirty activists who were having a circular meditation around a giant redwood. Scott slept only fitfully that night.

Rob was waiting for him. "Scott, want to go on a real assignment?"

"Yes sir. In a heart beat. Where?"

Ok, you know these forests activists, at least some of them. You joined them at the Thanksgiving road block, spoke to them. Maybe they'll let you in."

"In? In where?"

"Where those people were killed. There's been a stand off there for weeks. People keep slipping into the woods. Estimates run from four to seven thousand. There's a major standoff. The cops and the military have the perimeter, the activist are holed up in the woods, and no one want's to give an inch. You find a way to get past the authorities and then get the activists to let you in. You do a story from the inside. You get me an exclusive and it's worth a bonus equal to two weeks pay. Can you do it?"

"I'll try."

"Damn it, Scott! Can you do it?"

"No sweat. I can do it!"

"Good. Now go home and pack. Bring a backpack, sleeping bag, camera. Jacket, writing tablet, tent if you have one. Here's a map of the area. You can get this far by road. The rest is a creative endeavor. Get me an exclusive, and plant your name in the reporters' hall of fame."

Scott was fired up. "You can damn well count on me, boss. I'm on my way."

He drove home, packed and headed south, stopping quickly

153

at Jake's to tell Peaches about his assignment and telling her he'd be thinking about her and telling her to have fun.

Scott didn't have a clue as to how he'd get around the military blockade, find the activists, and convince them to let him in to talk. He wasn't familiar with the area, so he just followed the map to the site of the stand off in order to check it out before making a plan.

There was no doubt as to where the action was. Suddenly the road was filled with army trucks, and guards were stationed in the road with guns.

Scott wanted to turn around, but the guards motioned him to approach. He was getting nervous, hoping he wouldn't get arrested before he even got close to his story.

"This is a restricted area. What's your business here?"

"Well, I wanted to find out what's going on with the guys in the forest."

"Didn't you read the sign back there. This area is closed to civilians. Are you one of these people?" The guy pointed toward the thick woods.

"No, no I'm not. I just wanted. . . "

"Let's see some ID."

Scott pulled out his wallet with his drivers license, which was next to his press card. The guy studied it for a bit, then looked up and smiled.

"Press, huh? Why didn't you say so?

"I didn't know reporters were allowed."

"Sure they're allowed. The government doesn't mess with freedom of the press. We don't need any more bad press out here. There's a major in that tent over there. He has a complete press packet, and he'll answer your questions."

This was almost too easy. He decided to chance pushing it a bit further

"How about the guys in the woods? Any chance of talking to them?"

"Don't see why not. Look, just stop over there, and major will get it all set up for you."

Scott thanked him, parked and walked over to the tent, afraid that the major would be less accommodating.

The major was a hard looking man, with short graying hair. He looked to be mid-to-late forties, and he looked like he'd break a man's back just for exercise. He was sitting around the tent with a couple of lieutenants and a captain. They had a computer on and were playing video games. There was also a TV set tuned to soap operas.

"Sir, my name is Scott Mukis. I'm a reporter." He flashed his card.

"Sit down Mukis. Now, we intend to be totally open with the press. You've got access to anything that isn't classified."

Naturally, Scott had no idea what the criteria for classified was, but he had no intention of saying anything the major might take to be a smart ass remark.

The major continued. "The only thing we ask, and we do this because many people from the liberal press have been coming up here with their minds already made up. Their stories were written before they came. Anyway, we just want you to look at both sides, look at our operations, read our fact sheets, before you write your article. Is that fair?"

"Yes sir. That's fair."

"Good." The major handed him a stapled stack of papers to read. He then motioned him to follow, and they walked around a rather complex base camp that stretched up and down the road for over half a mile. Guards had guns, but there was no heavy weaponry, and no one seemed to be ready to shoot anyone. They just seemed to be guarding the woods, which looked peaceful enough.

"Major, have there been armed conflicts?"

"No. At first the terrorist forces threw rocks and sticks, and our boys arrested a few. We were trying to get them out of there without anyone getting hurt, but after that unfortunate accident with the chopper, we've been ordered to stand firm and hold our perimeter."

"Huh, sir."

"In other words, son, we're sitting out here, and they're sitting in there, and we're not arresting them until they get cold or hungry enough to come out."

"It looks to me, major, that you're using restraint and conducting your operation in a humane manner, and my story will certainly reflect that. However, is there any chance I could talk to any of the acti. . .terrorists?"

"Sure son. Any time you'd like. I don't have a problem with that, but they might."

"Well, how would I go about doing that?"

"See what looks like a foot path between those two big trees?" He pointed to a pair of giant redwoods. "You just go straight through there for the better part of a mile, and you'll run right into them. You'd best shout every minute or so that you are a reporter, and that you're alone. You don't want to be hit by a rock or a wine bottle. Oh, one more thing. You first have to sign this waiver, saying you understand the risks of interviewing a hostile force and that you absolve the military or the government of all liability."

"And they'll just let me walk in there?"

"That, or strip you down, beat you senseless and run you out. They don't like the establishment, but you look almost like one of them."

This was all too weird. They'd made an institution of this little war. He signed, and open his trunk to pull out his pack and sleeping bag.

"Hold on there, son." The major said. "We can't allow anything in there but what you need to do the story and some water. Tents, sleeping bags, lanterns, stoves, and all the rest can be used by the terrorists to continue their occupation of this forest. You walk in with the clothes on your back, pen and note pad, and a bottle of water, and that's it. You can't even take a flashlight. If you choose to stay with these people, they'll have to provide warmth and shelter. I'd advise you to be back before dark. Even on a clear night with a full moon, it's black in there. Have fun, son."

Scott pulled the hood of his Gore-Tex jacket over his head, stuffed his note pad in a waterproof pocket, and sloshed off through the mud and detritus and under a constant heavy drizzle into the forest.

After about twenty minutes of stumbling through wet duff and shouting, he was tapped on the back. He swung around to see a long haired young man in jeans and a sheepskin jacket. He had his finger to his lips, signaling Scott to be silent.

"You the reporter dude?"

"Yeah, Scott Mukis, down from Crescent City. Are you the leader here?"

"Leader? No man, that leader stuff's not cool. I'm one of the tribe. Follow me."

The stepped off the trail and wound among the trees. It was difficult to see more than ten feet. Scott wanted to make conversation.

"Perhaps you remember me. I spoke up at the road block."

"Hundreds of people spoke up. I didn't hear most of them."

"Well, how about the papers. I've written supporting your situation here."

"I don't read mainstream media propaganda too often. You don't get the real story. But it's cool that you speak up for us. Careful, you gotta hop over that stream."

Suddenly, Scott was in a small clearing, surrounded by several hundred young men and women. A beautiful blond in camouflage clothing walked up and shook his hand.

"I'm Cobra Lily. I've been selected to speak for the people. And you are?

"Scott Mukis, reporter. I've supported you at the road block, and in my articles. I'm here to tell the world your story." He thought he'd put it eloquently.

"Thank you Snot Mucous. Cool forest name. Many of these people have endured hardships to protect the forest. As you can see, we are living in tents and cooking in the open, even during these rains." She spoke in a soft, slow manner that betrayed no emotion. "Many of our tribe were lost during the bombings and when the helicopter crashed right over there. Some of those who stopped trucks with their bodies were also friends. We have, however, remained steadfast, and we will prevail." Her face blossomed into a expansive smile.

He was going to correct her on the name, but she seemed to be taken with it, so he just asked, "What do you do for food?"

"There are many ways into this forest, and the government can't watch them all. We've had people walk twenty miles at night with food. There is a network of people along various trails, helping and acting much like pony express riders, relaying needed supplies. I'm not going to give you details, as I don't want the authorities to know where to apply pressure. You understand."

"I won't reveal anything you don't want me to. You can trust me."

"Naturally, but as a reporter, you must report, and the government people are wise enough to read between your lines. In fact, I'd rather you be vague about our supply lines. Can you do that for us?"

She had a way of making him desperately wish to please her, to follow her suggestions as if they were commandments from the almighty. He swore to her that he'd say nothing that might in any way compromise their position.

But something else was bothering him. "Why don't they just come in here and grab everyone?"

"Ah, that part apparently didn't make the papers. Mr. Owl, could you come here for a moment and tell this young man about how we kept the military machine at bay?"

Mr. Owl was a skinny little guy with big glasses. He reached into his jacket and pulled out a hand grenade, held in up to Scott's nose and smiled.

"At first we were hard to find in here, but pretty soon they managed to track the main compound and stormed in. When they found us in this clearing, hundreds of us were holding these, with the pins pulled out. We were just standing there holding the levers. I told them that they would not take us alive, and that if they tried it, we'd simply release our grips and bang. One brave little dude named Jo Jo had brought in some dynamite, and he was standing on a very large box of it with his grenade. He shouted at the military leaders, saying that we'd all go up together. They backed off. Now they just hem us in, hoping to freeze or starve us out, but we're prepared."

Scott was amazed. It must be the same Jo Jo, and when he asked for a description, he was sure. The little hillbilly was crazy, but in a good way.

Cobra Lily took his arm and led him around the area. There were tarps and tents among the trees, cooking areas set up, and groups hanging out, talking. He was chilled and damp and amazed that these people could stay here day and night.

"Oh Snot, It's time for the forest spirits magic tree ritual. You must join us."

She said "must" as if it were a command.

"What is this ritual?" Some of these people were strange, and he didn't want to do something dangerous.

"We strip naked, hold hands, and dance around that grandfather tree over there."

"All of you? Naked!"

"Naturally. The body is a sacred dwelling place for spirit. We must allow spirit within to connect to spirit without."

"Naturally," Scott muttered. "But, it's cold and raining."

"Dancing warms the body, as does contact with other living beings. You will not have ill effects. Come, it is time."

Everyone started taking their clothes off. Hundreds more came streaming out of the woods. There must have been close to a thousand people milling around. No way they could all hold hands and dance around anything smaller than Mount Rushmore.

Soon, everyone within sight was naked or nearly so, and Scott felt as uncomfortable as if he were the naked one. He quickly stripped.

He was freezing his ass off. The trees had blocked the rain so that it dripped constantly off the branches and needles, rather than fell from the sky. Soon, people had grabbed his hands and they were off. It was more a milling throng, snaking in and out between groves of trees than a real circle around anything. In fact, it was like a blind crush of bodies in a Hieronymus Bosch triptych, an organic pulsing conga line, blood cells coursing through the capillaries of the forest.

Soon he was caught up in it all, no longer cold but feverish with the collective energy. He found himself chanting with the mob, although he had no idea what it was he was chanting. Things became a blur before stopping as suddenly as it started. Then everyone started milling around to retrieve their clothes.

Then he was pulled into a tent, where some smiling people passed him a joint. He smoked with these people for some time before going out again to find people playing homemade drums and wooden flutes. The music started filling all the background spaces between the people, around the trees and into the faint sky high above. The music was in him, and he was the music.

At some point food was served, and the vegetarian stew was delicious. They sipped homemade wine. More joints were passed and more music played, and suddenly Scott looked up and it was totally dark. How would he get back?

He mentioned his concern to the young woman to his right, and she waved it off as if it were nothing, passing him a bota bag of wine and a joint.

Scott woke to the first light, covered with blankets in a corner of a giant covered space. The great tarp flapped in the wind above him, and he was surrounded by sleeping strangers.

They fed him a tofu breakfast and talked more about their determined dream of a protected forest. The only person in the establishment world they seemed to admire was Senator Bambi Bottoms.

Soon, Scott had pages of notes and the realization that if he didn't leave soon, it would be a repeat of the day before, and he'd spend another night. There was a moment when he felt like giving up his job and simply staying, but he convinced himself that, besides being cold and wet, his words in the paper would do more good than one more body in the woods.

Before she showed him to the path leading out, Cobra Lily told him that he should also drive out past Ettersburg, near the Lost Coast. A land owner had allowed a group of forest activist to set up camp on his land near the river. This is the group that is planning media events, and they were in part responsible for the massive road block. She told him to say that Cobra Lily says that the wind in the trees whispers the cry of peace. They would know and welcome him.

As she parted company with him, he asked her if he'd ever see her again. She responded with, "Wherever you hear the gentle flowing waters refresh the parched roots of the ancient trees, there I will be, watching and smiling."

As Scott walked away from the forest compound, he kept thinking of how profound her statement was. Suddenly, Madd slipped off his mental pedestal. He was quite sure he could fall quickly in love with Cobra Lily.

After taking a couple of wrong trails and falling over a tangle of branches, Scott finally reached the road, only to find the two FBI agents waiting for him.

"Well, Mukis, you're finally back. So, what have you and your radical friends been plotting back there?"

"I haven't plotted anything. I went in to interview those people for my paper."

"We see. And it took you thirty-one hours and eleven minutes to do your interview?"

He didn't want to justify himself to these creeps, but he found himself answering with, "It got dark, and I had to stay over."

"Yes, I see," said the talking one, as the other scribbled furiously in his notebook.

Scott asked, "Am I free to go?"

"All in good time, Mukis. Now, about the conspiracy. What did you and your friends plan in there?"

"I didn't plan anything. It's their protest or sit in, or whatever."

"Fine, Mukis. What did they plan?"

"They didn't discuss plans."

"And how do they get supplies?"

"They mentioned some sort of supply network, but they didn't trust me with details."

"Of course. And who exactly is supplying them and how?"

Scott was more frustrated and angry than intimidated, and he snapped out the first thing that came to mind. "It's the IRA, and they have a late night airlift."

"The IRA?"

"Irish Republican Army."

The big guy started to warn him against sarcastic answers, but the silent partner whispered in his ear.

"Oh, yes, Mukis. Code. Well, we aren't the fools you take us for. IRA would be code for ALF or perhaps even ELF. Are we right?"

Scott honestly knew very little of these organizations and told them as much.

"I see. You are in there over night, conspiring, and you claim to be unfamiliar with the Animal Liberation Front or the Earth Liberation Front. Come now, Mukis. Do you take us for fools."

Tempted to answer yes, Scott instead tried a different approach. He put his hand to his mouth and gasped," I had no idea it was code. I thought they trusted me. I feel like such an idiot." He hung his head in an exaggerated effect, hoping they'd either be satisfied or realize he didn't take them seriously, and he'd be able to leave.

"Don't feel bad Mukis. You aren't the first idealistic young man who's been duped by radical organizations like this. You've been a pawn in their plot to disrupt the engine of commerce that keeps America great. I only hope that you can now do the right thing."

"Yes sir. I'll go back to my paper and write the clear, unvarnished truth."

"Good for you. You may yet become a patriot. Now,

remember, we're watching you."

Scott drove over to the 101 intersection, where he found a homey diner. He was looking over the menu when a stranger asked if he wouldn't mind company. Although he did mind, he extended a reluctant invitation. The guy, somewhere in his thirties identified himself as Bill, a local reporter, and asked Scott, "Weren't you down where the government and the activists are having the standoff?"

"Yeah, I'm a reporter too."

"Did you meet those dedicated young people?"

"Did I? Let me tell you."

The guy was all ears, asking questions each time Scott paused. He kept using terms like, "fascinating," and, "Very interesting."

Naturally, Scott filled the guy in on his columns and his suspicions about Buck and the mysterious calls taking credit for the events. The guy was so impressed, that he offered to buy Scott a steak dinner.

It was dark when Scott got back on the highway, too late to look for some camp out past Ettersburg. He checked into a motel in Garberville, and called Rob to tell him what he had and ask if he should send it ahead.

Rob told him to do a first installment, his encounter with the military and FBI agents and his meeting with the activists. Rob wasn't sure how much would be appropriate. "You write it all, and I'll edit it down. Get those people down by the Matole River as a second installment."

Scott was a reporter on assignment, a reporter on an expense account, a professional wordsmith, a player in the world of journalism. He thought about buying a six pack and taking it to his room, but he thought better of it. Not the thing for a pro on assignment. He walked to the bar on the corner and started drinking martinis, while he watched a movie on TV, a silly Christmas comedy.

The next morning, after a breakfast on the company, he started off to Ettersburg. Somewhere between Ettersburg and

Honeydew, he saw a group of old vans and some tents. There were signs ordering the passers by to save the forest and to save the earth. He pulled in and told the first person he met that he was a reporter sent by Cobra Lily.

The guy directed him to a tent in the middle of a field, the place where Mondo Banana Slug, the organizer dude was. Scott reached up to knock on the tent but realized that wouldn't work, so he pulled back the flap and called out.

A big guy with bushy blond hair and a wide grinning mouth came out. Scott repeated who he was and who sent him. The big guy smiled.

"Cobra Lily! Goddamn I miss her. She's my ol' lady, and we've been apart for weeks. How's she holdin' up?"

"She appeared to be thriving, in spite of some seriously adverse conditions." Scott wanted to ask the meaning of "ol' lady." Was she his wife, lover, steady girl friend. Whatever the relationship was, it was certainly a relationship, and he was again the man on the outside.

Mondo Banana Slug showed him around and introduced him to dozens of people. This was, Mondo explained, the nerve center for media action. When Scott asked what media action was, Mondo pointed to him as one example.

"Other stuff we do is stage roadside sign waving events, that big road block a few weeks back, sit ins on the steps of public buildings, and all that."

"Are you in charge?"

"Man, there is no in *charge*. We all just feel it and do it. I'm the organizer dude. That guy over there is the sign art dude. She's the bullhorn babe. It goes like that around here. Someone will say, "Hey, I can make posters," and he becomes the poster dude. Dig?"

Soon a bunch of people started cooking up a huge meal. The salad babe was making salad, the rice dude was cooking rice, and others were doing what they did best.

There was no meat, so Scott was glad he'd had the steak the night before and bacon that morning.

A few boxes of organic wine were brought out. A guy named Bear's Feet stood up and made a bit of a speech. It was a special occasion. It was the season of renewal, the days were slowly getting longer. It was a ritual of lights, Kwanza, Hanukkah, and quite incidentally, Christmas. He acknowledged all the major spiritual traditions and proposed a toast to the human connection with the divine spirit that makes everything such a cool groove. Everyone cheered and drank up.

Then it hit Scott. It was Christmas. Everything had been so off kilter and chaotic lately, he had totally forgotten. Then he thought of Peaches, and he suddenly wanted to be near her, to hear her babble, to feel her against him. She was all he had, and he hadn't remembered to buy her anything for Christmas, to send her a card, or to even call.

He pulled out his company cell phone and stepped away from the group. Then he realized that when he left, she still hadn't gotten phone service. He was going to call information, but then he realized that through it all, he never bothered to learn her last name. He tried to called Jake, but there was no service out there, miles from any real town. Scott was dejected. She would be alone and heartbroken on Christmas, and she probably wouldn't be speaking to him when he got back.

When he got back to the group, pot had been added to the box wine, and everyone was working themselves into a party mood. In a desperate attempt to lift his holiday mood, he joined in the party with a vengeance. Unfortunately, he had forgotten to set up his camp first. Late at night, when most of the others had crawled off to sleep, a half drunk and stoned Scott fumbled in the dark and the rain with his tent.

Everyone was up early. The Big Sign Dude had come up with the idea of hanging huge signs on the overpasses along the Avenue of the Giants, so people were putting the finishing touches on the signs, connecting rope and packing up. Mondo Banana Slug wanted Scott to come along, to participate or to write about it. It would make a perfect ending to the second installment, so Scott helped tie some ropes, jumped in his car and followed them.

They tied signs on three overpasses. Then people started disappearing into the trees or driving off. Scott was so caught up in it that he hung around, making notes, taking pictures, watching the faces on the drivers going by. Then the flashing lights came on and the highway patrol car pulled up. They said the signs were illegal. Of the dozen or so others still in the area, two called the patrolmen pigs and tools of the bastards who were denying the people the right of free speech. The patrolman got on the radio, and within minutes the whole bunch, including Scott, were on the way to jail.

It was late that evening before Scott, with the help of a call from Rob, got it all straightened out. Because he was a reporter, they didn't keep him overnight, but they did ticket him for littering a public highway.

13.

It was December 26, and just about everyone was home enjoying their families or dear friends. Scott was in a strange town, freshly out of jail, and renting the same room in the same motel he'd enjoyed two nights earlier. This time he had no interest in the bar or having a drink. He took a long, hot shower, typed the last of his article, picked up a magazine, and read himself to sleep.

Scott was back at the paper by ten the next morning, after driving through a storm. Rob congratulated him on his good work. Scott looked at the final version, which was cut to about half what he'd written. Most of the personal reflections were cut, leaving just enough to show a reporter intimate with his story. It wasn't literature any longer. It didn't convey the pain and the excitement that had been a big part of the experience. Scott went to his desk and quietly caught up on his work.

Exhaustion was overtaking him by four, and he started to leave for home. Rob stopped him near the door. "You can't go home."

"Rob, I'm beat. I can't keep working."

"No, Scott. You can't go home. A report just came in. I guess all the rain loosened the soil. A big redwood fell over the highway. Road will probably be closed until at least midnight."

"Shit! I don't know if I can stay awake that long."

"Look, Scott. Come home with me. I've got a guest room. It's not a problem. Besides, it would be nice to chat about our noble profession over a brandy."

"If you're sure it wouldn't put you out."

Rob and his wife, Kay, who was the mayor of the town of Smith River, had a ritual of fixing dinner together. Scott wanted to help, but they sent him off to the living room to keep Sandy company.

"Trust me Scott, you'll be helping. The baby in the family,

167

always the spoiled one." He shook his head to indicate that the girl was Scott's responsibility until dinner.

She was sitting on the floor in front of the TV. "So, Scott, tell me about your big journalistic adventure."

"Oh, Sandy, you wouldn't be interested."

"Trust me, I would. I've been following this. Give me the details." She got up and sat cross legged on the couch.

Scott told the story, actually glad someone really cared to hear it. Every time he skimmed over something, she motioned with her hands to give her more.

"Sounds like you did a good job and had some awesome adventures. I'd love to do that."

Being appreciated was novel enough to make him suddenly very solicitous toward the girl. He was about to make a profound comment when Rob came in.

"Food. Let's go for it."

All throughout dinner Sandy seemed very interested in Scott's work. He was flattered, but he realized that kids her age are easily impressed.

After dinner, as they sat around the living room, talking, Sandy made a suggestion.

"Scott, how would you like to be my date to a movie tonight?"

He grabbed the first excuse that floated through the air. "I work for your father. It wouldn't be appropriate."

Rob stabbed him in the back with, "Not a problem. I trust you to take good care of my baby. Besides, you need to get out and relax."

He looked lamely at Sandy. "There's an age thing."

"You're four years older. Calculating for different maturity rates between boys and girls, and we're the same age. Yes or no?"

Scott reluctantly agreed, and they drove off, not in Scott's compact, but in Rob's BMW. Rob cited safety in bad weather as the reason.

It was a disaster. It was some movie about a secret agent,

starring some guy with a shaved head who looked like a muscle-bound Elmer Fudd. It was all action, and damn little story, but Sandy was really into it. In fact, each time a dangerous looking stunt happened, she squeezed his leg. In spite of his mental take on the situation, these thigh grabs were getting him excited, not that he'd ever think of messing around with Rob's daughter, and not that she interested him at all. She was, after all, just a bubble headed kid.

On the way home, she talked about how cool the movie was, and Scott tried to be conversational without pushing his opinion of the film. At every opportunity he changed the subject, talking about how the government and the rich were making war on dedicated young activists who only wanted to make a better world. He also talked about his writing, and how he wanted to write about real people's lives and issues.

She managed to interrupt him from time to time to say that she agreed with him, but that he was on a soap box and it was a drag. "Like we're out together for the evening, sort of a date. Let's keep it light and fun."

Every attempt Scott made at small talk sounded hollow and trite. He had no skill at it.

As they arrived back at the house, she looked him in the eye and said, "If you weren't such a stuffy guy, you could be fun. We need to go out more often. My project will be to get you loosened up."

"I'm not stuffy," he said indignantly. "I'm serious and mature and concerned about the important issues in today's world. Besides, even though you're a nice kid, your only seventeen and the boss's daughter."

"It doesn't seem to be an issue with my father. And, wow, you're so old, you probably even shave once a week."

He didn't like being made fun of, and he was determined to deflect her crude advances. "Besides, Sandy, I sort of already have a girl friend." He started to open the car door.

She grabbed his arm. "I don't understand a sort of girl friend."

He explained about how she'd lived at his house and how they'd gotten kind of close, and, being unable to stop his mouth once in motion, he continued with how when she'd moved into her own place, he'd said they should both be free to date other people and not feel obligated or committed. And he added that he hadn't seen her since then.

"So, you broke up with her."

"No I didn't. I just gave her some freedom from any obligation she might feel."

"Bullshit. I don't know what you think you meant, but 'I think we should both see other people' is universal code for 'I want to break up with you.' Now you haven't seen her or called her through the whole Christmas holidays, right? Like no card or gift? You two are *so* over."

He tried to protest that it wasn't like that at all, but she just shook her head. This time she reached for the door. "You're a smart guy, Scott, but you are so totally clueless when it comes to women. You need me in your life. You can be taught, trust me."

Scott crawled into bed as soon as they got back, not wanting to deal with a girl that aggressive and self possessed, and resenting the idea that some kid could teach him anything.

He pulled into his carport after being gone almost six days. The house was dark and cold, and it seemed even smaller. He cooked up a frozen dinner and went over to Peaches' place.

It took the longest time for her to answer the door. She looked disheveled. He asked if he could come in, and she seemed hesitant. He told her he'd had a rough few days and could really use the company. When Scott got inside, he saw the reason for her hesitation. Buck was on the couch. There was a bottle of wine and a lit candle on the table. He looked at her and then at Buck, and she nodded yes.

"What did you want to talk to me about, Scott?"

" I just wanted to say I was so busy with the story and so far out in the woods, that I wasn't able to get you a Christmas present, and I'm sorry. I didn't even know how to reach you by phone."

"You've given me presents enough over the last few weeks. But here's something for you." She handed him a neatly wrapped package.

She'd given him a chain with a crystal in a beautiful setting. He thanked her, and would have reached over to kiss her had not Buck been there. After a awkward moment of silence he excused himself, not wanting to interrupt their evening.

She followed him out the door. "You seem hurt. I figured it wouldn't be a problem for you, since you pretty much broke it off before you left. That is what you wanted?"

He wanted to say no, but he opted for what he considered the noble gesture. "No, it's fine. I'm just surprised. I mean, Buck?"

"He's been really sweet to me, and thoughtful. He's kind of strange, but in a nice way. Are you sure you're fine?"

His mind screamed no, but he said, "I was serious when I said I wanted you to be happy and not feel any obligation to me. If Buck is making you happy, you have my blessing."

She touched his arm gently, "You know I'm here for you, Scott, if ever you need me."

He turned on the stupidest TV show he could find and let it bore him to sleep.

The next day he asked Rob to have lunch with him. They went down the street for a sandwich, and Scott told him about Peaches and Buck, and how it had been before she'd moved away.

Rob put down his sandwich and pointed at Scott. "I like you. You're bright, enthusiastic, a good writer, and a friend. However, your waffling is going cause someone to throttle you. You've got to decide how you feel about this girl. If you want her in your life, go after her. To hell with this other guy. But, if you're just lonely and don't really want her, but just don't want anyone else to have her, then back off. She's a human being, with emotions and needs. Be honest with yourself, and then be honest with her. Above all, don't assume anything about women. They are more complicated than we are. Trust me, I'm a married man with two daughters."

For the rest of the day he thought obsessively about what Rob had said. He wasn't sure how he felt about Peaches. When she moved in with him and couldn't hold a job, the sight of her in front of that TV surrounded with snack food drove him crazy. But now he felt affection for her. It didn't feel like love, not like the feelings he had for V.V. and Maddie, but Perhaps love can grow through shared experiences and just spending some time together. Then, as if two voices were having a debate in his head, the thought came that no, love is something that reaches out and grabs you. You meet someone, and you just know it. She'll have those incredible qualities that will generate love at first sight. But, then, the other voice insisted, "how could you love both V.V. and Maddie in such a short time?" He finally came to the decision that there was a certain set of qualities he must find in a woman for him to love her. V.V. and Maddie both had those qualities. They were very much alike, but very different from Peaches. Then again, Peaches was still young, and her life had been in upheaval. Now that she had a good job and a place of her own, she was starting to show things about her character he hadn't seen before.

He wanted to do anything to stop the maddening debate in his head. That night he went over to see Jake.

"Hi Jake. Just wondering how Peaches is working out."

The big guy pointed to a tattered chair, the same one he kept saying he was going to replace. Scott sat down and couldn't help noticing the big smile on Jake's face.

"The girl's a wonder. She has the hands of an artist, a Mozart on motorcycle engines. She's quick, and now that she's working at it every day, she just keeps getting quicker. You know, there are set times for each procedure. That's how we bill. Someone comes in for a certain repair, and you say that's a three hour job, like that. Well, if you've got someone who can do it in less time, you get more done in a day and make more money. Now, tune ups are her specialty. She's already saving nearly twenty percent per job."

"You mean she's better than you?"

"Faster, buddy. See, lots of us Harley mechanics are big guys with beefy hands. Plus we're part of the biker scene, been in too many fights, busted knuckles lots of times. These ol' hands are stiff, but she's got them little, nimble fingers. Swear to God man, never thought I'd talk up women bike mechanics, but if she's any indication, they've got themselves an advantage."

"Then you're going to keep her?"

"Hell yes. Even if I gotta make her a partner to do it. But don't you go puttin' that idea in her head. First of the year, she gets a fifteen percent raise, and she worth ever dollar."

"Fifteen percent. Wow! That probably means she'll be making more than me, and not just a little more. And I am a professional journalist."

"No offense Scott, but lots of people can write down what the school board says. Damn few can rip through a full Harley tune up as fast as that kid."

There may not have been offense meant, but Scott was offended. He wanted to say that there was more to being a reporter than just writing down what the board said, but he decided not to get in an argument with Jake. Instead he changed the subject.

"Broken knuckles, huh? You must have been one hell raiser back in Texas. Maybe I could do a story on you."

"No, not in Texas. My folks moved to California when I was five or six. I did spend some crazy years in the biker bars in Lodi."

"Five or six! Why the hell you go by Texas Jake?"

"Well, how does 'California Jake' sound, or maybe 'Lodi Jake'?"

"Yeah, I see what you mean. But about Peaches. How's she able to get around, living up here with no car?"

"Obviously, she walks to work. Does much of her shopping cross the road. If she needs to go to town, she borrows a bike."

173

"In the rain?"

"Real bikers ride in the rain. Sunday bikers ride on sunny days."

Since Jake had opened another beer for him, Scott started telling him all about his experiences with the people in the forest and along the river. Jake got a kick out of the naked dancing around the tree, said he wished he could have been there.

On the way home from Jake's, Scott wanted to detour over to Peaches' place, but he was afraid he'd find Buck there, and he didn't want to feel awkward like that again, so he went home and sat down to his novel, The project lacked the fire it had just weeks ago. Not being one to work on only one project at a time, He started writing his experiences with the activists, with the idea of turning it into a book when it all got resolved.

He went to work on New Year's eve and realized that he had no plans for the night. He was quite sure Peaches would be with Buck. He faced the possibility of sitting home alone, sitting at the bar in the Tree House alone, or taking a chance that Jake was home. The alternatives were depressing. He thought how wonderful it would be to go to dinner with Madd and then maybe do some dancing before going back to her place for the night.

Since he'd developed a personal relationship with Rob, he told him about how depressing the holiday was for a young guy alone.

Rob saved the day, or rather the night. He said he was having a few people in for the evening, some of his and his wife's friends and some of his daughter's friends. The oldest girl, who had her own apartment, would be coming over. Anyway, it wasn't a wild party, but it could be fun, and Scott was invited.

Scott snapped it up. He figured that Sandy wouldn't be making him uncomfortable, not with her school friends to party with. When they knocked off early, he went home to shower and change. Rob had insisted that once there and having a drink, he was to stay the night.

Rob had a full house. Sylvia was there, as were a few others from the paper. The guy who owned the local surf shop was there with his wife or girlfriend. The lady who owned the book store was there with her grown son. Rob's oldest daughter, the college girl up from Arcata, was there with her boyfriend, who claimed to be a writer. There were six high school kids there, and Scott was trying to tell which of the boys was Sandy's date, not that he really cared.

Curiosity propelled him over to Rob's older kid. He spent a gratuitous minute chatting about the paper before turning his attention to her boyfriend. "Tina tells me you're a writer. What have you written?

"Just got a book published. The timing was perfect. Four years ago, as a university freshman looking for some meaning, I did some tree sitting for Earth First!. While up there I started thinking about this whole *save the forest* thing and how long it's been going on and how it started. Well, I started doing research, interviewing people, looking at old news stories. Anyway, I was wrapping it all up when this forest war or whatever you call it started up. The bottom line is I got a five grand advance and the book comes out in January." He pushed his thin glasses up on his thin nose and gave Scott an insipid smile. Then he asked, "And you. I hear you're a writer too."

"Well, yes. Besides being a journalist, I'm working on a serious novel."

The guy leaned on the book case with one elbow and drawled, "Really. And what's it about?"

"It's about a dedicated social scientist and her writer boyfriend, and how they find themselves caught up in the critical issues of the day. The stresses in her life break them up, but he never loses hope, and they're finally united while in a fight to preserve basic human rights."

Tina and her boyfriend looked at each other and then back to Scott. "Interesting," He said, flatly. "Sounds like a it could be an exciting story."

The couple started talking to each other about skiing plans with some other couples, and Scott backed away and found

175

Sylvia, who informed him that she was thinking of retiring. She had plenty of money and wanted to move closer to her daughter.

Scott would really miss her. As caustic as she'd been, she helped hone his journalistic skills, as she'd apparently once done for Rob. She was also someone he could talk to when he needed to sort things out.

He wandered from conversation the conversation before finding himself in the middle of Sandy's group. She grabbed him by the arm.

Not being able to think of anything better to say, he asked which guy was her date.

"I don't have a date tonight, so no need to be jealous." She cut him off before he could protest. "So, what happened with the sort of girlfriend?"

"Well, she hadn't heard from me, and she kind of got the wrong idea." He was hoping to leave it at that.

"It's over, right? Come on, I can see it in your face. Let me guess. She's already seeing someone else."

Scott tried to hide his reaction, but he obviously wasn't successful.

"Oh, yeah. You got home, and she's doing someone else because you broke up with her. All that stuff about seeing other people. Oh, you are so clueless."

Scott found himself speechless. The smug little bubble head had him dead to rights, and he couldn't deny it or justify it.

Then she looked at her friends. "Scott here has the raving hots for me. He wants to be my boyfriend and have me teach him how not to be a dork around women. Problem is, he's too proud to admit it. Isn't that about right, Scott?"

She was having fun at his expense, probably payback for rejecting her. She obviously enjoyed making his squirm. If he denied her claim that he had the hots for her, it would just confirm it to her friends. She was a mean spirited, cunning ball buster, but there was something sexy in her brazen self confidence.

He immediately rejected the thought of her being sexy. She

176

was a bratty teenager, and they all seemed to love being snotty to others. The only response he could come up with was, "I'm sorry, but I need some adult conversation."

He managed to avoid her the rest of the evening, and he was almost having a good enough time to forget that Peaches was probably in bed with Buck.

As the party was breaking up, Sandy approached him. "Sorry I was so mean back there, but you deserved it after last time. I promise to be nicer on our next date." She blew him a kiss and strutted off to bed.

When he got home the following afternoon, the sun had slipped out from the clouds and the rain had temporarily stopped. He took a walk around the trailer park. Peaches was also taking a walk, and he asked her how if she had a good New Years.

"Well," she said coldly. "I thought you might come around yesterday and ask me that or wish me a happy holiday or something. Oh well, just like Christmas."

"I explained about Christmas." He protested.

"Oh, that's right, the busy newspaper man. Well, I had a great time, thank you."

Before he could determine if Buck had been part of her plans, she walked off.

As he watched her walk away, he figured Buck was obviously part of it. She'd found someone she wanted, and she no longer had any use for Scott. It was petty to expect him to come over just to let her flaunt her relationship with Buck.

He took a long walk until the rains started again. He spent the rest of the day working on his book.

The next day at work as he chatted with Rob about the party. Rob said, "I hear my little girl was pretty rough on you that night."

Scott tried to dismiss it but Rob continued. "Be careful of Sandy."

"No, please believe me. I have no intention of trying to take advantage of her."

"Scotty, Scotty. I'm not worried about her. I've seen the way she treats her boyfriends. I love her dearly, but she's a willful girl, and woe be to anyone who doesn't let her get her way."

Scott felt like a guy who spends his pay on lottery tickets. In every one of his relationships with women he'd come up with straight zeros. He didn't need grief from Sandy, and he'd be just fine if he never saw her again.

He was prepared for trouble with women, trouble with the FBI, trouble with Buck and his fuzzy connection to this forest war, trouble piecing together the complex story he'd been working on. He wasn't, however, prepared for the kind of annoying, tick in your underwear type of trouble he would have with his new neighbor.

A clean cut, slightly chubby guy in the last half of his thirties had bought V.V.s place. He was moving in as Scott came home from work. Scott stuck out his hand and said, "I'm your neighbor, Scott. Welcome to our strange little neighborhood.

The guy put out his hand. "Michael Vole. Pleased to meet you, Scott. Say, have you been saved?"

"Beg your pardon?"

"You know, have you heard the message of redemption, the word of the savior?"

"You mean, like Jesus?"

"Yes, have you taken Him as your personal savior?"

The guy got right to the point, and it was making Scott uncomfortable. He was raised with nominal religious beliefs and church attendance, but this guy was getting personal. "Well, I'm what you'd call a Christian. I went to church, did Sunday school as a kid. You know."

"Yes, yes, we all went through the motions. But, have you been born again?"

"I . . . I don't know exactly what that means. My personal beliefs are, well, personal. I've had a long day. Nice meeting you." Scott ducked into the safety of his house. Damn, he thought, and I was going to offer to help him move stuff in.

Weekends had become a problem. During the week, Scott

stayed busy, what with a full day at the paper and evening meetings to cover. But Saturday morning hit, and he had two days to fill, days alone. The rain continued to fall, making even an hour walk an ordeal. He thought about spending his weekends building an ark, figuring he'd need one pretty soon. He was also thinking about getting a larger place. Two nice places had come up, and he hadn't acted. V.V.'s place sold at a price he could have handled. Emily's place would soon be on the market, but Peaches was living there and should have first grab at it. He thought about offering her his place cheap, so he could buy Emily's. But, he quickly realized, Peaches was now making more money than he was, didn't have a car to keep up, and didn't have to commute. By the time probate cleared, the girl would have the necessary down. Well, Scott figured, women were more into nesting, and they needed a more homey home. All Scott needed was a place to eat, sleep and work.

It was his weekend for the bike, but the rain ruined his elaborate travel plans. He thought about Jake's comment and real bikers. Did he feel he needed to prove something? At ten in the morning and in no mood to write, he decided. Hell, yes. He had something to prove to himself. He went to Jake's shop.

"Hi, Jake. My weekend on the bike. Think I'll go for a ride."

"Streets are pretty wet." This said without any inflection.

"Well, Jake, real bikers ride in the rain."

"If they have a need to. Where you going?"

" I don't know. Arcata. Yeah."

"Long ride. Be real careful."

Scott bundled up, put on goggles, gloves, boots. He took off down the road and almost spun out on an oil slick. This wasn't a good idea, but he was damned well going to do it.

When Scott hit Redwood Park, he took the scenic route. A few miles down the road he went through a patch of redwood needles on the road, just as an oncoming car went through a puddle, spraying him. He touched the brake to slow and spun out. The bike slid off the road and into the mud. The leathers

179

kept him from getting a pavement burn, but landing and sliding hurt his left leg and hip. He was too sore and shaken to get the bike upright. He shut off the engine and stepped under a tree to get out of the worst of the rain. He felt his leg starting to stiffen up and knew he had to walk it off. Starting down the trail, Scott realized this was the same place he'd walked down to the beach several months before. Something propelled him down the trail, and the further he went the more it seemed the right idea. In the back of his mind, he realized that something was missing, and it was a good thing. Yes, he thought. There were no signs, no guardsmen. Apparently the government had started to back off this war with the trees. Perhaps he'd meet some activists. Maybe he'd join them, become a tree sitter. But this was a national park, so no tree sitting was necessary to save these trees. He kept going until he reached the beach, one of the most uncrowded beaches in the country. He expected to be totally alone, but he wasn't.

Right at the margin of forest and beach a small tent was pitched. In front of the tent, dressed in a big rain coat, sat a man. Scott walked up.

The guy was bearded and looked to be sixty-something, probably homeless.

"Excuse me. Are you OK out here?"

"Certainly. Couldn't be better. And you, what brings you down here on this lovely day?"

"My motorcycle spun out. I had to walk."

"Yes, walking's more peaceful that riding. Quieter too. You love the rain?"

"Well, I'd rather have nice weather. The bike might not have slid. Oh, I'm Scott, a reporter."

"I'm Ben, Ben There, a. . . well, a living being."

"Ben There, really?   Do you live here in the park?"

"Sometimes I live here. Sometimes in other places. I suppose this is a park. Something is always called something, park, private forest, back yard. Trees, beach, plants, animals, surf."

"Are you homeless?"

"My home tonight." He pointed to the tent. "I was further south, in the forest. But a big group of people moved in, and military people buzzed the forest in helicopters. One crashed, and it wasn't at all peaceful any longer, so I decided to come here. No one uses this trail and beach in the winter, at least until now."

"You were in that forest. Didn't you know about the closures, the military guard and all that?"

"That doesn't concern me. It's not in my reality construct."

"You were lucky. They were arresting people."

"I never pay attention to anyone called 'they.' Scott is real. Ben There is real. *They* are not real."

"They had guns." This guy was frustrating.

"Guns only have conditional reality, conditional upon your acknowledgement of whatever they symbolize."

Scott pulled his collar up and sat down in the wet sand. Suddenly, the rain wasn't a big concern. "Just a minute. Are you trying to say that reality is somehow relative?"

"Why not? You say you're a reporter. You could have said you were human, a male, a motorcyclist, a lover of rain, a madman, a son or father, or any of a million things. So all these other things aren't real to you, but being a reporter is. Guardsmen and guns are not real to me at this moment, but this beach and those waves are, at least at this moment."

It was then Scott noticed the surfboard leaning up against a tree. "So, you came here to surf?"

No, I came here, and I surfed. I also cooked food, and talked to that tree, and took some photos."

"You live in this tent?"

"I live on this planet. I sometimes sleep in this tent when it rains."

"I think you're bullshitting me. You can't just take everything as relative. This is a world of real things, facts that can't be dismissed."

"Ok. Name one of those facts." The guy smiled at him with yellow teeth.

"Well, the world. No the whole fuckin' universe. That huge universe that contains everything is real, a fact."

"That huge universe? Mathematically, the universe we experience as just about infinitely large is indistinguishable from its inverse, a universe that's infinitesimally small, say about ten to the minus thirty-fourth of a meter."

"That ridiculous." Suddenly, Scott saw himself sitting on a rainy beach having a conversation with a loony. He decided to walk back to the bike. "I gotta get out of here."

"From where you stand, how can you tell?"

Scott turned around. "How can I tell what?"

"The size of the universe. You're in the midst of it. You know nothing outside of it. How can you prove or even say what size it is, or even what size you are?"

"Well, It's obvious that. . . This is pointless. You're nuts."

"Relative to what or who? To you? You are the universal standard for truth and normalcy! Well, I'm glad I've finally met you. Perhaps you might tell me what time it was the day before time began? Who would you be if you weren't you? What is the sound of a perfect day? Why isn't the ocean ever still? Anyway, we can continue this the next time we meet."

Scott waved him off and started up the trail. When he got back to the bike, a highway patrol car had stopped. The cop helped him right the bike and asked him how he was. It was then Scott realized that Ben didn't have a car parked on the highway. How did he get there? Hitchhike? Then for a chilling moment, Scott considered the possibility that he only imagined meeting the man, that the fall had dazed him and caused him to hallucinate. He desperately wanted confirmation.

"Officer, there's a man camped down at the beach. I think he's a bit off."

"He'd have to be to camp in this weather. I don't think that's an official camp ground, and I'm not sure if that closed forest rule's been lifted, but this time of year there's no fire danger and no other people to bother. I'll notify the rangers, and they'll check it out on whatever regular patrols take them there, probably in the Spring. But, where's this guy's car?"

"I think he hitchhiked. He's obviously a transient."

"Hell, buddy, the woods are full of nut cases. Take that mob further south, camping out for weeks in this weather, having a stand off with the whole military. According to some touchy feely liberal writer, these people have nude dances around some trees for christsake. Which reminds me. Why were you all the way down there in the rain, with your expensive bike on its side up here?"

"I was too sore and dazed to ride."

The cop held a finger up in front of Scott's eyes and asked him how many. Then he suggested that Scott may have imagined the guy, and he'd be better off finding some dry place to get off the road.

Scott rode down to Trinidad and pulled up at the restaurant where he'd met Madd. Passing her house, he saw smoke coming out of the chimney and saw that there was an additional car in her drive way.

Scott had a couple of glasses of white wine and watched a golf game on the TV. He tried flirting with the waitress, who seemed almost too bored to notice. He had a late lunch before heading home.

14.

In the Sunday paper's book review, there was a hot new book about a young female lawyer who took on the entire United Nations to stop them from interfering with some country's government. There was a science fiction novel about a space age cop on the trail of a serial killer who has been killing transporter operators over a string of planets. A contestant on one of those reality TV shows wrote his autobiography and admitted to using steroids during the show. He looked over the entire review section until he discovered a small review of Tina's boyfriends book about the history of forest activism.

In the afternoon Scott saw Jake heading in the direction of the Tree House and rushed out to catch up. "Join you for a beer?"

Jake nodded, and the two of them, collars up, were blown up the road by the wind and rain.

Over a pitcher of that flavorless light beer Jake always ordered, Scott told him the story of the guy on the beach. "Really weird old guy. Called himself Ben There."

"Yeah, what was he like."

"Long white hair and beard. Had a tent and a surfboard and talked like nothing was real."

"Sounds like old Stanislaus Portfolio. He lives here, or he has a place here that he stays at now and then. He also goes by a bunch of weird names, but I don't remember anything about Ben There."

"I can't believe this. I run into this guy where you'd never expect anyone to be, and he's a neighbor. He said some weird shit. Is he on the level?"

"To be honest Scott, can't even say it's the same guy. Don't know much about him. Was already here when I bought the park. As I get it, he used to teach at some college near the Bay Area. Wrote some strange books, controversial I guess. Place he

184

worked apparently asked him to resign. Sold whatever he had down there and bought the only other twenty-four foot travel trailer in the park. Opposite corner from the lesbian band broads. Looks just like yours, 'cept it's a baby barf green color. Says he used to do lots of psychedelics. Figure he's a burn out."

"How's he live? Didn't seem like he worked or anything."

"Heard his books got some small cult following, so he gets this little check each month. Also, probably gets social security by now. Anyway, he's got a twenty year old car in front, and he don't drive it much. Spends a good part of his time camping God only knows where. Hell, probably don't exchange a dozen words with him in a month. Funny thing with all the names though. Warned me right off that he had multiple personalities, so I shouldn't be surprised if he don't remember me or gives me a different name."

Scott got the almost visceral feeling that he was in the eye of a weirdness hurricane, and that strange events were spinning around him at a increasingly dizzying speed. "I think I'm a magnet for weirdoes," he said without really planning to say it.

"You wouldn't have moved here if you didn't want to be. My trailer park is where the strange in society shakes out and settles. I mean, I don't plan it that way, but that's what shows up. Normal people don't live here, or if they do, they don't stay long."

"I consider myself normal."

"For around here, I suppose you are. I guess where you came from—what, Santa Barbara—you were probably the odd duck in the neighborhood. Hell, man. You gonna be a writer. We got some people to write about."

Scott saw Buck come in and hoped he wouldn't notice them.

Jake spotted him. "Look, Scott, it's Buck. Guess we got a party. Hey Buck."

Scott tried to wave Jake off, but he wasn't quick enough. Buck turned, smiled and started over.

"What's the problem, Scott?" Said Jake.

185

"He's been seeing Peaches."

"So what. You cut her loose, dumped her right good, I hear. Be adult about it. Yo, Buck, come have a seat."

"Good to see you two. Hate to drink alone. I do it, but I hate it. Scott, where the hell you been? I haven't heard from you."

Before Scott could answer, Jake sounded in with, "Seems he's got his nose out of joint cause you're fuckin' Peaches."

Scott felt foolish and couldn't think of an ego-saving way out.

"Jesus, Scott. I didn't think you had a thing for her. Hell, she's nothing to me. We're just hanging out and playing together. You want us to believe you're madly in love with this chick?"

"No, man. I don't know. I just felt uncomfortable. Like she was living with me, and now you two are playing house. I come over to see how she's doin', and I interrupt the two of you."

"Shit. I've been over there five, maybe six times. Most often a beer with a buddy counts as much as getting laid. But, if you want me to dump her."

"No, no. I'm just being weird. I guess it was coming back from doin' that story in the woods. I'm sorry. Don't worry about it."

"Did you read his story?" Jake asked Buck.

"Yeah. Liked it. Great part about all those people dancing round the trees in the nude. Made me want to go party with them."

Scott was loosened up now. The bad feelings about Buck evaporated, and he also realized that he could probably make another play for Peaches if he ever decided he wanted a serious relationship.

Scott shared the story about Ben There with Buck, and asked if he knew the old guy.

"Sounds like the same guy. Travel trailer like yours. I know him as Les Apt. The guy's got a wonderfully fucked outlook on life. Even though I've only talked to him a few times, he's the closest thing I've got to a hero."

They shared a laugh about the guy, whatever his real name

was. Then Scott remembered Michael Vole. "What kind of a character did I get for a neighbor?"

"The born again guy. Yeah, he's a bit much with his religion, but he seems ok."

Buck perked up. "You got a born again next door?"

"The guy started off as soon as I met him. Wanted to know if I had a relationship with Jesus, if I'd been saved."

"All right!" Buck was rubbing his hands together in glee. "I want to come over and fuck with his mind."

"Don't do it, Buck. I gotta live next door. I don't want a feud with the guy. Better I just stay out of his way."

As Jake poured another round, he looked at Buck and said, "Let me guess, atheist."

Buck laughed. "An atheist believes that there is no God. I don't believe or disbelieve anything. I guess I'm a skeptical agnostic." That must have struck him funny, as he started laughing hysterically.

"And you, Scott?" Jake asked.

"I dunno. I was raised sort of Methodist. We went to church fairly regularly when I was a kid. Then the old man got really involved in business, my mom in her social and civic things, and we went less and less. It's like, yeah, I guess there's a God, and that Jesus died to save us and all that, and I try to be a good person. Beyond that, I really don't think too much about it. How bout you, Jake?"

"Church of Divine Man."

"What? Never heard of it." Scott said.

"We believe we are co-creators with God. We're involved with learning to use our innate psychic abilities, see auras, balance chakras, meditate, run energy, and all that."

"New age." Buck observed.

"New age." Scott agreed. "I'm sorry, Jake, but that doesn't seem to fit with a hard drinking, hard fighting, hard doping biker."

"Man, I wasn't always into it. I took up with these ideas some seven years back. Went and changed my whole outlook. I

187

got a crystal on a chain, and I can balance your chakras with it. Now, I haven't gotten the psychic thing yet, but I'm working on it."

It was Scott's turn to laugh. "The more I know about you, the less I know about you. Wow, was that profound, or am I drunk?"

"You're drunk," Buck observed. "But then so are we, so it sounded profound, and in today's world, image is everything." Then Buck, who had just got his laughter under control, started cracking up again.

The beer-induced profundity was rising in Scott. "Jake, you are this long series of opposites of what you seem. I bet next you're gonna tell us you're a woman."

It was Jake's turn to crack up. "Yeah, man. The name's Jackie, not Jake, and you and me gonna make us a baby tonight."

By the time they left the Tree House, they were staggering, holding each other up to keep from slipping in the mud and falling in the mini lakes fed by the unrelenting rain.

The next morning Scott woke in a sort of dazed state, just a few millimeters below the hangover threshold. He stumbled out to get the paper, and saw that Buck had been up early and in typical form. Scott's car sported a new bumper sticker, big and bright and impossible to miss. It said, "Another Psychotic Axe Murderer for Jesus." Scott could only imagine Michael's reaction when he sees that.

That afternoon Michael made his reaction clear after loudly knocking on Scott's door. "Scott, you probably think that bumper sticker is funny, but it shows how little you value your immortal soul. These things build, blasphemy upon blasphemy, until you are so jaded that you become completely lost. Satan doesn't just grab your soul, you know, he steals a bit of it at a time." He thrust some pamphlets in Scott's hand. "Read this, and think about coming to a prayer meeting. Once the Lord is in you, this sorrow in your heart will be lifted."

Trying to be polite, Scott thanked him and promised to read

the literature. As soon as the door closed, a thought flashed through his mind. Perhaps becoming religious like Michael would really take away the loneliness and frustration he seemed to feel almost constantly. It was however, a momentary flash in a badly tarnished pan. Michael's approach was so off-putting that Scott couldn't imagine becoming like him nor even taking him seriously. In fact, while religion had always been a pleasant corner of his life, even as it sat on the back burner, Michael was making it distasteful. The man's approach cheapened the sacred Scott felt lurking just behind the church rituals. He tossed the papers in the trash.

Tuesday night at the school board meeting, one of the Trustees actually suggested banning the Harry Potter books on the grounds that they glorify witchcraft, which was evil. Luckily, the rest of the board dismissed her concerns with little discussion, but Scott felt, as a writer and recent victim of Michael's onslaughts, personally attacked. His report, written as soon as he got home, was anything but an objective chronicle. In fact, he started the piece with, "Censorship rears its ugly head again, and this time in our town." He ended the piece with a defense of freedom of speech and of the press.

Scott was still mad and spoiling for a fight. Unfortunately, the board member was not within reach, but Michael was. Scott marched next door and banged on the aluminum door.

As soon as the door opened, Scott thrust a copy of his article in Michael's hand and said, "This time I have something for you to read. I'd like your opinion."

He read carefully and slowly. When he finally handed the paper back to Scott, his eyes showed sadness. "While I don't believe in banning books, particularly books that are understood to be totally fantasy, I do agree with her that books like this are bad for children. They glorify the dark side. But what concerns me the most is the obvious anger in this writing. You are clearly fighting against the truth and the light. You're soul has become so corrupted with your decadent life, that you feel you must defend this absurd writing. I can only imagine what has led you to this place in your life. You are possibly lost in a world of debauchery, drugs, alcohol, and who knows what else. Go home and reflect, and I'll go inside and pray for you." With that he closed the door and left Scott pumped with adrenaline, with neither a victory of a defeat. The son of a bitch felt sorry for him and was going to pray for him. How can you yell at a fool like that?

He still needed to vent, so he called Buck, who agreed with him and said he'd be happy to come over and play all sorts of head games with Michael. Scott was determined to deal with this himself. Michael had become the symbol for all the intolerant people that condemned literature and ideas in every age. The man would have no books read but the Bible. He would deny Scott's very essence, the passionate writer of controversial human issues.

While Scott didn't yet know how he'd handle this guy, he knew he'd no longer allow himself to be the object of pity.

The next day Rob read the piece and agreed with him, but said it was necessary, seeing that Scott's piece was coverage of the meeting and not an editorial, to soften the language a bit.

Then Scott told Rob of his frustration with the neighbor, hoping the boss would have some words of wisdom.

"Scott, my wife's brother is the same way. I told him right off that I have a rich spiritual life that I would not discuss with him, and that I expected him to respect that and not discuss his religious views. Admittedly, it took a few times to get him to see my point, but now the subject is taboo."

They hadn't heard Sylvia walk up, until she joined the conversation. "A good journalist's most important god is truth."

Sylvia had a way of ending long, complex conversations with a single sentence.

Scott tried Rob's approach when he ran into Michael the next evening. The insufferable jerk responded, "If your spiritual life was that rich, you wouldn't be so defensive, and you would wish to talk of it. I'll pray for you."

As the man walked toward his door, the only retort Scott

could come up with was, "Don't you dare pray for me."

Scott hadn't really examined his religious feelings since he was a child. He thought seriously about them now, in the context of Michael and his pronouncements. He came to the conclusion that he didn't like religious ritual or religious people. He decided that if God exists, he doesn't need guys like Michael running around making all those pompous statements. God would probably prefer someone like Scott, someone who tried to make the world a better place, rather than someone who was holier than thou. With that thought, Scott severed his last connection to organized religion and made whatever beliefs he might hold truly personal.

That Friday night, having nothing better to do, Scott accepted a dinner invitation to Rob's. After dinner Sandy invited him down to the den to play some pool.

After a couple of games and some small talk about school, the forest standoff and the paper, Sandy asked if he'd changed his mind about them going out together.

Being still a bit edgy from the religious thing, he was in no mood to be diplomatic. "Look, Sandy, you're a nice kid, but I'm a serious adult, dealing with serious adult issues. I don't have time for sock hops, car crash movies, and the coolest new fashions."

"Are you saying I'm frivolous?"

"It's not you personally. You're just a kid. It's part of being your age."

"Man, get any kind of clue. Do, you even read the paper you write for?"

"Naturally. What's that have to do with anything?"

"You do, huh? I don't think so. I suggest you read the damn thing." She stormed up the stairs.

As he got ready to go home, Scott apologized to Rob. "I'm sorry if I said something to make Sandy mad."

"I'm the one who's sorry, sorry for you, Scott. You still think you're going to win an argument with that kid of mine?" He shook his head.

"She suggested I didn't read the paper. What was that about?"

"Oh, that." He laughed. "You don't know what she meant? Check the Wednesday edition, last Wednesday, next Wednesday."

He'd already recycled his week's papers, but made a note to look carefully in the following Wednesday's paper for whatever it was.

The lull between rain storms must have happened while he slept. He woke late on Saturday to the sound of thunder and the flash of lightning. The rain beat on the windows. Scott was restless and considered going to see Peaches, but he thought Buck might be there, or perhaps another lover, or she would still be upset with him, or he would have to confront his feelings for her, and he still hadn't sorted them out. He figured that if he tried to make up with her, she'd assume a serious, committed relationship, and he didn't want to go there unless he was sure. He didn't want to hurt her, to break her heart again, which he figured was the reason she turned to Buck. In the end he talked himself out of it, thinking that she would be there if he ever decided he wanted something permanent with her, so there was no hurry.

He stopped by the trailer where Ben There or Stanislaus Portfolio or whatever his name lived. The old car was in the drive, but there was no one around. He thought about leaving a note, but decided against it. He drove to town to catch a movie and spent the rest of the weekend writing and watching TV. His concentration was off. He missed having a woman in his life.

His ritual of going straight to the book review section was shattered by the headlines. There was to be a showdown on Senator Bambi Bottoms' forest bill. In the article she offered a fervent plea for healing the forest and the country. She quoted from a north coast journalist, Scott. In the speech she gave, she quoted his lines about saving the forest as a way of saving our mental health and the health of our society.

Suddenly, all his personal issues took the first flight to

Maui, along with his massive sexual frustration. Here was the pivotal figure in the major current domestic issue using something he wrote to drive home her point and to push the senate to voting her way. He had written of real life and had written well, and now it was his time to shine. He cut the paper out and made his weekly call to his parents.

His mother thought it was wonderful that the senator used his words, and she hoped he could get a job as one of her speech writers, so he could get out of that dreadful little newspaper.

That evening Scott was glued to the evening news. There she was in front of the media, talking about the upcoming vote on her bill. In her hand was a clipping, which she waved at the appropriate time. "A man, living and writing in the midst of these ancient forests, stated it eloquently," she said. "He has walked in the forests and interviewed the people who have risked their lives to protect it." She went on to read the bit about the forest's ability to heal the mental stresses of the individual and of the entire society. Then she launched into her plan to make this forest bill a reality. Scott was elated. He saw himself as a nationally syndicated columnist, and a best selling author. He drifted off to sleep fantasizing about his glorious future.

Yes, Rob and everyone else had heard the news, and they all congratulated Scott.

He picked up the phone and after a few moments got himself connected to the Senator's offices. A woman on the staff gave him the standard greeting.

"I'm Scott Mukis from California."

"Yes, and what can we do for you?"

"I'm the guy who wrote the article."

"The article?"

"Yes. The Senator read from my article on her news conference yesterday. She quoted my piece and mentioned my name. I'm the guy."

"Was there a problem? Did she misquote you or use your material without your permission?"

"No, no! That's not the problem. There isn't any problem. I just wanted to thank her for quoting me and for introducing a bill that means so much to us out here. I wanted to talk to her if I could and to offer my services if she ever needs them."

"Well, the Senator is not available at the moment. She's on the floor arguing her bill. I'm sure she will be pleased to hear your response. I will inform her of your call and your support. You will get a letter of confirmation in the near future. Thank you again and good bye."

"But," Scott protested, but it was too late. The phone was dead. That wasn't good enough, so he sat down and wrote a letter about how he'd been moved to write the piece, how he admired what the Senator was doing, and how he would be glad to help in this campaign. Not wanting to take the time for mail delivery, he faxed it to both her office in D.C. and her state office. He gave his address, phone number, and his home and office e-mail.

Then he wrote an opinion piece about how the Senator had vindicated the activists and their noble efforts. When referring to the activists, he used "we," placing himself in their company. He talked about being proud to stand shoulder to shoulder with visionaries like the Senator and those people who have dedicated months of their time and even their lives to guarding our ancient forests.

Then he had to sell Rob on the idea of publishing it. Rob agreed on the basis of Scott being in the middle of his fifteen minutes of fame, so this journalistic masturbation would sell some papers. Scott was hoping his boss would say that the piece's great literary value made publishing it a must, but Rob seemed unwilling to aspire to that level of praise. None the less, it would appear, and the public would be forthcoming with the adulation that Rob was too timid or conservative to offer.

His piece came out the next day, and Scott's whole being was tuned to the public's reaction and the Senator's response. In fact he was so single minded, that he almost forgot to check Wednesday's paper.

Scott would have forgotten, but Rob mentioned, almost as an aside, that this was the day Sandy had been talking about. He grabbed a proof and started looking for, he knew not what. Then he spotted it, her picture under the caption, "The School Scene."

Apparently she wrote a weekly piece about high school life, and he'd somehow always missed it, probably assuming that student writing was trivial.

This week it was about how many adults often discounted teenagers, assuming that, because of their age, they had nothing to say or to contribute. She then went on to cite students who had started businesses, found new heavenly bodies, become consultants, formed popular bands, volunteered in various areas and had other notable contributions. She'd concluded with the observation that everyone needs to be validated for who they are and for what they have done. She observed that lumping people together in stereotypical groups has been the basis for atrocities throughout history. She ended with a plea to see the person, not the demographic group.

Scott was stunned. She was making one of the points he'd always stood up for, and he'd been the kind of insensitive person he'd always opposed. He quickly dug up back issues and discovered that Sandy was a talented, insightful writer. She had depth and maturity, and Scott felt like a total jerk.

His new found respect for the girl grew as the hours passed, until when his day ended, and before he was scheduled to cover the planning commission, he drove to Rob's house to see Sandy.

She was doing homework when he arrived. Rob's wife let him in and he caught Sandy in the den. "I read your article. I'm sorry I never read your work before, and I'm sorry I didn't take you seriously. That isn't really like me, and I swear I'll never do it again."

"Fine, Scott, I accept your apology. Do you have anything else to say, or should I get back to this history homework?"

"Well, I do have something to say, if I'm not disturbing you."

In answer, she put her books down and gave him her full attention.

"I've been a jerk, and I see we have more in common that I thought. You were right all along. We would do well together. Let me start to set things right. I'll take you to dinner on Friday night."

"You're asking me out on a date?"

He swallowed hard. "Yes, would you go out to dinner with me on Friday?"

"No."

"No. What do you mean?"

"I'm not interested in going out with you."

"But, you said you wanted to go out with me."

"You got it wrong. I wanted you to want to go out with me. That's not the same thing.

"But. . . I don't get it."

"Yeah, what's new. Now you're interested in me. You want to date me. I'm more than some kid to you. I think I've made my point. Besides, you're like already a stuffy guy. You'd be a drag to date. You're not even much fun to read."

Scott stumbled out into the gray drizzle, stunned by the girl he thought had a thing for him. She was cruel and calculating, or maybe she was only reacting to his rejection. Maybe she was interested in him but was so angry that she wouldn't give him the satisfaction. Still, she apparently did set him up, and Rob had told him to be careful. Scott decided he'd never know the girl's deep feelings, but he knew that she'd deliberately tried to hurt him, particularly with the remark about his writing. He wouldn't consider chasing after a high school girl, particularly the boss' daughter. He was better off. What if they'd gone out, and he'd had a moment of weakness and had gone to bed with her. Disaster.

What was it about women, he thought, that made them want to hurt him. He'd always tried to be sensitive to their needs and feelings. What was it? Did they only want assholes who treated them like shit? In fact, the only woman who had cared for him without reservation was Peaches, and he'd let her down. He vowed to himself to make things right.

Scott turned on the windshield wipers and radio, in that order. Senator Bottoms' bill had passed the Senate, in spite of lobbying by the President. The day of the vote, several papers printed photos taken in the aftermath of the forest bombing and the helicopter crash, with captions questioning if these people had died in vain. Like it or not, most senators could do little else but vote to end the national embarrassment in the forest. The pundits were claiming that the bill would quickly pass in the House, with few changes. Passing this bill was the politically correct act of the moment. Bottoms had struck while the proverbial iron was white hot.

What was disappointing was that none of his writing on the issue, including his last, impassioned editorial, had gotten into the huge media frenzy surrounding the forest bill. Yet, he knew that the door was opening on a stage of his career, and recognition was about to jump him from behind.

Perhaps, Scott was thinking, things in general were taking a turn for the better. Maybe even his personal life was due for a change for the better. He parked and went straight to Peaches' place, hoping he wouldn't find Buck in her bed.

Peaches answered the door wearing a pink robe and motorcycle grease under her finger nails. She was alone. Scott tried to start out with some small talk. "Haven't talked to you for awhile. How's the job?"

"I'm working hard, but I love it. Jake says I do the best and quickest tunes he's ever seen. I got some job security, and I'm making plenty of money. You know, I even like the weather. What's up with you?"

"Well, you know. I care about you. Want to know if everything's OK and all. Like how are things going with you and Buck?"

"That asshole! I'm in bed with the guy, telling him about work, my feelings, my life, and he says all my chatter bores him, It's like, let's have sex but don't talk. I tell him if I'm

197

gonna fuck some guy, he's got to think I'm something special. Like he's my guy and really into being with me. Like I'm valuable to him. He says we're like playmates and it doesn't mean anything but sex. Then I ask him how he'd like it if all that sex just stopped, and he shrugged and said, 'whatever.' Well, I tell him to get his sorry ass out of my place, and that was the end of it."

Scott looked at this poor girl and thought of all the rough times and rejection she'd suffered lately, and it broke his heart. He took her hand and said, "Peaches, I really care for you. I don't know how deep those feelings go, but I want to explore them, and whatever happens between us, I'll always be there for you. I didn't want to hurt you by making promises I wasn't sure I could keep, but I can promise to open my heart to you and to try to build a relationship."

"It sounds like you're saying you don't think you love me but you want to try to, or something weird like that. I don't need all that drama. I care about you too, Scott, but I don't want a relationship with you."

"You're just saying that because I hurt you before."

"I'm just saying that because I'm in a relationship that makes me happy."

"But you said you broke up with Buck." Scott was confused.

"I'm not talking about Buck."

"Not Jake?"

"Hold on, Scott, not even a guy. You know Paula, the drummer for the Hot Licks Lesbians.?"

"The chubby little redhead? You're having a lesbian relationship!"

"Yeah. There was some mutual attraction when we met, and I kind of fantasized about the idea. Well, she pursued it, and I decided, what the hell, I'd give it a try, and it's really nice. She's soft and tender, and she understands, says the right things. She knows how to please me."

"But she was with Jules."

"Shit, they haven't been getting along for a long time. The three of them are hardly speaking. Don't know how the band stays together. Anyway, we both found ourselves free, and it clicked."

Scott was overcome with guilt. "Oh my god, I've driven you to homosexuality. I've really screwed up your life. I'm so sorry. What can I do?"

"You can start by getting over yourself. You didn't drive me to anything. I'm not your responsibility. I told you once that I loved you, and I did, I still do, but it didn't mean I wanted a fifty year marriage and kids and all that. It just meant I loved you because you were warm and giving, and I wanted to enjoy a relationship. But, you think you're the center of the goddamn universe. Jesus! You take yourself so damn seriously. You were with all this stuff about not knowing how you feel, like if you made a mistake, I'd fall apart or something. Lighten up. You know, somewhere between Buck and you is a half-way tolerable man, not that I want a man these days."

"Is this your anger speaking?"

"You make me wanna scream! This is me telling you the truth. I was having a rough time, and you helped, and that was a really sweet thing. I'm fine now. I have work I like and a relationship that works, at least for now, a nice place to live, and some friends. I'm cool, but you keep being your own worst enemy, and nobody can get through to you. If you'd let me, I'd like to help you, be your friend and all."

Scott was touched by the gesture of this brave girl. "You've got a big heart, but I'm fine. My life's getting better all the time. I worry that you'll be hurt, but remember I'm here for you." He kissed her on the cheek and said good night.

When he got home, he called Buck. "You rode over her pretty hard, and now she's turned to Paula. They're having an affair."

Buck gasped. "Oh, shit, Scott. You mean our little Peaches is dating a drummer. How low can she fall."

Scott wasn't in the mood to be taken lightly, so he excused himself and hung up.

15.

The inspiration for his novel about Maddie was out of his life, but it was as good as finished. But now, with Senator Bottoms using his words to hammer a revolutionary law through congress, he started on a novel about forest activists saving our ancient trees. Without a woman in his life, he poured himself into this new book, using himself as the model for the hero, an uncompromising reporter and activist. Cobra Lily was the basis of the female activist, the love interest, and he included aspects of Peaches, V.V., and Madd in her character. He also obsessively tracked the forest bill. All that, plus his work at the paper, kept him too busy for introspection. He also joined the gym that V.V. belonged to.

Between work, after work meetings, and an almost daily workout schedule, he rarely got home before nine or ten at night. He'd eat, work on the book and go to bed. It was a full schedule, but a satisfying one, leaving him little time to enumerate the reasons why his love life sucked.

As predicted, the House, in an effort to look like compassionate humans, passed Senator Bottoms' bill quickly, and with a big majority. There was nothing left but the President's desk.

Unfortunately, the President had been saying all along that it was a bad bill and didn't address critical issues, although he gave no particulars. Mostly, according to the pundits, he was concerned for friends in the timber industry and fearful of the Senator's growing popularity. He'd vowed repeatedly to veto the bill. So it arrived at his desk, where it sat, day after day, while the country waited.

A popular political cartoonist ran pieces showing a White House staff informing the President that another thousand young activists were killed, to which the voice of the boss stated that it wasn't a problem, as they weren't likely to vote for him.

Several nationally syndicated columnists asked if the President might try to make amends for all the bloodshed by signing the bill. The photos of burning and dismembered people were also splashed on the front pages of the big daily papers. Thousands more young people slipped by the military to join the people who had been camped out for most of the winter. Rallies and marches were scheduled all over the country for the following weekend.

Reluctantly the President signed, which started a week-long environmental celebration. Two days later, he recalled the thousands of troops camped out in the redwoods, which apparently disappointed many soldiers who had taken this assignment as a paid camping trip.

Rob dispatched Scott to the scene of the forest standoff to do a follow up on his story and to get photos and comments as the weary protesters came out of the forest. This was just what he'd hoped for, and he set out without packing a bag.

It was tough getting down the narrow road, with all the military vehicles heading out toward the highway. He had to pull over many times to make room for tanks and rocket launchers.

When he finally pulled into the recent staging area, the first group of protesters were poking their heads out of the woods to see if it were safe to come out. At about that time, two large trucks rumbled up and stopped. The signs on the trucks read, "R.S. Mukis Home Improvement. What the hell, he wondered, were his father's company trucks doing here?

Several young women in expensive looking hiking clothes opened up the backs of the trucks and started unloading signs. They handed one to each protester who came up the trail. The signs read, "Bambi Bottoms for President; she saved the forest."

As he got out his camera to take pictures of this, several other cars with reporters and photographers pulled up. Cameras started clicking, and tired and grungy protesters were being pulled aside for interviews. It was a media feeding frenzy, and Scott managed to grab a few scraps for himself, in spite of the more seasoned and aggressive news service people.

One thing he absolutely had to check on was the company trucks. He dashed over to them just as they were starting to pull out. He stood in the middle of the road, waving his hands, forcing them to stop.

The woman driving the first one declined to comment until Scott pulled out his ID and convinced her that he was the one and only R.S. Mukis Jr.

All the attractive, athletic looking, Asian woman would say was that the company backed Bottoms' bid for President, and that Becky had ordered the signs and had enlisted them to bring them down. The six women, it turned out, were all managers at various levels in the company.

It was, Scott had to admit, a great photo op. Each bedraggled protester came up the trail to the road carrying a sign insisting that this senator be made President.

On the way home, Scott wondered if his sister had made a unilateral decision to support Bottoms. He saw her as taking control without even asking anyone in the family. By the time he got back, he was pretty annoyed.

He'd dropped his story and film off at the paper just as Rob was about to leave. Then he headed quickly home and called his sister.

"Becky, I saw those women and all those signs. Whose idea was that?"

"Mine." She offered no explanation.

"Did you consult with Dad or Mom? I know you didn't call me."

"Nope. I just got the idea and went with it."

"Well, it's supposed to be a family business."

"A business you've rejected. I thought you were some kind of environmentalist and a supporter of these people in the woods."

"Of course I am."

"Don't you approve of the way Senator Bottoms solved the problem and stopped the bloodshed?"

"Naturally I approve, Becky. In fact she read a part of one of my articles in her news conference just before her bill went to a vote. I called her office about it, and I'm waiting for a response."

"So you support what she's doing? And, maybe you think she'd make a better president than the guy we got now?"

"Hell yes. I told her in a letter that I'd do what I could."

"So, what's the problem?"

"Nothing, I guess. You could have checked in with me first."

"The company's backing her campaign, but only if that's ok with you."

"Sure. I'm for her. You have my vote on this. Thanks for consulting me."

"Thank you for your approval. We stand united, little brother. Good night."

He felt better. Becky understood that his opinions must be taken under consideration. It's still a family business, he thought, and I'm still in the damn family.

His paper, along with just about every paper on the west coast and many from other parts of the country carried a photo of the weary activists stomping through the mud with "Bambi Bottoms for President" signs. The major papers wanted to know if the Senator had actually decided to throw her hat in the ring. As yet, there had been no confirmation from her office.

Within days groups within the Senator's party were organizing to make her the candidate. Columnists were singing her praises, and letters to the editor indicated that her popularity was growing. There was serious talk of the first woman president.

Scott was totally fascinated with the process, paying attention to little else. He felt he had a ringside seat on history. Then a letter came from the Senator's office. He quickly opened it.

It thanked him for his interest in her bill and in the forest issue. It also thanked him for allowing her office to use his written material in a public speech. It ended by welcoming his future comments.

It looked stiff and formal, almost like a form letter, and he suspected that someone other than the Senator had written it. He'd been hoping for something personal, perhaps with an invitation to an important function. Some clerical type, he surmised, had just sent out a letter without checking with the Senator, who would certainly have remembered reading his material and would have written a personal response. He decided he'd continue contacting her until he got past the minions.

He hadn't thought much about V.V. for some time, although some of the delightful moments they shared danced through his mind from time to time. It came as a complete surprise to Scott when she called one evening.

After the usual catch up questions about each other's working and social life, she came to the point.

"Scott, I've decided to buy a business. The bakery downtown is up for sale, and I've got a great idea for it." She left it there, waiting for Scott to pick up his cue.

"What's your idea?"

"I'm going for the healthy treats theme. I'll have pies and pastries, and all that sort of thing, but I'll be using whole grains, real fruit, fructose, instead of refined sugar. I'll have a line of low fat, low calorie. I'm also going to put in some computers with internet connections, gourmet, organic coffee, and perhaps I'll serve breakfast."

"That sounds like a wonderful idea. I like the idea of healthy foods and organics."

"How's this sound, Scotty. 'Goodies for You'?"

"I like it. When do you open up?"

"That's the problem. I've saved up some money, but I don't have quite all I need. I should have waited to buy the house, but you know, I wanted Sam to have a real home in a real neighborhood. Jake's wasn't a good place to raise a kid. You know that."

Scott agreed.

"I thought you'd understand. I have a business proposition

for you. You still have some money saved up?"

"About six grand, but I'm not really into business stuff."

"You don't have to get involved in business. This is an investment. The bank gives you interest. You invest the money with me, and you get dividends, and much more than the bank would give you."

"I don't know. The whole investment, business thing makes me uncomfortable."

"You know what a hard worker I am. You won't lose your money."

"Oh, I trust you, V.V. That not the problem."

"Put it this way. Now your money helps a big bank. This way it will help a friend, and it'll help put away a college fund for Sam. What are the career opportunities for a girl without a college education in Crescent City?"

She had pushed the right buttons, and Scott, given the choice between a big, impersonal company and a dear friend with a child, could only do one thing. He agreed. They'd meet at her bank to finalize things in a few days.

Maybe, after they got together again and he'd invested in her company, they just might start dating again. As a champion of healthy food, perhaps she had found her place in the world, her contribution to a better future.

V.V. looked very well, when they met at the bank. Her hair was shorter, and she dressed like a business woman. Scott was expecting and hoping for a kiss, but her greeting was a hand shake. She was friendly and genial, but all business.

After the papers were finalized, she took Scott to lunch, where she talked of her plans for the bakery and of Sam's happy adjustment to a neighborhood with other kids and good schools. She also said she'd been following Scott's articles and was very impressed with both his writing and reporting. "I knew you had it in you. You've become a fine journalist. I expect to see you working in San Francisco before long."

He confided that it was exactly what he hoped to do, that and get his novel published.

She asked what his novel was about, but since it was no longer the one in which she was cast, he gave her only a general outline.

The time slipped away, and he realized he was late getting back to the paper. As he excused himself, he took a chance and asked, "Now that we're partners, so to speak, perhaps we could meet for a drink after work now and then." When her brow furrowed, he added, "No pressure. Just old friends and business partners passing the time."

She conceded that she might be able to find a few minutes to do that.

Too much had built up in Scott behind his facade of nonchalance, and he confessed a small amount. "I've been too busy for a social life, getting tired of beer with the same folks at the trailer park, and a bit lonely for some interesting conversation. It would be nice to sit someplace other than the Tree House and have a quiet drink with someone I like and respect."

"Ok, Scott. Deal. Between the meetings you cover and my schedule, Monday's about the only day that works. Here's my card. Call me."

Scott felt good. They'd started out as friends before becoming lovers. At least they were friends again, and if they again became lovers, so much the better.

Back at the paper, news of Senator Bottoms came over the wire. She was giving a news conference, and Scott asked Rob to turn on the TV.

A group of reporters were interviewing the Senator, who was dressed in a lavender suit, skirt, not pants. Her plan had worked wonders. The tree sitters were all down and on their way home. Protests had stopped for the first time in years, and the timber companies were logging responsibly, under the watchful eyes of environmental inspectors. She was being referred to as a hero.

Then someone asked her if she had any other ground breaking legislation planned. She had, and she was ready to outline it. She was going to solve the Israel/Palestine problem. It was simple, according to her. Israel continues to get foreign aid, and an equivalent amount will go to Palestine. The condition for this would be that a firm border be drawn, delineating a boundary between the two counties, and all the violence would stop. If not, neither side got a damn thing.

Several people said that we could never cut Israel off, and she answered that there would probably be no need. The combination of carrot and stick should convince them that peace was in their best interest.

Again she was asked if she were running for President, and again she said that she still hadn't considered it seriously. However, this time she added that unfortunately Americans wouldn't elect a woman, no matter how qualified. To Scott, that sounded like a dare.

At the end of the conference, the network switched to the Capitol where a spokesman for the President said that her solution was simplistic and showed her severe lack of experience and knowledge of the complexities of foreign affairs. "A kitchen diplomatic," he called her.

Within two days it was clear who had the message that excited the country. Whether the President's people were right or wrong about her, she'd said something people had wanted to hear, that there was a solution and one that they could understand. More and more people were calling on her to run.

Pundits were debating her comment about the bias of the American voter. The women were fanning the flames by asking America if it were really that backward and provincial.

Sunday morning the papers carried a poll indicating that 57 percent had accepted her challenge and would vote for the better candidate without gender consideration. The poll also showed that 53 percent would vote for her. 14 percent thought that monthly bouts of PMS would render a woman too unstable for the job, and 9 percent felt that any candidate from the two major parties would be automatically untrustworthy. 3 percent said they intended to make a statement by voting for a cartoon character. Scott sought refuge in the familiar. He turned to the book reviews.

The *Slippers of Redundancy*, a new book by the author of *The Boots of Animosity*, was about a gruff but kind-hearted Interpol agent who was tracking a mad triple agent who was killing diplomatic couriers. Another book, *Naked Justice*, was the story of a handsome law student who was nominated for the Supreme Court by the first woman President.

There was a review of a non fiction book by a new author, Jojo Hoover. The book was *Sex Drugs and Redwoods: an Activist's Diary.*

Jesus H. Christ! Scott thought. That dumb ass little hillbilly wrote a book and got it published. He looked again and saw that the co author's name was also familiar. It was that arrogant college kid who was dating Rob's oldest daughter. Scott was so angry and frustrated that he slugged the wall as hard as he could. Since the wall was a thin piece of panel and the outer wall a thin piece of aluminum, his fist went through both, only to get rained on.

At the end of his emotional rope, Scott decided to take a walk and try to get his mind untangled. No sooner was he out the door than Michael Vole confronted him. Another man, one in a dark suit, was with him.

"Scott, this is pastor Pat P. Patterson of my congregation. I told him about you, and the Holy Spirit moved him to come here to reach out to you."

The pastor, who looked like a used car salesman from El Paso, Texas, offered a sweaty palm. "Brother Michael here says your faith is broken and you are angry at the Lord for not solving your personal problems. Remember, sometimes the Lord tests you to see if you are ready for the university of eternal life. If your SAT scores are too low, you have to go back and take Basic Faith 101."

Michael added, "Pastor Patterson was a University of California recruiter before he heard the word."

"Look, Pastor. The only problem I have is with Michael's lack of respect for my personal religious beliefs. If Job had to deal with this guy, the ending of that story would have been way different. Now, if you'll excuse me, I have something I gotta do."

Scott started walking, down the gravel road between the trailers, past Peaches' place to the cross street, down to the last row and left past Ben There's place, which still looked deserted. He kept walking down the bank, through the weeds and into the trees. He walked in ankle deep mud, through mixed forests, over a rise, up a small valley, and over another rise. He was trying to get himself lost.

He found himself in a thicket of ferns and rhododendrons. He pushed his way through and suddenly saw a light. It was the back door of the Tree House. He went in and headed straight to the bar.

"Shit. I can't even get lost. Give me a pitcher and a glass."

Scott saw Dusty at the end of the bar and walked over. He punched the big man on the arm and said, "Did you know that fucker, Jojo wrote a book?"

Dusty returned the punch to the arm, almost knocking Scott off his feet. "No, shit. Why that dude don't even read so good. Wrote himself a book, now did he?"

"Damn right. Now, next thing I know you'll be running for governor."

"I'd sure be a generous improvement over the weasel what's got the job now."

Scott looked at the lopsided grin on the big man's face, took in the homely wisdom of his statement, and he felt his anger dissipate. He felt a smile crack the icy mask of his face. "Damn you to hell, Dusty. I do believe you would make a better governor. My first contribution to your campaign will be to keep you in beer the rest of the goddamn day." Scott pushed his pitcher over to Dusty.

They made inane beer conversation for a few minutes when a young woman sauntered over to them. She was dressed in tight hip hugger jeans and a stretched, tube top, and she had a ripe body right out of Al Capp's famous "Lil Abner" cartoons.

The fullness of her melon-like breasts and thunder thighs was accentuated by her wasp waist. Her jeans struggled desperately to contain her. Her hair, bleached the color of straw, set off her full, pouty lips, covered with a quart of bright rid lipstick. Scott got an erection just watching her walk.

"Yo, Scott. This here's my little sister, Prudence. Pru, this here's my main man, Scott."

"Glad ta meetcha Scotty. Say, you one a them college boys?"

"I'm a reporter for the paper."

"Oh, I do like them professional boys. Buy a girl a beer?"

She sounded like a stereotypical hillbilly and dressed like a street walker, but she turned Scott on. He called for a glass and another pitcher of beer and filled her glass.

Turned out that she worked part time at the feed and seed store, the only place in the community Scott had never entered. She had a great sense of humor, telling one family story after another, mostly about family members getting drunk and getting into fights. Scott was both repelled and attracted, and the more she talked, the more they all drank.

At some point, Dusty winked at Scott and wandered off. With just the two of them, the conversation quickly degenerated to sexual banter. In spite of the voice of his inner prude, Scott invited her to his place. The rest of the evening was like a sensual dream or some X rated video. For the first time in his life, Scott experienced pure sexual pleasure without any notions of relationship or other distractions. They took turns on top, and they gave each other oral sex. They each tried things to drive the other wild. Scott found himself talking dirty to her, something he'd never considered with another woman, and it turned him on. She was screaming at him to fuck her hard. At some point they both passed out from exhaustion.

When Scott rolled over in the morning and saw Prudence sleeping, makeup smeared and hair tangled, he was bathed in a sea of conflicting emotions. As it all sorted out, he blamed himself for his lack of self control and self respect. He wasn't sure whether to cast her as a cheap slut or as the victim of his sexual excesses. He had assumed, based on just her appearance, that she was some easy woman. Was she just an innocent country girl whom he'd corrupted?

She was still sound asleep, and her purse was open next to the bed. He decided to have a peek to see what sort of woman he'd ended up with. He opened her wallet and found her identification. It wasn't a driver's license. It was a student ID. She was a junior in high school.

How the hell did she get served in the bar. Oh, yeah, she was part of the family. How come he didn't realize she was under age. He was drunk, and she was. . . He looked at her and thought that this didn't look like any school girl he'd ever seen. He looked at the clock. He needed to get ready for work, and she probably had to get to school. He decided to gently shake her.

"Huh, what? Oh, you, from the bar. Scotty. What's up?"

"I need to get to work, and you probably have to go to work or school, or something."

"Yeah, I guess." She stopped and listened to the tapping on the roof. "Shit, still raining. Drive me home."

"Sure, get dressed. Her full curvaceous body looked less appealing in the bright light of morning, with her age flashing in the air above her head like the welcome sign at the penitentiary. He watched her slip into her clothes and could only wonder if he were going to be arrested or shot by a member of the family.

She directed Scott to a rambling, two story wooden house with three very old sedans and at least eight pick up trucks parked on the lawn. He was looking nervously at the door and windows, expecting to see the flash of a gun barrel. She opened the car door and stopped half way out.

"You probably wanna see me again, but I gotta tell you about my boyfriend. He's on the football team, big and jealous, so you most likely get yo ass kicked, but I'm worth it."

Scott was about to say he wasn't afraid of some punk kid

football player, and if the kid wanted a piece of him, let him come on. Luckily Scott's brain clicked on before his mouth galloped away. This was his out. "I don't want to get punched out by some big ball player. Let's just forget we met."

"Why, you're chicken."

Scott swallowed hard and forced the words out. "Yeah, that's right. I'm chicken. Don't say anything, OK?"

"Hell, I thought you'd fight over me. Fuckin' wimp." She jumped out of the car and went in. Scott had no idea what she'd tell her folks or if they'd come looking for him with the sheriff.

He called V.V. from work, just as planned, and they arranged to meet at a downtown pub after work.

He had to tell her about his experience with Prudence, hoping she could calm his worries.

"What's your take on this girl staying out all night? What if her folks force the truth out of her?"

"Scott, you're from a nice middle class background. Parents set curfews for their high school kids, and they want to meet any boy who takes their daughter out. I've met these people. They don't come from the same place. It's likely the parents neither knew nor cared about the girl's whereabouts. The damn brother set it up, knowing you'd take her home."

"You think?"

"Well, yeah. Booze, sex and fighting are what the Hoovers are all about. If you hear anything more, it'll be from the no neck boyfriend. So, don't worry about it."

It was all logical, but telling Scott not to worry was like telling a dog not to bark.

She teased him for being a horn dog who'd go after anything female. Scott tried desperately to convince her that he really wasn't that way, that he'd just had a moment of weakness.

"Every time a cute young thing shakes her ass, men have a moment of weakness." She laughed like crazy.

Her accusations bothered him all evening. He wasn't just interested in getting laid. He really wanted a relationship with an intelligent woman with goals and a social consciousness. He hated to be compared to guys like Buck and Dusty. He was, after all, a sensitive artist, a man who wanted to tap the essence of real life and to add something of value to the human condition. He wasn't, goddamnit, just a horn dog.

16.

That Wednesday, when he got home, there was a phone message from Buck, informing him that Les Apt or Ben There, or whatever his name was, was home. Buck had seen him come in.

For some reason Scott felt he must see the old guy again. He walked quickly to the far end of the park, found the guy's place and started for the door, which opened before he could reach it.

The guy came out and smiled absently at Scott, apparently not recognizing him.

"Do you remember me?"

"Are you Scott Mukis, the man with problems steering his motorcycle and probably his life? I'm Roger Wilco."

"I thought you were Ben There."

"I might have been there, but that doesn't matter much with things happening on a different frequency. If you're here to ask about the surf, it wasn't very good, with the storm and all."

Scott didn't want to be rude, but he couldn't help blurting out what was on his mind. "Do you really have multiple personalities?"

"No. Actually, I tried that as a liberating activity, but I find having no personalities much better."

"That's silly. You have to have a personality."

"Why? It locks you in, limits who and what you can be. Without a personality, you can be anything or anyone you want at each moment in time.

"Is that your message?"

"Message? What do you mean?" The guy looked genuinely confused.

"I mean, what you're trying to tell the world."

"Goodness, Scott. I'm not trying to tell the world anything. I don't have words for the world."

"Well, you come off like some goddamn sage. You must

214

have something profound to share with humanity. I mean, you talk like you do."

"If we're going to talk, let's walk. It seems odd to just stand here exchanging comments." They started down the rows of trailers.

"Scott, I can't help you. I don't have anything profound or wise or helpful for the world or your condition. You and the world need to do your own repairs."

"I'm sorry if you thought I was asking for something for myself. I'm thinking of what you want to contribute to humanity."

"I'm not fond enough of humanity to want to contribute anything, assuming I had something humanity would want."

"Shit! What I'm trying to say is, why are you here?"

"My residence is here. You were just at my door."

Scott was frustrated. He waved his arms expansively. "No, no, I mean here!"

"Oh. So, why do you think there is a reason implied in being what you call 'here'?"

"There has to be, there has to be some reason why we were born and became who we are. Our lives have to mean something."

"Well, Scott, that might be, but it doesn't necessarily have to be. This ancient notion that God put us here to fulfill his complex plan seems rather like grasping for straws. Besides the comfort if offers, what other things underlie that assumption?" As he talked, he started making hand gestures at the trees, like a conductor with an orchestra.

Connecting it all to God's plan reminded Scott of Michael and his preacher, and made him feel that was talking like those insufferable boors. Could there be, he thought, some purpose or destiny apart from some almighty plan? Do we need a purpose simply because we are human and can think in terms of higher purposes?

What he said was, "No, I mean a humanistic purpose, something like Jung and his archetypes, something basic in the human condition."

"Do you really mean that, or are you just having trouble swallowing the standard religious package that goes with this whole purpose or destiny thing?" The old guy started to skip, and Scott had to hurry to keep up.

"No. Maybe it's like there this underlying human thing, and some people call it God, and others call it different things, but it's essential to a person's fulfillment."

The old guy grinned and stroked his messy gray beard. "So, because we're social animals, like the great apes, we find fulfillment in acts that are rooted in the context of the community. Then, if the human community evolves, the acts of fulfillment change. Purpose is relative. Higher states of living are relative. Virtue is relative. Good grief, Scott, you and I are on the same trip. Are you saying the only value is growth, which is change, which is fluid, which always eludes definition? So you believe that the late Mother Theresa and a junkie in the gutter are moral equals? Scott, you're a profound philosopher."

"No, damn it, that's not what I meant. There are values implicit in the human condition, whether they come from God or from... from somewhere else. You just sense it."

"If you are removed from all human societies, do you still sense it?"

"Well, I'm not... Yeah, it's part of being human."

"I'm human, and I don't sense anything at all, except for these lovely woods. So if you look into these woods carefully and tell me what you see, we may find a clue to this quandary."

Scott wasn't sure what he was looking for, but he peered intently into the woods, looking for something that would connect the ideas they'd discussed. When nothing seemed to manifest, he turned back to his companion, who suddenly wasn't there. He had taken those few moments to duck out, to slip between trailers and disappear.

It's the season of assholes, Scott figured. He wrote the guy off as an old burn out doper who had probably been brilliant before he fried his brains. Scott made a mental note to keep his dope use strictly moderated.

A phone call came in to both the paper and the police. It had been only a couple of days since the political poll in response to Senator Bottoms' challenge about the country not being willing to elect a woman. Some angry sounding guy claimed to be from an organization called GMMTL, which stood for God Meant Men to Lead. The guy said it was immoral and an affront to God to have a woman president. His group would take to the streets with guns to keep it from happening.

Within hours another almost identical call was received by the paper and the police in Eureka. Then, the following morning, the same calls came through in San Francisco and San Jose. The next day it happened in Sacramento. The various news services picked up, announcing that there was some radical group set to fight over a woman president.

Scott was surprised to have these reactionary calls come in from normally liberal Northern California. He could have expected something like this in other parts of the country.

In Saturday's paper, the same kind of calls started coming in to the media from isolated communities in Idaho, Montana, Utah, and the rural south. To Scott, this fit the profile. He assumed and hoped that this group was a very small minority.

As he read the paper, the sun came out for a short time, so Scott decided to take a walk in the state park to gain some perspective on his fellow man. The park was open again to the public, but almost deserted due to the weather. The dampness had brought out exotic mushrooms of various sizes and colors. There were a few people picking them. Some looked like people who collect to sell, some appeared to be gourmets, and others looked like hippies looking for an organic high. He wondered how many people died each year in these forests by mistaking one mushroom for another.

The trees had grown lichens and other tiny organisms that created streaks of assorted colors in the deep barks. The wet leaves and needles glistened on the saturated forest floor. A guy he recognized from the Tree House came out of the woods carrying a basket of mushrooms.

He walked right up to Scott and put out the palm of his hand. "Careful, don't step on it."

Scott looked down to see a small patch of tan mushrooms. "Are those edible?"

"Yeah, had four already today." He grinned broadly. "Magic mushrooms." He picked one, ate it, picked another and handed it to Scott."

"I don't want to take a chance getting poisoned."

"I've picked these for years. I've eaten them, sold them, and no one has ever been poisoned."

"Well, I don't want to freak out in the woods and get lost."

"Trust me buddy. You're the guy who sometimes drinks with Dusty, right? One will hardly get you a buzz. Are you getting into all the forest colors?"

When Scott nodded, he continued. "There's a saying, 'a few mushrooms for color.' It's true."

Scott was nervous, but at the same time he felt like a wimp. Finally, he reached out, took it and bit into it. It tasted good. He finished it, thanked the guy and continued on his way.

In a few minutes something subtly changed. The colors were more vivid, and the scene around him was imbued with more significance. It was like the way he imagined his life. Under the surface of the every day, there existed a level at which each action was important and touched on all aspects of the human condition. He liked the feelings. He spent the next hour or so feeling the important message coded in the forest, and he understood why people would camp for weeks or months to protect them.

Slowly the feelings slipped away, and the drizzle that would soon become a downpour started. Scott walked back to the highway and back toward home. He stopped at the store for some snacks and was waiting behind a no-neck kid at the counter.

As he stepped up, the clerk rang him up and said, "That'll be seven-fifty Mr. Mukis."

The no-neck stopped and turned around. "Mukis. You Scott Mukis, wimp reporter?"

"I'm Scott. What's it to you?" He was in no mood for some rude punk.

"You keep away from my girl or I'll kick your skinny ass."

"Your girl. Let me guess. Prudence?"

"Yeah, I know you want her, but you know I'll trash you if you even look at her."

"I don't want your girlfriend, and I don't want to talk to you. Get lost."

"Watch it reporter boy. I might kick your ass just for fun."

Scott turned to look squarely at him. He was almost as tall as Scott but outweighed him by at least thirty pounds. But he looked slow and clumsy like a high school defensive lineman and not a running back. He had a big smirk on his face, and he'd pushed Scott a bit too far.

Scott punched him in the face, and before the guy could recover his balance, Scott got him in the gut and then on the jaw. In less than a minute it was over. The big kid had only landed one punch and was now sitting on the floor, shaking his head and looking dazed.

"I told you I'm not interested in your girlfriend. Do me a favor and forget my name." Scott walked out, feeling decidedly better.

Sunday's book review promoted a confession book by a teenaged girl who'd had sex with over 600 adult men, for fun or money. Some were important businessmen, community leaders and even politicians. Apparently, she named names and described events quite graphically.

There was a new mystery thriller about a female detective who was tracking a woman serial killer who picked up men in bars, went home with them and cut their throats while they slept.

While he didn't think he'd get his throat cut, he was off women. His encounters were increasingly more and more disastrous. He vowed to concentrate on his routine of work, the gym, writing, reading, and Monday drinks with V.V., until the right woman came along, one he could have a healthy, real relationship with.

As was his habit, he turned to the front page only after reading the book reviews. It turns out that there was a sudden, nation wide backlash against the GMMTL people. Letters and calls had been pouring into papers and TV news stations. People were even saying that they would vote for a woman simply because it was damn high time a woman got the job.

This was another development Scott could obsess over. He couldn't get over that this GMMTL thing started in the same place that the activist suicides began, right in his back yard. He began to think that Northern California was the true heart of American craziness.

With people all over the country announcing their total opposition to the ideas of GMMTL, it was natural that the people who take polls would take another. This time 63 percent would vote for Bottoms. Of that group, 15 percent would do so just because she was a woman and to tell the GMMTL to fuck off. The same 9 percent felt that candidates from the two major parties are automatically untrustworthy, and now 7 percent still planned to vote for a cartoon character.

Over the next several weeks anti GMMTL demonstrations made the papers, but there wasn't any visible GMMTL activity. For Scott's work routine, the only breaks were stops at the auto parts store to replace wipers that seemed to wear out in weeks and his final religious confrontation with Michael.

Hardly a day had gone by without Michael advising him on the state of his soul or giving him some literature with appropriate Bible verses to consult. One Sunday Michael had come back from church particularly filled with holiness and had cornered Scott as he started out for his walk.

Scott had just gotten off the phone with Buck. He'd complained about what an annoying son of a bitch Michael had become. Then he'd added, "What do you think of those GMMTL characters?"

"What characters? Oh, you mean that anti woman president stuff. Haven't really paid attention, but it confirms my opinions about what assholes my fellow humans can be. I love to hear about this shit."

"Yeah, but what do you think about it all apparently starting in Crescent City?"

"No? Really? I'll be damned. We are the asshole capitol of the country."

Buck had switched the subject back to Michael, wanting to know every detail. He said he'd been wanting to mess with Michael's head for weeks, and this looked to be the day. He'd hung up the phone and had come up almost jogging.

He pointed to Michael, who was holding out a pamphlet, and shouted. "Hold on there."

Michael turned, pamphlet still in the air. He introduced himself and asked if Buck were a friend of Scott's, and if so, was he concerned about his friend's soul.

Buck asked, "You read the Bible and believe in Jesus?"

When Michael affirmed that, Buck launched his attack. "You believe in a prophet who died over two thousand years ago. You consider him divine and infallible?" He took Michael's Bible out of his hand. "Do you bother to read this? Jesus says in one scene that some people gathered there with him would live to see God's kingdom come to earth. He figured that it would happen in that generation, and he was wrong. He screwed up, got his facts mixed up, picked up the wrong message from his crystal ball. The spam filter had blocked his messages from the Almighty. He was fallible, a mortal like you. So get over it."

"You aren't interpreting the verses correctly. Come to our Bible study and learn the truth."

Then Buck's face lit up in a grin that spelled triumph and pure sarcastic fun.

"You claim to know the truth, God's will. Has he ever talked directly to you? Does he come to you at night in person to impart his secrets? No? I thought not. On the other hand,

Satan comes to me in person. He confides in me. I do his bidding on earth." He took a moment to savor the look of shock on Michael's face. " That's right!" His voice was getting louder, and he was gesturing wildly, which seemed to match the increasing violence of the storm. "This man's soul belongs to the Prince of Darkness, and the troops of heaven shall not prevail. I know this because," At this point he raised his voice to a howl and thrust his fists to the sky, "I am... I am, the Antichrist!"

Just then, as luck would have it, a flash of lightning went off over Buck's shoulder, and the roll of thunder followed his last word. Scott had to admit to himself that he was impressed and almost convinced.

Michael went ashen. "You're some kind of a madman. I'm not going to subject myself to this any longer." He started for his door, and Buck added to the effect by disgorging the most diabolical laughter.

"Don't think he'll be bothering you much any longer. Don't thank me. Buy me a beer tonight."

That night Buck persuaded Scott to publicly name him king of the assholes. An announcement was made to the bar in general, and everyone except a couple of Southern Baptists in the corner stepped up to buy a round. Several said they could hardly wait to try that on the next Jehovah's Witness who showed up at the door.

Dusty came over to get his share of the free beer. He slapped Scott on the back and said, "I hear you kicked ass on little sister's boyfriend."

"Yeah," Scott snarled. "You got a problem with that."

"Not at all, but I gotta problem with yo attitude. Jus' cause you whooped some kid, don't mean you kin get bad with me."

Scott looked up at Dusty. "I kinda like kicking ass. You mind your manners, or you'll be next." He flashed his best smug grin.

Dusty pulled Scott to his feet, and Scott came up swinging. Dusty could hit harder, but Scott's gym routine had given him more endurance. In the end, which came in two or three minutes, both men were spent and sprawled in neutral chairs. The consensus was that Scott had held the bigger and meaner man to a draw; therefore Dusty should buy the next round. Then came uncounted rounds of beer and lies that lasted until closing time.

Scott kept his alarm set for 6:30, which in itself is a stretch for someone becoming a night person, but one morning something rang that wasn't an alarm. Scott dreamed it was the back to work whistle in Hell, and it wouldn't stop. He finally opened his eyes and realized it was the phone, and it was quarter to six.

It was his sister. Becky was excited, talking a mile a minute. It started to dawn on Scott that the call concerned Senator Bottoms. She had announced in Washington DC, where it was almost nine in the morning, that she was indeed running for President. Becky was talking about the first woman President and saying she needed him to write about her candidacy. She saved the forests, so he'd do what he could, even though the idea of a woman President seemed to break a very comfortable and emotionally safe tradition. At not even six in the morning, things were still changing too fast for comfort.

February was touted as the rainiest month of the year in the Pacific Northwest, and the predictions were coming true. Scott hadn't seen a patch of blue in the sky for over a week. The trailer park roads had become mud and almost impassible. The highway was slippery, and wherever it was cut into the hill, mud slides were becoming regular events.

He had written about what a visionary the Senator was, and how the country needed her fresh perspective. In fact he had written two or three pieces about politics, all contrasting Bottoms with the same old, same old in the capitol. He'd also written a piece about his weird neighbor, Les Apt, Roger Wilco, Ben There, or whatever his real name was. The piece was titled "Burned out Brilliance." It was to be the first of a series about great minds that had imploded through experimentation, either mental or chemical. It was a great premise, but he had no follow up.

These few highlights held him together through weeks of routine. His career was stuck, and there was no easy way to rationalize it. He really cared for Rob and the rest of the crew, but he wanted to try his wings, and Crescent City was too small a cage to allow flight. He wrote up a resume, bundled up his best pieces, and sent them off to the San Francisco Chronicle and a few other California papers. In the weeks he waited for replies, he kept to his routine.

The workouts in the gym had actually added almost ten pounds to his thin frame, but only with the input of over four thousand calories a day. Scott had the metabolism of a humming bird. He was still thin, but in the best shape of his life, and he was poised for a career surge that would take him, running and swinging, to the capitols of the world.

17.

His routine was interrupted by an inevitable consequence of the incessant rain. A tree had come down, taking the power lines and two poles with it. Sputtering electricity, they'd blocked the highway to town, above the junction. He couldn't get to work. It was his first missed day in three quarters of a year. Scott called Rob, who wasn't worried. "You've got a computer and some meeting notes. Work at home. On second thought, no power or phones, so take a rest. You're caught up, we have enough weather news to fill the issue, and I can't remember the last day off you took. Don't think about the paper, and that's an order."

He'd never been home on a weekday that wasn't a holiday, and he wasn't sure what to do. He called the Chronicle, which hadn't made a decision on him yet. Then he realized he hadn't talked to Jake or Peaches in weeks, so he walked down to the shop.

He hadn't imagined motorcycle repairs to be a going concern in the middle of winter in one of the wettest places in the country, but the shop was filled with bikes. This apparently was the season to drop them off and get whatever needed fixing fixed.

Peaches looked cute in the coveralls that seemed too big for her. Smudges of grease made it look like she was wearing war paint. She gave him the hug that reminded them both that he had been her savior when she was down and out and that she would never forget it.

Jake was replacing a damaged crank shaft, and he'd just disassembled the entire engine and was taking a quick break. "Scott, good to see you. Pulling a sick day, or hemmed in by the downed tree?"

"Tree. How's business, and how's Peaches doing?"

"Best sit down, Scott. Peaches has turned this business

225

around, her, plus the time share thing. Anyway, I'm making her a partner, and we're opening a shop in town. It'll be a new and used showroom, and a one day tune shop. Yeah, we're a dealer now. Anyway, I'm staying out here, doing the heavy repair, and she's running the shop in town and doing tunes. Her little girl-friend, the musician, will work the sales floor. Your old girl friend, V.V., does the books for her new business and said she'd do ours for a small fee. We got a loan to help us open the new shop. You see, it seems there's this here fund down in Santa Barbara that makes loans to businesses run in full or part by women. Peaches talked to this gal by the name of Susie Takora, and we got the loan."

"Santa Barbara?" That was way too coincidental.

Peaches looked up. "Yup. Funny thing. She's like getting all this info on us, and all. Said we'd get a stack of papers to fill out, and those would be reviewed by their people, and we'd know in a couple of months. Three, maybe four hours later she called back to check on the name of this place and the location. Then she asked me if I knew you. I told her about how we met and you got me set up like this. Well, she said not to bother with forms. She's sending out the loan agreement. We fill it out, notarize it, and send it back. They get it, and there's a check in the mail. Don't know how they know you, but even when you're not helping me, you're helping me. I swear, if I ever go back to men, you'll be on the top of my list."

"What about me?" Jake demanded.

"You'll be twelve from the top, just below that hunk in my favorite soap opera."

His sister was behind this. The world was getting too damn small, and the family reached even up to the corner of the state. He saw himself as the prodigal, and Becky as the new godfather.

He stumbled out of the shop and couldn't believe his eyes. There was a patch of blue, and the rain had taken a long overdue coffee break.

He grabbed this opportunity to head for the park and a quick hike. Once in the woods, he realized that perhaps Peaches might have been the right woman for him, and he'd foolishly let her slip away. What other mistakes might he make? It was women. They simply didn't make sense. By the time he understood them and what they wanted, they were gone. It wasn't fair.

Scott saw all those mushrooms brought up by the rainy weather. They were colorful and intimidating. He wanted to feel what he'd felt that day, but every time he picked one and examined it, he found himself unsure and unwilling to take a chance. It was frustrating, knowing the ones that brought pleasure were mixed with the ones that brought painful death.

He'd enjoyed the solitary woods for almost an hour when he saw someone coming through the trees. It was Prudence, and it was too late to hide.

"Yo, Scotty. It was so cool how you stomped Cal. I'd a figured he'd a kicked your ass. I guess you must want me."

"He just pissed me off. I didn't mean to get into it with him. Say what are you doing out here? Aren't you supposed to be in school?"

"So I heard. School's boring, and I thought I'd get me some 'shrooms. Look at these beauties." She showed him a basket of the ones he'd been unsure of.

"You shouldn't be doing this. It's dangerous. It's easy to mistake the good ones for the poison ones."

"Oh Scotty. You's such a trip. I been pickin' and eatin' these since I was twelve. I maybe don't know history or algebra, but I know 'shrooms. Here, walk with me, and I'll show you."

Scott's first instinct was to get away from this girl, but he was fascinated by a really pleasant high free and right down the road from his house. He agreed to walk with her for a spell.

"She picked a mushroom and put it in the basket. Scott picked one, and she shook her head. After about a half hour, Scott was picking the right ones consistently.

She sat down on a log and popped a few into her mouth. "Here, Scotty, you picked them. Might's well enjoy them."

It took a few moments to get his courage up, but this girl had just popped a bunch into her mouth, and she'd been doing it for years, so he grabbed a handful and ate them.

They sat there for a few minutes making small talk. She was uneducated, but not stupid. She was mature and had a deep understanding of the world of the streets and how people have to relate in an effort to survive. In some ways, he thought, she was more experienced than he, considering his insulated, middle class upbringing. He was grudgingly starting to respect her when the mushrooms started to work. First it was the colors, and then he looked at her, and she changed from an innocent little girl, through each stage of growth, to a wizened old woman. He saw her entire history, past and future, and he was blown away. Even a seemingly simple person has almost infinite complexity, he thought. Having thought that, he reflected on it and decided it was totally profound. He suspected that he was high.

He said what was on his mind, that he'd underestimated her, and that there was more to her than he'd imagined.

That made her smile. "Am I a kid or a woman to you?"

Put on the spot, he answered that he thought of her as a woman.

She walked slowly over to him, popped a mushroom into his mouth, and smiled as he chewed and swallowed. Then she dropped her pack, unbuttoned her shirt and pulled it open.
Scott was face to face with those huge, firm breasts, nipples hard from the winter chill. She pulled him to his feet and pressed her body and her lips against him.

"Let's go back to your place. I'm gonna turn you into a big ol' mass o' jelly."

Scott had an instant erection. He wanted her so much his brain was on fire, but that little voice was screaming warnings. "I can't Prudence."

"Yes you can. You proved that last time."

"No, I mean I shouldn't. This isn't right."

"No guy says no to me. Well, there was one, but he was gay, an' even he was tempted."

She made herself sound so worldly. "No guys, like a sixteen year old's had a lot."

"At least a couple hundred, best I can recall." She licked her finger and ran it down his chest to his crotch. "And you. Had many women?"

"Half dozen or so." He was surprised at his own honesty.

"Oh, an' I'm the kid?"

"You're underage, jail bait. There's laws, and anyone your age having that much sex has got problems. You should get counseling."

"So somethin's wrong with sex. Ain't it natural?"

"That's not what I mean."

She kissed him hard again and ran her hand up his thigh. "You want me, and you can't say no to me, so let's go find your bed, lest you want to do it in the woods."

They started walking, and Scott was having that argument in his mind. She was a teen, and what he was thinking of doing was both illegal and immoral. He was also giving into his base urges when his mind and higher will were saying no. But, still, age is arbitrary. There are all kinds of child prodigies, like music talents, twelve year olds in college, teens winning the Olympics. That was it. She was a prodigy, a sexual prodigy. At sixteen she had more sexual experience then he may ever have, particularly at the rate he'd been going lately. Would he have denied Mozart the right to play a recital as a child? Obviously not. Why then should he deny her the practice of her one natural gift?

The argument was getting more and more convoluted as they stepped out on the highway. Within a minute, Scott spotted a sheriff's car. It was Marco, the local deputy who patrolled the neighborhood. He'd interviewed Marco a few weeks back for his weekly column, and the deputy had said he'd gotten to know almost everyone in the area.

Marco honked and waved at Scott. Then Scott realized that he may also been waving at Prudence.

He'd been spotted walking with an underage girl on a

school day, a girl with a reputation for being promiscuous. Marco would have no trouble putting two and two together. All he had to do was circle around and wait a few minutes. Then he'd kick in the door and catch Scott in the act, and it's prison for the next ten years. Scott felt the rising bile of pure panic.

He knew if he tried to explain this to Prudence, she would seduce him again, and he wouldn't get away. The shrooms, he decided, had weakened his will and resistance. His only chance was to get away quickly.

He almost screamed. "I can't do this. I can't see you again!" and before she could respond, he bolted across the highway, narrowly missing being run down by a logging truck southbound on 199.

Back home, Scott saw that the power was back, so he locked the door and turned off the lights. And to keep Prudence from luring him out with her seductive talk, he put on a CD and slipped on his headphones. In the relative safety of his bed, he started to relax.

An hour had passed, so Scott figured Prudence had gone home. He took off the 'phones and turned on his laptop. Then there was a knock on the door.

"Go away, Prudence. You can't come in."

"Scott, it's Peaches."

"Peaches. Are you alone?"

"Yeah."

"Are you sure?"

"I'm looking around, Scott. There's nobody around. Open up."

She looked bewildered by his behavior, but she got right to the point. "Why not take over my place?"

He told her he didn't follow her.

"When we open the other shop, there's no point making the commute. Paula and I found a cute place, rent to buy. I'd like to own some day. So, it's almost the same price to live in my place, and there's almost twice the room. You'd even have a real bedroom."

"But no bed. I don't have furniture."

"I'm leaving it all. It all belonged to Emily. We'll get new stuff."

Until that moment it hadn't dawned on Scott that he'd been able to afford a better place for months. He would have gone on the same way, the same guy who'd showed up months ago without a job and with little money. When Peaches pointed it out, it was obvious. Sure he'd take the place. He could bring respectable women back there. It was a place Madd would have come to. He sure as hell missed her.

The next day at work a story came in about a trucker who had just missed hitting a tree hugger activist. The guy was quoted as saying, "If it hadn't of been for my quick reflexes, I woulda killed the guy. I thought since that liberal woman senator had got that fool bill passed, this stuff was gonna stop."

Scott looked at Rob, who had shown him the story, and explained that he was the one, and he hadn't seen the truck coming when he made the dash.

Rob suggested that Scott might want to write his version, not that the major media would give it much space. Activists running in front of trucks make news; dumb reporters who don't look where they're going, don't.

None the less, Scott set about writing the truth of the matter and had almost finished when Rob came up with another wire story. Seems the anonymous spokesman for the highway suicide group had called the news service and made the following statement: "This brave and dedicated member of our group had no intention of being run over. This was done as a demonstration and a reminder. We want the timber industry to consider the consequences should they fail to abide by the new law."

Rob shook his head. "Your version doesn't sound as interesting, but by all means, tell it."

A small truth about perception and the ability of news coverage to make reality settled over Scott's consciousness. He shrugged. "What's the use."

When he got home, Scott called Buck. "It was you wasn't it?"

"It's always me, but I'm self absorbed. What are you talking about?"

"Me almost being hit by a truck. You said it was a demonstration."

"That was you. Wow, the paper said you're a brave and dedicated activist. I didn't know."

Scott raised his voice in frustration. "Damn it. Don't deny it. You planted that lame-assed story."

"Right, Scott. And I'm responsible for all those Elvis sightings and the stuff about UFOs landing in trailer parks. Love to talk Scott, but there's a woman here. You understand."

Before Scott could object Buck had hung up.

Scott entertained the possibility that perhaps it was coincidence and Buck wasn't the one after all. However, when he went out to his car in the morning, there was a new bumper sticker. It read, "The Truth is Only What You Make it."

It was a week before Scott and Buck talked again, and by then Buck acted as if he'd forgotten the whole incident.

As Peaches moved out, Scott moved in. It was great to have a place with a real bedroom. He set up his computer by a window in the living room. He had a view of the redwoods. The small TV was in the corner, and Emily's old couch was still comfortable. The double bed was no larger than his old pull out, but it was much more comfortable. The place was bigger, newer, and best of all, away from that religious fanatic, Michael.

Still, Scott considered himself an open minded man, and he understood that Michael was only trying to be helpful in his own, obnoxious way. He'd treated, or rather he'd let Buck treat Michael rather badly.

On his last load of clothes, he knocked at his soon to be ex neighbor's door.

Michael opened the door cautiously. "Yes, Scott, what can I do for you?"

"I just wanted to say that I'm sorry about the way my friend treated you. He's kind of weird sometimes."

"I rather think he's a dangerous nut, but your choice of friends is obviously not my concern. Where are you moving?"

"Two rows over and back four or five. Bigger place. Anyway, I know you were concerned about me, but we're all a bit touchy about our religious beliefs, me included. No hard feelings?" He stuck out his hand.

Michael looked at Scott's hand for a few moments, kind of like he was looking at a fresh turd. Then he shrugged and shook hands. "Anyway, Scott. You know where I am, and you know where I'm coming from, if you ever want to talk. By the way. Does your friend really believe he's the Antichrist?"

Scott thought about it for a moment and started to smile. "You know, I think he very likely does."

With few exceptions, the days were all the same. The sky looked like a huge piece of slate had been put in place about a hundred feet above ground, blocking the stars and the sun. Winter was thinking about retiring and turning the show over to spring, and still it rained. Scott hadn't dated or even cruised the singles bars. His routine was work, the gym and writing. He had set the Presidents' Day weekend as the deadline for finishing his novel about the sociologist and Easter for finishing the new one about the forest wars, and he'd made the first deadline. Left with only one project, he rested for a few days and then poured himself into the forest crisis book. The main character would be a reporter who follows the story and gets involved in it. He could take the facts and easily turn them into fiction. After all, he'd been there and seen the whole thing. He could also work in the character of Buck, making him the mysterious phone tipper. He cast Cobra Lily as the deeply committed female love interest. It would be great. He set up a daily writing schedule and began working on it at a minimum of a thousand words a day.

His routine was run through reality's document shredder with a phone call one night. It was Madd. Scott's heart skipped, turned flips, and danced the Texas two step before taking a long pause.

"Madd, I've missed you. I've been thinking about you. What's up?"

"I want to invite you to a book reading and signing. It'll be a week from Saturday at Northtown Books in downtown Arcata."

"Yeah, sure. I didn't know you wrote a book." Scott was curious, pleased, and just a bit envious that she had a book published and he didn't.

"Well, it's something I've been working on now and then, but I decided to make it a general reader work, not just something for other professionals or a class text. And, I'm inviting you because you were the inspiration for my finishing it and getting it published."

That got his attention. He'd inspired her, as she had inspired him. He'd always known they were made for each other. It was going to finally happen. "You know, I finished a book recently too."

"Bring a copy down. I'd love to see it. You are coming?"

"Naturally. What's the book?"

"It's titled *Changing Times; Changing Roles*. It's mostly concerned with the shift in women's roles in this country and how that shift has affected men's roles. You see, I've put men in three categories, and you know how I love to put men in their places. There are the men who have always supported women's equality and advancement. They've taken the partnership position, and for them the changes in the work place, political arena and the rest are natural and comfortable."

"Yeah," Scott replied. "The enlightened men." He considered himself in that category, which was obviously the reason he'd inspired her.

"Right, Scott. Then there are the men who think they are cool with the changes and voice support. But they are confused and a bit frightened by the new female roles. They are always trying to catch up, secretly hoping that when it all settles men's roles will remain much the same. And then there are the guys who deny anything is changing, who sit around with their buddies talking the macho talk and claiming a woman's place is in the kitchen. They find some traditional woman, one with no skills or career, and they ignore everything outside their little sphere."

"Sounds like a fascinating book."

"I'm making it sound too simple. There's a lot more to it, and those are only rough categories. Anyway, there's a lot of research and data involved. The book's actually selling, and the publisher is setting up a book tour, starting in my back yard."

"Wonderful. I'll see you on Saturday. Perhaps we could go out after, drinks, dinner, you know."

"Scott, you remember my situation. We'll talk on Saturday."

Ok, Scott thought. She wants to break up with this guy, but she doesn't want to hurt him. She needs a way to let him down easy. She needs me to reassure her that we do have a future and to give her the courage to make the break. She needs me to be a strong, take charge man, to be someone she can lean on. He vowed to guide her through her impasse and to re establish their relationship.

The day of the reading, Scott got an early start, after putting on his best jeans and shirt. He could have taken the Harley, but the rain, which had changed from winter storm to spring constant drizzles and sprinkles, had not let up. He arrived early, and the little store was already filling up. Madd looked good. Perhaps she'd lost a bit of weight, maybe a new hair style. She called him over and introduced him to the smug looking jerk she was going with. Scott shook his hand and mumbled some trivial greeting, but he was so busy sizing up the guy, that he didn't even catch the name.

Before Scott could engage in a male show of plumage that included comparisons of desirable traits, the store owner got up to introduce Maddie. He made sure the crowd knew that she was a respected professor at the university and had published extensively in scholarly journals.

Then she got up and talked about the genesis of the book idea. Along the way, she introduced Scott as the person who had made her realize that she should finish and publish the work. She talked and read brilliantly, before fielding questions.

When it was all over, including the book signing, Scott asked Madd if he could talk to her alone for a minute. After handing her a copy of his manuscript, he started in with the assumption that she wanted to break up with the boyfriend and get back together with Scott. Then he was about to launch into a scenario about how they'd break it to him and get rid of him. She stopped him.

"Scott, you and I never really were. We were a temporary thing. I'm engaged to be married. We're buying a house together. We have love, mutual interests, and all the rest. I'm really sorry, Scotty, if you came all the way down here expecting something else."

Then she rubbed salt into the wound by asking him if he'd like to join the two of them for dinner. He made his excuses and started to leave. She promised to read his manuscript and if appropriate, send it to her editor.

As she walked back to talk with her boyfriend and the others in her group, Scott watched her, wondering why he'd thought she'd lost weight. Her ass was definitely wider then he remembered.

The situation being what it was, he was sorry he'd given the book to her. His heart was splattered, like a rotten egg, on each page. The saving point was that she might get it to someone who could get it published. As it was, seven copies had been sent out, and he'd been waiting, none too patiently, for the replies.

The first polite rejection came the day before Maddie's next call.

"I read your book," she said over the phone. "Typed up some comments, and put it in the mail. I felt I should call. I guess that's because I'm the caring, maternal type. I guess the

Mary character is supposed to be me, and obviously Steve is you. Is that how you see me? That's not me, not even from the same planet."

Scott felt the need to defend himself. "I picked up on deeply hidden character traits and amplified them for the sake of the story."

"I'm not buying that at all. You pasted my image on your ideal woman, if that woman even exists. I don't think Steve is anything like you either. Scott, you've got real people to draw from, complex people. These characters are soap opera people. I'm sorry, but I have to be honest."

Scott argued that the truth of the story necessitated taking liberties with the characters, but she wouldn't accept that. He argued that he wanted to show them as the ideal people they could be, but she didn't accept that. He argued that there was a big "T" truth that took precedence over the small "t" truths, but she rejected that too.

In the end she simply wished him luck and said good bye.

Scott continued working on his forest novel, which was coming along nicely, but around nine one night he felt restless. He'd beat back the urge to walk to the Tree House, not wanting to run into Prudence or have to talk with her dim-witted brother. Instead, he did something he rarely did on a week night, he drove back into town.

The weather had improved. The rain had let up and had been replaced by a cold, wet wind off the ocean. He wore a ski parka.

Crescent City had at any given time one bar that had an active singles scene. Although he'd never been there, he was aware of the one currently in favor with the locals. He wasn't really on the prowl, just looking for some diversion, perhaps some company.

Week nights meant a DJ rather than a band, but the people who hung out there seemed to like it, as the guy played nothing but dance music. Scott sat at the bar, nursing a beer and watching the couples connect and disconnect around the room. One gal seemed to dance with a different guy each dance, hardly ever sitting one out. She moved very well, and it was a pleasure to watch her.

Suddenly, as he watched her, she headed straight for him, reaching out her hand as she approached. "Come on; let's dance."

Scott wasn't a dancer, but he couldn't think quickly enough to make a reasonable excuse, so up he went. Throughout the song, which seemed to run for twenty or thirty minutes, he felt he was moving like a chicken that had just had its head chopped off. He was painfully aware of his arms flailing up and down in an attempt to keep time with the music. He feet seemed to be making the same back and forth steps over and over, but their movements didn't seem to have any connection to whatever piece of music was droning on. He saw a couple at a table, heads together and giggling, and he was sure they were laughing at him. He glanced at the clock and figured the bar would close in three hours, and the song would have to end by then.

Finally it ended. He thanked the gal and started back to his stool. She remarked that he seemed to be all alone, and he could join her group if he wished. He didn't even know she had a group or that she'd actually sat down from time to time. It was then he realized that the DJ had taken a break.

He walked back, picked up his beer, considered his options for a moment, and walked over to the table.

His dance partner was Juliet, and her two friends were Kathy and Jen. As a way to break the ice, he called the waitress over and bought a round for the table.

By the time he found out that they all worked at the harbor department and had told them that he was a reporter, the DJ was back. Juliet promptly jumped up, grabbed another guy and was up on the floor. The other two seemed to be content to wait for someone to come up and ask them. Scott tried to make small talk to stave off having to ask one of them to dance.

Of the two Kathy seemed the most interesting and talkative. She appeared to be intrigued with the fact that Scott was a writer. Jen mostly sipped her drink and scanned the dancers, as if searching for someone. By the second song, Scott could think of no way out. He asked Kathy to dance. She wasn't much of a dancer either, so he felt more comfortable and actually started enjoying himself. He surprised himself by asking her to dance two or three more times. Between numbers they were hitting it off.

Apparently Jen's scanning paid off, as she suddenly became animated as a guy approached. She squared her shoulders and smiled. The man caught her message and asked her to dance.

Scott and Kathy had the table to themselves and took advantage of the opportunity to talk. She had a wealth of stories about life at the harbor department and about all the people who worked there.

After awhile Scott got the uneasy feeling that Kathy's cheerful chatter was forced and that when she relaxed her smile, a shadow of melancholy played over her face. Perhaps, he imagined, it was misgivings about getting close to a stranger.

In spite of having an attractive woman paying attention to him, Scott was growing aware of the time. It was late, and he was miles from home. Another beer and he'd have difficulty navigating the dark, wet mountain roads. Juliet and Jen weren't even close to slowing down, and it looked like they'd close the place. He couldn't postpone his exit much longer.

"Kathy. I've gotta work in the morning, and it's a drive home. I think I'll have to call it a night."

"I understand. I'd love to go home too, but once those two get in a mood, there's no pulling them away."

Scott was on his feet and about to turn toward the door, when an idea slapped him in the face. She would like to go home!

"I can drive you home." He ventured, as if it were a flash of brilliance.

She seized on his offer like a politician on a photo op. She dashed out to the dance floor to shout her departure to her two friends. In moments they were outside looking for Scott's car.

As the script dictated, she invited him in for a drink, "nightcap" not being a term used by young singles these days.

It was a small apartment, furnished with old, mismatched pieces. Her job paid well enough for this part of the coast, but she lived like she was broke. Suddenly the explanation came running through the door in the form of a toddler. She was a single mother.

The little boy, followed by the neighbor woman who'd been watching him, ran up and hugged his mother, and then toddled over and wrapped his arms around Scott's leg and looked up with a big smile. Scott patted him on the head and asked, in baby talk, how he was doing. A feeling of discomfort coiled around Scott like a snake. What was the appropriate thing to do or say?

She volunteered the delicate information. "I got married just out of high school. Things were going along pretty well 'til little Gus was born. Then the responsibilities of fatherhood broke our little bubble, and my old man just split." With few skills, she was forced to take whatever clerical jobs she could find to support herself and the boy.

The neighbor woman, satisfied that Kathy was in for the night, excused herself, leaving the three of them alone.

Almost out of the blue Kathy informed Scott that he could stay the night, but that he'd have to leave no later than five in the morning, as she didn't want Gus to be confused by finding men staying over. "Scott, when I have a man committed to being in my life, I can let Gus start forming attachments and expectations, but not before."

The message was clear. She'd gamble a one night stand, hoping that the guy would want to hang around long enough to become "dad." If not, that would be the end of it. The whole scenario seemed desperate and sad, and the more Scott looked around the room, the sadder he became. Sexual desire started to evaporate in the dim light of this woman's tarnished reality and his tarnished role in it.

"That's OK, Kathy, but I have a rough day tomorrow, and

I'd best go home."

A kiss without mutual feeling was followed by an exchange of phone numbers and empty promises to call.

On the road home Scott listened to one of those late night call in talk shows, where chronically lonely people fought their way through the long nights by staying on the phone. As he listened, his own loneliness drained his energy to the point where he could hardly make it to his door and into bed.

In spite of the futility of it all, he kept feeling that he should call her, that perhaps he was prejudging the situation. What would it hurt to explore a relationship? In the end, basic physics prevailed. A body at rest tended to stay at rest unless moved, and try as he might, he couldn't get the potential relationship to move him to call.

The last talk show call he heard before turning off his car was from a guy who claimed the aliens came at night and watched him, sometimes carrying him off to their ship while he slept. Obviously someone willing to take a bit of company at any cost. He hoped his life would never become that empty.

18.

While the visit to Arcata and Madd's reading didn't work out as he'd wished, the idea of going to hear authors talk about their work was compelling, and he wished there were venues in Crescent City like there were down in the college town. But why not, he thought.

During lunch one day he stopped at the local book store and talked to the owner. She thought it was a great idea, but she didn't know how to bring in authors nor how to promote the readings should a writer show up. Scott offered to help.

Deviating from talk of his mountain community, Scott used his column to run the idea by the readership and to challenge readers to suggest possible authors. In fact, he mentioned the idea in the next two columns.

He finally got some responses, some suggestions. He passed these on to the store owner and discussed possible guest speakers in the column.

Within weeks the store got it's first response. Turns out a rather well known novelist lived just over the Oregon border in Brookings. Her name was Paige Turner, and she agreed to come down to promote a new book. For getting the program started, Scott would be the one to introduce the writer.

He wanted to be prepared and perhaps to make a helpful contact in the business, so he picked up her latest book and read it. It was about a family from a small southern town who took a trip to some weird sounding resort in Tennessee, that sounded like some made up country western version of an amusement park. The oldest girl was eighteen and without prospects for either a career or a husband. In the week they stayed in this town, she meets a guy, has a romance, has it fall apart as they return to their respective towns. In the end, and with some interesting enough twists, they are reunited and fall in love. It was all fantasy escapism. There weren't any real life or real issues involved. It was, however, well crafted and a quick read. It was a page turner, and he was sure the pun was intended.

Paige Turner almost arrived late, having trouble finding the well-hidden little book store. She was in her early forties, but actually quite attractive for her age. Obviously, she had taken good care of herself. She had the full body of a mature woman, but she wasn't fat. Her shoulder length brown hair framed a full face with surprisingly few lines. She had an open and totally disarming smile that made Scott instantly like her.

When they introduced themselves, Scott added the terms "journalist" and "novelist" to his name.

"I'm pleased to meet another member of the writing profession. I'd love to read some of your work. Say, anyone ever tell you that you look like Jim Morrison?"

"Who?" The name sounded familiar but didn't trigger the right synapse.

"Not the Who, the Doors."

"Oh, yeah, the sixties rock band. I don't know what the guy looked like."

"Well, something like you. I had his poster when I was a little girl. Anyway, nice crowd you've assembled. Thanks."

Getting up in front of the small crowd, she explained, "I actually research parts of the country and try to create realistic characters and situations that fit the area." She added, "Many of my characters are based on interviews with people I've met." Then she read a bit and answered questions. It was the standard format. Within an hour she was signing copies of her books for the two dozen people who had purchased.

This was a boon for the store, which often had no more than one or two browsers at a time. The owner shook Scott's hand and vowed to make these readings a regular event.

After the people cleared out, Paige asked Scott if there was a decent place to eat before she hit the road. Scott, armed with his manuscript, offered to take her to a local coffee shop to thank her for coming.

Between bites of dinner Scott asked about her name.

"Actually, it's Pamela Gayle Turner, and I started out using P.G Turner. My first editor looked at that and noted that PG is page, so I should be Paige, and it stuck. I do use my real name for my poetry"

"Poetry?" He was curious. She seemed more like a formula romance writer than a poet.

"Yeah. That's my serious side. I send to all the literary publications, poetry journals. I actually have a pretty good reputation in the poetry world, which means I'm an unknown to most people." She laughed at irony of being a serious poet.

Scott ventured carefully into strange waters. "You write well, but I'd like to see more real life, rather than just romance characters."

"These lives are actually quite real. You ever been back east, maybe to the south?"

"Folks took us to New York City, to Cape Cod, and once to Disney World, but that's it."

"Well, Scott, I videotape the people and places before I write. You should see them. But, you say you write. What?"

Ah ha, his chance. He pulled the manuscript from his briefcase and handed it to her. "Finished this recently."

She flipped through it, stopping here and there to read a paragraph or two. "Hum, I'd like to have the time to read this over. Do you mind if I take it home?"

"Sure, please do. I would love to get your input."

"Is this the only one?"

"Well, actually, I've been working on a new one. I was very close to the forest wars last fall, and I've almost finished a novel about that."

"That sounds interesting, but you know someone's coming out with something on that subject, and the guy's a well known writer. Still, I'd like to see it."

"I didn't bring it along. Perhaps I can get it to you somehow." He didn't want to lose a possible connection to publishing.

"Look, Scott. I'll repay the dinner. You come up to my place a week from today and bring the other work. In the meantime I'll read this, and I can show you those tapes of real life in places other than California. They'll surprise you."

For the rest of the dinner, Scott worked at maintaining a literary, artistic conversation, mixed with a few reporter adventures. For her part, she had written ten books, all of which sold very well. She'd moved from Los Angeles after her divorce from a man would couldn't handle her new fame and fortune, and she moved to a sea cottage above the harbor in Brookings. It was a perfect place for a writer, a small and scenic community.

The next morning, during his Sunday call to his family, he tried to get Becky enthused about his hanging out with published writers, but she was too excited about news of her own. Apparently, she'd gotten Senator Bottoms to make San Francisco a stop on her early campaign trail, and Becky was arranging the accommodations and the venue. She asked Scott if he'd like to come down and be a part of it, meet the first woman to run for President. Bottoms did, Becky reminded him, read his story on a nationally covered new conference.

Naturally, Scott would do it. It was in three weeks, and Scott figured he could pull a day off plus the chance to cover it and get an exclusive.

Things were finally going his way. He had a famous author interested in his work and a chance to interview this controversial candidate. He could almost hear Mission Control counting down to the launch of his warp drive, interstellar career.

Rob was up for letting Scott go down to San Francisco, particularly if he could get a photo with the candidate. Rob saw a series of in-depth reports. "Don't just stand in the audience and ask the standard vacuous questions. Find out why she chose your piece to quote. Establish some sort of connection."

It wasn't necessary to tell Scott that. He had every intention of talking to Bottoms, finding out why she quoted him, establishing that they were both fighting for the same thing, using the fact that the family business was backing her if need be. He had a mental picture of the two of them on the stage, hands clasped and held over their heads in a gesture of victory. He had, after all, been a part of the process, part of the solution. His writing had ignited a spark, and the Senator had turned it into a blaze.

Winter had quietly slipped into spring, but the weather hadn't been notified. The sky was a filthy, dripping sponge as he pulled on to Highway One from Route 197. Entering Brookings, he drove up the hill overlooking the harbor and its gray, wind-whipped water.

Pam Turner had a lovely rambling rancher on a hill overlooking town and harbor. The whole look of the place advertised a successful person. Scott was just a bit intimidated. Although he considered her work somewhat superficial, she had sold to and attracted hundreds of thousands of readers. She obviously knew her craft. He was also a bit uncomfortable being invited to a woman's place for dinner. He didn't know if she had any ulterior motives, but she was twice his age, so he just couldn't imagine.

She came to the door wearing pants and a shirt that looked made of satin or some other soft, clinging material. It wasn't exactly a seductive outfit, but it did create a sensual look. She was smiling and inviting him in.

As he walked through the door, he thought of his mother, the two women being very close in age, and he started to feel weird about checking out her body. This was likely to end up being an uncomfortable evening.

Her living room was furnished with lush, contemporary furniture, rich, dark woods, and overstuffed, dark green couch and chairs. She pointed to a chair, and he settled deeply into it. Pam brought out a bottle of Cabernet and filled two fancy crystal glasses. There were trays of delicious looking finger food on the tables. Jazz was playing in the background. There was an ornate, Turkish Hooka, with six smoking tips snaking off, like an artists interpretation of an octopus, sitting in the middle of the glass covered coffee table.

"I'm glad you could come, Scott. I've read your manuscript."

He waited a few moments for the "but."

Instead, she said, "I see you've brought the new one." She reached out her hand, and he nervously handed it over, and she started skimming it.

After a couple of minutes, she looked up. "So far, I like it. I remember you saying you didn't think my book reflected real situations, real people, and I told you about my research. Ever hear of Pigeon Forge, Tennessee?"

Scott was really dying to ask her impression of his book, but he didn't want to appear overly anxious, so he replied that he'd never heard of the place.

She smiled broadly and popped a tape in her VCR. The forty plus inch TV came to life, and he was treated to the most bizarre looking main street he'd even seen. As the camera panned the street, he could see ornate miniature golf courses, amusement parks with little race cars in cement channels, miniature bungee jumping towers, arcades, home style restaurants, country western venues, tacky, gingerbread motels, monster signs that dwarfed the establishments under them, and the world's largest discount Bible store. All along the street, great mobs of families, dressed in tourist Bermuda shorts, gaped and pointed.

She interrupted the bizarre images with, "Watch the people, and listen to what they have to say. While this is on, I'll look over your new manuscript."

He was amazed at the hokey stuff that people seemed so excited to see. In the interviews, people often said they'd planned for several years to vacation here, or that once they'd discovered it, they came year after year. They talked of being able to see many of their favorite country singers in one week. They all seemed to be crazy about miniature golf and the little race cars. Everyone seemed to think that an amusement park called Dollywood was the highlight of the area. This park was on the edge of town, and had been built by a country singer named Dolly Parton, of whom Scott was only vaguely aware. A few people actually said they'd visited Great Smokey National

Park, only a half hour away, but none seemed to have considered camping. They all wanted to be in a motel in the heart of the action, as it were.

He was glued to the set, fascinated by a segment of society of which he'd been unaware. He groped the table for his glass, and it came up empty. As if on cue, Pam extended the bottle and refilled it without spilling a drop and apparently without missing a line of his book.

A couple being interviewed seemed familiar. They talked of how they'd met there several years earlier. He'd been in construction in Knoxville, and she'd come with her family from a small town in Georgia. They'd been celebrating her high school graduation. Seems they'd had a brief romance, and then the vacation was over, and they'd each gone home. They'd gotten in contact months later, written back and forth, and eventually gotten together. Now they had two small children, and she was a data input person in a Knoxville insurance company.

As he killed his second glass of wine, it hit him. This was the couple in her latest book. Pam had romanticized the story, making it more dramatic, but it was their story at the bottom of it. He voiced his surprised reaction. "My god, it's a real story. They are real people."

She refilled his glass again and clicked off the set. She carefully refilled her own glass and put down his new manuscript. She pointed at it and said, "This is more like it. This feels real. It has feeling and depth. Why did you take so long to write this?"

"I was working on the other one. I wanted to finish."

"She was shaking her head. You were there when it happened, writing about it for your paper. You could have written the book and got it out there first."

"First."

"I'm sure you know that Jack Graves just came out with a novel almost like this. It's what Jack does, and it's made him a must read for thousands. He did it with the plane that went down in the South Pacific, the toxic chemicals in the Indiana town, and the kidnapped tourists in Angola. He's always right on top of this stuff, churning out one best seller after another."

"Sure, but I was involved. I was there when it happened."

"You and I know that, but others will see you as an unknown trying to ride in on Jack's coat tail. It's doubtful you'll get published with his book climbing the charts, and if you do, can't say who'd buy it. You're three months late. You should have had a proposal and a draft in January. I could have sold this to my publisher."

Something golden had slipped through his fingers, but his major opus was completed and ready to publish. "How about the other book?"

She sighed. "It's a nice story, but it doesn't ring true. The main characters are too... to much like types, like characters from old westerns. They aren't fully rounded people, just heroic types, people in the white hats. This line, 'Don't despair my one and only love. Building a better world is a thankless and lonely job, but it's our destiny.' It's...it's melodramatic. It's... I'm sorry, Scott. I don't want to hurt you, but this needs some major rewriting to be viable."

His first instinct was to argue with her, defend his vision and the power of his writing. Still, she had praised his other book, and somewhere deep inside, he realized that his unfinished piece was the better book. She knew that and saw how good it was, so he couldn't claim that she didn't understand. He had to conditionally accept her opinion, but he wasn't ready to abandon his work. "I can rewrite it, fix it."

"Yes, I guess you can. Do that, and keep writing. You have ability."

It's not what he wanted. He needed her to say that with a few changes, his novel would be great, and that she would personally take it to her publisher. He wanted, no needed, more than an offhand sentence.

He tried to bring her back to his novel, but she squirmed away from any further comment.

In an end run, she countered with, "So, why do you write?"

249

She filled his glass as she asked.

He told her about his need to deal with real people and real, socially relevant issues, to educate and inform as well as entertain.

She said something that he felt needed to be tumbled in his mind until smooth. "I think the story is foremost. Any message will emerge naturally from the plot and characters, but they shouldn't be the foundation of the work."

His first instinct, as always, was to argue the point, but the point was complex enough to warrant thought first. He opted for asking her to expand on this a bit, desperately trying to be open minded.

"Before I start what might be a long and serious conversation. . ." She pulled out a bag of dope, giving Scott an inquisitive look. When he nodded in the affirmative, she filled the bowl of the hooka.

As they each inhaled a deep hit of the rich, acrid smoke, he looked over at her and saw how her languid pose accentuated her full curves, without being obvious. She was totally natural and totally feminine.

"Let's talk about the writer's craft." She talked about the underlying structure and the plot, while he argued for message.

"Like putting up a skyscraper," she said, "A writer should hang the decorative elements on the solid framework of a well crafted story."

He weakly maintained that the responsible writer used the story to nurture the germ of the message.

Without argument or pressure, she continued to explain her point of view, making his position seem less and less firmly anchored.

He was getting stoned and, quite frankly, losing his ability to be logical. On the other hand, the dope only made her more coolly analytic. She was, if nothing else, totally self possessed. There wasn't a gesture or vocal inflection out of place. But it wasn't forced. She was as relaxed and natural as an ingenuous child, her points made as observations, rather than truisms.

Very humbly, she noted that her success was based on getting people to like her characters. Once that happened, whatever happened to the characters, happened to the readers.

That was an astounding concept for Scott. At least it seemed so in his stoned condition. He couldn't be sure how he'd feel about it all in the morning.

The discussion started getting muddled, but one thing stuck in his slippery mind.. She said his opinion pieces had a strong message, and he'd done it well. A novel had a different purpose. It was like hard rock and new age music.

Yeah, he thought, that made sense. He was smiling and feeling rather full of himself and full of the moment. There was more to this woman than just a romance writer. He asked about her poetry.

She slipped a book over the table as she lit the hooka again. He read three poems and found them complex and deep, although he was far too wasted to concentrate on them enough to know what was going on.

He looked up and realized that he was talking to a fascinating, intelligent, creative woman. He was seeing layers and depth, and he was awed.

When she looked at the clock, he realized he'd lost track of time,. "Scott, it's getting late. I'm not a night person."

Instinctively, he started to get to his feet, but she held up her hand.

"Highway One isn't the best route on a sunny day when you're sober. On a rainy, stoned, and tipsy night, it's murder. I'd feel better if you stayed here tonight."

He must have given something away in his expression, because she added that she wasn't implying anything sexual. "I realize, Scott, that I'm like your mother, and that romantic or physical things are beyond whatever you imagined this visit to be. Please don't be uncomfortable. I have a guest room."

Scott tried to think of something to say. To acknowledge her comments would be to concede that she was old and unattractive, which she wasn't. Actually, there was something quite sexy about her. To argue against what she was saying would be to argue for something more intimate, which he wasn't sure he was up for. He was wedged into a tight spot. He was definitely stoned, and he got very horny when stoned.

She got up, almost effortlessly, in a flowing motion, from the couch. "Please don't feel uncomfortable. I understand about the age difference and all. I'll show you to the guest room. "

"I'm not uncomfortable.," he heard himself say. "I don't even notice the age difference."

"You're being kind." She moved closer to him, almost close enough for bodily contact. "I am, after all, a middle aged woman." He thought he detected a slight grin as she spoke the words.

He not only suddenly found her fascinating, but his sense of chivalry wouldn't let her self deprecate. He was, if nothing else, a traditional male.

"I don't think of you as middle aged. You're a very attractive woman."

"Thank you for being gallant. I'm guessing you're one those old fashioned guys, one who feels compelled to be a gentleman at all times."

He started to protest that it was more than that, but she took him by the arm and started leading him down the hall. She pushed open the door to a nicely made up guest room with a large, comfortable looking bed. "You'll be comfortable here. As I said, no uncomfortable situations. Sweet dreams."

She whispered the last only inches from his ear. He turned and looked into her eyes. It had now slipped beyond being gallant to having to prove he found her an attractive woman. He was also getting aroused. On impulse he leaned over and kissed her.

"Careful there. Don't start anything you don't mean." She flashed him a seductive smile.

"Oh, I mean it." He kissed her again, this time passionately.

She slipped a hand around his neck and under his hair and kissed him hard. "I warned you." She mumbled.

Dizzy from the dope and wine, he wasn't sure if he pulled her on the bed, she pushed him, or they simply fell. However it happened, there were locked in an embrace and rolling around.

"I want you." He grunted breathlessly.

"OK. Put your arms up." He did, and she pulled his shirt over his head. He reciprocated by unbuttoning her soft, satin shirt and unhooking her bra.

It was skin against skin, and Scott was so excited he was afraid he'd never last long enough to get it in. But she disengaged and slipped out of her pants, giving him a moment to catch his breath. He struggled out of his pants after having trouble first with the belt and then with the zipper.

She made love in a slow, deliberate way, getting him to a fever pitch and then easing back enough to keep him from coming. They went on this way, in a kind of slow sexual dance, for what seemed hours to Scott, although he realized that it probably was only a few minutes. They moved together, and she'd nuzzle his neck and move her hips slowly. He'd start to thrust, and she'd pull away. Finally he was beyond control and they came together in what felt like an explosion. Then he fell back and back, as in slow motion, finally hitting the bed. For a few minutes he couldn't talk at all, and then he could only drone on about how wonderful she was.

Try as he might, he couldn't stay awake for more than a few minutes. He slipped off with his arms and a leg wrapped around her.

He woke to sunshine and some kind of African Marimba music. He was alone in bed. His clothes were carefully laid out on the chair, so he got up and dressed. He felt kind of odd, like he'd done something wrong. Why else wouldn't she be there. Looking at his watch, he realized how late he'd slept, which could account for her absence.

Scott smelled breakfast cooking, so he followed his nose to the kitchen. Pam was in a robe, looking less glamorous than the night before. "Why didn't you wake me?"

She shrugged. "You must have needed the sleep. I've done

my yoga and written a few pages this morning, so it all worked out. Hungry?"

He was starved. She was being very matter of fact and business like about breakfast. He wasn't sure if he should kiss her and talk sexy or just make like a house guest. He was trying to read what she wanted, but he couldn't fathom it.

Standing there, needing to talk, he finally said, "I hope you realize I didn't come here last with plans to seduce you."

"Perhaps I seduced you." She shrugged, turned away from the frying bacon and winked at him. "Anyway, it just happened, as these things do when a man and woman have an intimate dinner with wine and dope. I found it delightful."

"Oh, yeah. Me too. You were wonderful. I never knew, realized how it could, well, you know."

She kissed him on the cheek. "I know. Sit down. Breakfast is ready."

They chatted about the joys and frustrations of writing, the highs of getting it right and the lows when editors want it changed.

It was a leisurely breakfast punctuated with serious conversation and laughter, and his vague sense of discomfort, one he felt with any new woman, was starting to evaporate. Then he thought about leaving. What, he wondered, was the right way to go about it, and when? If he rushed off right after eating, what message would that send. If he hung around, might she feel put upon, perhaps obligated to entertain him and feed him more meals.

As causally as possible he asked, "Pam, do you have plans for the day?"

"Matter of fact, I do. Meeting an artist friend for lunch. We're talking about a cover design for the next book. That was the book I was working on while you slept. As much as I enjoy your company, as well as your resemblance to Morrison," she winked as she added that, "I'm going to have to send you on your way in a few minutes."

Well, that saved him. The next social hurdle was the question of another date. He wasn't sure what she expected of him. Playing it safe, he said he'd like to call her again, and she said that would be wonderful. She kissed him goodbye, affectionately, but not passionately, and told him she'd be waiting to hear from him.

Scott considered stopping by to see V.V. as he passed her neighborhood. He wasn't sure what to do about Pam, and V.V. could set him straight. Only women, he figured, understood women. However, he wasn't privy to her social life, and he didn't want to show up at an awkward time, so he decided to continue on home.

All the next week he was plagued about Pam. The difference in age was awkward, and also she was successful in an area where he was still a struggling unknown. Would she be interested in a relationship with him? Would he with her? With the wine and the dope, it was all so sexy, but would there be that spark in the sober light of day. What would happen if the age thing bothered him and interfered with his performance? What if she just considered him an attractive young man, someone to stoke her ego for a time?

The more he looked at it from every angle, the more unsure he was. If he called, would that be telling her he was interested in something serious? She was inscrutable. He knew exactly how she felt about writing, but he was clueless about her feelings for him.

Friday found him no closer to a solution than he'd been on the drive back from Brookings. Getting away from work a bit early, he decided to seek Jake's advice. Jake had a homey wisdom about life that always managed to clarify things.

The biker's combination living room and office had been transformed since Scott's last visit. The old chairs with the springs dangerously close to the surface were gone. Comfortable modern furniture was in place over a new blue rug. The tables were metal and glass, solid, quality stuff.

"Jake, so you finally did it. I always figured you'd never get around to it."

"Didn't. Peaches just up and ordered all this stuff. Knew when I'd be out, and had it delivered. Now I says to her, 'I'm the senior partner here. You should be consultin' me before spending a fortune of company bread.' And she looks at me and says, 'What, you don't like it?' Well, I explain to her that I think the stuff is decent enough, good and comfortable in the bargain, but it's more the principle of the thing. Then she says that if it's just the money, I could take it out of her share, like I'd really do that, seein' she went out of her way to do me a favor and all."

"Well, I like it." Scott managed to inject. "The girl has nice taste."

"That she does, and quite honest and all, she's made us so much money, it don't really matter what she spent. Guess I just don't feel right 'bout a girl not old enough to drink, takin' over like that. Next she'll be tellin' me I gotta iron my coveralls or something." Both Jake and Scott found that funny and had a good laugh.

As soon as Jake put a beer in his hand, Scott managed to do a U turn with the topic of conversation. "I've got a problem concerning a woman, too, and since you're a man with lots of experience. . ." Scott launched into his story.

After relating all but the most intimate details of his encounter with Pam, Scott shrugged and looked helplessly at Jake.

"She's successful, funny, interesting, attractive, and a good fuck. And, by the way, forty-one or two ain't all that old. This time next year I won't be forty anything no more. Now, let's look at you. Skinny kid working long hours at a local paper, living in the funkiest trailer park on the coast. And women. Got all of those you can handle these days? Didn't think so. I figure you got two choices. Call that woman and do the horizontal tango, or introduce me to her. She sounds too damn good to throw away."

"Jake, you make a good case. I guess I should. Got nothing to lose I suppose."

"Good, the man's actually made a decision about a woman. Let's celebrate. Come on, we'll go over to the Tree House. My treat."

Scott had missed having a beer with the guys, and was hungry for some male bonding. They pulled their parka hoods up over their heads and headed out into the spring rain, which was much like winter rain, except it came straight down rather than at a forty-five degree angle.

In deference to Scott's taste, Jake ordered the Humboldt amber ale rather than his usual Bud or Coors lite. He took a healthy slug and his eyes widened. "Wow, this stuff's got some serious taste to it. Has a bit of a kick too, come to think of it. I see some serious drinking here tonight, though you know I'll be payin' for it in the morning.

Man talk over beer usually involves women, and Scott started to lament his ongoing confusion with the opposite sex. Jake's past was strewn with wives and lovers, so he must have some insights.

"Scott. Way I see it, you don't have trouble finding women. Your problem is keeping them. You're a personable sort, good gift of gab. Not a bad looking kid. Kind of remind me of some rock singer dude from the sixties. You're sayin' you don't understand them, but it ain't that hard. You just gotta listen to them. They'll drop you all kinds of not-so-subtle hints about what they want and expect. And it ain't stuff like diamonds and furs. See, all through history women been used to cooking, cleaning, taking care of babies, and mostly being ignored by their men, 'cept when the guy gets hungry or horny. So, you see they learned a long time ago not to expect a whole lot from us. So you pay them a bit of attention, tell them they look nice, pick up some flowers and candy, and you just climbed to the top of the list. Let's face it, since we're all for the biggest part jerks, the least jerky guys look like Prince Charming. Understand?"

"You make it sound so simple."

"It is, but it ain't. See, once you start living with one or get married, the old natural tendency to become a jerk gets the best of you. You start throwing your under shorts on the floor, belch at the dinner table, watch the game while she's trying to clean around you. You get the picture. Then one day she says you're not the guy she married, and that's true enough, cause that guy was sort of the 'best behavior' you, not the real you. So she leaves you, and it starts all over again."

"Then it's hopeless."

"Not so. Sometimes you get yourself a woman who doesn't feel she's gotta be too damn subtle. She'll keep you on the straight and narrow, cut you no slack, and if you can stick it out, you'll end up a better man for it."

"I don't know. Seems easier to stay single."

"Yeah, well, that's pretty much what I decided. Like those touchy feely counselors keep saying, 'relationships take lots of work.' I'm lazy, so I stay single. Too early in the game to say about you."

Just then Scott saw Dusty over at the bar, apparently at the same time Dusty saw them. He really didn't want to deal with Dusty, but the big guy was making a beeline toward their table. With him was old Ben There, or Les Apt, or Roger Wilco, or whatever the hell his name was.

"Jake and Scott. I wanna innerduce you guys to one o' my new best buds. This here's Al E. Gator, and he's changed my life." Dusty was, as always after dark, quite drunk.

The old guy, whatever his name was, said, "I do believe I know these gentlemen. Why we all live at the same establishment. Fact is, Jake's grandma and I were quite an item back during WWI."

Jake looked at him as if he were crazy. Then he relaxed as he recalled that the guy was indeed crazy. Jake laughed and went along with it. "Granny used to say you was quite a stud."

Scott motioned for them to sit down, and the barmaid showed up with two more glasses and another pitcher. She obviously knew the drill and was prepared.

Dusty was excited. "Al here jus' give me the secret of long life. I'm gonna learn me to surf right away."

Scott started to laugh but suppressed when he saw that Dusty was dead serious. He did manage to ask with almost a straight face, "So what does surfing have to do with living a long time?"

"Well, it's all pretty complicated, but it's like them waves are part of the flow of life and time, and the guy riding them waves, rides that flow an' don't get caught in it and pulled under. See dyin's bein' caught and pulled under. Al here been surfing for well over a hundred year. He's one hundred, thirty-six and don't look half that."

This time Jake decided to play with the bait. "So, how you know how old he is?"

"He tol' me all bout it. Showed me his first drivers license, issued in 1897 Got his boyhood photo on it."

"1897!" Scott exclaimed. "How can you be sure it's real?"

"I knows me a real license when I sees one. Hell, had me a fake one when I was sixteen." He stopped for a moment and glared at Scott. "Say, you best not be callin' my friend a liar, cause if you do, you an me gonna duke it out."

"No, my friend. You say it's real and that's good enough for me." Scott looked over at Jake and winked.

In turn Jake leaned over and said, "I don't believe they had drivers licenses in 1897."

"Since there probably weren't more than a dozen cars on the road, I would guess not." Then he turned to Al, or Ben or who-ever. "How's it feel to be well over a hundred?"

"Exactly how I felt at twenty-one. Trouble is, if I ever stop surfing, I'll die within two weeks. That's why I got to get in the water at least every other day."

Scott studied this enigma, and it seems he saw the corner of the guy's mouth turn up just a bit. This old guy isn't crazy, Scott thought. He's a damn prankster. He's been mind-fucking every-one. Suddenly, Scott felt a new admiration for this weird guy. He was an artist in his way. He said and did things to shock people into thinking in totally different ways, and he never preached or argued. He just wandered through the world,

259

destroying people's sense of what's real.

"I gotta take a piss." Dusty trumpeted, as he staggered off to the bathroom.

Scott took the opportunity to try to find a bit of truth about this old guy.

"Al E. Gator, huh? Is that what it says on that license?"

"I don't really have a drivers license, at least one in this century. I'm afraid I've bent the truth a bit."

"Don't tell me you don't have a license. You have a car, and you drive."

"Yes, but I don't have a license. You write. May I see your literary license."

"Don't you ever get stopped by the cops?"

"Occasionally. They ask for a license, but I give them a story. A good story is better than a license." Then, without taking a pause or breath, he changed the subject. "Surfing would be good for Dusty. It would get him out of the bars, get him fit, sharpen his mind and reflexes. Don't you think?" Then, he added parenthetically, "Might make him live forever."

Jake shrugged and threw up his hands. "Couldn't fault that logic."

Scott still wanted to get into the name thing, but he realized that it would just take him into a maze that he didn't want to enter. Scott hated things or people that couldn't be put into categories, labeled and explained. This guy drove him nuts.

The guy leaned over to Scott and said. "Learn to surf, and your problems with women will vanish."

Scott felt indignation rising. "And what makes you think I have problems with women?"

"You told me all about it that afternoon you spent in the woods with me, all those relationships that fell apart almost as fast as they started."

"Afternoon? I was only there for five minutes, or not much more. What afternoon?"

The guy put up his finger indicating quiet. "I won't say a word. Doctor patient relationship and all. By the way, tell Dusty

I had to leave."

He was up and out before Scott could object. Scott looked over at Jake, who'd been listening with interest. "Jake, I didn't spend the afternoon or tell him anything about problems with women. It was five minutes. Well, maybe more, but not the whole afternoon, and we talked, but not that much. He's just screwing with me."

For a moment Scott doubted his own memory. He thought that perhaps he'd been drinking too much and was losing track of the time and the things he confided in others. Suddenly he had no desire to be in a bar, pouring down beer. He excused himself by saying he wasn't feeling well, not too far from the truth.

The Sunday paper had a big article on Jack Graves' book, War in the Forest.

There was a photo of Graves, and Scott recognized him as the guy who'd pumped him for information in that little restaurant. The son of a bitch had picked Scott's brain for material for his bestseller. He vowed to get a copy of the book to see how much of himself was in there.

Looking at his watch, Scott decided it was late enough to call Pam. He expected a warm greeting; instead the icy voice on the other end asked him what was on his mind.

"Well, I said I call, and I was wondering if we could plan to get together, perhaps a date next weekend."

"I don't think so, Scott. You took a week to decide if you wanted to bother seeing me again. Maybe you flipped a coin. Whatever. It's too late. We had an intimate night. An man who was really interested would have called back within a day or two, not over a week later."

"Well, it was a busy week. I thought about you. I mean, it's only been a week."

"You may not realize this at your age, but I don't have any trouble getting men."

"Oh, I never thought you did," Scott interrupted.

"As I was saying, getting men in my life isn't a problem. A

guy's got to show me some enthusiasm, some real interest, and that wasn't you. Your loss." She sounded ready to hang up.

"It's a misunderstanding," he desperately blurted out. Now that she was rejecting him, his ambivalence was gone. He really wanted to be with her. "Can't we start again and maybe get it right?"

"No, Scott. There was a brief spark, and you didn't fan it. Now it's out. I'm not interested in seeing you. No hard feelings; just the way it is. Good luck. Scotty."

With that she was off the line and out of his life. He was stunned. It made no sense. Nothing about women seemed to make any sense.

No sooner had he gotten off the phone with Pam, then V.V. called him. Without waiting to find out the reason for her call, he started in about Pam and the brush off. He almost demanded an explanation, a glimpse into the secret code of women.

"To begin with, you're clueless about women. No matter how attractive and successful, there's something slightly uncomfortable in the older woman, younger man thing. You didn't call, and that sounded like hesitance, which, knowing you, it probably was. You really are easy to read."

"How the hell was I supposed to know all that?"

"Be sensitive. Rather than overlay an image of what you want her to be, see the woman as she is, listen to her, pay attention."

"I do pay attention! I'm a very sensitive guy!" He demanded.

"Yes" she agreed, "but to yourself, your needs, your feelings. I hate to say this Scott, but I don't think you'll ever really get it, and I feel sorry for you. You'll end up with a woman who'll play on your eccentricities and manipulate you by making you think that your version of things is what's really happening. You'll end up broken to harness without ever knowing it."

"Bullshit. I'm not stupid."

"Except when it comes to women. But what I called about is business, my business."

Scott was afraid she'd gone bankrupt, and was about to offer help when she stopped him and explained that it was just the opposite.

"My boyfriend is an investment banker, and he's enthusiastic about the business's future. He's talked it up to some of his investment friends, and they want to take us public."

"They want you to sell out to them?"

"No, Scott. Stocks, investors, money. We're talking a chain up and down the coast. They have the money to make that happen. What'll happen is that rather than having a pretty big piece of one store, you'll have a small piece of a big chain."

"V.V., please. These people eat small businesses. You'll end up with nothing."

"No, I've had it checked out. I'll still control the business. You see, your initial check, before dividends and all that will be several times you original investment. You, we, can't lose."

The whole big business thing really bothered Scott to his core. Talking about possible failure was only a cover for his basic distrust of the whole corporate world. He tried to argue it with her, but kept bringing it back to a secure future for herself and for little Sam. In the end he had little choice. It was illogical to tell people not to make money because he didn't like big business.

He was now a shareholder in a growing concern, and soon her little shops would be popping up everywhere, but she wouldn't be there, just some minimum wage clerk doing a routine she was taught at Corporate Training 101. There would be the merchandise but no soul, no personality.

Everything was getting that way, he thought, business, work, relationships, shopping. It was all just going through the motions, without and real connection, any pride in one's work. The more the real world became unreal, the more real the characters he hung out with at the Tree House became.

19.

He hadn't realized it, but the weekend of the Bottoms' campaign event was Easter weekend. While his family didn't celebrate Easter as such, it was always a time for a big family dinner, an attempt at closeness. He came to work that Friday only long enough to finish the police blotter piece and to check his schedule. Rob wished him luck and he dashed out the door and into his car.

There was only a fine drizzle, which cleared up as soon as he passed Fortuna. It remained overcast until somewhere south of Willits, and then the sun came out over the rich, fresh, green oak-studded rolling hills. Scott realized he hadn't seen the full sun, not hiding behind veils of cloud, for months. He saw the vapor rise from the road, and he felt the heat coming through the windows. He actually found himself becoming cheerful and optimistic.

Bottoms' campaign entourage was entrenched at the Mark Hopkins, a posh hotel way up on Nob Hill in San Francisco. A valet in a crisp uniform parked his car, and a bellboy picked up his luggage. He found that his room had been booked by the company and was ready for him. His bags arrived before he got there. There was a cheese plate and a chilled bottle of champagne waiting for him and a note to call his sister in a room on the same floor.

"Becky, thanks for the VIP treatment."

"Scott, why don't you take a shower and change. Bambi is giving an address in a couple of hours. I'll stop by in a few minutes, and we can open that champagne and have a toast. I've missed you brother dear."

Shower, my ass, Scott thought. This room had a deep tub with whirlpool jets. He settled in for a comfortable soak. This was so much better than his shower tub at home or his two by two shower at his old travel trailer.

He was still in the robe he found in the closet when Becky arrived. He was going to open the bubbly, but Becky insisted that she'd do it while he got dressed. There were schedules to keep. He threw on his clothes quickly and came back into the sitting room.

She looked him over appraisingly and pulled a tie out of her purse, draping it around his neck. "Now, this will look great with the suit in the closet."

"Suit?" he demanded.

"Little brother, this is a major event with major players. Come in a suit, or don't come at all."

Scott grumbled the entire time he was changing. He rationalized this absurd outfit with the fact that the paper was paying him to attend, and he had to be there. There was also the idea that once face-to-face with the Senator, he could finally talk to her about their common interest.

Once relaxed in the deep chairs, glasses of champagne in hand, Becky gave Scott the overview of the campaign. Becky had built a network of companies run by women and had convinced them to back Bottoms. Also, her network had been bankrolling new businesses ventures with women at the helm. As these companies grew, paid back the loan, and added their part to the growing alliance, the network had mushroomed into something quite large and influential.

Scott said that her group sounded just as sexist as the men who band together to support males. But, he did acknowledge, they'd done great by Peaches and Jake.

Becky crossed her legs and leaned forward. Her red hair hung just below her ears, and her suit was perfectly tailored. A string of real pearls hung around her neck. "This isn't quite the same thing, Scotty. We have never had a woman president, and we won't until women stand up and show their political clout. And, don't think there aren't many men behind this also. Everyone always says it's time for a change. The time's right for a real change, not only gender but about how the business of running this country is done. She's an independent, a populist.

She's not part of any establishment."

"So I get to interview her?"

"I don't know. Hope so. At least you have a leg up on the rest of the press. You are a paid guest at this $500 fund raising dinner."

"Paid! The company?"

She nodded and checked her watch, which was redundant, as there was a clock on the wall just above Scott's head. She told him that cocktails were at seven and dinner at eight, and then she bolted toward the door, champagne glass still half full.

She stopped at the door and turned back. "They've got a great gym here. How bout meeting me there at six tomorrow morning?"

"Six A.M.? Let me think about it." She left, and he finished her drink, as well as his own.

He paced nervously, watching the clock's hands crawl like a banana slug across a fallen redwood. This fancy, dress up thing made him feel out of his element. He'd rather have met this Senator at the site of the forest demonstrations.

He wandered into the fancy top floor room about half past seven. Well dressed waiters and waitresses inundated him with drinks and elegant finger food.

Milling through the crowd, attempting to accidentally bump into the Senator, Scott recognized a face, but he couldn't place from where. She was a trim and very attractive oriental woman, somewhere in her twenties. She was dressed in an expensive business suit.

"Excuse me, you look familiar. Have we met?"

"Susie Takora. Yes. You're the prodigal son, Scott. Yes, we met when those forest activists came out of the woods. You flagged down my van."

"Oh, yeah, you work for the company. I don't remember you from when I worked there."

"I've been there about a year. MBA, Harvard. I'm assistant VP in charge of sales and marketing."

"Wow, impressive. So you work for Collins."

"Collins retired."

"So, who's VP?"

She laughed. "The job's open. The person's been picked. Just have to convince him to come on board."

"Well, Susie," Scott stopped at that name. She hadn't introduced herself that day in the woods, but the name rang a bell. Peaches and Jake! "You were the contact for the business loan for Texas Jake's Harley Repair."

"Yeah, that another part of what I do. I'm sort of Becky's right hand. Anyway, I'm glad you could come. I have to talk to Mike from *The Journal*. See you later."

The Journal, Scott thought. He wondered if she meant the Wall Street Journal, and if so, her informality about a contact like this was impressive.

He recognized the Senator from her photographs and he hurried right up. "Senator, I'm Scott Mukis. I wrote that article."

"Nice to meet you Mr. Mukis. Becky's brother, obviously. Which article?"

"The one you quoted when you introduced your forest bill. I wrote that."

"Mr. Mukis, Scott. It was a well written piece and perfect for the occasion. I'm glad we both recognize the critical issues facing the country's forests. Keep putting your message in front of the public." She motioned to a member of her staff. "Ron, this is Scott Mukis. He's a journalist. Give him my position information." She turned back to Scott. "It's all spelled out there. If you have questions about any of it, please bring them up at the news conference. I want to be able to clarify anything that might sound ambiguous. I want to communicate clearly with the public." She accentuated her comments with that gesture that resembled a slow karate chop, the kind that gives emphasis to the accompanying statement. Then she shook his hand and was off to talk to another person.

Scott made a mental note of what she'd said and his comments: friendly, accessible, straight talking.

She obviously remembered his article and was impressed by it. He would certainly get an opportunity to talk to her later, a one on one, perhaps an exclusive.

The dinner was great, and afterward, Bottoms got up and thanked all the people in California who had worked to support her campaign. Among those thanked were his sister and several prominent businesswomen. There were men also, among them several congressmen and state senators from her party. Scott suddenly realized that he was perhaps the only one in the room from another political party. He'd registered as a Green in protest of the lack of difference between the major parties. He figured that this wouldn't be the right time to advertise his affiliation.

Her after dinner speech was aimed at her supporters. She talked not in political generalities, but about specific programs and legislation she felt was needed. Issues involving the environment, public health care, protections for the working people, and legislation preventing disparities in opportunities based on gender, race or ethnic background. She came right out and advocated for a health care system like the Canadian system. That, in his opinion, took political guts. He was impressed.

Even though the press was invited for the speech, she made it clear that a press conference would be held the next day, and that then the press would have every opportunity to ask questions.

She was whisked away by her people as soon as the post speech applause ended. A band started up, and the die hard party people started pouring down the drinks and getting social.

Scott was spent from the long day, the drive, and from being trussed up in a damn suit for several hours. He tried mingling, but these people seemed to run in the same circles, which wasn't Scott's circle, so he went back to his room, put on some music, and finished the champagne.

Breakfast was delivered without his ordering it. There was a message from Becky, apologizing for not having breakfast with him and reminding him he'd forgotten to meet her at the gym. Business and politics were holding her captive.

He had some time to kill before the conference, so he decided to take a walk. Half way down the hill he saw a woman jogging toward him, moving pretty fast up the steep street. It was Susie, wearing very trendy jogging clothes. She stopped short when she saw him. Apparently catching the question in his look, she ventured an explanation.

"Running is part of my day. Tunes me up; clears my head. Had to push the envelope a bit on this god awful hill. You run?"

"Hike mostly. Do the stair step machine at the gym. Where I live, it isn't running weather very often." Then realizing that she was not only friendly, but quite well put together, he added, "Headed any place special?"

"Just shower and change."

He ventured out a bit. "I'm exploring the neighborhood. Care to join me?"

"I'm in jogging clothes, no purse, money, you know."

"I've got it covered. Perhaps some coffee at one of those fancy coffee bars?"

She agreed and fell in beside him. She talked about how great it was to be working for such a socially progressive company, and she couldn't say enough about Becky. Apparently his sister was a brilliant, compassionate, innovator, who was going to revolutionize America's business climate. It was a blatant display of hero worship. And, she seemed so amazed that Scott was not associated with the company.

He explained his dislike for business and told her that he was first and foremost a writer.

They ducked into a cute coffee place, one with a view of the bay, and she hit him with something unexpected. "Lot's of great writers have had important, demanding day jobs. The great poet, Wallace Stevens, was a VP for an insurance company. Several famous writers were also doctors. You work at a paper and, I assume, work on your novels at night. You could work for your family business and do the same."

"You make it sound logical," He said. "But there's a flaw.

The world of business sucks your soul dry, turning you into an empty literary hack. The kind of writing I do requires a kind of purity that can't exist with the obsessive desire for wealth and power."

She very pleasantly disagreed with him and changed the subject to the sights and places of interest in the city. She said it was sad that he had to leave in the morning and that he should have the time to enjoy this lovely town.

Later, as he changed for the press conference, he thought that it was too bad she was a business type, with an MBA in the bargain. Otherwise, she was an attractive and interesting woman.

The press conference started out with a bang. There was a room full of reporters from the major papers and the wire services. He was probably the only one from a small paper, and the only one in jeans. Becky hadn't made any dress code demands about the conference, so he dressed as he wished, as he would back home this time of year, jeans and a wool plaid long sleeve shirt. Everyone was shouting.

One of the first questions set the tone for the rest of the afternoon. Some guy from one of the big back east papers asked, "Are you running as a woman?"

She turned on him like a hound on a fox. "I'm not at all sure what that question means. I am the gender that I am, but I don't know how one runs as either a man or a woman. If you'd asked a similar question of the person who is keeping my desk in the oval office warm for me, I'd be inclined to try to answer it. Apparently not. Let me set some perameters for this confer-ence. This country is the biggest economic and military power on the planet. We live in a critical time for the entire interna-tional community. Right now we are concerned with who will lead this country during these times. This is a serious matter, requiring serious debate. We are all educated people. Do ask me the tough questions, but make them serious questions. I will not equivocate."

For a moment you could have heard a fly land on the table.

Then the room was awash with a low murmur. Then the semantic walls came down.

She was hit with questions about her advocacy of universal health coverage, and she didn't back down from her position in the least. Someone asked about raising taxes, and she said definitely for the wealthy and the corporations, who could afford to pay. She was asked if she were a liberal.

"That's just a label, and it has meant many things during many times. I don't wear a label. I have positions I feel strongly about. Some of these might be called liberal, and some could be called conservative. I'm neither. I guess I'm a pragmatist. If it improves the country, the lot of our citizens, and it doesn't violate the constitution, I'm willing to take a serious look at it."

Scott was amazed, as others obviously were. There were no ambiguous sound bite answers. Each question was answered directly and candidly.

Finally, Scott raised his hand and got her attention.

"Senator. First I'd like to thank you for using my piece during the forest bill campaign."

"You're welcome, but is there a question there?" Her abrupt response caught him short. "Well, why did you take up that controversial issue."

"I thought that was all public record by now. But if you missed it, here's the condensed version. Forests are valuable resources. They provide clean air and water and habitat for biodiversity. They are also important for recreation. They should be banked for future generations. But, the most pressing issue was that there was something approaching a civil war being generated. We needed to find a workable compromise and heal the country. Yes, a question, over on the right."

Scott wanted to ask why she had chosen his piece, have that part of the media record, but she seemed impatient with any questions that didn't address current major issues. He was thinking of another approach. Perhaps he'd ask her if she labeled herself as an environmentalist. That was a good question. He was about to raise his hand when some gray haired guy in a blue suit asked his question.

"I don't label myself anything," she replied. "I care about the environment, as any thinking person should these days. There is a compelling argument for the position that saving the environment also makes sense economically. This work represents a vast area of growth, and if we can work out sustainable development, we can continue having economic prosperity for many generations. We also can have clean water, renewable resources, and abundant recreational opportunities. In that context, I guess you could call me an environmentalist."

Damn, she was good. Questions like that, he suddenly realized, were meant to put her on the defensive, make her backpedal. Instead, she went on the offensive. She reacted like a predator.

Someone brought up an obvious problem in her statements. "Senator, your positions are almost certain to leave you out of favor with most of the traditional sources of campaign money. How have you planned for the financing of your presidential bid."

She swung toward him and held out her arms as if to hug him. "Thank you for that question. Let me start by saying that everyone knows that presidents are bought by campaign contributions. Everyone says it's not right, but it happens every time." She pointed at the TV camera. "So, if you out there can't lick them, join them. Why should the rich be the only ones to buy a president? You, the working, middle class Americans can get me in your pocket and can be confident I'm in Washington working for you. And you can afford me. If every one of you who work for a wage or operate a small business or family farm sends me ten bucks, you'll put this campaign over the top and will have bought yourselves a president. If you're a student or retired, send five bucks, and if you've got some extra cash, send me twenty. Make your check out to Bambi for President."

For a moment the room was collectively stunned. Then a wave of laughter spread around the room. It was clear they weren't laughing at her, but with her as she pulled off something unimaginable. The few other questions that trickled in were just time fillers. She'd made her point, and it would either sink her or give her a massive win.

Later, as the press lined up to shake her hand and exchange pleasantries before filing out, Scott found Becky and expressed his admiration for the Senator's candor.

Feeling he should leave, but hoping he'd get one more chance to talk to the candidate, Scott began the process of excusing himself, saying he should join the other reporters filing out.

Becky grabbed his arm and motioned for him to stick around. In a few moments the Senator came out to talk with the people who had organized the weekend, and Becky was one of the players. Scott realized that unlike most political gatherings, men were in the minority. In fact only about a quarter of the people left in the room were male.

Champagne was opened and poured, leading to several rounds of toasts. Scott felt good being a part of it, being in the inner circle, if only for a few minutes.

After a couple of drinks, Bottoms noticed Scott. "Mr. Mukis. It seems you were concerned about my use of your article. Was there a problem? Did I misquote you?"

"No, on the contrary. I was proud that you used it. I was surprised, knowing that it only made a few papers in California."

"Oh, well, it seems that someone passed it to my campaign manager, saying it fit my speech. So I looked at it, and it did, so I used it."

"Someone passed it?" He wanted to know who.

"Yeah, I don't recall, but it was someone from this California group, probably someone in this room."

Scott looked over at Becky. She seemed to have her hand in everything, and he could see her touch on this. There was no point pushing it, if it meant having his suspicions confirmed. So, it wasn't the power of the piece that catapulted it into her hands. But, he reasoned, if the piece had been weak, she would have rejected it, so what did it matter how she got her hands on it. Yeah, the piece spoke for itself, and she'd quoted it to the whole damn nation.

He wanted to hang around to the end of the party, but he had an eight hour drive ahead of him, and it was well into the afternoon. He hugged his sister, shook hands with Bambi, and hopped into his car.

A couple of small papers seemed interested in Scott, but what they offered wasn't much different than what he had already, and he liked Rob and the other people he worked with. A couple of the major papers suggested that he continue to send stuff to them. They however, made no promises. One helpful editor suggested that he become syndicated. What he didn't receive was an offer to be a reporter or columnist for a major daily. Odd, as along with his resume and examples of his work, he always included the piece the Senator had read to the country. That should have earned him a prestigious position.

Although he was hungry to move up, to be a major voice in the shaping of the American consciousness, he realized his life wasn't too bad for the moment. He had a good job and the respect of the community. He had a nice place to live and a few friends. Some men might have been satisfied with that.

Just as Pam had predicted, his book about the forest wars wasn't accepted. He had come in behind a blockbuster by a popular writer.

With the forests saved and Bottoms' popularity in the polls rising each day, Scott needed another issue to focus on. He turned to the disparity between the sexes, between the whites and the minorities, and between the upper and working classes. He read passionately every respected source, and he called various professors who had accumulated research data. He was writing a column a week on the subject, and he'd started neglecting his local community coverage.

He'd launched into a series of pieces, and Rob was supportive at first, but as the weeks went on, the editor reminded Scott that Crescent City wasn't Detroit, Chicago, or L.A. There really wasn't a problem here, and perhaps Scott had made his point.

"You write with passion, but you overdo it. There are end-less issues. Do a different one each week. I can live with that, but keep it below 600 words."

He tackled health care, the CIA's involvement in other countries' business, corporate corruption, Over fishing the coastal waters, air pollution, and pesticides. He was on a roll, but even the heady feeling that accompanies getting his messages out to the public didn't quiet that little internal voice that constantly wondered why Rob had given him such a free hand. It was always hard to sell the editor on even one non regular piece, let alone a weekly editorial spot.

Scott didn't consider himself the type to look a gift horse in the mouth, but in truth, that was really who he was. When he could no longer contain his curiosity, he cornered Rob.

"Hey, boss. You've let me run with my columns for weeks. Don't get me wrong; I appreciate it, but that doesn't seem like your micro management style."

"I guess it's part of being a short timer. The next guy probably won't cut you so much slack."

"Next Guy! What are you talking about?" A shadow of foreboding, like a three ton black cat, crossed Scott's path.

"Didn't I tell you? Well, I was going to announce it at the end of the week anyway. I'm leaving."

"You can't do that! I mean, Why? Did you get canned?"

"Just moving on. This was a great place to raise kids and a great job to have while doing it, but the baby is grown now, ready to graduate and head for college."

Scott sat down to compose himself. "But, where will you go?"

"The big city, my boy. Portland. I miss a major daily, and they're offering me the Arts and Entertainment section."

"But what about me?" He hadn't meant to say that, but it was out, and he couldn't back track.

"You'll be fine. Just remember, you're starting over with a new editor. No history, so don't expect or demand. From the moment he walks in, he's the boss, and your year of service won't give you a single brownie point. He's Marv Peabody, out of Turlock, and he's rumored to be a hard-nosed editor."

Scott mumbled something about taking Rob out for dinner and drinks to send him off, and then he sort of shuffled back to his desk to ponder the possibilities.

On the way back up the hill after work, Scott didn't notice the magnificent forest surrounding him. It appears, he thought, that every time things started going well for him, a disaster sneaked up on him and bit him on the ass. For the last few weeks he'd been a hard hitting columnist, and he was reaching people, changing the country one reader at a time. Who knows what this next editor will be like, perhaps an arch conservative who didn't want the status quo criticized.

That was it, the only way this Marv could reject his work. If the man wasn't biased, he'd welcome Scott's writing.

20.

The presidential convention was starting, and Scott dropped his writing projects and turned on the TV. On the first day it was obvious that Bambi Bottoms was the favorite of most of the delegates. There was a bandwagon, and party movers and shakers were climbing on.

After the first day of convention coverage, the talking heads started their analysis.

"Well Diane, was that a group desperate for anyone who can challenge the incumbent?"

"That's pretty simplistic, Paul. The Senator has proven herself to be a leader and someone who can bring together various factions of the party."

Paul turned to the other man. "Now, Ed, I ask you, where is this so called proven leadership? The woman's a grandstander, with no political savvy at all."

"Well, Paul, you're right in that she doesn't understand the subtleties of the political game."

"Gentlemen," Diane interrupted, "You're obviously brainwashed by the good old boy maneuvers and can't see a fresh new approach, one that the public has been hungry for."

"Wake up Diane. This is just entertainment, the Bambi show. She has all the substance of the model she once was."

"That's it Paul. Toss out some labels when your argument fails to hold water. Or are you threatened by the notion that a woman can do a better job in the Oval Office than a man.

"Diane, your women's lib rhetoric is getting tedious. Perhaps you should let your head rule your emotions."

Scott turned off the TV, poured a tumbler of wine, and tried to celebrate Bambi's growing success, while trying to forget that he was a very lonely young man who had for many weeks substituted work for a love life.

A couple of glasses of wine later, he convinced himself that there was cause to celebrate, so he walked over to the Tree House. The regular guys weren't there, but there was an attractive young woman. His courage up from the wine, he offered to buy her a drink, making much of the fact that he was both a local and a local reporter.

Yvonne was striking, with long black hair and pale skin. She was a software programmer from San Jose who had left one job for a better one in the same neighborhood, one that wouldn't start for a couple of weeks. She'd decided on the spur of the moment to go camping, but was bored at the State Park, this being too early in the season for much activity.

Scott told her of his walks in the rain in the Park, even when it was off limits during the stand off. He added that he'd had a major hand in solving that stand off and that he thought he knew who was behind it all.

She seemed to be impressed with what he was saying, and with each round he bought, she became more attentive to his stories.

Yvonne talked about the stressful world of programming, and how it destroyed any social life one might want. In fact, she said, time off between jobs was just about the only time a programmer could have some fun. Then she asked if it was always so chilly in May. She'd apparently expected the evenings up here to be like those in the Silicon Valley.

Scott used her questions and comments to talk about how he camped and rode his motorcycle during the freezing winter rains, and she thought that was very manly and all, but she'd been wishing for nights sitting out by the fire, rather than in the sleeping bag.

At some point late in the evening, the alcohol and her strong hints about wanting accommodations other than in a tent got Scott thinking. He asked her if she'd like to stop by his place.

It didn't take very many wine enhanced minutes for the two of them to go from sitting side by side to kissing and groping. There was a short but robust sexual session, and then they both either fell asleep or passed out.

The next morning Yvonne stayed long enough for a cup of coffee before saying she had to go. He asked for her number, and she seemed to hesitate before smiling and scribbling a number on his note pad. He swore he would call in a week, when she was home again, although he had no idea how he'd manage a relationship with someone five hundred miles away.

Whatever the future held for the two of them, he had shared intimacy with a lovely, intelligent woman, and his spirits were lifted. He continued to enjoy the fantasy of a relationship with Yvonne until his call to her home actually connected him with the admissions department of Stanford University.

Rob was planning an exit in a couple of weeks in order to pack up and get his ball busting bitch of a daughter off to college. Scott had hoped that he wouldn't have to deal with the new editor until after Memorial Day.

With Rob's departure just over two weeks off, Scott was covering the police beat and saw Buck's name. He read the report. Buck had been walking downtown when a group of skateboarders allegedly ran into him and then cussed him out and threatened him for getting in their way on their sidewalk.

It was the only interesting altercation of the day, so Scott emphasized it.

Almost immediately the phone calls and letters started coming in from older citizens saying the skateboarders were just punks and delinquents, and the sport should be banned. At the same time skateboard groups called in, saying none of their number would behave like that, and that it was either a lie or some fringe outlaw type group.

Somehow other papers grabbed the story, and the anger and mistrust on both sides of the skating issue suddenly flared up in towns all over the state. Local skateboarders were saying, "skateboarding isn't a crime!" To that, other people said it should be, and that they'd take it to the city council.

Suddenly Scott was very suspicious. He called Buck one evening. "Is it true about those skateboarders?"

"Don't you fuckin' trust me? Damn, it's really turning into

something, almost a generational war. I see laws being passed in anger and then broken in anger."

"So, you made it all up?"

"I didn't say that."

"Then it's true?"

"Could be, Scott. Could be. But then truth is what everyone chooses to believe."

As soon as he hung up, Scott connected the dots. Buck was obviously connected to the Mahatmas of the Forest brouhaha, and it was likely he was behind that GMMTL bunch that never materialized but only served to hype Bottoms' campaign. This was another attempt to agitate and fuck with society. He sat down and wrote a piece about Buck and his machinations. It was one of the last things Rob ran before leaving, and his only comment was, "I hope you can back up these allegations."

The new editor, Marv, called Scott into his office. "I see all these columns. Was Rob planning to print them?"

"Well, he'd been printing them for several weeks."

"This isn't your main job around here?"

"Well, I do the police, city hall, water department, and school board beat, plus I write a local interest column. You see, I live up the hill past the State Park."

"OK, Mukis. That's the stuff we need you to do. This other. Well, I can't use it."

"I don't get it. You object to my point of view?"

"Not at all. In fact I agree with most of it, as do dozens of syndicated columnists who tackle the same subjects, well known and respected columnists. We're a local paper. Our staff does local news and local issues. If I want this sort of stuff," he pointed to Scott's work, "I buy it from the services."

"Wait. You've got to give me a chance here." Scott was indignant and had jumped to his feet.

"No, I don't. I'm the editor; my decision; end of story. You're an adequate reporter. Just do your job. On your way back to your desk, send Carol in here."

Scott found himself out in the hall, feeling like a stranger in the place he'd spent the last year of his life. He felt like walking back in there and giving notice, but he figured he'd better get something else first.

He'd no sooner sat down and calmed himself enough to get back to work when Marv yelled for him. What now, Scott wondered.

"Mukis. You know this Charles 'Buck' Rogers?" He was holding a copy of Scott's piece exposing Buck.

"Yeah. He's a neighbor and an agitator." He pointed at the column. "Look at all the crap he's stirred up."

"I hope the hell you can prove that. I just got off the phone with him. He wants a full retraction. He's threatening to sue."

Scott started to sputter that Buck can't do that, that's he's nothing but an habitual trouble maker, low level criminal type.

"Prove it. This guy wants a retraction and his record made public."

Fired up, Scott banged his fist on the desk. "I'll have his damn record by the end of the day."

Scott enlisted old Ron at the paper who was good at this sort of thing, and the two of them dug for dirt on Buck. By the end of the day, Scott had determined that Buck had never been arrested. He'd never even had a ticket. Scott couldn't believe there hadn't at least been a pot bust.

Ron also came up empty handed. The chamber of commerce had Buck listed as a partner in A.H. Printing, a reputable local company. He also worked for two local contractors who praised his work and punctuality. Scott had to slink into Marv's office with his figurative tail between his legs and admit that he had nothing but his own suspicions to back the story.

"You've been around here long enough to understand the term, 'responsible journalism.' If you value your job, do not screw up like this again. Now write a very contrite retraction, highlighting his immaculate record, and hope to hell that satisfies this guy."

As soon as he'd finished the retraction, Scott called the couple of papers who had shown an interest in his resume a month or two before. Both had filled the positions, but assured him they'd be in contact if something else opened up. Scott spent the following weekend, ignoring spring and sending out a new set of resumes, including one to the Arts and Entertainment section of the Oregonian. He was ready to take a job at the first paper that made an offer.

21.

It was a year from the day he'd first moved in, and Jake called him to invite him over for a drink to celebrate. When he walked into Jake's totally redecorated combination office and home, the little place was full of people yelling "Surprise!" V.V. was there, as well as Peaches and her lover, Paula. Buck and Dusty were there, along with Jules, and even Michael, who told Scott that Forest Walker, who turned out to also be Ben There, Les Apt, etc, had opened his eyes and enriched his spiritual life.

Michael pulled Scott aside and explained that Forest was a minister as well as a Zen master and had explained that the Buddha and Christ were the same being, that the Son of God had come first to India, but then had to return once more to take his message to the western world. Forest had claimed to have seen ancient texts that predicted the unification of Buddhism and Christianity in the twenty-first century, ushering in a golden era. Their talks had been so moving and inspiring that Michael was going to study and become a Buddhist as well as a Christian.

The man was caught in a fit of ecstasy, and when he started to preach his newly expanded spirituality, Scott excused himself and went to tell V.V. of his new situation at work.

V.V. advised him to simply quit. Scott argued that it might take awhile to find another job and that a long delay could hurt his credibility in the business.

"Scott, your investment in my business is paying you enough to live on, and I'm sure there's money set aside for you in your family's business. You can stay home and write your novels."

"But, you don't understand. I need to work at a paper, to reach an audience. I can't just let investments keep me. It would be immoral, like the idle rich who play all day."

She kissed his cheek and said, "I hope you find a way to

make yourself content some day. Being the tortured writer must get dreary after awhile."

He was going to explain how she didn't understand him when Peaches grabbed his arm and pulled him into a corner.

"Scott, I thought this whole sexual orientation thing was settled, and I love Paula, but I'm not really past men yet. Understand?"

Scott was sure she was leading up to restarting their old relationship, an idea that appealed immediately to him. But she continued, "So, I've been seeing a guy on the side. He's the salesman from the tee shirt and hat company, you know, the ones with our logo printed on them. Paula doesn't know, and I don't want to mess things up by telling her, but I don't want to give this guy up. What do you think?"

Several suggestions came to mind, things about honesty, about realizing that he was obviously the one she wanted, but when he followed the logic of each, they all lead back to reuniting the two of them. Finally he shook his head and said, "With my track record, you are probably asking the wrong guy."

Buck was speculating on the kinds of media events that could turn Bottoms' political momentum into a landslide. He wanted to see her as President.

"So, Buck, you double dealing bastard, you do believe in something. You must either believe it's time for a woman in office, or you believe in her program."

"How quaint, Scott. I just love the way her presidency would stir everything up, blow away the status quo, mess with the minds of the far right."

"Yeah, Buck, and maybe you can follow the election with a skateboard war. I need a beer."

Scott was reaching for one of the Coors Lites Jake had in the box, when Jake came up and took it from him. The big man opened an ice chest and showed Scott the selection of a dozen or more micro brews. "I stocked the kind of swill you like, my boy. Have at it. Buck and I will carry you home if needed."

Forest, Les, Ben, or whomever came quietly in, and Scott

immediately went over to him. "I didn't know you were a Buddhist."

"Buddhist? Not at all. I did read a book on Buddhism by Alan Watts some decades back, but I don't practice religion or much of anything else, except surfing."

"But, Michael said."

"Oh, yes, Michael. We had some interesting speculative conversations regarding metaphysics or gardening or something."

"Come on now. You fucked with his whole point of view, made him even stranger than he was. Aren't you going to own up to that?"

"Should we take responsibility for other people's lives? Do you feel that humans are sheep, or that they can think for themselves, if they choose to do so? Do you think you can break or fix anyone else?"

"Sure you can. That's the whole point of a society. People interact in positive or negative ways with others. They help or hurt others."

"OK, so you can have an effect on another's life. You change him, and he changes the next person, and so on until your action has touched the entire world, changed everyone, made the world a paradise or a purgatory. That kind of power is frightening, but you seem to handle it well."

"Well, that's not really how I meant it. That seems kind of extreme. I don't think one person can. . . Well, maybe a great leader."

"Scott, perhaps you are the second coming of Christ. You'd best consider the possibility before interacting with anyone. I'm glad I don't have that heavy load on my shoulders. Take up surfing. It will simplify your life, and you'll do better with women. Oh, look at the time. Gotta go." He turned and walked out.

Scott's head was reeling. He turned back to the crowd to see Jake go to a closet, pull out a keyboard, and set it up. He started playing an old Aerosmith tune, and one by one, people started

285

singing. Finally, even Scott joined in. After a half dozen popular songs, Jake stopped playing and went for another beer.

Another facet of his landlord, Scott thought. "Jake, I didn't know you played."

"Don't much any more. Was in a band when I wasn't more 'n a kid. Used to play gigs in the Sacramento area, where I worked as a bike mechanic."

At some point in the evening, Rob came by and had a beer or two. He didn't stay long, and after he left, V.V. realized it was late, and she had to go. Peaches and Paula followed her, and soon it was just Jake, Scott and Buck. They continued swilling beer until they were quite drunk, and then Scott staggered home to bed, still unable to get Buck to confess to his elaborate plots.

The next morning there was a news flash. The president had been addressing some group, and the press had been there, asking the usual questions. At the end, and when the president apparently thought there was no camera on him, a reporter shouted a parting question. "What's your response to the polls indicating that Senator Bottoms will almost certainly win the election?"

Apparently reacting without thinking, the Commander-in-Chief snapped back with, "No blond bimbo's gonna beat me!" The words, along with the pugnacious expression and the look of shocked realization that immediately followed it, were played back for the viewing public. Scott was thinking that this must have been what it was like to watch the Titanic sink. It was pretty clear that five months hence this country would elect its first woman president.

Naturally, the pundits volleyed his statement for the rest of the day, with his avid supporters claiming that it was a slip and would soon be forgotten. Unfortunately, they didn't sound as if they believed it themselves.

He caught the commentators Paul and Diane long enough to hear her say that the election was all over, only to have Paul reply that Diane didn't jump to conclusions, but rather she jumped first, hoping a conclusion would be there when she landed.

Naturally, Becky called, all excited about the turn of events. She was getting hooked on politics and was now running for city council. She planned to be in the state assembly by the end of the decade.

All her good news was making Scott crazy. He tried to sound upbeat, but he finally broke down and told her about the new editor and how he'd clipped Scott's wings.

"Take a few days off. Come down for your birthday. You've got to have some vacation coming. Maybe the bastard will appreciate you when you're not there to cover all the stuff you cover. Besides, like it or not, you're in the family, and we really need a family meeting.

She was right, and besides, he was so pissed at Marv that he was close to telling him to shove the job. A few days cooling off might put it all in perspective. He agreed.

He showed up for work Monday and told Marv he needed to take a week's vacation.

"Scott, that's kind of short notice. You need to give me time to rearrange schedules to cover you. You're supposed to make vacation requests a month in advance."

Rather than fight, Scott lied. "Got to go now. My father is sick. Heart problems, you know. If I wait, he might die before I can see him."

Marv gave him a look like he didn't believe a word of it, which was likely, as Scott was a terrible liar, but there wasn't much he could do but grudgingly agree.

Suddenly anxious to get home for reasons he didn't understand or wish to delve too deeply into, he decided to leave that night. He drove to Orick, and checked into the $40 a night Palm Motel. Scott still thought of himself as the broke young man who rented a travel trailer a year ago, so he always opted for the cheapest prices.

Tuesday morning he had breakfast when the motel coffee shop opened at six, and headed south with the desperation of a man who believes the answers to all his questions lie at the end of the road.

Pulling into Santa Barbara, Scott realized that he'd forgotten that June was warm in the southern part of the state. It was nice to be outdoors with only a tee shirt again.

At the big family dinner Scott's father treated him differently, with respect, almost as an equal. He actually said he admired how his boy had carved a niche for himself in journalism in only a year. "I always knew you had it in you. It's in the genes, boy. We're a go-getter family."

As uncomfortable as the term "go getter" made him, Scott grudgingly realized that his passion for writing was much like his father's and his sister's passion for business. Suddenly, and for the first time in several years, he felt part of this family, and not some kind of outsider. This, he figured, was what he hurried home for, a reconciliation. They actually backed him and his chosen career. He had wanted his father to understand his choice and to respect it, and he finally had.

The next morning Susie Takora showed up for breakfast. Becky had invited her. They sat her next to Scott, and she seemed pleased that Scott had come down. In fact, she said, "I'm so glad you decided to join us. I hope it's a long association."

That seemed odd to Scott, seeing that he was leaving on Sunday. Perhaps she assumed he returned for good.

Susie nodded to the tennis court in the back of the house and asked Scott if he played.

"It's been a couple of years, but I guess I can still hit the ball."

They played a set, and even though Scott was out of practice and Susie was very athletic, he won. It felt good to play a sport again, and it felt good to have a woman act as if he were special.

After the game, they went walking on the beach and stopped at the State Street mall for a glass of wine. Over the wine she mentioned that the company was trying to come up with a catch phrase that could be identified with the company in its advertising. She said, "You're a writer. Maybe you could think of something."

After saying that business writing wasn't his thing, he saw her look of anticipation and tried to think of something. To stall, he ordered another round and commented on the lovely weather. "Good God, I've forgotten how warm and sunny it is down here. I could tell you stories about north coast weather."

He wanted to be terribly clever to impress Susie and also his family. Family! That's it. He tossed out a hasty idea, "How about this: 'From our family to your family, R.S. Mukis Company?"

"That wonderful. You're a natural. Perhaps we've found our VP of advertising, my new boss."

"Thanks for the compliment, but I have a job. I'm a journalist. Wait. You said the company had someone in mind for the job. Did you mean me?"

"If you want it. Becky and your dad would love to have you back in the company. They miss you."

Scott changed the subject, talking instead about their common experience with the forest activists.

Later that afternoon, Scott sat down with his parents and Becky. His father said that this was both a family meeting and a meeting of the company board of directors.

"Even with you working elsewhere, you still own your piece of R.S. Mukis, which builds interest in the goddamn bank, but you have a vote. Oh, by the way, I like the 'from our family to your family.' Anyway, we're growing almost too fast, and we need to make a decision. Do we keep the business strictly in the family and borrow extensively for our expansion, thereby making us vulnerable if the economy sours, or should we go public, keeping the majority of stock for ourselves?"

Scott was floored. This was something big. "Dad, I don't know much about the business, and very little about business in general. My gut says a family business is somehow a better business than a public one."

"Your mother agrees." Scott's mother nodded. "Becky

thinks selling stock will help us expand even faster. I'm undecided."

"Scott tried to sound knowledgeable. "Don't some business that grow really fast tend to collapse?"

"Occasionally," Becky injected. "But the key is good management, and we have that."

"Our own family can't agree on things," he observed. "What if outsiders have a vote. Besides, with the country soon to get its first woman president, might the economy go through a shaky period?"

Becky looked thoughtful. "I hadn't factored that in. Perhaps we should exercise some caution in our expansion plans, at least until the aftermath of the election."

"Oh, yes, Bottoms as President." His father added. "The stock market doesn't like things that are too different. I'm going to go with keeping it in the family at least until next year. That's three to one. Sorry Becky."

"Well, perhaps it is for the best at the moment. So, little brother. Since you seem to be a market analyst now and are making decisions for the company's future, you should be here making it happen. Obviously Susie and you had a talk."

"I'm not really ready for that right now."

"Tomorrow I'm taking you on a tour of the company offices and a few of the stores. No pressure. We'll talk about your future association with the company at the end of the week. Deal?"

Scott was impressed with how much the place had grown. The company offices took up twice the space they did a year ago, and there were lots of new people, mostly young, professional looking women.

At the sites it was the same. The new stores were bigger, more modern, with a huge selection. Becky had been right when she said that they had changed from hardware stores to home improvement centers.

"With stores like this you have all the customers you want."

Becky laughed. "With stores like this we can struggle to

compete with some of the big chains. You've been up in the boondocks too long. One reason we haven't gotten into the L.A. market is the domination of the really big chains. But, we have an aggressive policy. We key the store to the needs of the location, and we push the personal service. That's where your slogan fits in so well. We want people to thinks of us as the local, family business, which we still are."

Scott sighed. "And soon you'll be just another big chain, a big, indifferent profit generating machine."

"Not exactly brother dear. We are socially responsible. Besides helping a populist candidate like Bambi, we've started a group that funds small businesses, generally businesses owned by women. Don't say anything yet. You know that women still don't have their share of the top jobs, their proper percentage of businesses, and you've certainly heard of the glass ceiling. We're not working to put women at an advantage. We're working for equity."

"Come on, Becky, you know I support the feminist cause. Hell, I've written columns about it. I think what you're doing is right. I'm just afraid that R.S. Mukis will go the way of all other businesses once it gets really big."

"That's why it's family run, and that's why you could damn well make sure that doesn't happen by taking an active role and running it. Your personal integrity would help keep us on the right track."

"Well, Becky, that's true, but I'd have to give up my writer's life, and. . ."

"And what? Your new editor has taken away your forum. Your writer's life is covering the traffic ticket scene and living in a trailer. Here, you'd work less hours, giving you time to really write important novels."

"Look, don't pressure me. I'll think about it, and that's all I can promise."

"Susie would like to talk to you again about the ad campaign she's working on. She wondered if you could meet her for drinks and brainstorming at the Mexican restaurant at the corner. I promised Tom I'd be home early. We have guests, and he's cooking something special." She started to walk away before he could even agree to meeting Susie, something he'd gladly do without a special reason. As she walked out the office door, she turned and said. "I won't be able to get over to the folk's place tonight, but I'll buy you lunch if you show up tomorrow at noon."

After a couple of margaritas, Scott seemed to ooze clever ideas out of every pore, and Susie seemed enthralled by his agile mind. She took notes and smiled. As they parted to their respective cars, she reiterated how she would really enjoying working for him.

Scott's mother had instructed the cook to fix one of his favorite meals, and his clothes were freshly laundered and ironed. He showered and wandered off to his father's study, where he'd been terrorized only a year before.

"Come in son. Hope you had a good day. We got a special thing for your birthday, so don't make plans for your last night in town. By the way, your boss called."

"Marv? What did he want?" Scott sat down in one of the deep, leather chairs, sinking almost out of sight.

"Some stupid file he couldn't find in the computer. Something about the school board vote. Wanted to know what you filed it under. Said to e-mail him. Damnedest thing too. The guy says he's sorry to hear that I'm sick. Well, I told him I never felt better in my whole damn life."

"Jesus, Dad. Didn't you pick up that I'd used you as an excuse to get some vacation time?"

His father looked away for a moment. Then: "Hell, I guess I'm getting a bit slow on the uptake. Haven't had to lie to the boss since I was younger than you. I told your grandpa some whoppers to get a bit of time off. Damn, hope no damage was done."

"I might lose my job."

"Oh, hell." His father bellowed. "I'll talk to the damn guy. Get it all straightened out."

"No, Dad. I'll take care of it. Really."

Scott arrived early for his lunch with Becky. As he walked into the outer office, he could hear Becky and Susie talking.

"Susie. That's above and beyond the call of duty. You certainly don't need to get involved. You just want to sell him on the damn idea."

"No, Becky. You don't get it. I've been thinking about this, and I think it's worth exploring."

"But, but, you and . . .Come on. Seriously now."

"I look at what you and Tom have, it's unique, and it works. You're happy. I'd like that too."

"Hope I'm not interrupting." Scott poked his head through the door, not wanting to interrupt any business strategizing."

The two women stopped abruptly and looked startled. "How long have you been here?" Becky asked.

"Just arrived. Big deal cooking?"

"You heard?" Becky seemed concerned, like it was some secret deal.

"Not much. Susie's hustling some business, and you and Tom have something that she'd like."

Susie jumped in with, "Yeah. It was, well, it was about art. Yes art. You know that big Evyand Earle serigraph Becky has over the fireplace, the one with the multi colored tree. Well, I want one of those, and Becky was trying to talk me out of it."

"I don't know the painting, but why talk you out of it?'

The women looked at each other. "The colors." Becky said.

"Right," added Susie. "See, the colors don't go with my furniture. I'd have to replace the couch and chair. Yes, the furniture. I mean, what do you think. If you love a picture enough to pay seven grand for it, what's another thousand for a new couch and chair? Right?"

"Well, yeah, I guess. Art's important, more so than furniture. But, like I said, I don't know anything about this guy and his work."

Susie looked puzzled. "How can you miss it. As soon as you walk in the door, pow!"

Becky touched Susie on the arm. "God, I just remembered. Scott's never seen my new place. I know the big birthday bash will be Saturday at the folk's place, but you've got to come over Friday for dinner. I want you to see our home. You can look at the painting too. Susie, perhaps you could come too? Scott, would you mind if Susie joined us?"

"Well, sure, fine. We can talk about art. What the hell. I don't have to dress up, do I?"

Scott had almost forgotten what Tom was like. He was a quiet young man, but really handsome. Becky had obviously been a sucker for good looks. He still worked in the accounting department, but as a supervisor now, and with shorter hours. They'd agreed that as soon as they had a baby, Tom would stay home to care for it. The business wouldn't survive if Becky took more than a couple of weeks off.

The guy was an excellent cook, and he knew his wines. He could easily have a career as a caterer or head waiter. Scott wasn't into clothes, but the sweater Tom was wearing was great. It looked like it cost around three hundred bucks.

Susie complimented Tom often on his taste in clothes, the food, and the whole gracious host thing.

Funny, as much as they'd made a big deal about the picture, it was Scott who brought it up and insisted on discussing it. Until seeing that picture, Scott had only wanted to write. Now he also wanted to learn to paint. It was vivid, stunning, and it dominated the huge, expensively furnished room.

At one point in the long discussion of the serigraph's merits, Susie laughed and said, "I guess I'm buying art tomorrow."

Scott had mailed off the location of the missing file to Marv prior to driving to Becky's place, just down the hill then their parents place. The next morning, he got on his father's computer and checked his e-mail. Marv had written to say that he wasn't happy with Scott and that they needed to discuss his future with the paper.

Damn, Scott thought. What now?

He saw the local paper on a chair, and decided to check it

out. It was bigger than his paper, with better national and international coverage. Maybe he'd drop off a resume.

Then he saw a piece that was way too familiar. Apparently a Charles Rogers of Crescent City had complained about being harassed by skateboarders, and now he claims he's been getting threatening phone calls, even death threats. Also, some unknown skateboarder had sprayed on the wall of City Hall, "You'll get our skates when you pry them from our cold, dead fingers." An anti skateboarding law was on the council agenda.

Scott saw Buck wearing both hats in this game, but he didn't care any longer. His games started something in motion that ended up saving the forests and will give the country its first woman president. Hopefully, some good will come, way down the line, from this skateboard fiasco. However it worked out, there was nothing Scott could do to stop it.

Becky called. She apologized for butting in his life, but since she had a good working relationship with the managing editor of the paper, she'd shown him Scott's writing portfolio. She was just proud of her little brother and wanted to see if the editor was as impressed with his writing as she was. Well, Becky told him, the guy was interested. He didn't need another reporter right now, but he might be interested in contracting with Scott for a regular column, part of the regular board of contributors.

At first Scott felt a wave of resentment toward his sister for interfering, but then he realized that even if she was using her connections, the editor wouldn't consider it unless he genuinely liked the writing. "Which writing did he like?" He asked.

"The forest stuff. The columns on equal treatment for women and minorities. The political and human rights pieces. I showed him your best stuff, Scott, like the piece that Bambi read to the media. God, that was powerful."

Yes, Scott thought. The editor liked his writing. It was just a matter of getting someone to look at it. Becky had done that, but after that, the writing spoke for itself.

Perhaps he would be fired. Marv was a jerk. At best, he was

covering the local meetings and writing about traffic accidents and drunk driving arrests. Here, perhaps he could make a difference. He could make sure at least one big company stayed socially responsible, and he could reach a readership of over a hundred thousand, rather than less than ten thousand. And, it was obvious that Susie liked him. Perhaps they could have a relationship. He was already tainted by money. V.V.'s stock had given him an income, and the family business paid him a dividend. His father was right the other day when he'd said, "Hell, son. You could sit on your ass the rest of your life and still live well."

But, what of V.V., Peaches, Jake, and Buck? If he decided to stay, and it was a really big "if," he'd damn well make sure he could take time off to go back and see his old friends. In fact, he'd keep the trailer as sort of a get away, a place to write when the business world got too much. The family would have to accept his occasional retreats if they wanted him. That would be the deal. He wouldn't back down on that.

Well, tomorrow morning he'd have to decide. He'd either start driving north or he'd call Marv and quit. He'd sleep on it and make his decision in the morning. Tonight, the family and Becky would gather to celebrate his twenty-second birthday. He'd come a long way in the last year, and he saw only wonderful things for the future.

But, he still had a few hours to kill before the birthday party. He thought about the strange old guy with many names, the guy who went surfing when most people wouldn't even be outside. Then he thought of the solitary surfer at the mouth of the Klamath, catching waves while a great white shark circled just yards away. It was absurd to think that surfing would make one immune to shark attack or drastically increase one's life, but there was a mystique that he found attractive. He picked up the phone book and looked under "surf boards."

He entered the Santa Barbara Surf Shop. "Hi, I'm thinking of buying a board and learning to surf. Is it possible to get lessons?"

The kid behind the counter assured him that lessons could be arranged. Then he showed him a selection of boards, advising him to start with something fairly long and easy to learn on. Later, he could buy a shorter, high performance board.

"You know," he told the blond kid behind the counter. "I'd never given the sport much thought until I met this crazy old guy up on the redwood coast. He seemed to have a different name each time I talked to him. Claimed to be really old, but looked to be sixty something. Told me surfing would make me live longer. Weird old guy.

"'Bout six foot one? Curly gray hair? Short beard? Talks about stuff that sounds like science fiction?"

"Yeah. You've heard of him?"

"Sounds like the Tripper. The boss and him used to surf together back in the late fifties. Guy's been around near forever. Last I'd heard he was in Peru. So, he's up north now? How about that."

"The Tripper, huh? And he's been around for who knows how long? Look, how about that fancy board with the bright red stripes? And give me the application for that surf school. You know, I'm a writer. I write about real life, real issues. Perhaps there's a really important story in surfing that needs to be told."

Other Books from Eclectic Press

***Cosmic Coastal Chronicles*, by M.L. Fischer**
A passionate love affair with the west coast. Travel, adventure, and reflections on the art of living.

***Essential Love* by Patricia Easton Graves**
A primer on the basic concepts of a spiritual life.

***Shattering the Crystal Face of God*, by M.L. Fischer**
Further adventures on the west coast, with philosophical reflections of the nature of life and the universe. Living as artistic expression.

***Walking the Dog*, by Ann Menebroker**
A major name in the poetry world for over 40 years, Menebroker has assembled a personal selection of her favorites from the first three decades. She takes the funny and sad moments of daily life and turns them into something universal.

www.baymoon.com/~eclecticpress
eclecticpress@baymoon.com (e-mail)